# ARISTAR

## ETERNIGY SERIES, BOOK II

# ZANE KAYLANI

Editing, design, and distribution by Bublish

ISBN: 978-1-64704-944-7 (paperback)
ISBN: 978-1-64704-945-4 (hardcover)
ISBN: 978-1-64704-943-0 (eBook)

# CONTENTS

## PART I



## PART II

AMPHORA
RAE CITADELS
PRISM
STAR LEAF
THE ORIFLAMME
THE DANTE
STAR NEEDLE
BOLIDES
Illustration by Brandon W Broadfoot

SOLIERE NEBULA
THE PALE
GNOST BAND
NANJ CLOUD
MAGNA BAND
ELRED'S WORLD
SYNTHA BAND
SYNTHA DARK PATH
THYRRENEAN BAND
THYRRENEAN DARK PATH
MAELSTROM
EMPYREAL BAND
CORE OF SOLIERE THE ARISTAR
EMPYREAL SEAL
ADNAN & RISHNA
MAGNA DARK PATH
GNOST DARK PATH

# PART I

# CHAPTER 1

# METEORS

He wanted to dive right into those clouds. Something deep within them, he was sure, was calling out to him, had been trying to reach him for some time. He longed to reach back, but Aurorno Augustine sat at the flight controls of his little vessel and remembered what the prefect had said before he had embarked: *"You think something awaits you in the nebula, which has brought us only fire. The watchers, too, sense something stirring behind it. You may search out what simmers there. But you are not to enter the clouds, no matter what comes, no matter what you see."*

For over two hundred years, his people had lived at the edge of the Soliere Nebula. Swirling clouds, great plumes of dust, a rich mosaic of colors—yellows of sunlit gold, reds of dawning skies, icy rivers of blue. Along the frontier, where the clouds dissolved into black space, asteroids clustered, a beach of shattered rock on the shore of a fluorescent sea. One of those stony orbs—really a space vessel—differed outwardly from the others only in its perfectly spherical shape and the swift precision of its flight. Its interior held an atmosphere, a gravity field, an electronic grid embedded in the inner walls. And two occupants.

"Auro!"

The ringing of his name jolted the pilot as he maneuvered around the drifting rocks. His face, pale as his shoulder-length hair was raven dark, was porcelain smooth except for a brow creased by grief and the brooding to which he was prone. Though just in his twenty-fifth year, the recent loss of his parents had etched a sadness in his eyes.

"Look there," his shipmate continued, drawing up beside him and entering new commands into the console. He was Auro's age, rounder of face and body, but little less in perception and grit.

"There's nothing, Bailyn."

But his mate persisted, and their view screen homed in on a dynamic region where some torrent was scattering the clouds. An object emerged: a ship unlike any they had ever seen—metallic, sleek, tapering into an intensive engine that emitted a blue exhaust. Ominously, it was speeding their way, and their home city lay just beyond the rocks.

The copilots gripped the controls. Their vessel, which Auro had named the *Meteor*, accelerated smoothly with no outward sign of an engine. As they cleared the asteroids, losing their camouflage, a new distortion churned the clouds and knifed through them in a blaze. It was another space rock nearly the size of their own, but this was a bolide, enveloped in a red fire that burned wildly over the stone, streaking behind it like a comet's tail.

They had seen such comets before. A few months ago, a swarm of them had burst from the clouds and, with their terrible fire, destroyed an entire array of stations along the nebula. Auro had suffered a traumatic loss in that attack, and it had left their city deeply frightened of the danger that lay across a border they could not see beyond or even think of crossing. But this lone comet seemed to be after the mysterious silver vessel. Swiftly, it overtook it, flames licking the metallic hull. Protruding guns on that hull fired lasers at its pursuer. The bolide staggered but resumed the chase, its flame even more ravenous.

Suddenly, the silver ship halted its retreat. Slowing and turning, it released a new weapon. A pulse of energy, even redder than the flame, emanated from its port side and flashed manically around the bolide like an insect over a fire. The silver ship seized its chance to slip out of the flame's reach while the pulse continued its flurry, circling its adversary, leaving streaks of crimson light in its wake. The bolide surged again, and it looked like its flame might simply engulf the pulse, but instead, a lone spark jumped from one of its rippling fingers, presenting the crimson point of energy with a fiery counterpart. The little lights charged at each other, collided like photons, were thrown back, and charged again. The two vessels stood still as their strange offspring clashed.

Auro and Bailyn sat in astonished silence. Their eyes flitted between each other and the dueling vessels on the screen. They weighed the risks of attempting contact with either. Tentatively, Auro opened a general channel that he knew would reveal their presence. No answer came, but the silver ship suddenly veered around, guns pivoting, one still pointed at the bolide while the other swung toward the *Meteor*.

"They're firing!" Auro exclaimed just before the barrage hit their stone hull, throwing them both across the cabin.

Regaining his senses, Auro felt himself being lifted and realized Bailyn was helping him up. "They stopped after one volley," Bailyn said. "Since we didn't fire back, they seem to be hesitating. I don't think they're looking for another fight."

Their scopes showed the two pulses more clearly now. They were shocked to see both were human-shaped, with heads, arms, and legs. More distinct features were obscured by light. Each was struggling against the aura of energy that surrounded the other. They nearly touched. Suddenly, a great flash erupted between them that flung both into the depths. The two vessels remained inert, as if acknowledging their stalemate.

"Let's head back to the city," Bailyn muttered in disbelief.

Auro had a different notion. "I'll need a space suit," he declared.

Bailyn instantly began to protest; it was Auro's turn to persist. The situation, he thought, spoke for itself. "Two unknown vessels have come from the nebula. It seems each has sent some sort of scout to confront the other. I don't know why they are fighting, but whoever wins may go on to our city. We may not be able to stop them, but we might make a personal appeal, either to the vessels or to one of those entities. We can't turn back without trying."

Bailyn nodded stiffly. This was Auro's mission, and he had placed a great deal of trust in Bailyn when he had asked for his help. Though Bailyn would do everything he could to protect his friend, he would not inhibit his captain.

Auro was soon garbed in a stretchy, soft fabric, dexterous and warm, enameled with glassy metallic scales. A transparent helmet and breathing apparatus covered his head and neck. Equipped to leave the ship, he strode through the air lock and launched into space. A thruster unit on his back propelled him.

He saw the bolide, the silver starship, and the nebula beyond. Behind him, the void appeared to swallow his own vessel of dark stone. He had no real plan and little to wield in defense, apart from a deflector shield and a small laser emitter. He hoped the sight of a single person, an individual life, might convince these combatants to venture toward some understanding.

Neither of the crafts showed any sign of detecting him. He veered toward the silver ship, impressed with its design, but he did not forget what a simple hail had triggered. Danger indeed flashed before him, but not from its guns: A ribbon of flame suddenly streaked over the top of its hull and descended toward him. It was the fiery entity from the bolide. Beholding it up close, Auro saw that it truly was a human figure.

Reversing his thrusters, he shot back in an upright posture. When he twisted around, he saw the other entity coming at him from the opposite way. It, too, was a humanoid of red energy, but not of fire—more like a glistening plasma. Caught between them, Auro dropped out of their paths as they collided. They continued their struggle above him. They were so vivid now, like dueling gods. The flame surged with devilish strength, and its adversary appeared limp. The fire burned fiercely into it.

Auro faced a fateful decision: Retreat or choose a side. His presence was obviously known to both vessels and to the entities that had come from them, all too embattled to pay him much heed. To make contact would mean helping one at the expense of the other. Instinctively, he spurred to defend the plasmic being. Although the silver ship had fired on him after his peaceful hail, he was more disposed to see a grave threat in the bolide and its coarse red fire. He felt a dread of it. Of the entity that wielded it, he felt something more, as though it held a profound secret that he was not ready to know. The starship, on the other hand, had been the one in flight. It was an elegant construction, and the plasmic being's energy was lucent and serene.

Auro routed power to his deflector and braced for impact, zooming to maximum speed. But he was unable to reach the entity, for the bolide sent out a flare that seared over him. His suit barely protected him from being scorched. He stopped dead in space, his jets overloaded.

Faced with two adversaries, the fiery entity fled straight back toward its bolide, disappearing into the surrounding fire. The bolide began to move again toward the nebula, picking up speed until it vanished in the clouds.

After a few moments, Auro managed to regain some maneuverability. Cautiously, he approached the limp form covered in crimson plasma. It was stirring weakly. The silver ship moved toward them, its guns ominous. Auro could not locate the *Meteor* and assumed that Bailyn was frantically trying to get through to him.

The injured entity was still a potential threat, but as Auro came within reach, it extended a hand. They gripped in a sparkling moment of connection. Auro felt the plasma's heat even through his gauntlets. The being seemed to regain some strength and began to move, pulling Auro along. The silver ship careened closer. Before Auro could process what was happening, he found himself inside an interior chamber that promptly sealed shut. The currents of an atmosphere swirled and hissed around him. A pull of gravity took hold, a floor caught his feet, and another door opened to reveal a well-lit corridor.

Dazed, he peered into the entranceway. At the threshold stood an imposing figure: human-shaped, clad in an armored space suit that gleamed where the polished metal caught the light. The face was concealed by a helmet. Each of its forearms bore what looked like laser emitters. A human voice spoke through the helmet in a strangely accented form of Auro's own language, "Did you mean to bring him, Jaimin, or did he force his way in?"

"He saved me," was the reply. "I wasn't going to leave him out there."

Auro swerved his head back and forth. He was standing between the plasmic entity at the air lock leading out and the armored figure at the door leading in. The latter's helmet slid up and receded, revealing a stern brown face, smooth head, and dark eyes.

Now the glaze of plasma dissipated from the body of the one who had brought Auro on board, revealing a slender youth with yellow hair and blue eyes. His body showed no sign of injury. He scooted past Auro to stand by his shipmate. They were almost equal in height, the fair one younger and slighter; the other looked to have a frame nearly as substantial as the armor that covered it.

Auro removed his own transparent helmet and tested the air. It was breathable, fresher than the air in the *Meteor*. Putting his hand to his chest, he repeated the short version of his name, trying to approximate their accents.

"I am Jaimin," said the fair one who, until a moment ago, had looked so supernatural. "This is Kelmin," he continued, indicating the man in the armor. "Are you hurt?"

Auro shook his head, though he wasn't really sure. "I have a shipmate," he said. "Could we contact him? We tried to hail you." He did not remind them how they had responded.

"Come inside," Kelmin said. "We have your ship on our monitor."

Auro followed them into the corridor through a tunnel-like hallway until they came to a wide room that appeared to be their main flight center, housing several stations and screens. Another person stood near the far wall, leaning over a console. It was a young woman with black hair braided down her neck. She turned to greet them. Auro guessed she was no older than himself or Jaimin. Her face had some of Kelmin's sternness, but her eyes were green and soft. Shanna was her name. She was clad, strangely but somewhat regally, in a sort of armor made of what looked like a purple ore that Auro could not identify.

They exchanged more greetings, all trying to understand what had transpired. The bolide was still the immediate concern. "Let's see if we can track its course," Jaimin said.

"It went back into the Pale," Auro said.

"To where?" Kelmin asked.

"The outer clouds of the nebula," Auro explained, stepping closer to the console where Jaimin had set to work at various instruments. Suddenly, the inside of the *Meteor*'s flight cabin appeared on the main view screen, and Bailyn's face filled the frame.

"I saw them take you aboard their ship!" he exclaimed through the speakers when he saw Auro. "Are you all right?"

Auro nodded. "Did you mark the comet's last position? Can you still detect it?"

Bailyn affirmed the first question but not the second. Having reentered the nebula, it was beyond the reach of sensors.

"What was it?" Jaimin asked.

"We have a lot of data to sift through," Kelmin said. "Rocks rarely burn like that in space." He turned to Auro. "But then, your vessel is no ordinary rock. Neither was that bolide, nor was it covered with ordinary fire. And this nebula . . . it's masked from a distance, like a black hole might be. It has some characteristics of a small planetary nebula, about a light-year across, full of clouds and dust and rock fragments. I presume it has a core star, though we can't see it. The clouds are very dense. Even our sensors can't penetrate them."

"I know," Auro said wearily. He sighed and sat back contemplatively as Bailyn stared at them through the screen. "Could my shipmate come aboard?" he asked quietly. "I think we all have questions."

✳    ✳    ✳

Within an hour, five emissaries from two far-flung civilizations were gathered at a conference table on the lower deck of the silver vessel, which Auro and Bailyn had learned was called the *Astraeus*. That they could communicate so easily was remarkable, the imprint of a common ancestry. As guests on the ship, Auro and Bailyn were prepared to give their account first. But with an insight that inspired trust, the three mates of the *Astraeus* understood that they were the visitors there, voyagers who had come to a new world.

Jaimin spoke. Auro already felt a connection with him and listened intently as he delivered, as concisely as he could, a chronicle of their history.

They hailed from Gemma—one of the Bioplanes, the spacefaring continents forged in the centuries after humanity had left Earth. He reintroduced himself and the others—Jaimin Caraggio, Shanna Oneen, and Quantus Kelmin—and explained how some of the fissures in their society, the tensions between science and mysticism, had produced sectarian movements that had unleashed what they called the Eternigy, of which the three of them had by chance been infused. The Eternigy had given them distinct powers in the facets of energy, matter, and technology. In Jaimin, it manifested as a red plasma; in Shanna, the ability to conjure a mystical, marble-like matter; in Kelmin, a telekinetic control over all forms of technology. Jaimin recounted how they had used their new powers to resist the machinations of their government and journey to a neighboring Bioplane, where they had become embroiled in yet another conflict that had brought about the creation of a new star near their world. He ended with their construction of this vessel and its experimental engine that had transported them as far as this very place of their meeting.

"I set our instruments to take us to the farthest point where we could detect human life," Kelmin said. "We wanted to discover and map the most remote human settlements and, of course, make contact. The coordinates showed no sign of a nebula here or even a star. We were unconscious during the journey and emerged within a nexus of clouds that surrounded us like a thick fog. Before we could decide what to do, that flaming object came at us. It appeared to be a fiery asteroid but moved like a vessel. It answered no hail but released bursts of fire that burned our hull. Then it began to encircle us in streams of flame. Our lasers staggered it long enough for us to accelerate away. It pursued. We hoped to lose it in the clouds. Then we broke through into open space with it still on our tail."

"That's when I came out," Jaimin explained. "My plasma can sustain me in space for a time. Kelmin wanted to go with me, but since his technological perceptions make him almost one with this ship, Shanna and I convinced him to stay here, and I ventured out alone. I thought if I could withstand the flame, I might be able to drive the bolide off or perhaps make contact."

*Just as I had thought to do.* Auro smiled to himself.

"Well, as I think you saw, a spark of fire came out of it and tried to fend me off. I thought it was actually human. Anyway, I think you know the rest. I fought with it. Our energies clashed, and we kept throwing each other back. Finally, we touched. I absorbed some of its fire, and I think it absorbed some of my plasma. I still feel the burning."

Jaimin's voice drifted off, and he sat back with a troubled expression. His shipmates looked concerned. "I'll examine you at the medical station," Kelmin said. But nobody moved. There was an uneasy silence.

"That red fire comes from within the nebula," Auro said. "We have encountered it before."

"Who are you people?" Shanna asked rather bluntly. "How did humans come to colonize a nebula this far from Earth?" The young woman had listened as her shipmates had offered up their story, and she clearly thought it was time Auro and Bailyn reciprocated.

"We didn't come to the nebula," Auro replied. "We created it." He let out a deep breath and continued. "Our ancestors also left Earth during the exile. But while most of the refugees ventured outward, our people remained in the interior of the solar system, unwilling to leave the sun. They were drawn to it and inched closer with each generation, building vessels and stations that could withstand the intense heat. Over many generations, they stored vast surpluses of solar power, including gravitational waves and stellar winds, creating new technologies.

"Moreover, the energy was changing them, and some more than others. Whether they were simple mutations or something more mysterious, they found they could withstand fierce heat, gained strength from the gravimetric pressure, even developed sharp perception and a far-seeing sight. These were some of the characteristics of the great families, the Empyreans. It was the highest among them, venturing ever closer to the corona, to whom the blinding brightness brought a new vision.

"They began to propose the unthinkable: leaving the sun to which they were devoted and on which they were dependent. They had reached an epiphany. The boundless energy could be channeled through these devices to generate a field that would carry them great distances. As they journeyed through the cosmos, they would collect yet more energy, and at the end, they would ignite a new star in some dark corner of the galaxy, a newborn sun as much a part of them as they were of it.

"So they fused all their stations, vessels, and collectors together and began to draw the energy they needed. They did not drain the old sun fully—it still exists—but they absorbed such power as no humans had ever dreamed they could wield. Then they activated their combined vessel. It is not known precisely how much time passed—they were semiconscious—but when they revived, the entire colony had been transported here. The Empyreans' claims proved true. The energy that carried them had coalesced into a single churning ball. A new star emerged in what had been a void. It's said that a great halo flashed out from it in a golden ring of stardust, which formed a new planet within the habitable zone."

Auro paused and saw that his tale was resonating deeply with his three foreign listeners. They had themselves played a role in creating a small star near Gemma, but the feat Auro described was beyond their imaginings. Even more, here was proof of what many scholars and sages of the Bioplanes had long maintained: that not all the exiles had ventured out of the solar system. Some had indeed stayed in the interior and accomplished great feats, harnessing the solar energy that their ancestors had forsaken. Yet evidently, all had not gone well, for the star they had created had apparently gone nova, and there was no sign of any planet.

Auro had another chapter to recount. "This nebula is the remnant of that star," he continued. "Our own exocity is the last crumb of the world that formed in its wake. Having made the Great Journey, most of the arrivals settled the planet, which they named Edda. The star they named Soliere, the heir of Sol. Both were somewhat like their precursors. Soliere was smaller than the old sun, formed in part from its fire and supplemented by new energies from across the galaxy. Edda was smaller than Earth but ripe for terraforming. The Eddans raised a biosphere, cultivated its lands, and seeded it with such life as they had preserved from Earth, and they and their descendants dwelled there happily.

"But it turned out that the Great Journey had only sharpened the divisions that had emerged in the earlier exile in the glare of the sun. They all shared a connection to the star, but some found fulfillment in starting anew on a planet of their own making, whereas others felt cold again and yearned for greater heat and brighter light. Most of the higher Empyreans ventured off-world to live in new stations near Soliere as their forbears had near Sol.

"The rift between them only widened. The Eddans embraced a terrestrial life, tilling the soil and building cities. They even renounced the Empyrean name. Having created a sun they could gaze on with naked eyes, they were content to enjoy its blessings from a distance. Yet those who still claimed the Empyrean legacy sought to tap into the new sun's power. But Soliere is no ordinary star. The Eddans never fully grasped what was happening, but from the surface, they saw that their sun was changing as though infected by a disease. The first signs were subtle: the dimming and flashing of light. Then came the flares that affected Edda's climate, then the fluctuations. The star heaved and pulsated in convulsions that began to jostle Edda's orbit and threaten its atmosphere.

"The Eddans tried to send emissaries, but the Empyreans were now so close to the corona that direct contact was impossible, and the flares even interfered with transmitted messages. Finally, open conflict raged between them. Exactly who fired first has been lost to history, but each side had its own methods and means. The Eddans had powerful surface-to-space lasers and frantically unleashed them at the Empyrean stations, hoping to at least get their attention, to make them see that their thirst for energy would destroy the planet their brethren needed to survive. Sadly, the Empyreans answered fire with fire. The star itself became their artillery. They sent out huge flares that battered their way through the planetary shields. However, the Eddans had a vast surface on which to find shelter, while one by one, the Empyrean stations were destroyed.

"The Eddans believed they were achieving victory, but it was a false hope. The delicate balance between star and planet had finally ruptured. Soliere was churning more violently than ever. According to accounts, Edda's tectonic plates rumbled; its skies were full of fire. The star swelled to frightening proportions and flashed unnatural colors. As the planetary cataclysms raged, the inhabitants began to evacuate.

"Although they lacked the Empyreans' mystical connections to star energy, they had advanced capabilities in terraforming and gravitational fields, and they initiated a feat that would make your Bioplane builders proud. Converging in their greatest city, they opened a crack in the surrounding lands, digging deep into the crust, lifting the entire metropolis from the surface, from its deepest foundations to its tallest buildings. The city itself became their vessel, its power cells the engine that carried them off. A great force field shielded it from the void. It stands today as an exocity living in space. They renamed it Amphora, for in it lay the hope that the civilization it preserved and contained might bloom again.

"The surviving Eddans, now the Amphorans, retreated from the expanding energies of the wounded star. The few among them who retained Empyrean perceptions strained to see what was happening, and their worst fears came true: Soliere went nova. On Amphora, we mourn our lost star and world and give thanks to our forebears that they reached a safe distance. In the centuries since, we have existed on the edge of the nebula, drawing power from its energies but otherwise closed off from it."

Auro paused, wondering what else should be said. The three shipmates of the *Astraeus* had just heard a history that seemed to dwarf their own in magnitude and achievement. They had wondered how humans had come so far into the galaxy. Here were descendants of those who had never journeyed outward to build the Bioplanes, who had stayed home by the sun. Yet through its energy, they had ultimately traveled farther. However, they had noted that this nebula and the fiery vessel and entity they had encountered in its clouds were nearly as mysterious to Auro and Bailyn as they were to the Gemmans.

"That bolide," Kelmin said, finally breaking the silence, "came from within the clouds. And since our ship brought us here, we can surmise the nebula contains life. Your people have never explored it?"

"The outer clouds form what we call the Pale, the frontier beyond which our sensors are blinded, our ships disintegrate. While the Empyreans among us can see much through time and space, the nebula is closed off even to them. Our probes don't remain intact for long inside the clouds. They are toxic to flesh and steel and will quickly dissolve a ship's hull. Only the ore of the asteroids, the broken remnants of Edda, can withstand them, as Edda was spawned by the star. Our scientists had long theorized that we might construct vessels from such rocks, but until recently, we lacked the ability to power them.

"But in recent months, rocks covered in red fire have been sporadically appearing just inside the clouds. We once had an array of observatories along the Pale. They were called the Pearl Stations because of the way they glittered white and silver in the nebula light. A few weeks ago, a swarm of bolides burst out of the clouds all at once and destroyed every one of them. Our fleet pushed back the invaders before they could approach the city. But observing them and eventually fighting them has helped us make strides in our own designs. The *Meteor* is our first attempt to create a vessel in their fashion—without the flame, of course. My team and I hollowed this asteroid and equipped it with field propulsion. I am of Empyrean blood, and while I don't have the deep perceptions of my ancestors, I have spent my life studying the technologies they used to tap solar energy. Bailyn and I were out testing the *Meteor* and monitoring the Pale to see if we were ready to take the first plunge inside."

"Observers back on Amphora were monitoring us," Bailyn said. "I don't know how much they saw of what we encountered, but now we'll have more to report than contact with an entity from the nebula. We will be escorting back a delegation from another world."

"I am not ready to go to your city," Jaimin said. "Not ready." He stood up. His hands glowed with red plasma and a faint trace of fire.

"We'll rest first," Shanna said. She reached out to Jaimin, but he stepped away.

"I don't want to rest. I've felt fatigued in the past after expending a lot of energy, but this is different. That bolide seared its flame into me. I want to follow it. I need to know who wields this fire and what it is doing to me. This is what we came out here for."

"We came to find fellow human beings," Kelmin reminded him. "Here they are, and there is their home." The image of Amphora was coming into focus on the screen, beautiful towers set against the stars.

But Auro stood up as well, his eyes level with Jaimin's, and seemed to share his conviction. Neither was of a mind to engage in politics or diplomacy. The nebula beckoned. Somewhere within it dwelled what each of them had lost, though what Auro was truly looking for he was not prepared to reveal. "That flame," he said, looking squarely at Jaimin, "took something from you while infusing something alien and unsettling. You need to be purged of it, made whole again. I'm also ready to go into those clouds. This is the time."

"We'll all go," Shanna declared.

Jaimin was still edging away. She drew up to him, clasping his arms. "Sooner or later, Kelmin will tune our sensors to see into those clouds. This time, we'll be ready for whatever is in them."

Jaimin looked back at her gravely. To his surprise, Auro gave voice to his thought: "You and Kelmin should go to Amphora with Bailyn in the *Astraeus*. Jaimin and I will enter the nebula in the *Meteor*."

"We stay together," Kelmin protested.

"They can see us just as we can see them," Bailyn said of the exocity twinkling distantly on the screen. "We owe them an explanation of your appearance here and what transpired with the bolide. And we don't know how long your ship can last in those clouds."

Now Kelmin walked over to Jaimin and Shanna. The three of them had been linked by a shared purpose ever since they had been infused with the Eternigy in a cavern on Gemma. They all knew they were weakest when apart. But Jaimin had left their vessel alone to face the flame and had been touched by an energy beyond theirs. He felt the imperative to face a new frontier, one that lay outside their personal bond.

"If you're sure this is the way," Kelmin said, "very well. We'll make contact with this city while you explore the clouds. Hopefully, we'll each find a new understanding of where we have come."

"We may not get far anyway," Auro acknowledged. "We'll see how deep we can go and head back if the clouds prove impassable."

Auro refastened his space suit and conferred with Bailyn while the three Gemmans huddled and whispered together. A few moments later, Auro and Jaimin exited the *Astraeus* and flew to the *Meteor*.

The friends they had left behind watched them enter the stone sphere, which began to move toward the colossal storm of light and cloud. Kelmin turned the *Astraeus* around and set the course toward the great city that was a faint light in the distance. Each vessel went its way.

# CHAPTER 2

# PILLARS

Shanna and Kelmin were at least glad to be on their own ship. Hosts for this brief journey, they would be guests at the destination. *Amphora,* Auro had called it, an exocity. True to its name, it looked like an ornate vase floating in space just beyond the nebula. Several miles from top to bottom, the base swelled into a long body of smooth rock speckled with lights, narrowed into a short neck, and widened again in a broad rim, from which sprouted the gleaming towers of a cityscape.

Locking eyes in a moment of reflection, the two Gemmans who had ventured in search of the farthest reaches of human abode marveled at what they had found. Instead of a populated planet, here was a nebula, a ghost of a manmade star, and this haven of the descendants of its creators. Jaimin's absence heightened their anxiety. The intense conviction that had spurred him to join Auro on an expedition into the clouds had been hard to contend with in the moment; now the separation weighed heavily. They could only carry on together, drawing strength where they could.

"How will they receive us?" Kelmin asked Bailyn, who had rejoined them at the console after pacing around the cabin. Before he could answer, the instruments signaled an incoming transmission.

A new image filled the screen of what appeared to be some sort of dignitary: a man in early middle age whose eyes flickered with recognition as he exclaimed Bailyn's name. "So, you are on that ship!" his voice sounded through the speakers. "Have they taken you hostage? What happened to the *Meteor*? Where is Aurorno?"

"I'm all right, Sultaan," Bailyn said quickly. "This ship is not from the nebula. We've received an embassy from another world. They arrived just as . . . we saw . . ." He started to stammer. "There's been a new incursion," he began again. "These visitors helped us fend off a fire comet. I stayed on their vessel to escort them back to the city. Can we assemble the other prefects to receive them?"

Despite this momentous report, a look of relief came over the official's face. But he was not entirely satisfied. "Where is Aurorno?" he asked again.

"He entered the nebula," Bailyn said gravely. He hung his head in trepidation.

The face on the screen did not change expression. "Did he go alone?"

Shanna and Kelmin exchanged a tense look. Auro had said they were being observed, but if these people didn't even know where Auro had gone, how could they know about Jaimin?

Bailyn hesitated. "We can explain everything when we arrive. Well, almost everything."

Relenting from his questioning, the official addressed the foreigners. "Forgive me," he said in a sincere tone. "I am Sultaan, a prefect of our governing council. Bailyn is right; we should talk in person. I will transmit a landing location and greet you there."

His image dissolved. Bailyn looked surprised when he saw the coordinates come through. "I don't believe it," he said. "We are summoned to Simeon Tower."

"Is that where we'll find these prefects of yours?" Kelmin asked.

Bailyn shook his head. "Prefects like Sultaan are civil administrators. They are advised by an order of Empyreans, the Stylights. Their perceptions have made them stewards of our greater interests, and they keep close watch on the nebula. I would not have thought the prefects would surrender the honor of receiving our first foreign guests or that the Stylights would open their highest sanctuary to foreigners, or even to me."

Bailyn's words stoked a hundred questions, but the Gemmans' desire to probe further was muted by the wondrous sights that filled the screen as the *Astraeus* soared over the shimmering skyline. This, Bailyn told them, was the crown, the summit of the world. Planted in a great basin, the lower buildings nestled along the rim while, farther inward, the great towers descended deeper and reached loftier heights. This world had no farmlands or wilderness or seas, yet it evidently supported a substantial population. The buildings glowed in myriad colors. Some had minarets, and there were domes and obelisks and narrow pyramids. The city slumbered in an unending twilight with no tint of blue in the sky, only the dark cosmos and the sheen from the nebula clouds and faraway stars.

"Scintillating, isn't it?" Bailyn said. "Most people actually live below the crown. Auro grew up along the rim facing the nebula, where there's a mesmerizing view of the Melosian Dust Cluster. On the other side, you can see stars in every direction." He paused. "I've never looked on the city from above."

"You didn't take off from here?" Shanna asked.

"We left from a hangar down in the stem. Ships usually aren't allowed to fly over the crown."

They were heading toward the central district with the highest towers. Their destination was the loftiest of all. Its four sides inverted up and up, culminating in an apex of several levels without walls, each lined with massive columns supporting the level above. The topmost floor was a platform open to the stars.

"Simeon Tower," Bailyn whispered. "Where the city touches space."

Shanna and Kelmin had seen enough temples on Gemma to recognize a spiritual sanctuary. On this sky-piercing perch, the mystics of this world could view the heavens. The nebula gave the firmament a vibrancy to shame a starry night on Gemma and no doubt inspired them to stretch their perceptions.

"We are directed to land on the floor just under the upper platform," Kelmin said. "There's just enough room between the columns for the ship to get through."

They began their descent. Kelmin deftly guided the vessel to touch down near the base of the colonnade. The sensors confirmed they had passed through a force field. There was life support, though to all appearances, the square was open to space. With mounting anticipation, they exited the air lock and stood for a moment in wonderment, looking out at the nebula. Bailyn, no less than the visitors, marveled at the sights.

Footfalls echoed, and Sultaan appeared out of the stillness. Studying his two guests, he beckoned Bailyn aside, and the two conferred in voices too low and speech too rapid for Shanna and Kelmin to follow, but they heard Auro's name.

Sultaan broke away with what sounded like a cutting remark and strode toward them, leaving Bailyn off to the side. The prefect bowed his head and formally addressed the foreigners. He explained that the Stylights awaited them on the upper level. The great mystics had been aware that something from far away of human origin was traveling toward their world. "But seeing you here now," he marveled, "I can barely believe my eyes."

Shanna and Kelmin felt no less overwhelmed. They had come flush with a sense of destiny, convinced they had the power to bridge the disparate lineages of humanity. They were chagrined to discover that the people here already knew of them and had worthy powers of their own, perhaps even beyond the Eternigy.

"What do you know of us?" Shanna asked with a bluntness more characteristic of Kelmin, who looked at her, startled.

"Our ancestors knew of the Bioplanes," the prefect answered. "But they chose to stay near the sun and, in time, absorbed some of its power while your worlds receded."

"Yes, we have learned something of your history," Kelmin said. "You are descendants of sun-cultists."

Although he still felt a sense of awe at Auro's narrative, there was a trace of contempt in Kelmin's voice. He and Shanna well knew that one of the first cults to arise after the exile was one with a strange fascination with the sun—the aspiration to harness its energy and employ it to reignite the human soul. The sun was the closest thing to a known deity, unlike Earth, too mighty to be destroyed by its children: the endless well, the unquenchable reality. There were strains of similar beliefs even on Gemma, but the fanatical endeavor Auro had described represented everything the Bioplane builders had rejected. Those engineers believed humanity had to move away from its cradle to evolve and seek new sustainment. It was true that there was a nostalgia for Earth and Sol, made all the more painful since the old sun was usually the brightest star in the Gemman sky. But these were mere sentimentalities. The enduring legacy of the Bioplanes served to rebuke the misplaced obsession with the home of their infancy.

Kelmin was aware he had overstepped the bounds of courtesy. "I didn't mean . . ." he faltered.

Sultaan replied with a disarming smile. "I understand. You have encountered so much so fast. We must seem strange to you, a little outpost far away with different inspirations. I would add that while we may be sun-cultists to you, you are Noctarians to us. That is the name our histories gave to those who migrated from the solar system to roam the twilight. Your ancestors were great builders; ours were great conductors. What you see is the salvaged city of a lost world."

"It is glorious," Kelmin conceded, looking over the dazzling metropolis and out at the clouds that showered the buildings with their lights.

"All of the exiles," Shanna said, "no matter where their travels took them, had to evolve and make new worlds, harness new energies."

"That is how we have come together now," Sultaan affirmed, "with all that we have to learn from one another. Let us take the first step."

He pointed to a spot in the center of the room. There was a brass-colored circle etched on the floor, big enough for a group of their number to stand in. When they converged upon it, it began to lift them all up. They had stepped onto a protracting column that was carrying them to the level above. For a second, it looked like they would all be dashed against the ceiling, but a circular space opened directly above them, making a hole for them to rise through.

In an instant, they were standing on the topmost platform they had seen from the ship. This truly was the summit. The towers of the city glowed below them like a candelabra nested in the sprawling bowl, with the lights of the cosmos a canopy above.

This level was also lined with columns, but these were only wide enough to support a single person and were about six feet high. They served as pillars, for on most of them sat solemn figures, still as statues, with eyes closed and hands on their knees, clad in cloaks, some with circlets around their heads. At the opposite end, facing them and the nebula, perched a man whose eyes were open, looking intently at them. He was flanked on either side by a man and a woman, also awake.

Sultaan started toward these three personages, beckoning the others to follow, and addressed them. "Your vision was true," he called. "Our brethren separated for so many centuries have found their way to us!"

Sultaan came to a halt near the foot of the pillars, with three mystics looking down on him. They reminded Shanna and Kelmin of the High Organon on Gemma. Yet these figures had a different gravity about them. Far from being estranged from the political powers of their world, they seemed firmly on their thrones, both temporally and spiritually.

The man on the middle pillar was named Falconhyn. He was evidently a leader of these Stylights. The woman to his left was Etemeena. Her hair and gown were silver, a golden circlet wound about her temples, and there was a jeweled medallion upon her breast. On the right was Sumero, a younger man. Falconhyn was robust and broad-shouldered, with thick brown hair and beard. He bowed his head graciously.

"For centuries, we have been aware of the Bioplanes," he said. "Some of us have even glimpsed them. We have long believed that, in time, one of our peoples would build a bridge to the other. Our ships do not venture far from this city; from here, we probe the depths, and we sensed your energy drawing closer. It seems you were diverted into the nebula, and we cannot see behind the clouds."

Kelmin stepped forward. "As far as we know," he said, "we are the first of our people to travel beyond the Bioplane archipelago." Drawing a breath and putting his thoughts in order, he explained what the immersion in the Eternigy had done to him and his fellow travelers; how human technology had become like wet sand in his fingers that he could shape into wondrous creations; how he had created the *Astraeus* and Jaimin had kindled its engine, harnessing the Eternigy to break the light barrier even as the forebears of the Amphorans had harnessed the power of the sun.

"We are honored to stand before you now and reunite our two branches of the human family," Kelmin continued. "I confess we knew nothing about you. We simply believed we were heading toward the farthest point where human life existed. I wish circumstances were such that we could simply learn of one another, but it seems we have arrived in the middle of a crisis that has even claimed our own shipmate. As we speak, he and Auro are exploring the clouds out there."

Falconhyn took a moment to consider these words. When he spoke, it was to bid Bailyn to come forward. Guessing why he had been addressed, the youth drew up beside Sultaan and reported what he and Auro had encountered near the Pale: the Gemman starship and the bolide, the dueling entities of flame and plasma, and Auro and Jaimin's hasty expedition.

"You found what you were intended to find," Etemeena said. "Aurorno thought he was given leave to watch the Pale because we sensed more raids were imminent. In truth, it was the coming of these travelers. Still, we forbade him from entering the clouds."

"He was drawn in," Bailyn explained. "Their shipmate, the one who went with Auro, has an energy that rivals the red fire. He lost some of his power in the struggle and felt driven to reclaim it. I think Auro took their arrival as a sign that this was the moment to enter. To seek—"

"The decision was not his," Sultaan cut him off sternly. "I made that clear to him."

There was a silence. The mystics appeared to be studying them all. Then Falconhyn spoke again to the Gemmans. "We have lately sensed new energies within the nebula, just as we perceived yours from afar. We feared the two would soon converge."

"You knew we were coming," Shanna said, "or at least that *something* was coming. You sent Auro to retrieve us?"

"Aurorno has Empyrean blood," Falconhyn revealed. "He has been at the forefront of the new sciences—hollowing asteroids into ships, studying the gravimetric arts we lost when the highest Empyreans split from us. He served on our stations along the Pale and helped defend them. We feared that if he entered the clouds, he would bring the danger back to Amphora. But sensing your imminent arrival, we allowed him to go monitor the Pale. From our pillars here, we saw your vessel emerge and the flame that followed.

"We can indeed learn from one another. We are brethren, not only in heritage but in the energies we wield. You were touched by life energy as we were touched by solar. Your power may provide the lens we need, the extension of sight into the clouds. If we look as one eye, we might pierce the veil."

Suddenly, the mystics' three pillars began to push upward, somehow growing taller.

"They lift you into space," Shanna said with a gasp.

"The Stylights ascend, body and mind," Falconhyn declared as he receded on his extending mast. "You, too, can see as far." As he spoke, two new columns appeared out of the floor just behind Shanna and Kelmin.

"You are rising beyond the life-support field," Kelmin called, projecting his voice so that they might hear him. "I can endure the vacuum in my armor, but Shanna has no protection."

"The Empyreans braved the sun's heat," Falconhyn called down. "We brave the dark void. You may find that you can as well." His voice was lost to the vacuum.

Shanna and Kelmin turned toward Sultaan and Bailyn, who looked as dumbfounded as they. The other mystics, to all appearances, remained deep in meditation on their pillars, which were still at their modest heights. The seats of Falconhyn, Etemeena, and Sumero now towered some hundred feet above.

Tentatively, Shanna and Kelmin approached the pillars meant for them. "Let's go on one together," Kelmin said. "I can generate a support field around us if we need it."

For the first time since they had left Gemma, Shanna harnessed her power to create a widened platform atop one of the pillars. She and Kelmin perched upon it, joined at the hip, clasping each other around the shoulders. As if sensing their presence, it began to rise. The floor receded beneath them; the cosmos widened above. Soon they faced the three mystics again, who now appeared to be in the same trance as the others down on the platform.

Shanna and Kelmin felt like they, too, were falling asleep. Their bodies numbed and their eyes closed. Yet they could still see, as though they were peering into a telescope showing images distant in space and time, changing scenes fading in and out. Their pillars seemed to be floating in space. Even the nebula was gone. The city that had been glittering below them had vanished.

Now they saw a great mass of energy hurtling through space. Then it halted and blazed in the distance. Awestruck, they guessed they were witnessing the arrival of Soliere at the end of the Great Journey, as Auro had described it. And the star was not alone. A conglomeration of ships came in its wake, oddly fused together like a vast space station that had traveled along with the star. Looking directly at the great yellow-white ball of light, Shanna and Kelmin felt the pride that must have swelled through the colonists at the fruition of their journey. Also as Auro had described, a great flare swept out of the new star, a spinning ring of light that gradually dimmed to reveal clumps of dust that congealed into spheres, forming new planets. It was an accelerated creation of a new solar system.

The scene changed again. Jumping ahead in time and distance, they were now closer to the star, looking out at the planets, one of which had the blue sheen of an atmosphere. There were structures around the star with shiny hulls that both reflected and absorbed its light. But then there were signs of strife. Lasers fired from the planet toward the stations, and the stations channeled the star's energy back toward the planet in great flares that flashed over its surface. Again, all as Auro had described.

But then they saw something peculiar: What looked like a human figure, far bigger than normal scale, emerged from the closest station and flew toward the star. Despite the heat that should have eviscerated it, it kept its form and speed until it disappeared into the corona. The star convulsed. Now they were witnessing the nova itself, seeing things Auro could not know, things that no human outside the nebula had ever seen. The star's corona and outer gases burned out into space; it shrank into a denser white core that then began to stretch outward as though pulled by some force in multiple directions. Five great rays stabbed into space, each a different color. Streams of light issued from them and spiraled around the star, forming layers of colored clouds.

Shanna and Kelmin began to move through those clouds at breathtaking speed, clouds so thick they felt gelatinous as they skimmed through them. First, there was a vibrant purple that rippled like a fabric. In it shone a strange disk-shaped object full of pulsating lights. They pushed on into a blue cloud that felt more like water. It had a great depth, and in its thick currents, they thought they could glimpse vague monstrous shapes moving in shadow.

The blue then became green, and they saw two long winding and glowing lines of light, one green and the other silver, which bent toward each other to form a shining arch. They appeared to be trees. One had green leaves and the other had silvery needles. Shanna and Kelmin passed under the arch formed by their adjoining tips, which led them into a new cloud that was red and full of fire. Flaming comets streaked across the crimson vista, and there were enormous asteroids with smoldering volcanoes. They guessed that the bolide they had encountered must have come from there. The same coarse red fire was manifest all around, and they felt its scorching power.

In the distance was yet another cloud, tinted orange. In it, they could see a fan-shaped mass of red fire burning over an oblong base of dark ore. It looked like an old seafaring vessel with a fiery sail. A red bolide circled over it, and between them was a tiny flickering spark, like the entity that Jaimin had fought.

As they drew closer, it stopped and seemed to study them. They could clearly see the human shape submerged in the rippling fire.

Suddenly, it shot away and headed farther into the orange cloud. They followed it, gaining speed, and it led them into a cloud of soft yellow. There were space rocks there, too, of plain stone, and they saw a cluster of large rocks that held what looked to be buildings, including great domes of glowing gold.

But now they saw a dense cluster of clouds ahead, like a storm-front. It flashed and sparkled, a swirling mix of all the colors they had seen along the way. This was the very region in which they had emerged when they had arrived. Auro had called it the Pale, the border of the nebula, beyond which was normal space.

They were still following the fiery entity. It stopped before the Pale, turned, and looked back at them. Then, to their astonishment, the fire around it dissolved to reveal a human figure: a woman, neither young nor old, tall, with long silver-black hair and shining red eyes. She floated before the storm and reached out her hand to encourage them on. Then she turned and disappeared into it. Without taking time to think, they followed her.

The Pale indeed stormed so violently, they should have been buffeted or crushed. But this was a vision, and they passed through it with little regard for real distance or danger. Finally, they broke through into normal space. Coming full circle, they saw their own vessel, the *Astraeus,* and another object coming toward them, a bare spherical stone: Auro and Bailyn's vessel. Behind it lay a swarm of asteroids, and farther on, the sharp lights of Amphora.

That was where they really were, on tall pillars at the summit of that city. They sensed that their dreamy tour was returning to where their physical bodies resided. Coming out of the asteroids, they floated up to Amphora's shining crown and, in a strange way, felt like they were coming home. They stopped moving, opened their eyes; all was still.

The vision had taken them through space and time, traversing in a few moments hundreds of years and millions of miles. From the end of the Empyreans' Great Journey to the creation of a new star and planet, then to the formation of a peculiar nebula through a nova caused by an ancient conflict and a mysterious being. A nebula that had many regions infused with different lights surrounding a core star with colored rays.

Shanna and Kelmin were still on the platform atop their shared pillar with the three Stylights arrayed before them. The city sprawled beneath them again. They were all awake now. Falconhyn looked at his guests with a penetrating intensity. Suddenly, all their pillars began to lower them to the platform where Sultaan and Bailyn and the other Stylights were waiting. Down they went until their seats were once again just a few feet off the ground.

The other Stylights were now awake and peered knowingly at them as though they had shared their vision. Bailyn walked up to Shanna and Kelmin while Sultaan came before the three aligned pillars that held Falconhyn, Etemeena, and Sumero. "What did you see?" he asked. "Did you glean any insight into where the fire comets came from and why they have attacked us? The prefects have a right to know."

The mystics were silent. Shanna and Kelmin were still bewildered by sights impossible to describe. What had they seen? Was any of it even real?

At length, Kelmin spoke up, his scientific mind ever analyzing whatever he encountered. "We saw the star your ancestors created," he said. "Someone or something went inside it. That evidently triggered the nova and created the nebula. But there was something else. Rays extended out of the star of different colors, and the lights of each permeated different regions. One of them was red and fiery, with volcanoes and bolides. I think we saw the very bolide and fire entity we just encountered."

"All we saw . . . is that what Jaimin and Auro will find in the nebula?" Shanna asked.

"In all the years we have meditated on this tower," Falconhyn said, "we have never seen so far and so clearly into the clouds. Your power and presence have expanded our perceptions, as we foresaw. You have helped us lift the veil, a great leap forward. I believe our future meditations will reveal even more."

"But what did it all mean?" Shanna asked. "Who was the being that entered the star, and who was that woman? Was she really the one who attacked us and enticed Auro and Jaimin to enter the nebula?"

"That was most unsettling," Etemeena agreed. "She turned human for a moment."

"Did you recognize her?" Shanna asked, remembering the ethereal face before it was swallowed up by the fire.

"Yes, indeed," Falconhyn said. "Now we know what voice has been calling to Aurorno from the Pale. She was his mother, Armarna. She was lost to the clouds when the fire comets came. It was she you encountered on the edge of the Pale, and she awaits them inside."

Shanna and Kelmin slowly climbed down from their pillar and fixed their eyes on the clouds in the distance. From their fleeting glimpse of what lay behind them, they were more worried than ever about what Jaimin would find.

Bailyn had similar concerns for Auro. His friend, too, had stepped into that abyss, which he feared held powers beyond his ability to handle and secrets that would only bring him sorrow.

# CHAPTER 3

# THE BANNERMAN

"That is the Pale," Auro said. "We mean to go beyond it." All his life, he had gazed at it from the spires of Amphora and the stations in the outer clouds. Entering it had long been impossible, always unthinkable. Was he just following the doomed course of the Empyreans, whose lust for energy had destroyed so much life and potential? *No,* he insisted. He and Jaimin merely sought to become whole again. Each had lost something they believed still existed somewhere within those clouds.

Jaimin felt a different guilt. He had abandoned the friends and fellow travelers with whom he shared the Eternigy. But as the distance between them increased, his thoughts dwelled more on the terrible flame burning inside him.

Auro was piloting solo while Jaimin looked pensively at the controls. "I was a pilot back home," Jaimin said. "With a quick training, I'm sure I could help you out." He marveled at this vessel carved into rock, which gave it the feeling of a cave, and how it harnessed the properties of space to move through the void like a billiard ball rolling on a baize table.

Auro appreciated the gesture but shook his head. "No time for a lesson. Once we hit those clouds, it will be all we can do just to stay intact."

The Pale loomed before them, forbidding and forbidden. Auro had seized the moment to answer a call only he could hear. Despite the prefects' orders and the Stylights' warnings, he was about to take the great plunge. Hovering for a moment on the precipice, putting his faith in this remarkable vessel forged from the remnants of a lost planet, he closed his eyes and resolutely took them into the clouds. Then the turbulence they had been dreading began to buffet them.

"I can't see far enough ahead to set a course," Auro complained. "For now, we're riding the currents, but one bad bounce could send us spinning."

The ship Jaimin was just admiring for its smooth flight now trembled as though a tsunami had crashed over the hull. The scopes were blinded by a swirl of raging clouds. They were inside the great storm the Amphorans had long observed from a safe distance. So far, their vessel persevered, but could it hold indefinitely?

Jaimin was at least unburdened by the long history that weighed on Auro as he struggled to keep the ship under control. "I've been here before," he said in an almost dreamy state, as if somehow communing with the currents and energies, knowing them in a way Auro could not despite all the instruments at his disposal. Rather than strapping in, Jaimin let his plasma flow so that his body glowed and steadied amid the tumult. "Our ship withstood the clouds; I believe I can, too. I'll go out and see if I can disperse them."

"Out there?" Auro couldn't believe what he was hearing. "Every probe we've ever sent in lost integrity within minutes."

"I'm not a probe," Jaimin returned with a grin.

Auro sputtered, but he remembered Bailyn's disbelief when he had ventured out to meet the dueling aliens. Acquiescing, he opened the air lock, and Jaimin streaked out and left the ship.

Jaimin's vision filled with a mosaic of colors. Dust particles crackled as they touched his blazing body. Channeling his plasma to propel himself forward, he became a streaking light and was surprised to feel the stormy currents retreating and the clouds parting before him. He turned back and saw the stone visage of the *Meteor* at the end of the tunnel he had just created through the clouds. Something was moving around it.

Straining his eyes, he discerned what looked like a cable flapping near the spherical hull. Auro must have released it, and Jaimin quickly deduced its purpose. As the clouds began to coalesce again, he lunged back toward the vessel and grabbed the cable in his searing hands. It seemed to be made of rock but was segmented and flexible. With the line in hand, he spurred forward again, pulling the vessel in tow. Unable to see very far, he lost all sense of distance. His limbs and back were strained, and he didn't know how long he could maintain his plasma. If it sputtered out, he would likely die quickly.

But as his strength gave way, so did the clouds. Shaking his head, he was beginning to feel that they had cleared the storm. The surrounding space was changing. He saw warmer colors than the murky blends of the Pale, mostly a soft yellow. He even saw stars, though they were hard to make out in the amber sheen.

Jaimin paused to take in the sights. The cable tightened and nearly slipped out of his grip. Seizing it again, he realized it was retracting and pulling him back toward the vessel. Before he knew it, the *Meteor*'s rock wall closed in on him. The air lock opened and he dove into it.

Drained and weary, his feet touched the floor with a sense of release. His plasma dissipated in exhaustion. It would be another day or two before he would regain full strength. In human form, he stepped forward woozily and was only then conscious of Auro reaching out to steady him. "You did it!" he exclaimed. "The storm is behind us. I believe we made it through the Pale."

They hurried back to the central cabin to activate the scopes. Now they were fully inside the nebula, if still only a shallow way into its vast depths. "No more storms ahead," Auro observed with growing excitement. "At least, nothing like what we just passed through. We seem to be inside a yellow cloud. It's quite serene." He paused. "There's an object ahead, not very large, giving off some sort of energy."

Jaimin gave him a quick look. "The bolide?"

"Maybe," Auro answered quietly.

They would need to work out a fast plan if they were going to come across the fire comet again. There was no city to run back to now. Auro pored over the instruments; Jaimin looked at the view screen and studied the new light. At first barely perceptible against the yellow backdrop, as they drew closer, it took on a distinct form. Much larger than the bolide, about a mile across, it, too, appeared to be enveloped in flame, but not red. This fire was a deep yellow, only a bit darker than the surrounding cloud, and it seemed to be fixed in position like a space station. The fire flowed horizontally, resembling a great flag rippling in a breeze.

"What could that be?" Jaimin whispered. "Do you detect the bolide anywhere nearby? It could be affiliated with it."

Auro shook his head. Suddenly, he looked alarmed. "We're accelerating again. It's not my doing. That thing is manipulating the currents, pulling us in. I can't steer away."

Possessed by some unknown force, the *Meteor* rolled right up to the object until the strange fire seared the hull. The heat was surprisingly mild, doing no damage. In a flash, they passed right through it and found themselves in a small pocket of space surrounded by a wall of yellow flame. In the center was a space rock of similar composition to the *Meteor*, though considerably bigger and more elongated in shape. As they drew near it, a portal opened on its surface, large enough for their vessel to enter, and resealed behind them.

They were now suspended inside some sort of cavern with a breathable atmosphere. At the foot of the opposite wall was a small archway that apparently led to the interior. They decided they had little choice but to accept this forced invitation. Auro donned his space suit, and Jaimin swelled his weakened plasma as much as he could. Together, they exited the *Meteor* and flew toward the archway. As they touched down at its threshold, a figure suddenly emerged from the darkness behind it.

"Out of the clouds, into the flame!" the man called to them. His speech was similar to Auro's. "Few have ridden the storms intact. Please come in."

With a wave of his hand, he turned and disappeared into the passageway. Auro and Jaimin hastened after him.

The tunnel-like path turned a bend to reveal a wide hall with a vaulted ceiling lined with wooden beams. Along the left side, windows looked out at the yellow fire, and on the wall on the right hung a series of embroidered tapestries. The hall culminated with a large fireplace, and in its hearth burned a yellow fire, presumably the same that surrounded them.

Their host, now halfway down the hall, turned back toward them. He had auburn hair and wore a fur-lined coat of the same color. His skin and eyes had a slight yellow gleam. His smooth face was guarded but not menacing. Clasping his hands behind his back, he watched them for a moment as they looked around.

"My name is Leone," he said. "You have come to the Oriflamme, beacon and banner of the Rae Citadels. I am its bannerman. I know that you are from beyond the nebula. In fact, one of you is from very far beyond." He paused and studied them again. "Please join me at the fireplace."

The fire was quite inviting. The tapestries lent the hall a monastic earthiness, most of them woven in the colors of the nebula clouds. A few depicted scenes and people. Auro and Jaimin also noticed a striking ornament mounted on the mantelpiece above the hearth: an engraving of a star with five thin rays extending from the center, each capped with a shining gem. They both sensed, as they had in space, that the yellow flame was the source of the comfort they felt despite their unsettling circumstances.

"You seem to know us," Auro said as they gathered. "All the same, I am Aurorno Augustine of Amphora, a city of Edda preserved from the nova. And this is Jaimin . . ." He paused, trying to remember the surname.

"Caraggio," Jaimin completed. "And you guessed right, I am from beyond. Specifically, from a Bioplane some light-years from here.

My people recently obtained the ability to make the voyage." He did not elaborate. He couldn't explain exactly how he had come to be there since he didn't really understand how Kelmin's engine worked or even the nature of the Eternigy that coursed through his body.

"Marvelous," Leone said. "Much has happened lately, inside and outside the nebula. I have a better view than most. Lord Raelight established this outpost to monitor the frontier and to welcome outsiders. The flame shelters me, but it also attracts those my lord wishes to know."

"Attracts?" Auro said. "You brought us here. But I take it you are not among those in the nebula who have assaulted my city?"

"If I were, would I offer you a drink?" He bent before a cabinet built into the mantel and retrieved a bottle and glasses nestled in the shelves, along with a tray that held a pile of what looked like an assortment of biscuits.

He led them toward a sofa off to the side of the fireplace with a low table before it. Neither of them had thought about food in a while. Jaimin reflected that he had not ingested anything since leaving Gemma. How long had it been? The drink was crisp and tart. Some of the biscuits were fruity and sweet, others a meaty protein, and still others were like bread or cake.

"Tell me," Leone probed as his guests sat and sampled the refreshments, "what do your people know about the interior of the nebula?"

"Not much," Auro admitted, leaning forward, clasping his glass in both hands, and looking into the fire. He didn't see any point in denying their ignorance. "The Amphorans have studied the outer clouds for as long as the nebula has been there, but we can't see through them. The Pale has always been inscrutable. We've only recently developed a vessel that could enter it, and I am the first to make the attempt."

He paused, trying to fit together myriad fragments of information and experiences. "You mentioned citadels. How many people live in the nebula? Are you all descendants of the Empyreans who brought on the nova? And what are these strange flames that permeate it?

There is the yellow around us here, and we have encountered a red fire that covers fearsome bolides, fire comets."

"I know something of the red," Leone replied. "Of course, this is the yellow band."

As he said this, he drew from a nook by the fireplace a long, thin poker and extended it over the flame. The top ignited, creating a torch. With this instrument in hand, he started back toward his guests. "After the nova, we were trapped in these clouds, but we were blessed with this fire, the first of the new energies released when the star was reborn."

"Reborn?" Auro said, a rash of bitterness suddenly pouring out of him. "Soliere was lost. The Empyreans destroyed it, and Edda as well—our chance for a new life—all because they couldn't resist drawing more energy for themselves. Was this fire your reward? For this, you condemned our people back into exile, stranded us in this dark corner of the galaxy with no star to sustain us?"

Leone waved his flaming wand in a circular motion, streaking yellow until it formed a golden circle between them. "Do not forget that the Empyreans created Soliere and its planet. Do not think that none of us mourned their fate. Our interests inevitably diverged, but we all suffered. The clouds have separated us for centuries. Now you have crossed over and can bring your sight to us."

The area inside the circle darkened and took on the likeness of a portal or view screen. Peering into it, Auro at first saw only an indistinct, crackling light. Then he could make out little silver objects glittering amid streaks of red. He gave a start, realizing what he was seeing: the Battle of the Pearls. The red bolides bursting out of the clouds and descending on Amphora's border stations, the fleet rushing to protect them, the Pearls consumed by the flames.

Auro had been in one of the Amphoran ships that had fought the invaders, too late and unprepared. The image focused on the last station to be engulfed, then one lone vessel as it was ensnared in the fiery tail of one of the comets and pulled with it into the nebula after they completed their infernal work. Auro cried out and reached into the circle, but its image dissolved, replaced by Leone peering back at him.

"Why did you show me that?" Auro asked.

"*I* didn't. The flame reached into your mind, searching for the trauma that drove you here. The yellow fire does not burn, but it does penetrate. Lord Raelight calls it the Gnost, the flame of self. He brought it to us from the star."

"Flame of self," Auro repeated. Wrestling with his emotions, he tried to gather his thoughts. "Your yellow fire may be soothing, but the red burns with an unnatural heat. Those bolides destroyed our stations, and we lost a good many people that day, including . . ."

He faltered. A memory had been pulled from his mind, but there was still the deeper question that haunted him, the mysterious call that had brought him there. But he was not ready to reveal his inner turmoil to this strange self-styled bannerman.

Leone looked at him as if sensing that he held a secret. "The red flame is the Magna," he explained. "The flame of discovery. The people of the Gnost have long contended with it as you have. It is hotter than the Gnost, more dangerous in some ways. A different energy altogether."

With that, he stepped back, leaving Auro to his bewildered thoughts, and turned to Jaimin, who was still on the sofa sipping his drink, showing no reaction to the little ordeal Auro had just experienced. "You have brought a different kind of power from outside," Leone addressed him. "What do you think the flame would show *you*?"

Jaimin shrugged. "I don't know. Right now, I don't even feel like myself." He was still fatigued from his exertion in the clouds. Mostly, he felt the lingering inner burn from the red fire. It was a queer feeling since he was used to reveling in the heat of his plasma and had thought his body could no longer be burned by anything.

"You were wounded by the Magna," Leone said.

Jaimin nodded. "It looked like fire, burned hot in space, intense beyond belief. And those who wield it may not be wholly contained within the nebula." He gestured toward Auro. "As for me, I just want to find healing." He shrugged again. "Anyway, I felt compelled to enter the clouds, and here I am."

"You wield a fire of your own."

Jaimin set down his glass. "Not fire. A sect on our world discovered a new source of energy unknown to our science. Our mystics think it is some manifestation of life energy. It first appeared in a cave as a diamond of light. I and two others were enveloped in it. We seemed to enter some new dimension filled with echoes of the human story. After a brief moment, it spit us out, but it left a peculiar imprint on each of us. In me, it manifests in the form of plasma."

"It does not burn you," Leone said, "but the Magna did." He held the yellow torch between them. "If you seek healing, the Gnost may provide it. Will you bring forth your power?"

Slowly, Jaimin stood, somehow feeling there was nothing to fear. He closed his eyes, and his skin began to glow crimson. Auro leaned forward, watching intently.

Leone's amber eyes widened and glinted in the scarlet light. He pointed his fiery baton at Jaimin's chest until it touched. There was a crackle as Gnost touched Eternigy. Jaimin felt soothed and serene on contact with the yellow fire. Then Leone withdrew, and Jaimin's plasma dissipated. His body and clothing were as they had been before. He could feel the new fire inside him, cooling the heat of the alien Magna and refreshing the strength of his plasma.

Leone smiled at both his guests. The yellow fire had disappeared from the tip of the poker, as if he had blown it out. He placed it back down by the mantel.

"Rest now," he said. "We can talk more in the morning. You will want to resume your expedition. Not far from here, Lord Raelight is waiting."

He led them through a door between the sofa and the last tapestry, into a hallway lit by cressets of yellow fire. After a short walk, they turned a corner into an alcove that contained a cabinet, a table, and chairs, with two doors on either side, all facing a large window. Both doors opened into little bed chambers, cozy and simply furnished. In the cabinet were trays of the same sorts of foods they had sampled before.

"Break your fast when you wake, and then join me again in the hall," Leone said. With that, he turned back around the corner and disappeared.

The offer of quiet repose made Jaimin and Auro aware of how tired they were. Each entered their selected room to be alone for a while with their thoughts before passing into a restful sleep.

※　※　※

The lights in his room gradually brightened, and Auro awoke feeling refreshed. He donned his full dress and slipped out into the alcove. Jaimin was already at the table, having poured himself a drink, and was sampling the biscuits.

"The same as before?" Auro asked.

"The drink is citrusy," Jaimin answered. "Good for breakfast. There are biscuits for every taste. Try the brown ones; they're a warm dough, and the orange ones taste like melon. I guess it's too much to hope for an omelet."

"I wonder who does his cooking?" Auro said wryly. He thought they should talk privately again before going back to the hall. The yellow flame that surrounded the station shone vibrantly through the window. "Well, we know this fire has some potent properties," he noted, reflecting on how Leone had wielded it. "Did he really heal you with that touch?"

Jaimin did seem more at peace. "I no longer feel the burning," he professed. "It seems to have soothed that. But I still feel incomplete. It's strange. I never really communed with the Eternigy the way Kelmin could, but I think I hear it now. It wants me to retrieve the part of it I lost."

With a tinge of guilt, Auro felt relieved that Jaimin still had a motive to continue exploring the nebula. He was not ready to turn back and might have need of his power.

"I still don't understand this place," Jaimin continued. "Leone called it a beacon, a repository of the flame. *Bannerman* is a strange title. He seems to be a lone sentry here, like a lighthouse keeper.

Evidently, there are cities of some sort farther inward, led by this lord he mentions. But these are not the people of the red fire but rather of the yellow? There are evidently different peoples within the nebula. Are they all descendants of the Empyreans, or do some come from elsewhere?"

Auro slowly chewed a doughy square, washed it down, and set his glass firmly on the table. "Let's go learn some more," he said.

They walked back to the main hall to find it empty. The yellow fire still danced in the hearth. For the first time, they looked closely at some of the tapestries. One depicted a striking scene: a man with a yellow beard standing on the rocky surface of an asteroid with his arms outstretched and a crowd of people before him. Yellow fires burned over his hands, and a star with five colored rays shone in the distance. Evidently, this was the same star that was emblazoned over the mantel. Jaimin was struck by how the five rays resembled a person, the top purple point like a head, arms green and blue, legs yellow and red. While they pondered the meaning of this and the other beautifully embroidered fabrics, Leone entered the room from the opposite end. They turned to see him walking toward them.

"I trust you rested well?" he asked.

"Yes," Auro said. He pointed up at the tapestry with the star. "Soliere?" he asked. "Is that what it looks like now?"

"It is indeed," Leone replied. "That is a depiction of the full star, though that is not how it appears in this band. You'll notice that one of the rays is yellow. Lord Raelight is greeting his pilgrims, the Empyrean refugees caught in the nova. My parents were among them. We are now in the very asteroid you see them huddling on. Lord Raelight came from the yellow ray and brought the Gnost."

Jaimin furrowed his brow. "What do you mean he came from the ray?"

Leone stepped back and looked squarely at Auro. "What do you know about the events that brought on the nova?"

"Our histories are less than clear," Auro admitted. "They focus on the heroism of the Eddans in surviving the cataclysm and saving our city. In truth, we don't know how the nova happened or what guilt our own people might have shared in bringing it about. All we knew was that the Empyreans had rejected life on Edda and took to the old ways of trying to live as close to the sun as they could. But whatever they were doing affected Soliere, which in turn affected Edda's climate and stability. Then came the war and finally the nova."

"That is all essentially true," Leone said, "but I can fill in the story a bit more.

"The Empyreans indeed wanted to be close to their new sun, though most were content to remain in their stations and go no farther. However, a core of the most powerful, the Light Lords, looked unflinchingly into the corona. They would link arms and glide out together, bearing technology that could absorb the starlight and even break it apart, drawing in different facets of its energy.

"Many Empyreans realized the danger that this courted. They ached at the prospect of Edda's destruction, but they could not resist the energies that the Light Lords drew to them. Eventually, almost all had fallen under the sway of the five greatest lords. There was Raelight and Romeon, Thyrr and his wife, Vitruvia. Greatest of all was Aris. By this time, he was the eldest of the Empyreans, the last survivor of the Great Journey. He had been born just before it began, and his young body at his mother's breast absorbed the most power along the way."

"Aris," Auro intoned. The Amphorans had lost the name, at least among the common public, but the legacy of the Empyreans' mad leader lingered like a fragment of a dreaded history.

"He was revered as the last living link to Sol," Leone went on. "He started the Journey as a babe and thereafter aged so slowly that the following centuries were like decades to him. The other Light Lords followed him, and eventually, by the power of the star, they fused their five individual bodies into a single form. In this fusion, known as the Pentheon, they ventured closer to Soliere, oblivious to all that was happening behind them.

"As the conflict with Edda broiled, many back in the stations were alarmed and sought to come to an accommodation. But in the end, no Empyreans could bear to be away from the star. The Pentheon was bringing about changes that made Soliere at once more terrifying and enticing. The time for choosing had come. All now followed the Pentheon to their fate.

"The star erupted, releasing energy in a multitude of colors. Then the rays shot out of the core, each a distinctive hue. But the nova broke the fusion. The constituent beings of the Pentheon, with the possible exception of Aris, were ejected through the rays and hurled into the nebula. In their brief moment inside the star, it was like they had become embryos in a great womb, and they retained little more memory of it than one has of his own birth. Soliere still existed but was reduced to its core, an intense white light with five colored rays, and the nebula was filled with much of its energy in the form of swirling clouds.

"As for the rest of the Empyreans, most emerged not far from here. They didn't know it yet, but they had been caught in the path of the yellow ray, the very ray that had sent Lord Raelight out of the star. The Gnost light traveled farthest and formed the outermost band. But some of our people had ventured closer to Soliere as the Pentheon took flight and may have been trapped in bands farther inward."

Leone walked over to one of the other tapestries. It depicted a circular shape against a background of space with concentric rings of darkening colors. There was a yellow rim, followed by a thicker red, a green, the blue widest of all, and then an inner ring of purple. Finally, at the center was the five-pointed star. Auro and Jaimin realized they were looking at a picture of the nebula itself.

"This is our realm," Leone said, pointing at the yellow ring. "The Gnost Band. The light of each ray circles the core star. The Light Lords were each infused with something more than light: the great flames. The Gnost is the coolest and brings healing, reflection, inner peace. Lord Raelight used it to soothe our loss. Though he could not take us out of the nebula, he helped us create a new home within it, and so we built the Rae Citadels here along the farthest edge of the star's reach."

Auro studied the tapestry. He pointed to the next band, the red, bordered by the yellow and green on either side. "So Lord Raelight presides here with his Gnost flame, and I take it the red bolides came from there?"

"The Magna lord is Romeon, the only lord we have seen since the nova. As you may have guessed, Lord Raelight's followers have never been able to leave the Gnost Band. The outer clouds keep us in the nebula as much as they have kept you out, and another kind of barrier separates us from the Magna.

"There is a point where the yellow light can go no farther, where it runs up against the red with a fraction of space between them, a dark film devoid of light and impenetrable, or so we thought. In time, Romeon achieved contact with Raelight and even crossed the barrier to visit our band. From him we learned that all the lords, save Aris, had been hurled out of the star and infused with the light of one of the rays, each confined within their band. While the Gnost can see inward, the Magna sees outward. Romeon knew many things Raelight did not. He even shared his flame with some of our people, and it kindled new desires in them, though it also burned."

Jaimin nodded and rubbed his chest.

"Romeon wanted to combine the red and yellow flames," Leone went on. "He thought that would be the first step to reuniting the Pentheon and reaching the core of Soliere again. But Raelight resisted. He did not want to pollute the Gnost's serenity with the Magna's restless burning and seeking. But some of our people were drawn to the red fire and went with Romeon back to his band."

"So Romeon controls the bolides?" Jaimin asked. "Do you know what the flame did to me?"

Leone shook his head. "No one from the citadels who touched the Magna has stayed in our band. And in any case, your power is as foreign to them as it is to me."

"Then I should seek out this Lord Raelight," Jaimin declared. "If he is in conflict with Romeon, perhaps we can help each other."

"I've already sent word that you are coming," Leone said. "I think he will be intrigued. Only once before have we received visitors from beyond the clouds, and they were not from one of the legendary Bioplanes."

At this, Auro stood up. "Others have passed through? Who . . . when?"

"I will leave it to the lord to reveal what he will."

Auro turned away from the tapestries, walked to the other side of the hall by the tall windows, and gazed out at the yellow fire. He reflected on the fact that the nebula was not actually very old; indeed, he would soon meet a being who had taken part in its creation. He looked back at Jaimin and the keeper of this strange banner.

"Can you tell us any more of what awaits us out there?" he asked. "We have already done the near impossible in crossing the Pale. The Amphorans regard the nebula as something deadly, unknowable. Now we know that the Pale can indeed be crossed and there is life beyond it. But what is this yellow space of yours like? Do any new storms or dangers lie ahead?"

Leone folded his arms and stood between his two guests in the middle of the hall. "The clouds are most violent along the outer edges, what you call the Pale. When Soliere went nova, the energies that did not collect in the bands combined in a stormy crust. Few beings or ships can pass through it as you did. But to my knowledge, there is nothing like the Pale anywhere else. From here to the Rae Citadels, your vessel will be bathed in the Gnost light, an experience our people have found to be most purifying. And you will see the star but not its entire visage. Throughout this band, it appears solid yellow, for the yellow ray and its light are all we see."

"How do people live in here?" Jaimin asked. "This is a sort of space station with life support, but you said the Empyrean refugees were floating out there until Lord Raelight gathered them on this rock. They had no space suits, if the picture is accurate. How did they survive?"

"They wore suits when they followed the Pentheon out toward the star, but after they were enveloped in the Gnost, they found they didn't need them. The concentrated starlight, filtered through the yellow ray, changed them more than the Empyreans had been changed through all their centuries of exposure to solar energy. Then Raelight completed the transformation when he touched them with his flame. The Gnost courses through our cells, its currents fill our lungs, its force acts like gravity, and its waves even carry our voices."

"You mean the cloud essentially simulates an atmosphere?" Jaimin marveled. "What about newcomers like us? Will we be able to breathe out there, even talk to each other?"

"You, too, have been touched by the flame," Leone replied.

"Yes, and I have touched the red as well as the yellow," Jaimin said. "If each band is a reflection of a different facet of the star's energy, what do you know about the other bands?"

Leone turned back toward the tapestry and drew a breath. Even he seemed to struggle to comprehend the mysteries of these colored rings and the core star they circled.

"What lies beyond the Gnost, beyond the self? None who remain in the yellow band, save Raelight himself, have been outside it. With good reason. But if you are destined to push on toward the core, despite all the barriers in the way, I can tell you what little I know.

"The Magna Band I know best. It is said to be full of red fire, with great volcanoes and lava flows. I have not touched its flame as you have, but I have met Lord Romeon, and he lured some of our brethren away. He is a man of great ambitions and the flame to stoke them. Just as the Gnost kindles self-reflection, the Magna agitates one's drive to discover. Romeon broke through the barrier to come to us and mixed the yellow and red to create a new cloud between our bands through which his vessels can cross."

"Is that how his bolides have been able to sweep right through the Pale toward Amphora?" Auro asked.

Leone nodded. "So far, the Gnost-Magna barrier is all he has been able to breach. His flame is not powerful enough to carry him inward toward the star. That is why he wants to fully combine the Gnost and Magna flames, but Raelight has refused him. Then Romeon learned of your city, the remnant of Edda outside the nebula. First, he launched scouts and then a full fleet through our band to reach it. He thought you might have technologies he could use, and I think he was also interested in the outer clouds, for they have traces of all the rays."

"And what about the bands beyond his?" Jaimin asked.

"The lord of the green band is Vitruvia, and the lord of the blue is Thyrr. Vitruvia wields the Syntha, the flame of growth, which we believe is a force for life, perhaps like your Eternigy. Thyrr's is the Thyrrenean, the flame of depth. His band is vast and ocean blue, and though we know it has limits, it also has an endlessness in which one can lose oneself.

"Vitruvia and Thyrr were once married and greatly enhanced their powers through their union, but they were of different temperaments, and it is said their affection diminished as their powers grew. Vitruvia wanted to have a child and was sure their offspring would be greater even than Aris. While she became more nurturing as she grew in stature, keener on creating and developing life, Thyrr grew colder and more unyielding. He grasped how unimaginably vast the universe was—how, in a sense, futile that made our existence in it. This insight made him bitter and all the more determined to do the impossible, to overcome the endlessness. In his struggle, there was no place for a child. By the time of the nova, they had drifted apart. Yet both remained devoted to Aris. Lord Raelight says that it was from them that Aris first thought of merging the Light Lords into the Pentheon."

"And the purple?" Auro said. "That is the band that contains the star itself?"

His voice intoned it as a question, though he didn't know exactly what he was asking. The nebula that had long been hidden behind the clouds of the Pale was starting to take on definition and reality in his mind. The bands, colored rings in the strange map, were now filled with personalities and even some history. But his eyes were still drawn to the center, to the pointed star immersed in its purple yolk.

"We call it simply the Empyreal Band," Leone replied. "Lord Raelight believes Aris still dwells there. He may even remain inside the star. When Raelight was sent out through the yellow ray, he only fleetingly experienced the Empyreal light. He thinks it is the densest band, almost solid, where all states of existence are one and all energies converge."

Auro and Jaimin looked at each other and back at Leone, taking in all they had heard. "And we are free to explore all this?" Jaimin asked. "You say that Lord Raelight's people have neither the ability nor the desire to leave this band. But Auro and I are from outside, and between us, we have powers and motivations quite different from Empyreans."

"I think I speak for Lord Raelight in saying that you are under no power but your own," Leone said. "Of course, not everyone beyond our borders may share that mind."

An ominous statement but fair enough. There was silence as Auro and Jaimin stood in the center of the hall with Leone. The yellow flame shone through the window, illuminating the tapestries that mapped out the nebula and perhaps their futures. Leone led them back to the fireplace, where they relaxed with another drink and talked of many things relating to the history of the Empyreans, the Amphorans, and the Bioplanes. They agreed that their stories were about to converge, as perhaps they were always meant to.

"There is something I'm still wondering about," Jaimin said. "My shipmates and I came here without knowing what we were heading into. Through Kelmin's technology, we channeled the Eternigy to find the farthest place in the cosmos where we could detect human life. We ended up in the Pale. But if there are humans inside the nebula, why didn't we emerge in one of the inner bands, or even near the star itself, if Aris is there?"

"Maybe your ship tried to take you there," Auro said, "but the Pale obstructed its flight, threw you off course."

Leone tilted his head. "Or it may have fulfilled its mission too well. If its directive was to find human life, you may find that the farther you go toward the star, the less human the life is."

These words brought a chill to his guests, even in the soothing warmth of the yellow hearth. It seemed there were forces within the nebula that wanted something from them even as they were searching for their hearts' desires. But if they proceeded farther in, they might be confronted with desires beyond any that inflamed a mere human heart.

# CHAPTER 4

# THE DIAMOND DOOR

The lights twinkled in harmony with the music. Capering among the tables, minstrels strung fiddles and blew into flutes while the overhead lamps brightened and dimmed to their rhythms. Waiters in tunics whirled around, carrying trays of meats and fruits and cakes covered with cream. Amphora's elite had gathered in the rotunda at the narrow tip of the neck just beneath the bowl of the crown, ringed by a transparent wall that looked out into a glorious panorama of stars and colored clouds. Shanna and Kelmin, along with Bailyn, were the honored guests at this festive dinner, seated at a triangular table on the central dais.

Five days had passed since the Gemmans' arrival and their vision with the Stylights. Since then, they had met all the prefects on the governing council. Word had spread of the arrival of a trio of the half-legendary Noctarians who called themselves Gemmans, travelers from the faraway Bioplanes. They were inundated with embassies from scientists and scholars in all manner of fields asking about their world and how they had made their voyage. In return, their hosts showed them much of their splendid city, touring a succession of laboratories and greenhouses, facilities and observatories, all of which sustained a community that had existed for centuries with no planet or sun.

Kelmin was intrigued by the feat of extracting a city from the crust of a doomed world. Shanna was less interested in the details of how the place functioned. She did not doubt what humans could accomplish; her ancestors had created a bountiful continent out of barren rock. The exhilaration of their mission was fading. From the moment Sultaan had appeared on their view screen, she had felt a gnawing apprehension that they were being drawn into some intrigue in this world that they didn't understand.

But this dinner set her at ease, and she enjoyed the food and lovely views. Her thoughts drifted back to their experience on the pillar high above the crown. They had not seen any of the Stylights again until this evening. Falconhyn and Etemeena were seated near the far wall, and neither came to greet them at their table. Glancing at them from time to time, Shanna always saw Falconhyn looking out the great window as he ate, lost in thought. She exchanged a nod with Etemeena, who looked as regal and radiant as before, the lights reflecting off her white gown and golden circlet.

The guests of honor hardly spoke to one another amid the music and flutter of well-wishing dignitaries. As the evening wore on, the feasting subsided, the music quieted, and to close out the affair, Sultaan and a fellow prefect named Ormonde stood upon the dais and delivered a gracious address, marveling at the historic occasion of two cousin worlds finally coming together.

The people had been told about Auro and Jaimin, but only that they were exploring the Pale, not that they had entered the nebula. Auro was widely known, as Bailyn was not, and many were aware that his parents' ship had been lost at the Battle of the Pearls. If Auro and Jaimin returned, they might bring news of what lay behind the clouds. If not, the people could be told they were lost to the storms. The prefects were politicians, and after several days in their company, Shanna missed the serene explorations of the Stylights.

Sultaan and Ormonde finished their speech and lingered with the guests as the throng of diners paid their final respects and began to file into the elevators built into the wall around the rotunda, which either lifted their passengers up to the crown or descended into the lower levels of the stem. None of the prefects had asked about what had transpired up in Simeon Tower and seemed to regard it as beyond their purview. Shanna and Kelmin were left to wonder what Sultaan might have told them.

With the great room cleared, the three guests were left alone with the two prefects. Ormonde, a silver-haired man with an elegant manner, turned toward them and said, "After so many official meetings, I trust this evening gave you a more pleasing view of Amphora."

"It was lovely," Shanna said sincerely. "I only wish we were more worthy ambassadors."

"You could not be more fitting. Your arrival has touched our people like nothing in our history since the nova."

"No less for us," Kelmin admitted. In truth, he and Shanna were overwhelmed. They had embarked on this journey with a similar mindset as when they had explored a neighboring Bioplane, but this really was quite different. These people were not only separated from Gemma by millennia and light-years, but by a whole different history and way of life.

"Gemma is called the jewel because of its crystalline mountains," Shanna said, "but humans have wrought other world-jewels. Your city is beautiful. In time, we may take some Amphorans back with us and return with more Gemman representatives. With our ship's engine to bridge them, Amphora and the Bioplanes can become one community. Speaking of which, we would like to board our ship again. It's time we tried to contact Jaimin. Maybe we can join him and Auro in the nebula and see what they have discovered in there."

At this, Sultaan shifted and glanced sidelong to where Falconhyn had been sitting, but the Stylight had slipped out.

Ormonde clasped his hands and gave them a diplomatic smile. "We agreed in council not to take any further actions in these matters until we hear more from the Stylights. They have been trying to extend their sight through the clouds. We have made appointments for you to meet with more of the guilds."

"We don't plan to run out on you," Kelmin said. "Well, not unless Jaimin is in some dire need. But it's time we tried to make contact."

"I'm afraid that won't be possible," Sultaan said stiffly. He backed away, his eyes shifting between them and the window with the nebula swirling in the distance. "Aurorno defied us when he entered the Pale. While the Stylights are probing the clouds, we cannot afford to attempt communications, given the threat that lurks within."

"What threat is that?" Shanna asked.

"You know," Sultaan replied coldly. "You have seen it yourself."

An uncomfortable silence fell. Shanna's suspicions roared back to the fore of her mind. All along, she had known something wasn't right—the Stylights' aloofness, the prefects filling their days with tours and meetings, showing them much but telling them little, formality without substance, deflection and delay. Their hosts had kept them occupied while the powers on this world had spun their hidden machinations. Shanna and Kelmin had tried more than once to assert their rights without insolence. Now the two prefects were also eying each other and seemed to be engaging in some nonverbal parley. While Sultaan stood rigid and distant, Ormonde opened his arms to the Gemmans.

"Of course, we understand your rights to your ship and to your friend. We also worry about Aurorno. Our laws are binding to us, but you are ambassadors here. I'm afraid we are unaccustomed to the subtleties of diplomatic relations." He paused and addressed Sultaan. "Will you relay to Simeon Tower that our guests would like to board their ship again and send a message into the clouds? My friends, give us until tomorrow to gain the consent of the Stylights and the governing council. Once we have it, and I have no doubt we will, you will be back on your vessel and may seek your answers."

Sultaan pursed his lips and bowed his head. "Forgive me," he said to the Gemmans, looking and sounding like the shifty official who had first appeared on their screen as they had flown toward the exocity. "These are uncertain times. All the leaders must be informed before any signals are sent into the clouds. But we should work things out by morning." With that, he turned with a billowing of his cloak and entered an elevator to take him up into the crown.

Shanna and Kelmin turned back uneasily toward Ormonde, though they felt a bit relieved to be left with him because he still exuded some sense of trust. "We understand your need to protect your city," Kelmin said. "The last thing we want is to cause any strife among the prefects or the Stylights. But the *Astraeus* is our vessel. You have no right to withhold it from us, and we have the right to try to find our friend."

"That I do not dispute," Ormonde replied. "But I cannot speak for all." He looked around warily, then lowered his voice to a whisper. "I know why your request is delayed and why you have been kept on such a rigid schedule, apart from a sincere desire to exchange knowledge."

Ignoring their puzzled looks, he motioned them to follow him into one of the elevators. Instead of taking them up into the city where they had been staying, the lift descended.

"Your ship was moved," he admitted. "They were never able to get inside it, but they succeeded in lowering it from the landing pad under Simeon Tower deep into the stem for further study."

Kelmin was incensed. "If you wanted a look at our ship, you could have asked," he growled. "All this time you've feted us, all these meetings—it was just a diversion to violate our property?"

"It was not my decision," Ormonde said gravely. He looked troubled.

Kelmin was about to say more, but Shanna quieted him with a glance. She wondered if this had anything to do with their vision with the Stylights, the revelation of whom the fire entity they encountered may have been.

The elevator came to a stop and opened into a dim and deserted corridor. Although he was among the highest-ranked administrators in the city, Ormonde was watchful and anxious. "I will bring you to your ship," he whispered, "but I will need your help. Will you trust me?"

Kelmin scoffed. Shanna looked at Bailyn. He, too, had been swept along with the events ever since they had returned from the Pale. "What do you think we should do?" she asked.

Bailyn's eyes darted between the prefect and the Gemmans. "I would not wait for the Stylights' permission to attempt contact with Jaimin and Auro," he said. "Auro is my oldest friend, though he was born with warmer blood. Our parents were fellow scientists studying the nebula, and I was with him at the Battle of the Pearls. When he decided to enter the Pale, he trusted me to escort you back to Amphora. If what you saw with the Stylights was true, Auro is on a personal mission that he never confided in me. We are all groping in the dark, blinded by the veil of the clouds."

Ormonde said nothing, and the others sensed that he did not know what they had seen.

Shanna nodded. "We have no idea if that was real, but it's time to search out the truth. We can begin by analyzing the sensor records from our time in the clouds."

"The follow me," Ormonde signaled. He led them down the winding hallway. Kelmin took the rear, his sensors and weapons ready. He didn't see any way of getting the *Astraeus* into space without being detected. Whatever Ormonde's motivations, he was taking a big risk.

The hallway wound on until Ormonde stopped them by an indentation in the wall between two windows. He pressed his hand against a panel just above it, and the wall opened into a shallow chamber. The sides and even the ceiling and floor were composed of a green but transparent crystalline substance that gave them an all-encompassing view of space and the nebula clouds in an emerald tint. As they filed inside, Shanna and Kelmin realized they had entered another elevator that began to slide down the outside of the city.

"These exterior lifts are for officials and others who earn the privilege," Ormonde said. "There are no residents where we are going." He instructed them to grab the handles along the wall as they accelerated rapidly, dropping more than a mile. Beneath their feet, they could vaguely make out the bottom point of the world. For a moment, it looked like the lift might fly into the depths, but suddenly, it began to slow down and finally came to a stop. The chamber locked in place, and Ormonde opened the door to pitch darkness.

"I'd rather not illuminate the whole level," he whispered to Kelmin. "Do you have a small light?"

Kelmin took a device from his armor that projected a sharp beam into what seemed like a vast, dark basement. Ormonde led them on. Veering toward a side wall, he ran his fingers along its surface, with Kelmin shining his light on it.

"Fifty years ago, there were research centers down here," Ormonde remarked. "Now this bay is used for storage and for keeping things out of sight." His body tensed as his fingertips detected something.

"It's a door," Kelmin said, activating his scanners. "Heavy composition. An alloy I'm not familiar with."

"Yes," Ormonde affirmed. He pressed his hands against it. Kelmin's light revealed an image chiseled into the surface under his fingers. A simple triangle.

"Not this one," Ormonde declared. "Let's move on."

They resumed their pace, and the prefect continued his tactile inspection. They came upon another door made of a different material. It, too, had a shape etched in its center: two stacked triangles, one pointing up and one down, forming a diamond.

"It seems to be made of diamond, too," Kelmin observed.

"This is our door," Ormonde said. "Now is where I depend on you. Can you open it?"

Kelmin stepped back. "To open a locked door," he said, "you either need a key or enough force to break through."

"A key I don't have. But locks are mechanisms; one who perceives the mechanism might make a key."

Kelmin considered this. What sort of key could open this door?

He pressed both hands against the etching and closed his eyes. His gauntlets vibrated, and a faint ringing echoed across the surface of the door. It began to glow.

Ormonde, Shanna, and Bailyn stepped back. Kelmin pressed with all his strength as the surface shuddered under the energy and pressure. Grudgingly, it began to give way. The right side swung inward; Kelmin lunged forward with it. He regained his footing with the help of his propulsion jets and turned back to face his shocked companions. "You were on the right track," he said to Ormonde. "Sonic vibrations. It took all my intuition to find the right frequency."

"Your success speaks to the truth of your power," Ormonde said. "The Stylights have a real key that fits right over the etching, which I suspect works much the same way."

"If you wanted it, you might have asked, good prefect," came a voice from the darkness behind them.

It was Falconhyn's voice, and as it sounded, dozens of lights illuminated across the ceiling, revealing the leader of the Stylights standing on the other side of the bay, with Sultaan beside him. He held up an object on a chain: a square slate etched with the shape of a diamond just like the one on the door. "Our guests were given fine lodgings up in the crown. Why would you bring them into our deepest rooms, which even you do not have clearance to see?"

Ormonde stepped forward. "The prefects' writ runs the whole length of our city, save only the highest point of Simeon Tower. You claim to deny my rights here. Why? Because you have hidden away the property of our guests?"

"And you tell them that we are thieves?" Sultaan rejoined sharply.

Before Ormonde could say more, a contingent of troops stormed into the bay. They wore leather jerkins over gray fatigues, with thick metal belts that bore an array of weapons and tools, and each held a rifle that Kelmin discerned could fire formidable lasers. Forking left and right, they spread out behind their two commanders, who represented Amphora's highest administrative and spiritual authorities.

Kelmin's armor hummed and his weapons locked, but he held his fire. Projecting his voice through his helmet with the authority of a former captain of the Gemman Security Corps, he called out, "Hear me! We have no intention to interfere with your affairs or do anything that would endanger this city. We ask only to reclaim our ship and seek out our friend."

"Your intentions are not at issue," Sultaan said. "You have powers and technologies that can help us extend our sight beyond the clouds. For generations, we have lived on the edge of the nebula with no ability to see inside it, never knowing what threats might lurk within, and lately, threats have come. The Stylights sensed that a new power was heading our way that might be our salvation. This also came true: Here you are."

"You had no right to take our ship," Shanna said. "Don't we want the same thing: to find Auro and Jaimin? If that means fighting those bolides again, we'll be with you."

"They don't want to find Aurorno," Ormonde interjected, his eyes darting from Sultaan to Falconhyn. "That has been clear for some time. Why don't you finally reveal what you learned from our visitors on Simeon Tower?"

Falconhyn stepped forward. "The ones lost at the Battle of the Pearls may still live."

Ormonde let out a breath of comprehension. "Armarna?"

"Yes," Kelmin said. "Evidently, it was Auro's mother we encountered outside the Pale. She flew out of the bolide, and Jaimin fought with her until Auro interfered. It seems he didn't know it was her."

*Or did he?* Shanna wondered. But she said: "Jaimin entered the nebula because he sought healing after the flame injured him. Maybe Auro is looking for his mother. But why should any of this mean we cannot board our own ship?"

"Something or someone in the nebula wants to draw us in," Falconhyn insisted. "In our vision, we saw glimpses of its interior and history, but only glimpses. Descendants of the old Empyreans still live behind those clouds, separated by different energies that reverberate from the core star. Indeed, it seems that they have been trapped within those clouds, at least until recently. Do you think it a coincidence that you Noctarians acquired the power to come here just when powers within the nebula were starting to make their way out of the clouds?"

"I don't know," Kelmin said, bewildered. "You fear that our contacting Jaimin might draw out another attack from the bolides or that they might draw us in and use us against you? It doesn't have to be that way. If Auro's mother is in the nebula, we might be able to reach her, too. Learn who controls these bolides and what they want. Maybe there's a way to seal off the nebula so that whatever's in there cannot threaten you again."

"These people are on their own journey," Ormonde declared. "We have no right to impede them because we fear the unknown."

"Events will take their course," Falconhyn replied. "But the Noctarians must remain on Amphora. We have need of their power, and we must probe the nebula again before we try to reach within it."

The soldiers arrayed behind Sultaan and Falconhyn fixed their weapons. All were saddened at the breach of trust that had occurred this fateful evening, which had begun with a celebration of friendship, yet all were determined to stand their ground.

Ormonde appealed for calm, but Shanna preempted him. "We won't continue to help you if you prevent us from finding Jaimin," she said. "We want nothing from you or your world, your towers or pillars. We want our ship!"

With a wave of her hand, a dark-purple substance materialized halfway between them and the armed throng, running across the floor from one end of the bay to the other. About a foot thick and initially just as high, it continued to rise, reaching a height of several feet. But then its growth abruptly stopped. Something was interfering with Shanna's ability to generate the matter. Falconhyn's eyes pierced her from across the room. Somehow, he had blocked her. As she looked over in confusion, the soldiers rushed past their leaders to scramble over her half-finished barrier. Then came the crackle of laser fire.

"Come, Shanna!" Bailyn shouted from behind. He and Ormonde were dashing through the diamond door. She doubled back to join them, seeking refuge in the room behind it.

Kelmin activated his jets and flew up nearly to the ceiling, fully armored and shielded by a force field. Compared with the Gemman Security Corps, which he had trained and led and later fought as a renegade, these troops were lightly armed and had no power of flight. Keeping his weapons on a light setting, Kelmin fired wide stun beams upon them. Half of them fell, and the dismayed remnants retreated back behind the wall.

Kelmin landed atop the wall, an imposing armored centurion facing down a legion. Yet he found himself inhibited from further action. Falconhyn was hindering him just as he had stymied Shanna.

"Quantus!" Shanna cried out. She rarely used his first name.

Jolted out of his paralysis, Kelmin's jets lifted him back and through the door. Bailyn slammed it shut. "This won't keep them out," he said. "They have the key."

"I will," Shanna replied. "Stand back."

A massive grid materialized over the door, grafting to the wall on either side. This time, Shanna completed her work.

Momentarily secure, they all looked around the room. It seemed to be a hangar bay about fifty yards deep. The far wall was curved, no doubt the outer wall of the cylindrical stem. It had a rectangular opening to space covered with a force field. Parked in front of it was the *Astraeus*.

"They moved it here?" Kelmin asked Ormonde.

The prefect nodded. "They towed it down from the tower. They tried to open its air lock but found they could not get in unless they forced it, so they gave up the attempt."

"I doubt they could have forced it, either," Kelmin grumbled. "But just like your door back there, it's easy when you have a key." He pressed a nodule on his right forearm, and part of the silver hull jutted out and slid down, forming a ramp to the opening.

They hastened into the ship. Bailyn was now familiar with the vessel and helped Ormonde along as they followed Kelmin and Shanna to the flight deck.

Kelmin activated the main view screen. Resting his hands on the console, he bowed his head and seemed to be in communion with the sensors and processors. The screen flickered, the nebula appeared, and the scopes zoomed in on the clouds.

"How far can the sensors reach?" Shanna asked.

Kelmin seemed so deep in meditation, she only half expected him to answer, but at the sound of her voice, he shook his head and backed away from the console. "I'm trying to configure the instruments to locate Jaimin's distinctive energy signature, but there's too much interference."

"Is there anything here that might enhance our own connection to him, enough to relay a simple message?"

"No," Kelmin said dejectedly.

"Perhaps we can find the *Meteor*," Ormonde suggested. "That vessel has a beacon designed to pierce the clouds. Our scientists thought your instruments might be able to pick it up, even use it to communicate."

As they pondered this, there came a rustling from the air lock. Before they had time to react, a lone intruder strode right in. It was Falconhyn, surprising them for a second time. "And what will you say to them?" the Stylight inquired as he stepped through the door.

"You!" Kelmin cried. "How did you get past the wall?"

"The young lady made it well, but it is only as strong as her will. With an eye for where it is weak, one may find he can walk right through what appears to be solid."

Shanna shuddered. She glanced at the screen showing the outer bay. Her grid was still there. Of the powerful beings she had encountered since her immersion in the Eternigy, none had ever simply walked through one of her creations. "But only you," she noted. "You couldn't bring your troops through."

"They are cutting through as we speak. I saw no reason to wait." He sighed. They all sensed he had come forth alone to talk through their differences.

"Ever since you arrived," he said, "the Stylights and the prefects have discussed what to do. Aurorno dared attempt the forbidden and entered the nebula. Since your shipmate accompanied him, we believed it was only a matter of time before you would seek him out. Aurorno is driven to find his mother and explore the clouds, but the prefects fear he is exposing the city to danger. If Armarna is truly the entity you encountered, she has likely been corrupted by powers that lie within. If the fire comets can break the confines of the nebula, nothing outside it may be safe, perhaps not even your Bioplanes."

"Aren't they coming anyway?" Shanna asked. "They have already threatened Amphora. If we can pierce the clouds, why not try to reach them?"

Suddenly, the console beeped. Kelmin gasped in shock. "I don't believe it. We're picking up a transmission. It's from within the nebula!"

The speaker crackled with static and the hissing of what might have been a voice.

"It's very scrambled," he said. "But there seems to be enough data to modulate it into a form we can decipher." He muted the speakers and activated a new screen whose presentation of the clouds warped into a blurry picture that sharpened into the image of a young girl.

They all stared dumbfounded at the child. She looked to be about a decade in age, with dark-blonde hair and a pale face. Her eyes glowed with an orange light.

Kelmin reactivated the speakers, and the static morphed into a child's voice. "Is anyone there? Is this the ship from beyond the clouds? Jaimin's ship?"

The girl seemed to be waiting for a response. Her glowing eyes made it hard to read her features, but her voice was in distress.

"We can't answer her," Kelmin said. "She's just talking to our signal. She can't see or hear us."

"If you're out there, please help us," she continued. "We are trapped by the fire. I'll send you a path to find us."

Her image vanished. Static swelled up again through the speakers, but the console also lit up as if each circuit had been activated to a frenzy.

"We're receiving something," Kelmin said breathlessly.

"It could be a trick," Shanna said, though she ached to believe they had found a way to reunite with Jaimin.

At that moment, a blast from outside the ship filled their ears and rocked the vessel. They all stumbled toward the walls to steady themselves.

Shanna knew at once what had happened, sensing her wall had been breached. Looking up at the screen, they saw the soldiers pouring into the bay with their weapons drawn. Sultaan, his face grim, strode in behind them.

# CHAPTER 5

# GOLDEN DOMES

Auro and Jaimin stayed one more night in the Oriflamme and, the next morning, said farewell to its enigmatic bannerman. Boarding the *Meteor*, they launched off the station's cavern-like port, passed through the surrounding yellow flame, and plunged deeper into the nebula.

As Leone had explained, they were well inside the Gnost Band of Lord Raelight, and with his leave, they were heading toward his citadels. The clouds no longer buffeted them. It was as though they had left a stormy shore and found smooth sailing in the open ocean. As they ventured deeper into the band, the amber glow intensified into a richer bronze. Soon, in the distance, they saw the bright visage of the core star, but only its yellow face.

"Soliere," Auro whispered with the longing of an exile glimpsing his old home. Even Jaimin felt exhilarated at the sight.

This was not just any star but the spawn of their ancestral sun, albeit a remnant left after a nova and a fraction of its former size, though still massive to human scale. Its yellow ray bathed this part of the nebula. Most striking was how it made them feel. They recalled the Oriflamme's gentle fire that had soothed and welcomed them.

Lit by the Gnost, space no longer seemed dark and cold but a warm haven that kindled hearts and affirmed life. Jaimin felt like he could fly into it even without his plasma. But he noticed Auro suddenly tense up at the controls. The sensors at last signaled something ahead.

It looked to be human-made. As they closed in, they realized it was a string of golden lights. To Auro, they looked rather like the Pearl Stations, yet these resembled glittering buttons embedded in the fabric of space.

Auro slowed their craft to examine the peculiar sight. It was a cluster of five large space rocks arrayed one after another a few thousand miles apart, each only about twenty miles across. Upon them, buildings arose right out of the rock. Like Amphora, these were exocities, but much smaller and with a more earthy appearance, built on asteroids shaped like tidal islands and gradually rising in elevation, with walls and towers winding up the sides. The golden buttons were actually gilded domes in the center of each, capped at their apex with a yellow flame that shone even in the tint of the surrounding space.

They hovered directly over the middle and largest citadel, about a hundred feet above the dome, the antigravity propulsion locking them in place. The flame at the apex appeared to be the same yellow blaze that surrounded the Oriflamme. There was no sign of any people below.

"I'm getting atmospheric and gravity readings," Jaimin noted. "Maybe it's the cloud itself, as Leone said, or some technology. We should be able to walk and talk down there, and you'll be in your space suit anyway."

"Where are the inhabitants?" Auro wondered. "If Leone sent them word, they should be looking out for us."

They flew out of the air lock and landed on the gleaming dome, touching down near the flame that was like a great candle erected upon a plinth. From this central point, they could see the two nearest citadels on either side. The outer clouds of the Pale were distant and not quite as opaque when viewed from inside the nebula. A few faint stars even pierced through. The vista was dominated by the yellow gleam of the core star. The closest clouds were mostly amber and bronze, but one region stood out with its orange color. It seemed to be seeping closer, with the yellow retreating before it.

Their immediate business concerned the city below, an empty abode set in an amber sky with wild cosmic clouds in the distance. The buildings seemed to grow out of the rock. Some looked like castle towers with pointed arches; others resembled classical temples with colonnades. There were cobbled streets and open areas, as well as entrances into the interior of the rocky cliffs. But no people. All was still.

"The Oriflamme at least had its bannerman," Jaimin mused. "There's no one here at all."

"I told them to take refuge," a deep voice sounded from across the dome.

Jaimin and Auro nearly jumped. They turned to see a strange man standing on the opposite slope. A tall and imposing figure, he yet radiated a sense of peace and compassion as well as power. He looked familiar, clad in a yellow cloak that matched his blond beard. Jaimin and Auro recalled the tapestry of the man greeting his pilgrims with the pointed star gleaming over his shoulder. Suddenly, they felt like they were in that tapestry, one of a throng of refugees who had just lost their sun, which in its dying moments had sent them a savior with a gift, a yellow fire to kindle a new beginning.

"Lord Raelight," they said together, with no doubt of whom they beheld.

The great figure nodded. "And I need not ask for your names, Aurorno Augustine and Jaimin Caraggio. My bannerman sent word that two travelers had found their way to us." He looked up at their vessel hovering over them like a little moon. He looked especially at Jaimin, covered in red energy so different from his yellow fire. "You are from a lineage that left the solar system early in the exile, and now you wield an energy no less potent than my flame."

Jaimin nodded. "Auro and I decided to enter the nebula together in his stone vessel, which proved able to withstand the clouds. Then your bannerman diverted us to the Oriflamme. We stayed there for a while, and he gave us leave to come to your citadels. I suppose we're trespassing on your roof. Seeing no one, we were drawn here." He indicated the fire between them. "Leone showed us the Gnost and even touched me with it. It soothed a wound I received from the red fire."

"Indeed," Raelight said. "The Gnost came from Soliere. I am merely its custodian. It is not for me to withhold it from those in need. I only defend its purity."

"From the red fire?" Auro asked. "The Magna? We have seen space rocks covered with it. They travel through space like fiery comets, carrying entities also enveloped in flame. They have attacked my city, but they also inspired the design of my vessel, which enabled us to travel here, just as Jaimin's people have a ship that can bridge the distance between his world and ours. We came here to explore the nebula and find the origin of the red fire." He paused. That was as good an explanation as he felt comfortable giving.

Raelight walked up the slope of the dome toward the plinth. They could see he was a head taller than either of them, with a broad and sturdy build, easily as robust as Adventus Borno, the consul-tribune of Gemma. Yet he had a deeper quality than that fierce statesman, a serene old spirit. He ran his hands through the fire as if warming them and looked thoughtfully at his visitors.

"My lord," Jaimin said, not knowing how else to address him, "might we retire somewhere to speak?" He looked around. "We are eager to see your citadels, but they look deserted. Where are your people?"

"In the catacombs, where I urged them to go," Raelight replied. "Now that you are here, our neighbors will be coming." He pointed toward the orange cloud. It appeared to have darkened and continued to swirl closer like an oncoming storm. Auro and Jaimin wondered if that cloud was the home of the bolides, or at least where they came from.

They looked back at Raelight and were astonished to see that another small figure had suddenly appeared beside him. It was a young girl, perhaps his daughter. Evidently, she had somehow scurried up the dome while they were looking away. She appeared to be a year or two shy of her teens, slight and limber, with a face much like the lord's in a feminine and childlike form, though her hair was darker. Her eyes also glowed, but not solid yellow; they twinkled eerily from yellow to orange to red, ever changing, and had a distant quality, as if she was not seeing what was in front of her.

Raelight bent down, and the child whispered something to him. "Just as we feared," he said. "This is what they have been working and waiting for."

Jaimin and Auro looked at the orange cloud again. It still seemed a safe distance away, but then they saw a trio of bright objects streaking out of it. They were deep red with tails of fire.

"Bolides!" Jaimin cried. "Fire comets! Three of them!"

"They come from the Magna Band through the Nanj Cloud," Raelight answered. "Lord Romeon and his people possess a different flame, but they desire mine, just as they desire yours."

Jaimin shuddered, realizing his presence may have attracted this danger. "Will they attack your cities?" he asked.

"It is power he wants, not violence, but when the lust takes hold of him, he may ill-use those who stand in his way. I presume you do not want him to wring your energy out of you. I do not, either, for that could tip the balance between his power and mine. He has long coveted my flame, but I have guarded it. Fire can resist fire."

With that, the awesome figure stepped up and onto the plinth and immersed himself wholly in the yellow flame. The fire coiled around the outline of his body. The girl had vanished just as suddenly and mysteriously as she had appeared.

Meanwhile, the bolides were accelerating toward them. Auro and Jaimin remembered their narrow escape from just one, when they had had a second powerful ship at their command. What could they do against three, stranded on the summit of a strange city that seemed empty and defenseless? Then, to their astonishment, the domes of the two citadels on either side lifted off their very skylines. First the two on the right and then the two on the left. All four arose into space and flipped upright, and each of the pairs joined together to form two golden spheres with yellow flames shining at their poles. They had combined to form spherical vessels and launched toward the oncoming bolides. Auro and Jaimin presumed that Raelight, now totally subsumed in the fire, was somehow controlling them.

Standing at the edge of their dome, they watched the golden spheres quickly intercept two of the bolides, unleashing streams of yellow flame at them. That soothing yellow evidently had some offensive bite, for the streams stymied the bolides' momentum and held them in place. However, they only stopped two. The third continued on.

"He can't contain them all," Auro said.

"Let me see what I can do," Jaimin replied.

His plasma surging, he leaped off the dome and flew as fast as he could to meet the oncoming bolide not far from the edge of the city. He braced for a potentially fatal impact, but the foe slowed before him. Its fire glared, and Jaimin felt its heat even through his powerful plasma. He hesitated. Had this fiery comet, or whatever controlled it, truly come for him? Maybe it was waiting for him to strike so that it could absorb his plasma.

As he wondered this, staring into the foreboding yet compelling flame, something burst out of the bolide: a human-shaped figure like the one he had fought before. Jaimin reeled back. But to his further astonishment, the entity flew past him and continued toward the citadel. Jaimin's first instinct was to follow it, but before he could spin around, a searing wave came at him from the front. The bolide's flame was surging over him. Jaimin felt a burning unlike anything he had ever imagined. Then he felt no more.

✳   ✳   ✳

Back on the central dome, Auro watched helplessly as the golden spheres held two of the bolides at bay. Jaimin, who appeared as a pinprick of red light, seemed to have halted the third. All he could make out of Jaimin's struggle was a slight blinking and flashing.

Raelight was still submerged within his Gnost blaze. The only way Auro could help Jaimin would be to go out there in the *Meteor*. He leaped off the dome toward his hovering vessel. He had just opened the air lock when he saw something streaking toward him, crimson in color. It wasn't Jaimin but a fire entity.

Before Auro could leap inside for safety, Raelight suddenly stepped out of his yellow flame as one might pass through a waterfall. "Wait!" he shouted, both commanding and entreating. "The Magna will engulf your ship!"

"What should we do?" Auro shouted back. "It's coming straight for us! Your vessels are too far away, and Jaimin is out there with them."

Their time ran out. The entity arrived, soaring over the *Meteor* and the dome. Somehow, Auro sensed this was a different being than the one he had encountered before. Its outstretched hands touched the *Meteor*, and as Raelight foretold, its flame spread over the hull. Auro watched his beloved vessel become the face of the enemy, a red bolide. Raelight stood warily at the foot of the plinth, apparently too drained to act. But having transformed the vessel, the entity declined to enter it. Instead, it took a sharp turn and dove down the slope of the dome and out of sight.

The red fire around the *Meteor* seared Auro and forced him back. He felt weak and realized he was falling. The ground far below the dome seemed to rush up to him until he felt the sharp impact and lay stunned on the ground. His space suit and thrusters had blunted the fall, and the helmet had kept his skull and wits intact.

Rising slowly to his feet, he stood for the first time on the proper ground of this world. The dome from which he had fallen loomed hundreds of feet above. He would have to get some distance out from under it to see its apex again. He was standing on a street that stretched on about a mile to a ridge at the very edge of the citadel.

On foot, he started toward the ridge, hoping to get a clearer view of the orange cloud and the bolides, to see what had become of Jaimin. But before he was halfway, a crimson streak soared overhead. The entity had forced Auro down there, and now seemed to be coming for him.

Auro lifted his laser emitter and fired a fine beam at the moving target. The entity twisted and spun off course before quickly getting its bearings. Auro braced himself for another assault. But when he looked up, he was shocked to see the girl who had briefly appeared at the dome now standing before the ridge. Her eyes were pulsating even more vibrantly, and to Auro's astonishment, a streak of orange flame emanated from them and hit the invader in midflight. It faltered again for a moment but then redoubled toward them in a swift dive.

Despite the power the child had just unleashed, Auro felt compelled to try to protect her. He sprinted toward her and scooped her up in his arms; then, activating his thrusters, he launched into a low flight away from the ridge into the heart of the citadel. With the entity scouring above, he zipped past several buildings, slowing down near a templelike structure carved into a cliff, with steps leading up to a row of columns lining its edge.

Auro landed at the top of the steps just inside the threshold and set the child down beside him. There was a shallow interior under the roof with little yellow fires flickering along the back wall but nowhere to escape or hide. Expecting the entity at any moment, Auro knelt beside the girl, who clearly had a formidable power of her own. Before he could figure out what to say, he noticed that her eyes were no longer aglow but pure white and dull. They had no visible pupils, and she was looking past him as if barely aware of his presence. Auro suddenly grasped that the fire exacted a toll for inhabiting her eyes: She was blind. But apparently, she had senses beyond physical sight, for she said in a clear whisper, "Father is coming."

Auro looked up in anticipation. Indeed, a new object was descending from the direction of the dome, a blazing ball that looked like one of the bolides but covered with yellow fire. It was indeed the *Meteor*. Raelight must have rekindled it with his own flame, replacing the crimson.

The red entity seemed equally startled and none too pleased. Diverted from Auro and the girl, it released a stream of its flame at the vessel, but the yellow absorbed it with barely a flicker. The entity retreated, flying beyond the ridge into the void, toward the orange cloud. Rather than pursuing, the *Meteor* hovered over the ridge.

"He's calling to us," the girl said.

"Let's go and see him," Auro replied. "He is in my ship, after all."

He held her and leaped up, ascending toward his transformed vessel, drawing up to where the air lock should be, submerged under yellow flame. The Gnost was warm and inviting, and he took himself and the child right through it and found Raelight waiting for them.

"Romeon believes his forces can still come and go as he wills," he observed. "The Gnost is peaceful but resilient, and these quiet citadels can muster a defense."

"And you have brought that resilience to my own vessel," Auro said. "The *Meteor* is a bolide now." He set the girl down, and she walked over to her father. Auro stood silently for a moment as the two seemed to commune by some means beyond words. Finally, he said, "Let me see if Jaimin is still out there. I may be able to track that entity and the bolides." He wasn't sure if this was still truly his vessel, transformed as it was, but Raelight stood aside, allowing him to slip through the corridor, and followed him in, taking the girl by the hand.

When they reached the central chamber, Auro sat at the console and began sifting through the strange readings of the yellow fire that surrounded the vessel like a second hull. Then he fixed the scopes at Jaimin's last known location. Sure enough, several objects were still arrayed before the orange cloud. The two golden spheres of the citadels still held two of the bolides in place. The middle bolide, unmolested, was also stationary, making no attempt to free its fellows. But the fire around it had doubled in magnitude and ferocity.

Auro could pick up no sign of Jaimin. He looked back at Raelight. "Should we go out there?" he asked. "Now that my vessel also has flame, can we go to the aid of your domes?"

Just then, the console beeped, and a new object streaked across the view screen, a spark of red fire moving at high velocity. "That's the entity that attacked us," Auro said.

They watched, too late to act, as the spark flew right into the red bolide, disappearing into it. There was a flash, causing Auro to shut his eyes. When he looked back at the screen, he saw that the golden spheres had been knocked out of position, and the bolides they had stymied were moving back toward the orange cloud. The middle one moved fastest, its fire very intense and streaking behind it in a long tail.

"They're getting away!" Auro cried. "What became of Jaimin?"

"They are taking him," the girl answered. Her eyes were glowing again.

"Can we pursue?"

"We cannot enter the Nanj Cloud or the Magna Band," Raelight said. "They have what they came for."

"You can't enter their band, but they can enter yours?" Auro asked.

"They can," he answered gravely. "They gained more power when your mother joined them, and now that they have your friend, they can gain even more."

# CHAPTER 6

# THE NANJ CLOUD

Caught in the comet's tail, Jaimin felt like a hot wind was carrying him through a storm. He had tempted this fate when he had leaped off to intercept the bolides that had burst out of the orange cloud. One of them had engulfed him in its fire, and he had blacked out. Now he awoke to find himself ensnared in its fiery tail. It was apparently towing him into another part of the nebula.

As his head cleared, his puzzlement grew. In his encounter with the entity outside the Pale, a mere touch of the Magna flame had grievously wounded him. Enveloped in it now, despite its heat, he did not feel the deep burning he had felt before. His own plasma retained its strength and shielded him. He could barely move as it swept him like a tidal wave across the expanse. But as he began to see more clearly, enough to perceive the clouds turning from yellow to orange, he realized the bolide was slowing down. The streaking tail receded as its momentum waned. Finally, it released him and continued into the depths. He was free.

He struggled to orient himself and to comprehend where they had taken him and why. The first clue was a new object before him. Much larger than a bolide, it also blazed with red fire. A wide fan of flame curved over a dark mass of ore, a long tub of a body, and many dots of firelight shining across its sides. It looked like a sailing vessel, a galleon such as once crossed Earth's oceans. Jaimin blinked slowly to make sure of what he was seeing. The hull and masts were of space rock; the fiery sail heaved and flickered over them.

Not knowing what else to do, he flew straight toward the mysterious vessel. Soaring over its fiery sail, he looked down upon it like a seagull might have descried a real galleon. Its long deck was composed of dark stone. How quickly it would sink if sailing on water! Jaimin knew of sail-like technologies that could propel spacecraft, though he had never imagined a sail of fire. He wondered what Kelmin would make of this.

It was not only mysterious but ghostly, too, with no sign of life. Yet unlike the bolides, it offered a place to land. Perhaps there were people below deck. Resolved to see for himself, he suddenly descended past the sail, down toward the front tip of the deck, landing on what he believed was the prow. Leaning over the railing with the sail blazing above, he looked into the garish clouds and the few stars that peeped through the swirl.

The horizon was less comforting than the vista seen from the golden dome. These clouds, orange and red, were stormier. His eyes found the core star. It was so striking that he was surprised he had not noticed it immediately, even with the sail to distract him. Larger than it appeared in the yellow band, it was not yellow but crimson, like a clot of boiling blood.

The bolide that had brought him there had circled back and was hovering high above the deck. Jaimin was jolted by a rumbling coming from the deck itself. A multitude of people now thronged on its surface, emerging from lower levels and matriculating across its length. One who possessed the unmistakable air of leadership started boldly toward him, with several others clustering in his wake.

Was this another sort of lord? He was not as tall or as broad as Raelight and lacked the imposing beard, yet he cut a robust figure with his strong chin, bald head, and red-tinted eyes. Dressed in black and red leather, an emblem of a comet with a long, fiery tail was emblazoned on his chest. The people behind him, evidently his crew, were dressed much like him except for the crest. Their hair and complexions were of various shades, yet all their eyes and bodies radiated a crimson light.

"You burn as red as our flame," he said. The voice was deep. A captain's voice. "But your flame is not of the star."

Jaimin returned the man's gaze with his own blazing eyes. "It's not a flame at all, as far as I know," he replied. "I am Jaimin Caraggio of the Bioplane Gemma. I was also known as the Red Flare on my world. I possess what we call the Eternigy. You are right; it is not star fire, though it may be as powerful or more. But I think you already know all this. I presume this is your ship, and it was your bolides that brought me here. You are the Magna lord?"

"I am Romeon. I claim no lordship. I conduct the Magna fire, but I am not its source, as you may know." He pointed to the red star. "It comes from there."

"The star was yellow where I saw it last," Jaimin said. "Why have you brought me here?"

"You are here because you meant to come here," Romeon replied matter-of-factly. "Of course, I helped you along. I thought we might help each other."

At first, this remark seemed glib, but Jaimin was unnerved to realize the truth in it. "I was burned by your fire," he explained. "With two shipmates, I journeyed to this nebula from our Bioplane, harnessing the power I wield before you. When we arrived in the storms of the Pale, one of your fire comets attacked us. I fought with someone who wielded your flame. Was that you? We drew energy from each other, almost like an exchange of blood.

"An Amphoran vessel helped us drive off your bolide, but some of the Magna was left within me, and some of my Eternigy was gone. Shortly after, I entered the nebula again with one of the Amphoran pilots. We successfully navigated through the outer clouds to come to Lord Raelight's citadels in the Gnost Band. But almost immediately, more of your bolides and fire entities came out of this orange cloud and attacked us again. As far as I know, Auro is still back in the Rae Citadels, and I am here. Was it me you really wanted?"

Romeon's red eyes flashed at Auro's name. But he said: "Indeed, I sensed your vessel coming from your faraway world, harnessing energies not seen since the Great Journey. As for you and me, this is our first meeting. The red entities you encountered were scouts."

Jaimin noticed that a man among the crew, with an air almost as commanding as that of the lord, had stepped up just behind Romeon's shoulder.

"This is Captain Thomoly," Romeon said, responding to Jaimin's glance. "He was the one who immobilized you and transported you here. He also paid a visit to the citadel to look in on your fellow traveler. However, he was not the one you initially encountered in the outer clouds."

He gestured up to the mast, and Jaimin looked up to see a woman staring down at him from where she sat upon a rigging about twenty feet up. She had raven hair streaked with silver that glittered under the flaming sail. Suddenly, a red fire swelled over her body, as though she had been ignited by the sail at her back. Aflame, she leaped off the rigging, circled overhead, and streaked down to the deck to stand blazing by Romeon and Thomoly.

Jaimin shut his eyes, and for an instant, he was back in space, feeling her fiery touch. His lids opened, and the aura of flame around her was gone. Looking at her human face again, he knew that this woman retained the part of the energy he had lost.

"This is Armarna," Romeon said. "It was she who brought us back a little glimmer of your power."

"You were waiting for us in the clouds," Jaimin said.

"Romeon asked me to go into the Pale," she replied. "To observe your arrival, make contact if I could."

"You attacked us!" Jaimin exclaimed. "You tried to ensnare us with your fire and then gave chase. Auro told us how bolides like yours have raided their stations, how the Empyreans brought on the nova, all to satisfy a lust for energy you could not control." He looked at Romeon. "You were one of Light Lords, one of five Empyreans who fused together to form the Pentheon, which entered the star and brought on the nova. Now you have stolen my energy."

There was a murmur among the crew lining the sides of the deck, but Romeon remained impassive and raised his hands. "You know a great deal," he said. "I was indeed one of the Pentheon, as was Raelight. We were born after the Great Journey and followed Aris as he spurned a planetary life and resolved to reach Soliere. Eventually, we succeeded in entering it through the glory of our fusion. But all of us except Aris were hurled out of the star with the rays. If only I could describe to you that moment when we were all inside it."

"You don't need to," Jaimin said. "I and two others from my world had a similar experience when we entered a vortex of the Eternigy. This is what such energies do to mere humans. We were not meant for this."

Romeon looked at Jaimin as though, for the first time since reconnecting with Raelight, he was dealing with one he could consider a peer. "We were meant for exactly this!" he exclaimed. "We had every right to enter Soliere, for we created it. Yet even as we drank in its energy, we could feel it contorting, about to implode. Instead, it flashed outward to form the nova, breaking our fusion. Each of us was ejected through one of the five rays. Their lights spiraled out from the star, and we were each imbued with one of the flames. Raelight possesses the Gnost, which illuminates the path to self-knowledge but also lulls one away from many things external to the self. I have the Magna, which sharpens our vision even as it burns our flesh."

"But we are not quite in your band, are we?" Jaimin noted, looking around. "Lord Raelight told us of the Nanj Cloud. We saw it from his citadel. It is a mix of Gnost and Magna, is it not? It allows you to move between the bands?"

"It does breach the boundary," Romeon affirmed. "When I finally succeeded in merging yellow and red, the result created a connection between the bands. The Nanj enhances the strengths of the Gnost and the Magna, blurs their weaknesses. This cloud is a place of deep memory as well as thrilling discovery. It has enabled me to complete my greatest project. I meant to bring you here. I believed that in this little cloud, you would be most receptive to our gift."

Jaimin looked back at him in silence, trying to comprehend.

"But you say we stole from you," Romeon added. "What makes you think this?"

"Do you deny that you sent this woman to siphon away my Eternigy?" Jaimin asked. "That you have raided Raelight's citadels and the Amphoran city?"

Romeon studied him carefully. "You think us raiders?" he asked. "Look around you. Describe what you see."

At first, Jaimin felt exasperated by this, after all he had heard. But already, he was beginning to think that this Romeon was not quite the fanatical warlord driven by a harsh and unnatural fire that he had first imagined. And these people seemed to regard him as more of a curiosity than a prisoner.

Suddenly, he felt out of place standing there covered in plasma and desired to face them as a human being, as vulnerable as that would leave him. Rather impulsively, he dissolved his second skin of energy to reveal his plain body dressed in simple fatigues. As Leone had said, he was able to stand and breathe and speak there in the cosmic cloud. Romeon's entreaty seemed so genuine, and his surroundings so mesmerizing, that he began to step cautiously down the deck along the side railing and looked into the cosmic colors swirling around this archaic-looking vessel adrift in the heavens.

"This is the third place I've visited in the nebula," he said as Romeon followed him, with Armarna and Thomoly close behind. "Each stay was too brief to fully comprehend. What do I see here? A red star. Red-and-orange clouds. Red fire that can serve as the tail of a comet or the sail of a ship. Not far from here, the star is yellow, and the yellow fire partially soothed the burn I received from the red."

He paused again. "Auro called you Empyreans, but there seem to be different tribes of you. The most powerful, the ones who went closest to the sun, made possible the Great Journey that brought your people here. They convinced the others that they were creating a new home with a sun and a planet, but I think they really wanted to create a star whose energy would be entirely theirs. Whether you Light Lords intended it or not, that triggered the nova. The star split five ways, forming bands around it, each with its own color and properties.

This band has the red flame, hotter than the yellow, perhaps more powerful, but I don't like it half so much. You make bolides out of it, space galleons, who knows what else. You desire the Gnost and, evidently, my energy, too. Obviously, you know something of the people outside the nebula since you have attacked them as well."

His mood hardened again. "What do I see here?" he concluded. "I see a pirate ship full of corsairs and raiders. And you have taken something from me. I want it back."

Jaimin considered that he had thrown down the gauntlet at his captors and expected Romeon to respond with threats and force. But to his surprise, the woman now spoke with her soothing voice.

"I know how you feel," she said. "I am from Amphora, no more native to the nebula than you. I was a part of the fleet that fought Romeon's bolides when they came through the Pale."

Jaimin looked at her in a new light, and his clash with her started to take on new meaning. He had questions but held his tongue as she continued.

"My father was of Empyrean heritage, but our ancestors stayed on Edda. They thought it folly to reach into the new star. After the nova, the Stylights meditated on the pillars of Simeon Tower, probing the nebula for its secrets. I had strong Empyrean perceptions and, even as a young girl, found that I could tap into my father's meditations. For years, I secretly shadowed him and the other Stylights, sharing in their visions. But I lost my connection to them when my father died. I married a man in the engineering guild, Torrorno Augustine, and we had a son. I joined Torro's guild, and in Amphora's deepest facilities, we studied the nature of the clouds and tried to see what lay behind them.

"While the Stylights meditated on their pillars and the scientists pursued their empirical inquiries, a few of us harnessed the highest arts of both. We examined the old solar collectors used to make the Great Journey and revived energies within their stores. From them, we generated a powerful new emitter, with which we meant to clear a path through the clouds. On the verge of being discovered, we ventured out toward the Pale and released a great beam into it. By this time, observers on Amphora, both prefects and Stylights, could see what we had done and gathered a fleet behind us among the asteroids. We shut off the beam and waited. Soldiers boarded our ship and accused us of endangering the city. What they knew of any such threat that might lurk within the clouds, they would not say.

"Weeks passed as all of us—scientists, spiritualists, and various officials—sat out there in anticipation. Torro and I were joined by our son, who was now an apprentice in the shipping guild. The clouds looked no different, but our sensors detected new energies churning just behind them, and the Stylights began to have vague new visions. Finally, the reckoning came."

"We came," Romeon said. "But to understand how and why, I must tell you something of my history here. For long after the nova, I had to come to terms with my imprisonment in the Magna Band. I was not alone. A group of Empyreans had been swept up in the red wave and ended up here with me. Not so many as were in the Gnost, but the few who had drifted farther in behind the Pentheon. Most of them are here as the crew of this vessel; some are scattered on the habitable crags of our band, operating my great furnaces.

"The Magna was like a lens that helped me glimpse beyond the band, but only glimpse. I knew that most of our people were with Raelight. He took them under his paternal care, soothed them with his flame, and built his golden monasteries. The people of the Gnost focused on healing, abandoning the thrill of discovery. On the other side, the green band was harder to see, but I sensed Vitruvia was there.

"I resolved to connect with Raelight, but for a long time, I could not cross the barrier between our bands. With the Magna, I could kindle space rocks, and I created the first of what you call bolides and fire comets, which I used to explore the full breadth of my realm. But I needed a greater vessel to carry more people over greater distances. Shaping the flame itself into a great sail that could absorb the nebula's energies and gravimetric currents, I created the very vessel upon which we stand. My finest achievement, save one. I named it the *Dante*, for it is a ship with a form from storied history, even legend, and it will lead us through many circles to a fiery destiny that once went wrong but can now, I believe, be set right.

"Ruminating long by the border with the Gnost sharpened my perceptions, and I finally found a path through which I could defy the barrier and cross into Raelight's realm. That led to a period of contact and mutual exposure of our flames. Some of Raelight's people, once they touched the Magna, chose to come back with me. Through them, I was able to combine some of the yellow with the red to create the Nanj, this very cloud that now straddles both bands. Through it, I can more easily traverse them. I paid more visits and tried to convince Raelight to fully combine our flames. We were only two of the Pentheon, but perhaps together, we could rejoin the others, even reach Soliere again.

"But Raelight refused. He declared that we must no longer meddle with powers we could not control. He was blessed with the Gnost, which healed his people's spirits but gave them no larger vision. Most of them had turned inward and desired only to rest and seek within themselves. But there were a few who had not completely suppressed the spark of inspiration. They saw that the Magna offered them new frontiers. I offered them its touch." He gestured to the people on the deck behind him. "Some of those you see here are from Raelight's citadels. They came back with me to take part in our journey."

"But not her." Jaimin pointed to Armarna. "She is from Amphora. What is your interest in the city outside the nebula? Why did your bolides attack them and destroy their stations? Why did you send her to intercept my vessel?"

"I began my sojourn through the nebula with Lord Raelight and the healing power of the Gnost," Armarna said. "But I came to see that the Magna possessed the enlightenment I sought."

"You were among the ones who disappeared when the bolides raided Amphora's stations along the Pale," Jaimin said. "The Amphorans didn't know what happened to you."

"You can be sure the Stylights know of our fate. They are secretive and not above duplicity. I speak as one of their line." She looked past him for a moment, out at the clouds.

"For some time," Raelight said, "during my expeditions in the Gnost Band, I had sent bolides into the Pale. Its stormy clouds proved too turbulent even for my vessels. But now the Amphorans had lit and cleared a path through the outer clouds that we could cross. I personally led my entire fleet of bolides in. We had to pass through Raelight's band to reach it, but he dared not hinder us. Several times, the storms hurled us back. When we finally broke through, we charged right into the Amphoran stations, and our flames damaged them. The Amphorans determined that we were hostile and attacked us."

"That was the Battle of the Pearls," Jaimin said.

"I tell myself it was all part of some greater good and not just a result of our foolishness," Armarna sighed. "Lord Romeon is right: Part of us has always been with the Empyreans. Those of us who brought on the tragedy were forced to watch our ships incinerated by flaming space rocks. Torro, my husband, rallied us. Seeing the demonic fire we had brought so close to our home city drove him to a passion I had never seen. We took our ship into the fight.

"I now know the bolides were attempting to contact us even as we fired at them relentlessly and they darted around, spewing flame. All the Pearl Stations were destroyed. The Amphoran ships fell back to defend the city. Torro navigated close to the Pale in pursuit of one of the bolides. As it turned out, it was the one Lord Romeon himself was in. It unleashed a barrage that disabled us. Torro was injured. I felt an unbearable heat swell over me and then blacked out.

"When I came to, I was in a strange place carved into rock, surrounded by a yellow fire. With me were two men who had been on the vessel with Torro and me. Romeon was there, along with a tall, radiant man whom I learned was Lord Raelight. Romeon had surrounded our vessel with Magna fire and towed us through the deadly clouds to Raelight's border station, the Oriflamme, where he healed me with his fire. But he could not save Torro. I wept for my husband and for my son, who had lost a father. The yellow flame soothed me but could not ease my grief.

"We spent some days there and then went on to Lord Raelight's citadels with their great domes of gold. On top of the central dome, we built a pyre for Torro and gave his body to the Gnost. Lord

Romeon lamented what had transpired. He had taken our beacon as an invitation, not knowing that our guild had acted on its own. Torro and many others had paid with their lives. As I mourned, I learned more about this nebula created by the boldness and folly of my ancestors. Romeon and Raelight had been inside Soliere and became custodians of the star's great flames, even greater than the Light Lords of the Pentheon had been before the nova. But they did not see eye to eye.

"At first, I and my two surviving shipmates, Angevin and Montefore, assumed that we would return to Amphora. I had to tell my son of his father's sacrifice. But then I thought of my own father and his visions, and I wondered what he would think of my being there. I came to believe I was brought into the nebula for a purpose. Meanwhile, the tensions grew between the Gnost and Magna lords. We heard rumblings of fierce debates under the great dome.

"One night, Lord Romeon came to us and declared that he had to return to his band, but his plans included a role for us if we would join him. I told him it was our duty to return to Amphora, and since Raelight's flame was healing us, we would continue to convalesce in his citadels before heading home. Romeon replied that while the Gnost could heal, only through the Magna could we come to our true purpose. Then he extended his hand, and I touched his red flame. At first, it brought pain, but as it seared into me, I saw new visions. I knew that if I stayed in the nebula, my son would find his way to me, that he would bring a new power to us from another branch of humanity that had left Earth all those ages ago."

"Auro!" Jaimin stepped back. "You are his mother! That was why he wanted so desperately to enter the nebula. He is looking for you!"

"Yes," Romeon said. "Soon they can be reunited, and I will cross the bands and sail toward the star."

Jaimin now clearly saw the woman's kinship with Auro: the same dark hair and eyes, the same earnestness and intensity. She started to speak again, and it even sounded like Auro talking.

"For many centuries, you Noctarians have been cut off from the heat of a star, cold and incomplete. Then, seemingly by chance, you found a power that sun-starved mystics had been seeking for centuries. Your plasma is a mere candle compared with what awaits us. You will help us reach the core star and profit as much as we."

"It's true," Jaimin admitted. "The Gemman mystics, myself among them, sought the Eternigy, but it has never burned me as your fire has. I see why Raelight distrusts you. I will not use my power to help you spread your flame. I would fly right back to him and out of this nebula before I would help you sail this ship of yours out of this cloud." He looked hard at Armarna. "I want you to return what you took from me."

"You can have it now," she replied. "Join me up in the cloud."

The red fire flared over her again, and she rose above him, a streak of raging flame.

Jaimin stood hesitant. He looked at Romeon and Thomoly, scanned the faces of their crew. None of them spoke, but their shining red eyes seemed to encourage him to follow the beckoning woman, to seek out his purpose there.

Jaimin reignited his plasma, heaved his chest, and flew up after Armarna. She now embodied his reason for being there, the source of the inner emptiness he wanted to fill.

She seemed to be flying toward the crimson star. That could not be her true destination, for Jaimin knew it was in some sense a mirage, like the yellow had been. The core star was far away, in the very center of the nebula, and it had five rays. Even the Light Lords could not reach it. This band was lit by the red ray, and from here, it was all they could see of the star. But Jaimin could hope to reach the fiery woman. Soaring through this orange cloud, his own crimson plasma surging to a healthy power again, he began to catch up with her. Actually, she had slowed down and was waiting for him on the edge of a new horizon.

They appeared to be at the cusp between the Nanj and the Magna, like the seam between two fabrics, where orange gave way to red. In the distance was a sight out of the pages of the namesake of Romeon's galleon: a vast region of red space, lit by a shining ruby of a star—hot, invigorating, alive with flame, full of fiery rocks, some nearly planetoid in size, belching bursts of fire out of their craters and lined with rivers of lava. It was like looking at Hades. Yet for all its unnerving power, this was not a place of doom. Jaimin sensed that the beings there were not suffering. Indeed, they were exhilarated, literally fired up, ready to meet any challenge, explore any unknown. He, too, felt this. For the first time, he found himself wishing that the burning in the pit of his stomach had not been soothed. What he had once regarded as pain now seemed like the spur needed to pursue a greater satisfaction than the sleepy balm of the Gnost could provide.

The flame over Armarna's face flickered away, revealing her dark, human features. "Do you see now why I came with Romeon? Because he is still on the journey my ancestors began. You have been a twilight wanderer, but you are on a journey, too. Here, we may find ourselves on the same path, and we can both take the first step."

"What step?" Jaimin asked. "So far, Romeon's only progress has been back toward the Gnost Band, toward the Pale, toward Amphora, all away from the star. He has only succeeded in going backward."

"But with my help, and now yours, that can change," she said. She pointed to an object he had not noticed before, moving toward them. It was no asteroid or volcano; it was not composed of rock but had smooth, clear sides and a wide base that slanted up into a point. It was a pyramid, forged with great craftsmanship, perhaps of crystal or a kind of glass. It moved through the cloud as smoothly as any space vessel.

"My finest achievement," a proud voice said from behind them. "A gift from the Nanj."

Romeon gently rippled up to them, enveloped in a red fire deeper and richer than Armarna's. "I have made comets out of asteroids and kindled volcanoes. Once the Magna grafts onto something, whether stone, metal, or flesh, it stays, not consuming it but joining with it. When I first arrived, the Magna lived only in me; now it thrives all over the band. But my craftsmanship has grown, and I have surpassed even the *Dante*. This is a space rock painstakingly worn and crystallized. By the power of the Magna, it was melted, frozen in the void, melted again, each time becoming smoother, clearer."

"It's beautiful," Jaimin admitted. Geometrically perfect to his eyes, it glittered in the red-and-orange clouds. "The Gemmans were masters of crystal, a key foundation of the Bioplanes, growing and shaping them into magnificent mountains, but we never created anything like this. Is it another sort of vessel?"

"In a sense," Romeon said. "But of a special kind. It is a prism."

The word hit Jaimin like an epiphany. The bands around the core star were the broken facets of its light. Such a device might further break or recombine that light, harness its power for a new purpose. He looked at Armarna. "He means to use this device to complete his journey, or at least to finally take the next step, and you are helping him?"

"I brought a scientific perspective, along with a fresh burst of Gnost fire that Raelight had used to heal me. Together, in the Nanj Cloud, we completed the prism. Now we will bring it to the far reaches of the Magna Band and put it to use."

"And what do you want of me?"

"A prism is only as powerful as the light that passes through it," Romeon replied.

"First, we'll cross this band," Armarna said, "then breach the barrier, take a step closer to the star. My father never left Simeon Tower, but he strove all his life to see through the Pale. We will go where even he, where even the Light Lords themselves, were never able to see."

On a more visceral level than words could convey, Jaimin was beginning to understand and found himself agreeing to take part in the great venture that this Magna lord and his cryptic convert planned to undertake. The three floated there silently on the edge of the Nanj Cloud on the threshold of the Magna Band, full of the vibrant, intriguing fire that had lured Jaimin into the nebula. A spark of it still burned inside him. To his own surprise, he now felt like it belonged there, but soon it would be fully purged in exchange for the service he was about to render.

# CHAPTER 7

# A BLIND GUIDE

Three days Jaimin had been gone, with Auro left as a guest in Raelight's citadel, unsure of what to do or where to go next. He had declined lodgings and used the *Meteor* as his living quarters. On his ship, he could probe the clouds for Jaimin's distinctive energy. In return, he promised not to leave without notice and to share whatever he learned from his investigations. When not on the ship, he was free to go about as he pleased.

In some ways, he felt at home there, and not only because the Gnost light that filled this band was as comforting as ever. The Gnost powered all five citadels and infused everywhere that feeling of inner peace and contentment that Auro had felt on the Oriflamme. Like Amphora, these citadels were small urban settings fixed in space, but they were not on the edge of a swirling storm. There, well inside the nebula, bathed in soft yellow light, all was calm and contemplative. Although the darker clouds in the distance were a reminder of how fragile the tranquility might be, they were not close enough to belie it, except perhaps the Nanj—where Jaimin likely was if he lived—which loomed like a perilous dawn.

Each of the five citadels had its domed edifice where the citizens could gather and arbitrate. This central one was Raelight's home and where he held his councils. The society was curiously organized. Raelight was clearly the leader, and his people revered him, but he did not seem to head a government. There were no soldiers or security men. Auro was told that no one had ever committed a crime. Most of the people lived in caverns in the hills; the outside buildings were mostly common spaces: storehouses, temples, botanical gardens.

Auro spent some hours walking the streets and greeting citizens as they went about. They all bore the signs of being high Empyreans. Their skin gave off a subtle yellow light and their eyes glinted amber, especially when deep in thought. Even the most ordinary of them could have been among the greatest Stylights on Amphora. They told him of their deep connection with the yellow star. They knew of Amphora and even of Jaimin's Bioplanes, but only vaguely, for they did not focus on things far away.

But events within the nebula concerned them greatly, and they regarded the Nanj Cloud with apprehension. Romeon and his Magna flame had lured some of their kindred away. There were other realms as well: bands farther inward, closer to the core star, with flames even more peculiar and powerful. They were not concerned with trying to reach them but worried that outsiders would disturb their peace. The Gnost had gifted them with self-knowledge and contentment, filling spiritual holes and quenching the appetite for energy that had driven their ancestors to madness and destruction. In the aftermath of catastrophe and cataclysm, they had found enlightenment.

Auro had to concede that these people were more content than his own. But Amphorans had a different history, having been left to fend for themselves with no Light Lord to guide them or mystical flame to ennoble them. Perhaps Raelight's people were too insular and complacent, the Gnost a little too soothing. Even in his brief time in their company, Auro was starting to feel restless. There was more to see in the nebula, much more, and he still felt that whatever he had heard calling to him from the Pale was somewhere in these depths. He felt torn between a desire to explore the bands and his lingering fear of the red flame and the fire comets. But the longer he stayed in this golden sanctuary, the more he was convinced that the Gnost power would be needed to hold back whatever threats lay within these depths.

The attack that had come almost immediately upon Auro and Jaimin's arrival had been no ordinary raid. Jaimin had brought a new power into the nebula that was not of the core star, with implications not even the Light Lords could foresee. Still, Auro was sure Jaimin would not readily volunteer to whatever designs his captors had for him.

Burdened with so many uncertainties, on the third evening, Auro hastened along the streets leading to the central dome where Raelight was set to hold council. Up the steps, a little crowd surrounded the lord and his young daughter—whose name, he had learned, was Haelia—and a few elders of the citadels. All took notice when Auro started up from the street. Even the blind girl was somehow aware of him.

Raelight led them into the rotunda and gathered them all under the dome. There was a yellow flame on the floor directly under the center, just like the one on the outside surface, and the curved interior ceiling reflected its soft light. The lord beckoned Auro forward and began to speak of the events around his fateful arrival. "From the moment you left the Oriflamme, we knew the Magna vessels poised in the Nanj Cloud would strike here. I think they came for both of you, but Jaimin in particular."

Auro had never shaken the feeling that the invader had also been after the girl, which was why it had gone down to the surface after inflaming the *Meteor*. But he said, "I have not detected any activity from the orange cloud since we drove off the bolides. Have you?"

The lord and all the elders indicated they had not, but like the Amphorans looking into the Pale, they had a sense of foreboding. "Those who have been touched by the Magna are ever restless," Raelight lamented. "Serenity is not one of its gifts, but Romeon has derived a measure of patience from many years of challenging the confines of his band. He has before him a new source of power and will take time to study it."

"I know you will not go into the Nanj," Auro said. "But as long as I have my ship and my freedom, I feel I must try to go there. Jaimin and I came here together, and I can't abandon him."

Raelight's face was grave, and the elders stirred. Auro fell silent, fearing his resolution on this matter could lead to a break with this venerable lord who had shown him all hospitality despite the consequences his arrival had brought. Haelia stepped back from her father and tilted her head sightlessly up toward the dome.

"Romeon is not evil," Raelight said. "He is driven to explore and longs to reach the core star. I don't believe he will force Jaimin to help him, but he will tempt him, either with the return of the energy he lost or the promise of something greater. We all know how the Magna can tempt us. The Gnost has brought us inner peace, but we are still Empyreans. Bred in the glare of the sun, touched by its fire, each of us retains the desire to reach out to the star. But it is Aris's star now. I believe he dwells alone in the innermost band, perhaps in the star itself, and part of me feels we belong there with him.

"When Romeon first crossed into my band, I gave him leave to come and go, but I was wary of his flame. I warned my people that it would disrupt the life we had built here and set us back on a path to ruin. Romeon wanted to combine our flames. That I would not allow. He agitated in secret, and through him, some touched the Magna and joined him. Thus, he was able to mix Gnost and Magna to create the Nanj. I communed with the Gnost for guidance. It taught me how to wield it as a weapon, and I armored our citadels. Then a new jolt came from a surprising direction: a beacon from beyond the clouds."

Raelight had come to the point of this assembly. The fire on the plinth stirred, and Auro's gaze fixed on the yellow flame that reached up like a finger toward the dome high above. For the first time, the fire seemed to produce smoke, like an amber vapor that sweetened the cool air of the wide room. Auro thought he could see something within its depths. It was a vision very similar to what Leone had shown him on the Oriflamme. Again, he saw the clash between ships and bolides in the Battle of Pearls and, again, the ship that his parents had been on, but this vision took him further. He saw the vessel pulled into the Pale, and his eyes followed them in. The clouds dissolved and were replaced by a series of still images like snapshots in time flickering in quick succession.

He saw the Oriflamme and a room that he had not seen when he had been there that looked like a medical bay. There, a man lay on a table with some people standing around him. Leone was there, as well as Raelight himself. Across the table was another striking figure dressed in red and black, smaller in stature than Raelight but more dynamic in his aura. Three others huddled at the foot of the table, dressed in Amphoran clothes.

Auro willed the image to focus on them. One was a woman, and a gasp came to his lips as he realized that it was his mother. But neither of the two men comforting her was his father. He forced the vision to show him the table and saw that the one lying on it, his body marked and scalded with burns, was indeed Torro Augustine.

Auro sank to his knees, still enraptured by the vision. He saw the yellow flame again. It became a cloud from which emerged the golden domes of the Rae Citadels. He saw a funeral atop the greatest dome, the very one he was currently under, where his father was given to the flame. He saw his mother walking the streets in grief, her eyes shining with yellow light. Then he saw her in a different setting, with the strange man he had seen by his father's body. His hand touched hers, burning with a red fire. Auro surmised that this was the Magna lord.

The vision began to glow with a crimson light. He cried out and reached into it, still kneeling on the stone floor. Then Raelight spoke in his anchoring voice: "She's not here."

The vision dissolved, leaving the yellow flame no more than fire to the eye. Auro would have burst into tears but for the soft light of the Gnost soothing his despair.

"I should say that she is not here now," the lord added. "Your mother *was* here, brought through the clouds by Romeon's bolides after his expedition to your city was turned back. She stayed with us for a while, healing, learning. Ultimately, she and one of the men with her decided to follow Romeon back to his band."

As Raelight finished, a fragment of the vision stepped around the fire before Auro: an Amphoran man in the flesh, a living connection to his home.

"Angevin!" Auro exclaimed. "Pierre Angevin!"

Auro didn't know him well but recognized him immediately as one of his father's colleagues and one of those who had been lost in the Battle of the Pearls. Auro had no idea that he had ended up in the nebula. But all that mattered now was that he had been with his mother the night she had decided to leave this citadel.

"Armarna wasn't simply lured by the red fire," Angevin said as if sensing his mind. "It was a means for her to continue a journey on which her heart had been set from the moment we gave your father to the flame. She did not need the Magna to kindle that in her."

Auro smiled at this. "And you did not feel impelled to join her, either by the fire or your own urge to explore?"

"I was once at the forefront of our efforts to enter the nebula," he replied. "But when I found myself here, even with the Magna spurring me on, my thoughts were not with the star but back home with Amphora and my family. When Armarna and Montefore went with Romeon, I resolved to stay here and await their return, as they promised they would come back. In the meantime, the yellow fire and the temples here have much to offer."

"Pierre is one of the few who have touched the Magna and not been consumed by it," Raelight said. "Not that your mother was consumed. I believe the fire merely emboldened her." He rested a hand, warm with the Gnost, on his shoulder. "Come—it is time to talk of the state of things."

The room darkened, and the lord entreated all to look up at the dome. Its gilded interior seemed to vanish, replaced by amber clouds flecked with stars, as if the dome itself was a lens into the nebula. But that image quickly morphed into something else: concentric colored rings culminating in a five-pointed star in the center, a depiction of the nebula much like the tapestry in the Oriflamme.

"The five bands were created with the nova," Raelight began, "with the breaking of the Pentheon and the fusion of the Light Lords. We followed Aris, for he alone was left of the elders who had brought about the Great Journey. The Eddans saw Soliere as a new sun, but we Empyreans never forgot that we had spawned the star and regarded it as the instrument with which we could finally merge flesh and light." He drew a long breath, recalling an experience so visceral yet so remote, it seemed to belong to a mythical past.

The room was silent but for the flickering of the fire. Auro spoke as he looked up at the vista spread out above them, his head swimming with questions. "The Empyreans are fallen heroes in the history of my city. They made the Great Journey possible, but they were not content with a new chance at terrestrial life. After Soliere was destroyed, the Amphorans only survived through the genius of our scientists and the insight from the few among us who retained a bit of the Empyrean power and perceptions." He paused and looked at Raelight. "What did you do to the star? What happened to you and the other Light Lords when you entered it?"

"Aris was a man of great gifts," Raelight said, "but still subject to a timeless failing: the corruption of power. When the Pentheon pierced the corona, the five of us, for so brief a moment, existed in an inconceivable energy. But the star reacted to our presence, perhaps like a body to an invading organism. Just as we were beginning to become one with the blaze, something within the core seemed to split it apart. The star broke our fusion and shot us away, purging much of its own energy as well. Each of us kept a facet of it that was most alike to our own being. You see, I am most like the Gnost, just as Romeon was most like the Magna. The star threw me farthest because I was most distant from it in spirit. But through the yellow flame, I have been able to fill the sense of incompleteness that Romeon feels, that human beings have always felt. I have come to understand that this is a fragile gift, for some of my people who encountered the Magna found that its spark made them feel empty again."

At this, Angevin recounted more of the night Auro had glimpsed in his vision, when Romeon had come to the three Amphorans on the eve of his departure. "The red fire burned over his hand, and he touched each of us. I know what stoked your mother's heart to continue this journey. We Amphorans have such longings, as you know, living in a city of endless night, our rightful sun shrouded behind impassable clouds."

Auro shook his head. "I don't believe she's acting on her own will. That infernal fire changes people, makes demons of them. This

Romeon has corrupted my mother, maybe Jaimin now as well, and through Jaimin, he will have even more power." He turned again to Raelight. "Your citadels may be the only good that came out of Soliere's destruction. You must defend them and not allow the Gnost to lull you to sleep, or eventually, Romeon or some greater threat will cross into your band and seize your flame, and all its capacity for good will be lost."

"This crisis has been long in coming," Raelight sadly agreed. "You and the Noctarians were the catalyst. You may also be the power that saves us." He pointed up again at the picture of the nebula spread across the dome. "Look there. We can see the Gnost and Magna bands and the Nanj Cloud nestled between them. Inside the Nanj, Romeon has gathered his bolides. His eye has thus far fixed on us, for this is the only other band he can reach, but his ultimate aim lies the other way. To reach the core star, the center of the nebula, he must cross the inner bands."

Auro studied the map. As the Oriflamme's tapestry had shown, each band was thicker than the next, except for the innermost, the purple, which all the star's rays drove into like daggers. It was a long way to the core. For now, Auro desired only to go into the Nanj, where he believed his mother and Jaimin could be found.

"My power is not enough to get you to them," Raelight said as if he sensed his thoughts. "I'm afraid the Nanj Cloud is a one-way gate. Romeon and his people can use it to pass from the Magna Band to the Gnost, but we cannot enter it from the Gnost side. However, there may be another path we can take—and one among us who can help us take it."

He waved his hand over the plinth and its yellow fire, and the ceiling flickered again. Then, across the colored bands, from the star's rays to the outer edges, there appeared dark, meandering lines like the splinters of a shadow.

"How Romeon initially crossed into our band had long been a mystery, but in spreading the Magna among us, he unwittingly gave us the answer. When the Light Lords were thrown from Soliere, our paths cut streaks through the clouds, dark paths that formed tunnels through the bands that remain even to this day. They appear to be interdimensional pockets where the star's light does not reach."

"They have not shown up in any of my scans," Auro said. "If they are there, can we use them to travel to other parts of the nebula?"

"We believe they originate from each ray of the star, save the purple. Romeon discovered them with the help of the Magna. As the Gnost Band is the farthest out, its path runs across the entire nebula. A power greater than Romeon's has blocked him from using the paths to travel to the inner bands, but he has used them to enter mine. I could not find them, even though the Gnost path was the very course I traveled from the star. But that has recently changed.

"When Romeon returned from the outer clouds with your mother, he urged me one last time to join him. The time had come, he declared, for the two outer Light Lords to act as one, to break the barriers and push on to the star. I was steadfast in my refusal, which he had heard many times before, but never had he taken it with such ill will. Here, under this very dome with Haelia at my side, he unleashed a burst of red flame upon us. I was able to filter it out, but some of it entered Haelia's body. It has robbed her sight but given her a deeper vision than that possessed by anyone in these citadels. She is the reason the paths are included on this map, for she can sense where they are, and she can lead us through them, at least as far as the Magna Band."

"Would she accompany me, then?" Auro asked. "It will be dangerous."

"I will be with you," Raelight said. "When Romeon realized what he had done, he said he could not heal her, but we should not despair, for her new perceptions would lead us to new possibilities. As usual, he was sincere but wrongheaded. Just as your friend Jaimin has sought to purge himself of the red fire, I seek the same for my child. Now, with your vessel and Haelia's perceptions, we may confront the Magna power in its own realm. My daughter may regain her sight, you can find your mother, and we can see how fares your Noctarian friend."

✻　　✻　　✻

The next day, the *Meteor* embarked on a new voyage with a most unlikely crew. It was a somewhat different vessel than the one Auro had first flown into the Pale, for now it was a bolide, enveloped in the yellow flame. Auro was at the controls, Raelight and Haelia with him in the flight cabin. The girl sat beside him at the console while the lord stood pensively behind them. By some manner he could not fathom, Auro felt the child guiding his hands, steering the vessel along.

He was beginning to understand that this was not truly a nebula but a singular realm of space created when the Empyreans had triggered the nova of their star. The Nanj Cloud loomed ahead. Skirting along its fringe, near the border of the red band, they slowed, hovering before the great barrier.

Haelia tensed in her seat, her eyes pulsating intensely, as if searching for something. "I see it," she said. "I see the darkness."

*You're blind, girl. That's all you see,* Auro thought.

But as if on cue, a black line suddenly traced across the view screen like a two-dimensional plane. It could not be seen until they passed across its edge, cutting through the yellow space as if with an ink pen. It thickened as they approached it, and suddenly, they were surrounded by pitch black, as though some great force had swallowed up all the light.

"Where are we?" Auro asked with a gasp, turning back to Raelight.

"This is indeed one of the dark paths," Raelight observed. "Free of the star, it is a realm unto itself and can lead us between the bands."

All Auro understood was that they were in some kind of inter-dimensional space, a sort of tunnel that seemed to be pulling them forward. Soon the darkness was pierced by a crimson glow in the distance. Haelia sprang to her feet, her eyes now a deep red. "We're clearing the path," she said. "Entering the Magna."

Indeed, they were now in a cloud lit in a deep crimson, and across the expanse were flickering lights of red fire. They could see the core star again, larger and brighter there—and red, as they expected. There was no more yellow, except for a vague glow behind them that was quickly drowned out. They could also see the Magna side of the Nanj Cloud.

Auro took a moment to study the sensor data. There was no trace of the dark tunnel they had just exited. Unless the girl could find it again, they might end up trapped there.

"Romeon is in the Nanj," Raelight declared, as if sensing his presence from afar. "Can we enter it from here? We shall find out."

"It's about a day's travel," Auro noted. "Near it, I'm detecting some unusually large rocks. Could be asteroids, maybe a colony similar to your citadels. I can't isolate precise life readings."

They could only go forward. Auro navigated alone, as Haelia could no longer guide him. She and her father were gravely quiet.

Hours passed. The Gnost flame around the *Meteor* sizzled and crackled as it soared through the Magna. Auro set a course for the Nanj, then left the console to take time to sleep. Raelight veered between mediating and pacing around while Haelia sat against the far wall. Sometimes she drew up to her father, who gently stroked her head.

Some hours later, Auro returned to find the great orange cloud glowing through the screen. The Nanj had a softer light, between the sleepy Gnost and the intense Magna, in a way more appealing than either.

"Do you sense anything?" Auro asked the lord. "I see no sign of any—"

He stopped. The sensors were flashing. On the outskirts of the Nanj, a faint object was emitting a peculiar light: a mix of red and orange, but also yellow and white.

Haelia raised her head and stood up. Raelight led her over to the console, running his fingers through his beard but saying nothing.

Haelia let out a slow breath and closed her blind eyes. Auro felt her control coming over his hands again. They accelerated toward the flashing object. It had a triangular shape and appeared to be a glass pyramid, its gleaming surfaces both reflecting and refracting the cosmic lights.

The screen now showed two red bolides coming out of the Nanj, their flames streaking in the fiery tails. Auro considered that his mother could be in one of these bolides. The *Meteor* now had a flame of its own, and Auro remembered how Raelight's domes had held the Magna comets at bay, but he didn't know how to wield the Gnost as a weapon. From behind the pyramid, they unleashed fire directly into its transparent walls. The flames converged inside it, then burst out in a concentrated beam, blindingly white. The *Meteor* shook; its fire flickered.

Auro looked over at Raelight and Haelia. Father and daughter seemed oblivious to him, and he assumed they were tapping into their connection with the Gnost that surrounded their hull to firm their defenses. But the *Meteor*'s flame seemed to be weakening. Just as Auro thought he had to find a way to rouse the lord or even the child to some plan of action, Raelight's eyes shot open. They were bright yellow, his face pale and grave.

"This is not the Magna," he said. "This is an energy I have never encountered." Without another word, he turned and left the room.

"Where are you going?" Auro cried, starting frantically after him.

Raelight halted just before the air lock. "You've just received a transmission," he said, looking back at him with a queer expression. With that, he opened the vacuum-sealed chamber and disappeared.

Auro stood there bewildered, debating whether to follow him. He was not prepared to brave the strange environment outside, and he was certain that Raelight did not intend for Haelia to be left alone on the ship. So he returned to the flight cabin, and to his surprise, he found Haelia sitting at the controls and conversing with someone at the communication station. Had the bolides contacted them?

As he went up to the console, Haelia stepped away, turning toward him. "They will come," she said. "I've shown them the way."

In no mind to ask questions, Auro sidestepped the cryptic child and went to see if he could trace the transmission or retrieve a record of what was said. The vessel rumbled again. Auro activated the scanners and scopes. The screen showed Raelight hovering just outside the ship, his body enveloped in Gnost, trying to deflect the alien energy issuing from the pyramid. He unleashed a broad burst of his own flame that forced the bolides back and scattered their fire. Then the lord directed his flame into the pyramid itself, adding its yellow to the red and white inside.

The bolides quickly recovered and moved back into place. Then something emerged from each one: more fiery humanoids. At first, Auro thought both were Magna, but one of them was covered with a smoother glistening energy. It looked like Jaimin's plasma but was tinged with red fire. Both entities flew from their vessels on either side of the pyramid to advance on Raelight, who was still guarding the *Meteor*, his flame nearly exhausted.

Auro doubted the Gnost lord could hold them off and didn't know what he or Haelia could do to help. He wondered if that plasmic entity was truly Jaimin and if he was aware of what he was doing. Perhaps his will had been subsumed by the Magna. And why had Raelight gone out there in such a fruitless gambit, perhaps a suicide mission, leaving his daughter behind?

He cursed the whole expedition, the stupidity of coming there in one little vessel. Once again, he had been convinced to cross a dangerous frontier in the company of someone with greater power and different motives. Ever since the Battle of the Pearls, he had been flying blind.

He knelt and looked Haelia squarely in the face. "Tell me the truth," he insisted. "What did your father hope to accomplish? I can't believe he brought you out here to get you both killed."

"They won't harm him," the girl answered. "They need us to reach the star. They need light for the prism."

Auro looked again at the screen. The pyramid was clear again except for a multicolored glow still shining in the center. The plasmic and flaming beings were moving toward Raelight and the *Meteor*. Yet as they came upon them, Auro felt sure that he was not destined to be conquered by the Magna or whatever energy had come from the pyramid. In fact, he was more convinced than ever that his journey through the nebula was still just beginning.

# CHAPTER 8

# RED RENDEZVOUS

Kelmin knew his ship's every feature and function. The *Astraeus* was his prize achievement, the embodiment of all the powers of creation the Eternigy had given him. But now, he was helpless to ignite the magnificent engine he had ingeniously designed, for he lacked its fundamental power source. "I built it," he said, "but Jaimin made it go."

He turned and faced his audience: Ormonde, Sultaan, Falconhyn, and a smattering of guards. Shanna and Bailyn stood quietly aside. No weapons were drawn; this was a peaceful parley. The astounding transmission from the nebula with the message from the mysterious girl had been enough of a jolt for the two sides to realize their common cause.

Shanna and Kelmin finally understood the intrigue that had been swirling around them since their arrival. All throughout the activities of the last few days, there had been a factional struggle over how to deal with the visitors and their technology. Some of the prefects and scientists had conspired with the Stylights to seize their vessel, learn its secrets, and perhaps eventually take it into the nebula themselves. That is, until Ormonde had preempted them, for he was aligned with another group that wanted to keep the vessel out of the Stylights' hands and work with the Noctarians in planning any future expeditions. But after a tense standoff in the close quarters of the flight deck, they had all listened to the unexpected and perplexing message that had come out of the blue, pondered its meaning, and came to see that they needed to find common ground.

They struck a new bargain. Kelmin and Shanna would take the *Astraeus* into the nebula to find Jaimin. Bailyn would accompany them to represent the prefects and contact Auro. Falconhyn would go as well to reconnect the Stylights and the Empyreans. The overall mission: to initiate Amphora's first official embassy into the nebula and to recover Auro and Jaimin, or at least learn of their fate. But first, they had to make sure they could safely enter the clouds. Kelmin was already at work strengthening the shields, but it was the propulsion that troubled him most.

"Your engine has no power?" Ormonde asked, marveling at its glossy blue panels.

"It can get us into the nebula for sure," Kelmin said. "But if current readings and our last foray are any indication, we won't last long in there unless we're well fortified by the Eternigy, and for that, we need Jaimin."

"Don't you and Shanna possess that same energy?" Bailyn asked.

"It takes different forms within each of us," Shanna explained. "I can conjure matter. Kelmin can manipulate technology. Jaimin's plasma powered the engine."

"What about the clouds themselves?" Sultaan inquired. "They have properties neither the Stylights nor our scientists fully understand. Perhaps the ship could harness them as it travels through them."

Kelmin raised an eyebrow. "Maybe so," he mused. "I could construct a port to conduct the ambient energy into the engine's panels. That might enable us to withstand the clouds."

Shanna took Falconhyn and Bailyn back to the flight deck to continue scanning the Pale while Kelmin worked in the engine room with the scientists. Sultaan and Ormonde disembarked, representatives of the two factions that had chartered this expedition. They had much to explain to the rest of the governing council and to the people.

Feeling in his element for the first time since he'd left home, Kelmin made dizzying alterations to the engine and outer hull. The Amphorans were astounded at the uses to which he put their tools and the speed at which he worked, producing innovations that would have taken them years of research. Using the limited data the sensors had managed to gather from their short time in the Pale, Kelmin modified the shields and created vents that could channel the cloud's energies into the engine.

When the preparations were complete, the scientists also departed, and the four remaining occupants of the *Astraeus* prepared for takeoff. Kelmin and Shanna were at the controls, with Bailyn and Falconhyn behind them. Kelmin set the course and ensured the instruments were integrating all his enhancements. With a deep breath, Shanna fired the thrusters. The vessel passed through the bay door and accelerated toward the beautiful and dangerous clouds. The exocity shrunk to a twinkling light behind them. Navigating through the asteroids, they closed in on the Pale and flew right into it.

The currents stormed; the ship held steady. Kelmin felt the flush of success. "The new shields are resisting the clouds' corrosive effects," he said, "and their energy is channeling into the engine at the right amounts, carrying us smoothly. I should have worked some more on the sensors. I can't read much of anything around us. However, we are following the course the girl provided."

Shanna sighed. She never doubted Kelmin's ingenuity to solve any technical dilemma. Her fears were turning from whether they would reach Jaimin to what they would find when they did. She remembered their arrival in these very clouds, their encounter with the bolide and its strange fire. It must have exerted some sinister influence on him. No natural urge would have pulled him away from them just when they had reached a new world. Or was that only what she wanted to believe?

They were still just inside the Pale, not far from where they had originally emerged to find themselves in a cosmic storm and then under attack. This time, they were fully alert and prepared. The clouds, of which the Amphorans had an almost primordial terror, did not dismay them. Though the sensors could not give them a clear picture of what lay ahead, onward they went, and the *Astraeus* carried them through the worst the currents could throw at them. Gradually, the clouds became more peaceful, both in temperament and in color, and the swirling jumble of hues a more uniform and reassuring yellow. They traveled at top speed for several hours until, finally, the view screen homed in on a patch of darkness ahead. It would not have been visible at all in normal space but stuck out like a hole in the amber tint.

"That's where we're heading," Kelmin confirmed. He turned back toward Bailyn. "Any idea what it is?"

Wide-eyed, Bailyn shook his head. Falconhyn, too, was silent. Kelmin looked back at Shanna. "Well, Jaimin headed into the unknown, and now we're following."

Into the blackness they went, as though they were entering a dark tunnel, not knowing if they were in another region of the nebula, another dimension, or some illusion. They continued through the darkness until the screen showed a new light in the depths: a red light, growing bigger and brighter. There was a flash, and they appeared to have exited the tunnel. Space now had a crimson tint, just as the region they came from was yellow, and before them were dots and streaks of red fire. In the distance swirled a distinctly orange cloud. Farther out was the piercing glare of a red star.

They had completed the course they were given. There was no sign of the tunnel from which they had come; they were now deep in an abyss with no path back. Shanna lurched forward, alarmed. The sensors confirmed that some of the fires were indeed bolides and seemed to be moving away from them. "Are there any near us?" she asked Kelmin. "Any heading this way?"

"No," he replied. "They're all going out ahead. But I'm detecting something else, something big, near the edge of that orange cloud."

"What is that cloud?" Bailyn wondered. "It looks out of place, like it isn't natural."

"This whole nebula isn't natural," Kelmin growled. "At least the cloud isn't shooting fire at us. But I'm reading something that might. There's a big concentration of red flame, too big to be a bolide."

Closing in on the orange cloud, they came upon a cluster of space rocks, smaller than the asteroid field near Amphora. Clearing through them, they gaped to see a massive rock on which was a mountain, miles tall, rather like a volcano. Its underside glowed molten red, and the peak belched up lava and ash. The *Astraeus* flew between this drifting object and the orange cloud, trying to get readings of both. Then they saw another manifestation of the red flame flickering in the currents, a wide fan of fire glowing over what looked like the hull of a sailing ship.

They were puzzling over these bizarre sights when the console notified them of an incoming transmission. Kelmin input some commands into the dashboard, and the image of a man appeared on the screen, a striking bald-headed figure with glowing red eyes.

"I'm glad you have come," he said. "The child summoned you. I doubted whether you would decide to answer her plea or be able to make the journey, but here you are."

"Yes," Kelmin replied, bewildered. "We came for our friends, led here by a child's message. Who are you, and who was the girl who contacted us?"

"I am Romeon. You have come to the Magna Band of the nebula. I wield the red flame that created it."

Falconhyn stirred. "You are one of the Pentheon? So it is true . . . the Light Lords did enter the star."

Romeon nodded. "And I recognize a fellow Empyrean, even one long left out in the cold." The crimson eyes flickered.

Kelmin wanted to ask about Jaimin, but Falconhyn cut him off with a glance.

"I know the questions that brought you here," Romeon said. "I regret that my overtures to the Amphorans and the Noctarians were so misunderstood. I did not desire conflict with either. The comrades you seek are indeed here with me. You will be reunited with them. But first, they will help me fulfill a great purpose. Come down to my vessel, the *Dante*, and all will be explained."

"We will meet with you down on your ship," Falconhyn confirmed. The transmission ended.

"We will?" Shanna said indignantly.

"He does seem to be the power here," Kelmin conceded. "We'll have to deal with him to have any hope of finding Jaimin."

"Is he down on that ship?" Shanna asked hopefully. "Why don't we see him?"

Falconhyn went over to the console and fixed the scopes on the volcanic asteroid. "Aurorno is there, somewhere," he said. "I also sense a power akin to yours out in the distance."

Kelmin scowled and examined the scanners. "Even if we could pick up Jaimin's signature, there are too many bolides. We couldn't go around looking for him."

"Bailyn and I will do what we can," Shanna said, far more interested in finding Jaimin than the doings of that galleon with the flaming sail.

Bailyn nodded. "You and Falconhyn can go meet this Romeon in person. We will watch from here and keep searching for Jaimin and Auro."

They all agreed. Kelmin and Falconhyn prepared to leave the ship. Kelmin was clad in the most advanced shell of technology ever devised, and Falconhyn had his space suit and whatever other mysterious powers he possessed.

Leaping from the air lock, they dove swiftly toward the galleon. The heat of the fiery sail swelled over them. They touched down on the deck at the foot of the mast. Kelmin reached into his sensors to record all the data he could—the ore that formed the hull, the nature of the crimson cloud, and the flame itself. The Magna indeed resembled a fierce red fire, yet it was something more.

Romeon came toward them. Before speaking, he pointed up the deck to the prow. Kelmin and Falconhyn turned toward it to see a tall, broad man with a yellow beard encircled by a ring of red flame. Romeon halted a few yards from them with a group of attendants clustered at his back.

Falconhyn stepped forward. "Are you indeed one of the five who entered Soliere over two centuries ago and brought on the nova?"

"I am. To my knowledge, all the five yet live, though Lord Raelight there is the only one I have seen since our fusion was broken. We were in the star together and were both expelled from it. Since then, we have been confined within our bands. I have endeavored to escape mine with some success. The Magna flame lights our passions and sharpens our sight. Raelight's yellow Gnost is cooler and robbed him of his hunger for energy. Suffice to say, we do not see eye to eye."

"The descendants of the Eddans who survived the nova now dwell in an exocity just outside the nebula," Falconhyn explained. "Lately, we have come to know your flame. You clearly know of us."

"And I am from a Bioplane called Gemma," Kelmin added. "We set out on a mission to find other humans in the far depths of space, if people infused with star energy can still be called human. When we arrived, one of your flaming vessels attacked us. One of my shipmates, Jaimin Caraggio, entered the nebula with the Amphoran Aurorno Augustine. Are they here?"

"They are. Jaimin is helping us make our next journey. And we are human enough—as human as you, I daresay, but we are Empyreans. Powerful energies have been searing into us for centuries. Even before the Great Journey, we were no longer quite what we were. You are mistaken if you think your power belongs solely to you. Energy is free. No physical being can lay a lasting claim."

"None of us knows what rights we have to any power," Kelmin said. "We do not ask for yours, nor will we turn ours over to you." He paused and looked back at the prow where the yellow-bearded figure stood transfixed by the fiery ring. "You have taken captive your fellow Light Lord? I suspect you've put Jaimin to some similar fate." Kelmin raised his arms, locked his weapons.

But Romeon laughed. "Fighting is the last thing that should be on any of our minds. Why should any of you want to thwart our endeavor here when we will all end up with our hearts' desire?" He spoke now with a booming confidence. "Come! I will take you to your friend, and you can ask him if he has any qualms about his task."

The fire sail above them rippled. Suddenly, the vessel began to move like a seafaring ship catching a gust of wind. Kelmin looked out from the prow, past the captive man and into the distance. They seemed to be heading toward the red star. He sensed that they were indeed traveling to wherever Jaimin was. Then he remembered Shanna and Bailyn. Turning, he could only see the volcanic asteroid and the orange cloud, both tiny in the distance. The *Astraeus*, if it was still there, was lost to sight.

"Get up!" Shanna snapped at Bailyn, reacting to a sudden and alarming movement on the screen. "That sailing ship is moving away."

Bailyn was crouched on his seat, trying to meditate as Auro had taught him. Oblivious to all else, he thought he had heard a faint voice when Shanna's sharp command jerked him up. Quickly, he caught sight of the galleon sailing off.

"We've got to follow them," Shanna insisted, and she prepared to set a course. But then two fire comets burst from the orange cloud.

"Oh no!" Bailyn cried. "They must have been hidden in there, ready to come out if we moved."

"They're not going to stop us," Shanna declared.

The *Astraeus* thrust forward, at first evading the streams of fire the bolides unleashed until one coordinated barrage sizzled over their shields and sent them spinning. Regaining control, Shanna found they were now directly over the asteroid's smoldering surface. Cautiously, she reduced speed, looking for somewhere among the molten crags where they might lose their pursuers.

"I hear him!" Bailyn cried. "I can hear Auro!" The voice he had reached in his reverie was calling back to him.

Shanna looked at him, bewildered. Another burst of fire flared across the hull. Their shields held. Shanna fired back. The red flames absorbed their lasers without effect.

One of the bolides came around behind them while the other bore in from above. Then each veered around, their fiery tails encircling them in a thick ring of flame. Shanna brought the ship to a near-sudden halt. "They're ensnaring us, just as that first bolide tried to do inside the Pale."

"How did you escape?" Bailyn asked.

For a moment, Shanna looked uncertain. But while she lacked Kelmin's mystical connection to the flight controls, she was a worthy pilot, taught by Adventus Borno himself. As the bolides swung back for another circle, she took the *Astraeus* into a new dive, through the one opening in the fiery net they could still get through. Drawing the flame's energy in through the new vents, she blasted the engine, igniting a huge fireball that dissipated the net and blew back on the bolides, sweeping them away. She continued on at top speed, flying around the volcano.

"I hear him again!" Bailyn exclaimed. "Auro is down here."

"Down where exactly?" Shanna asked skeptically. "Can you pinpoint where he's calling from?" She didn't know what to think of this unexpected fruit of Bailyn's meditation. In any case, it was Jaimin she wanted to contact. But Auro, if they could reach him, might know where Jaimin was, assuming what Bailyn heard was not some trick of Romeon or of his own mind.

"There," Bailyn said, pointing to a large crevice at the base of the volcano where lava was pouring down the sides like a waterfall.

Bailyn was certain. Shanna nodded grimly. They had to find some cover anyway. The bolides would likely regroup. Again, she took the ship into a dive, descending into the canyon, maximizing the shields, and avoiding the gushing lava as best she could.

Bailyn was trying to trace the voice in his head. At his signal, Shanna slowed the craft and hovered. "Through there," he said, pointing to a wall of lava. Their sensors confirmed that it covered a tunnel.

"It's a huge risk to take the ship through there," Shanna noted. "That's no ordinary lava. Can you speak to Auro, maybe get him to come out to us?"

Bailyn shook his head. "It's the faintest of connections. We are aware of each other but cannot communicate directly."

Shanna was wary. They would have nowhere to run if the bolides followed them in. But she remembered her own power; the boldness at the heart of her character surged forward. "There may be a way yet," she said.

"Can you strengthen the shields?" Bailyn asked, thinking of the wonders Kelmin had worked.

"No, but I might be able to go in myself." She stretched out her arm and conjured a sphere of her peculiar marble-like matter, which hovered above her open hand. "I command a substance that few energies can breach if I bend all my will to defying them."

Leaving Bailyn to man the ship and admonishing him to stay alert, Shanna quickly donned a space suit and entered the air lock. What emerged outside was a purple sphere some ten feet in diameter, enough to fit one person or two. Inside it, Shanna focused all her thoughts on keeping the shell intact, intent on piercing the falling Magna and discovering, for good or ill, what was on the other side. Her marble could conduct or deflect heat according to her purpose. For a moment, she felt like she was in the center of a great furnace about to melt her down. But in an instant, she was through.

She let a part of the shell in front of her eyes dissolve away and saw that she was in a cavern bright with the glow of red Magna. Judging that her space suit alone could sustain her, she let the shell completely vanish and stood with her own feet on the ground. Then she gasped to see a figure sitting against the far wall, legs dangling down a sloping crag. It was Auro. His black hair glistened through his clear helmet. His eyes were closed.

Shanna rushed to him, shaking him awake. He stirred and looked at her in recognition.

"You came," he said in a tone of bewildered relief. "How did you find me?"

"Bailyn and Falconhyn." Auro's eyes widened at the names. "They heard you or had some intuition of your presence. You can ask Bailyn yourself. He's on the ship. What are you doing down here?"

"This is where they brought me. Romeon said I had no energy to contribute to his prism and my part in all this would come later. For now, he seems to want me out of the way."

Shanna didn't understand but gripped his arm with one hand and re-created her shell with the other, making it a little larger, with a doorway-size opening. "I can take you through the lava flow," she said. "Our ship is just behind it."

"How did you enter the nebula?" he asked.

Shanna sensed that he would not move unless he knew more, as though he didn't fully believe it was really her. As quickly as she could, she recounted their stay on Amphora and the transmission from the mysterious girl who had sent them the course to come there, how Kelmin and Falconhyn had gone to treat with Romeon on his archaic sailing vessel, and finally, how Bailyn had steered them to this cavern as they evaded the bolides.

Auro was astonished. "Romeon wanted Jaimin; if he now has Kelmin and Falconhyn as well, he might find use for them."

"They may have been taken captive when that vessel sailed off," Shanna replied. "Who was the girl who contacted us? Do you know where Jaimin is?"

"Haelia is the daughter of Raelight, the lord of the yellow Gnost Band where Jaimin and I first came. The red Magna flame burned her eyes but gave her deeper perceptions, and she found a path by which we were able to cross the border. We came here to retrieve Jaimin, but our worst fears were realized—he seems to be helping Romeon—either of his own will or under the Magna's influence; I am not sure. Romeon has constructed a prism of sorts, which he thinks can help him move into the interior of the nebula, toward the core star. Just after we arrived, two bolides concentrated their energies through the prism to disable our vessel. Raelight tried to fend them off, but two entities overpowered him. I think Jaimin was one of them. Romeon himself boarded our ship. He immobilized me with a blast of his flame and eventually brought me here. Jaimin and the girl were taken to the other side of this band. Romeon also knew that Haelia had transmitted a message outside the nebula, so he stayed back near the Nanj Cloud to see if you would come."

"Let's not tarry anymore," Shanna said, beckoning him again toward the shell. "Bailyn is waiting. Those bolides could return at any moment."

Auro finally got up and cautiously followed her into the peculiar little pod. "Romeon is gathering his forces at the frontier. I think he is about to unleash a fire that will burn everything in its path."

Shanna closed the opening behind them. "Let's go get what we came for," she said.

✳    ✳    ✳

Kelmin was an engineer but had never experienced movement like this. He was on the top deck of what looked like a sea vessel; the wide Magna sail bulged and stretched high upon the mast. Gemman scientists had dabbled in theories of cosmic sails, but this was space travel by a means beyond even his understanding. His body stiff and his mind dull, he could not use his instruments to determine their heading or how fast they were going. He and Falconhyn were encircled in rings of fire, like the yellow-bearded man at the prow, and like him, they were somewhat paralyzed. He assumed Shanna and Bailyn had seen them take off and wondered if they were trying to pursue.

The red star was larger now, gleaming dark red with hints of green in the depths beyond. The *Dante* slowed. The bolides that had traveled with them were darting above the mast like flaming birds. Falconhyn, who seemed to have been meditating, suddenly opened his eyes.

Romeon walked up to them. "We are coming to the border," the Magna lord declared. "Even I have never been able to cross it. However, you have brought me a new power." He turned toward the captives and raised his hand. The flaming wreaths around them dissipated, releasing them.

High above the sail and the hovering bolides, a new object descended toward them. The transparent pyramid was familiar to Raelight but a shocking sight to Kelmin and Falconhyn. Though smaller than the *Dante*, it appeared gargantuan over the deck, refracting the sail's fiery light. Moreover, they saw three figures floating inside it. One of them appeared to be Jaimin, fully immersed in his red plasma.

There was also a smaller figure in a yellow-and-orange blaze. They couldn't be sure, but they thought it might be the child who had hailed them. There was a third being covered in pure red flame, like the entity Jaimin and Auro had encountered outside the Pale, perhaps the same that they had seen in their vision on the pillars. They reflected on whom the Stylights believed it was.

Kelmin's first instinct was to fly up toward the pyramid, but he was preempted by Raelight, who let out a harrowing cry of "Haelia!"

"She is unharmed," Romeon said. "Since she absorbed my flame, her body has contained Gnost and Magna, and therefore Nanj as well. It's time for her to release it. When she does, her sight will be restored."

Raelight looked back at him plaintively.

"Yes," Romeon confirmed. "And the Noctarian will be purged of the Magna that has so distressed him. In return, they will channel their energies through the prism and open a portal through the border of this band. We bent all our power to bring you here. The purpose of your journey now comes to fruition."

"Where is Aurorno?" Falconhyn asked.

"His is safe, back by the Nanj Cloud. He fulfilled his purpose in starting your journey into the nebula and will receive his reward when we're done. After we break the barrier, you can cross through the Nanj into the yellow band and go back to your city if you wish. The rest of us will proceed farther into the nebula, to the star itself."

"I must see Haelia," Raelight pleaded. Kelmin and Falconhyn could see the conflict in the Gnost lord, the desire to free his child and the hope that playing her part in this scheme would repair her.

"Soon enough," Romeon answered. "And she will see you." He turned to Kelmin. "Will you come up for a closer look?" he asked with a hint of boast. "Even a scientist of your peerless caliber will be awed by what we are about to do."

Without waiting for an answer, he flew up above the sail in a burst of red flame, past the bolides, to the very top of his pyramidical prism, straddling the apex. As Kelmin hesitated on whether to follow, Raelight blazed his own yellow fire, and though not invited he, too, shot up like a spear of molten gold. But he stayed off to the side, watching Romeon and the prism in apprehension. The rest of the *Dante*'s crew spread out along the sides of the deck, climbing the riggings to observe the momentous events above. Kelmin and Falconhyn activated their jets and flew up together, along the way getting a better look at its occupants, or prisoners, floating inside it like fireflies in a glass jar.

Inside the prism, Jaimin, Haelia, and the other fire entity floated there in a row, three points of light, then began to release synchronous discharges of their energies through the clear wall. Their beams combined into a solid white that emanated into space. Concentrated, blinding, it speared the dark, dense barrier of the band, which, after a few moments, flashed as though hit by strikes of lightning.

The discharge continued until all three ceased their energy flow, either out of exhaustion or by Romeon's command. The Magna lord, still perched atop the prism, on the verge of fulfilling his great endeavor, outstretched his arms as if in ecstasy. Now a swirling field formed in the barrier where the beam had burrowed into it, vibrant colors blending and spiraling into a dark center.

Kelmin sensed it might indeed be a portal to another place, yet something told him it did not lead where Romeon intended. In any case, it seemed to beckon them all toward it, a pull both gravitational and psychological.

Meanwhile, Raelight drew closer to Romeon. As if in response, the bolides hovered ominously over them.

"That is not the way to the Syntha!" Kelmin heard Raelight shout. "What have you done?"

Kelmin and Falconhyn also propelled themselves toward the two lords. Romeon's feet were still planted on the pyramid, with his three adversaries and his bolides poised around him. Raelight and Romeon both dissipated the flames over their heads so that their faces could be seen.

"We have opened a pocket between the bands," Romeon said. "Therein lies the Syntha, where Vitruvia awaits us. I can feel her energy. We must go through while we can."

The portal did appear to be shrinking. With every rotation, its currents spiraled in a slightly smaller width.

"Enough!" Raelight shouted. "I take Haelia now!"

The two lords were unyielding. Romeon again covered his head with fire and looked ready to discharge a barrage upon his fellow lord. But Raelight struck first, unleashing his yellow fire and sending Romeon hurtling off his perch into the crimson void.

Kelmin and Falconhyn now shared Raelight's determination to break the prism and free Haelia and Jaimin. The Gnost lord also seemed intent on thwarting any crossing through the rift between the bands that the prism had made. But the bolides were still there to oppose them. Rather than join in the quarrel, the *Dante* started moving toward the portal.

Kelmin and Falconhyn hastened over to Raelight. "We've got to hold off those fire comets to have any chance of freeing Jaimin and Haelia," Kelmin said urgently.

As he spoke, two of the bolides descended upon them. Kelmin extended his armor's deflectors and returned fire—not with lasers but with a gravitational damper that sent both vessels spinning away. A third bolide swooped in from another direction, but Raelight staggered it with a barrage. However, they could all see that the fire vessels were only momentarily stunned and would swing back at them in seconds.

Falconhyn turned to Kelmin. "You have another door to open," he said knowingly.

While he knew nothing of Kelmin's feat with the diamond, Raelight seemed to grasp the intention. He touched his flaming hand to Falconhyn's shoulder. "My fellow Empyrean," he said, "we can hold off the red flame. Our soldier here can see about freeing those in the prism."

Nodding, Kelmin ignited his aft thrusters and descended along one of the smooth triangular sides, evidently composed of some crystalline substance. He planted his hands flat against the surface, peering through it to see the three exhausted occupants floating limply in the center. His eyes caught Jaimin's, and he saw recognition in them.

Feeling a new burst of momentum, Kelmin reached into the astounding capabilities of his armor. A vibrating energy issued from his gauntlets that shook the prism's sides to their molecules. He had been experimenting with frequencies for a while and had confirmed their usefulness in opening the heavy door on Amphora. The structure heaved but would not give. He looked up and saw that Raelight and Falconhyn were indeed keeping the bolides at bay; the Stylight, like the Light Lord, issuing streams of yellow fire from his hands.

But then Kelmin was jolted by a burst of flame that suddenly came at him from around the pyramid. It was Romeon. He was still some distance away but seemed to have recovered and was heading around. Kelmin's shields held, and he bolstered them as much as he could, not daring to take his hands off the crystalline wall for fear of losing the cumulative pressure he was building. Again, he felt it heave. Then, with another redoubling, it cracked and shattered. The blast knocked Kelmin back. His armor deflected countless exploding shards.

The occupants of the prism lunged toward the hole he had made. The rest of the structure was still largely intact. Kelmin suddenly found himself face to face with Jaimin, who flew out, holding the girl in his arms. Now Romeon was almost upon them.

Jaimin extended his left arm and managed to charge his plasma through it, faintly, to fire a weak stream at the Magna lord, which Kelmin supplemented with his laser fire. Once again, Romeon was hurled back. Up near the apex, Raelight was aware that his daughter was free, but he could not come down to her without releasing the enemy vessel he held fast with his fire.

"Quick, cover the opening with a force field," Jaimin said. The third captive, covered in Magna, was about to dart through the hole when a white light emanated from Kelmin's gauntlet and adhered over it. The being was stymied, fluttering around Kelmin's barrier like a fly at a window.

"We need to help drive off those bolides," Kelmin said, "then make for the *Dante* before it goes through the rift." He gunned his thrusters and ascended to the apex where Raelight and Falconhyn were struggling. Jaimin followed, still holding the child. Kelmin fired his lasers on wide beam, and Jaimin released every iota of energy he could. The bolides flickered and finally retreated, receding into the distance.

Jaimin handed Haelia to Raelight. The lord scooped her up and let the flame he could still muster flow over her and warm them both.

"Quick, while we have time!" Jaimin cried. "Head for the ship!"

With Jaimin leading the way, they all launched off the top of the prism, heading toward the distant flicker of the fire sail. The *Dante* was closing in on the shrinking portal in the barrier between the Magna and Syntha Bands. The clouds thickened as they approached the frontier. Kelmin scanned behind them, worried that Romeon would recover quickly. His fears were confirmed. The Magna lord had returned to the hole in the prism he had hastily patched.

"They have broken through my force field!" Kelmin called to Jaimin. "Whoever was in that pyramid with you is out now!"

Jaimin twisted around. He saw that Romeon and the other flaming being were in pursuit, with the bolides close behind. Jaimin knew they were in no shape to fight them all off. He and Raelight had exhausted much of their power, and Raelight was encumbered by his daughter. Ahead, the *Dante* had stopped before the rift, presumably waiting for Romeon to catch up before it entered.

Jaimin and Kelmin regrouped with Raelight and Falconhyn, and they all looked back at their pursuers. But before they could confer, a new object came soaring toward them, not red but a more familiar blue. Kelmin recognized it first. Jaimin shut his eyes in a moment of deliverance. When he opened them again, the beautiful sight of the *Astraeus* with its gleaming silver hull and azure engine soared between them and their oncoming adversaries.

"Get up under it!" Kelmin cried. "Hopefully, they can extend the shields around us!"

All five evacuees got within the vessel's protective envelope as the bolides charged and a barrage of red flame hit the shields. The *Astraeus* shook but held firm. Kelmin reached the hatch under the keel. He pushed Falconhyn, who was close behind him, up the ladder. Then Raelight came, holding Haelia. They helped the girl up, and the lord followed her. Jaimin went next, and Kelmin took up the rear, closing the door behind him.

They all filed through the air lock into the corridor that led to the flight deck and were astonished to encounter Auro standing at the threshold.

"Hurry," he said. "We accelerated out of range of the bolides as soon as you were all inside. We have to close up that rift before Romeon's ship gets through."

They dashed into the flight center. Bailyn and Shanna were steering at top speed toward the edge of the band. "The bolides are closing in," Shanna said. Despite the frantic moment, she swung her head back in delight to see Jaimin.

Kelmin took Bailyn's place beside her at the console, then turned to Jaimin and Raelight. "The prism focused your energies into a beam that cut into the barrier. How can we close the rift it created?"

It was Haelia who answered. "That portal doesn't lead to the next band. We can cross through it and seal it from the other side, but we will be trapped in there."

"Where will we be?" Shanna asked.

The girl offered no answer. They were just closing in on the *Dante* when the screen showed two of the bolides overtaking them. In addition, the two flaming beings, Romeon and the one that had been in the prism, were soaring along with them.

"The fire comets have never been much impressed by our lasers, but they haven't reckoned on our new engine," Kelmin noted.

There was a rumble from the rear of the ship as energy poured through the vents, and in a sudden acceleration, the *Astraeus* shot right past the bolides and dove at the *Dante*. The spiraling portal was directly before them. Disregarding all caution, Kelmin charged into it, with Romeon's galleon right on their tail. Red space became black, and they streaked through until Raelight cried, "Wait, go no farther!"

Kelmin brought the engine to a stop and activated the rear scopes. They had gone through the rift and were now surrounded by black space with a sliver of red behind them, perhaps the reverse side of the opening to the Magna Band. Through it, they could see the faint flicker of the fire sail. The *Dante* was following them.

Shanna understood. "Can we conduct more energy into the engine?" she asked.

Kelmin pointed to a panel at the top corner of the console and grinned at Jaimin, relishing the advantage of having him back with them. Jaimin placed his hand on the panel and channeled his plasma into it, which Kelmin conducted through the engine. It blazed on impact with the rift. When the light flickered out, there was no sign of a red cloud, a barrier, a rift, or a fire sail. Only dark space.

"It is sealed," Haelia declared.

At least briefly, now they could relax and try to figure out where they were. There seemed to be normal space around them, even stars, as if they had been transported outside the nebula. They didn't know how that was possible.

For the moment, all in the company were just glad to be reunited. Kelmin and Shanna embraced Jaimin with great affection. Bailyn put his arm around Auro, and they marveled at the disembodied connection they had achieved through Bailyn's meditation. But the deepest connection was felt when Raelight picked Haelia up in his strong arms and held her tightly.

"Stars, child," he whispered, holding her before the view screen. "I wish you could see them." But he realized his daughter's eyes had pupils again and were a soft yellow like his own, as they had been before they had been changed by the Magna.

"I can," she said. "What a wonderful sight."

# CHAPTER 9

# STARS OVER GREEN HILLS

They were clear of the red band, maybe of the nebula itself, in what appeared to be normal space. The stars looked real enough, yet they had a ghostly glint, their patterns constantly changing. They reminded Auro of the projections on the inside of Raelight's dome on a much vaster scale. If Raelight thought so, too, he did not say. As for Haelia, her ordeal in the prism had restored her eyes but seemed to have dampened some of her otherworldly mysticism. She could offer no insight as to whether they had found their way back to the dark paths or had taken a very different road.

They still took comfort in their reunion. Jaimin, Shanna, and Kelmin were back together on their ship; Auro and Bailyn were glad to find each was safe; Haelia was again at her father's side. Falconhyn encouraged the spirit of communion, but he also focused their attention on the grave business that lay before them.

"The star patterns tell us nothing," Kelmin said in frustration. "But our flight is smooth, and I don't detect any other ships." He looked back at his fellow travelers, arrayed behind the console. "If we're still inside the nebula, we're in a peculiar region where the clouds don't penetrate. We have a clearer view of the stars, though I can't fathom why they're shifting like this."

"That portal felt much like the dark path we took to get to the red band," Auro said. "We were meant to cross from the red to the green, but we seem to have arrived somewhere else."

"This region seems boundless," Kelmin observed. "But looks and even readings may be deceiving. We can see stars, but I can't get a fix on any of them." As he checked his long-range scanners, suddenly both the dashboard and his eyes lit up. "I have something!" he exclaimed. "Of significant mass." He fixed their course to it like a buoy, as if it was the only thing in all this cosmos that was real. Putting the ship on autopilot, he scoured the region with the sensors while the others rested.

Three hours later, he called them all back. They were approaching a planetoid. It orbited nothing and gave off a curious green light. "It's solid," Kelmin said, "with an atmosphere." As they drew closer, they saw that it had a landscape rippled by highlands and valleys covered with grass and trees.

"How could a rogue planet with no sun have such vegetation?" Shanna marveled.

"Are you aware of any human colonies beyond the Magna Band?" Jaimin asked Raelight. The yellow lord shook his head.

"Well, there's someone down there," Kelmin said. "I'm reading life signs, including humans." He trained their scopes on a region along the equator where there were many rolling hills dotted with wooden structures.

Kelmin brought the ship into the atmosphere. They descended through green clouds to land on a bed of moist grass. Exiting the ship, they were all invigorated by cool air that smelled of dew. The planetoid was small, perhaps the size of Earth's moon, but it had an atmosphere and gravity close to those of the human norm. The sky was a light, shiny green.

They landed near the bottom of a slope. Perched on the hilltop was the largest of the houses they had seen from above. They decided to walk to it together so as not to startle the inhabitants and to take some time to comprehend this little world.

They had not gone halfway when Kelmin detected some movement. They looked up to see a group of people lining the edge of the hilltop. For a moment, the travelers stopped in their tracks; then they spurred up the hill until they found themselves standing before this curious set of figures. They numbered less than twenty and did not appear threatening. They were all aged, with white hair or bald heads, yet they stood tall and erect, their bodies lean and strong.

Raelight spoke first. He proclaimed himself a member of the old Pentheon, keeper of the Gnost, and founder of the Rae Citadels.

One among the throng stepped forward, the tallest man, with a ribbon of silvery hair around his temples. He walked nimbly and showed no fear at the sudden appearance of these strangers. A warm smile creased his bright, leathery face. "By the flames," he said. "At last, we have word of what we left behind."

Suddenly, Raelight sprang forward in recognition, recalling long-dormant memories of this man and his people. "Elred!" he exclaimed. "You found your stars."

The old man nodded. There was a thrilled murmur among the throng around him. "My old lord," he said. "You look the same as when we first saw you emerge from the yellow ray. The Gnost is still bright in you. Although we left your band, seeing you here, feeling its warmth again, brings a joy we've not felt since the clouds obscured the star."

Elred beckoned Raelight forward. As he did, with Haelia at his hand, the other natives quietly dispersed, most in the direction of the wooden house at the center of the hill. The rest of the visitors followed a short distance behind. Elred explained how he and his people had come to be on this secluded world.

As Soliere had collapsed, they had been among the Empyreans caught in the path of the Gnost and gathered by Raelight when he had proclaimed the founding of the citadels. But unlike most of the others, the Gnost did not bring them peace. In later years, the people of the Gnost would contend with the rival Magna seducing them away, but for some, the yellow flame never held any lasting allure. Rather than entreating them to embrace its gifts, Raelight had allowed them to take one of their remaining vessels and go where they would.

"At first," Elred said, "we tried to leave the nebula and see if Edda still existed, but the outer clouds were too harsh and stormy to traverse. Then we journeyed to the opposite border, but the barrier stopped us cold. There seemed no way to leave the confines of the band. We traveled round and round it while pondering our fate. Eventually, we came across a curious phenomenon: a great black path in the yellow light, pulling us in like an undertow and enveloping us in darkness. Unable to see, we were conscious of a voice speaking from the void. Later, we realized we had come to some kind of pocket between the bands."

"You came upon a dark path," Raelight explained. "These are the routes the Light Lords traveled when we were hurled from the star. They cross the bands and remain free of the lights and fires of the five rays. Just recently, I was able to find my own path again. It looked and felt like a dark tunnel, but this appears to be a wide realm of endless space, and there are stars."

"Phantom stars," Elred noted. "Visions from all over the cosmos. They are ever changing. We have observed their patterns since we arrived."

The whole company marveled that the very cosmos there could be a mere mirage, but if it wasn't real, what was?

"There are many things about this world I cannot explain," Elred said. "We believe it is interdimensional space, both within the nebula and somehow outside it. It is watched and was probably created by the being who led us here. The voice."

Raelight's eyes glinted, but Elred said no more. He led them across the grassy field to a stone hearth not far from the house. It contained a pale-green fire that did not feel like Gnost or Magna. More stirring than the former, less agitating than the latter, it was restful yet reaffirming.

The grass and clover around the hearth were thick and soft. The hill was surrounded by lush valleys. Elred described how the green sky rained emerald drops that enriched the soil, and the light of the fire permeated the sky, lit the world, and provided the conditions of life. But just as the planet was small, the days were short, and in fact, this day was almost done.

They could see other houses on hilltops across the vales. There weren't quite two hundred people, all the same ones who had arrived nearly two centuries ago. They aged slowly and lived a quiet life, tending crops and flocks, living on grains and vegetables grown in gardens, on sheep and wild deer. Their vessel had contained livestock and seeds preserved using the technologies their ancestors had employed in the exile. Everything they had revived and set loose to grow or roam across this little world had thrived beyond all their expectations.

There on that hill, in front of yet another mysterious flame, the visitors were left to rest as evening set in. The green clouds dimmed, the sky darkened, and the stars they had seen from their ship began to dot the expanse overhead. Elred smiled and walked toward the house, disappearing inside.

They looked to Raelight to see if he had anything more to say, but Haelia had already fallen asleep in his arms, and he laid his head on the grass, his amber eyes gazing up at the peculiar heavens. As the stillness wore on, they all nodded off under the phantom stars shining high above.

✳  ✳  ✳

Auro woke first. It did not seem as though the night had been very long, but his sleep had been deep. The fire still flickered in the hearth. The stars were fading, and the sky was filling with a greenish daylight with no discernable source other than the clouds that began to illuminate the rolling hills to the edge of the horizon. Morning had come, and the respite from his thoughts and recriminations had ended.

He no longer questioned what Jaimin had done back in the Magna Band. Romeon had used his and Haelia's injuries, and the seductive power of the red flame, to enlist their help in what they both had come to believe was an endeavor for a greater good, and Auro had played his own part in the events that had brought them to this point. His thoughts turned to what he had learned under Raelight's dome, that his mother still lived and was still with Romeon. But most of all, he pondered his own purpose there. Was his mother truly the source of the voice that had lured him into the nebula? Did she want him to find her?

The others were beginning to stir. Elred reappeared from the house, carrying a sack in one hand and a kettle in the other. He placed the kettle over the fire and took an assortment of wooden bowls and spoons from the sack. The kettle contained a porridge that heated quickly over the flame. Elred filled the bowls and passed one around to each of his guests. They all gratefully received their breakfasts, thanking him and murmuring among themselves.

They asked more questions about this planet and the community that called it home, as well as whether Elred knew of any way to return to the nebula proper. Their host revealed that he had not been off the world's surface since the day they had landed and could not explain even how they had come to be there, much less how to leave.

"That path you entered took you a long way," Jaimin said between spoonfuls. "You started from the yellow band and must have traveled the whole length of the red, unless you sidestepped it somehow. We came directly through a rift Lord Romeon created."

Elred sighed. "Only the voice from the darkness knows."

"There is a voice," Haelia said. "I can hear it, but I don't know what she is saying. She seems so far away."

They all looked at her in surprise. The girl had barely spoken since her release from the prism, quietly taking in sights long denied her. Perhaps her extra perceptions had not been entirely lost after all. She turned to her father. "Do you hear her, too?"

"I hear her, my dear." Raelight stood up and faced Elred. "It is indeed Vitruvia. I have heard nothing of her since the Pentheon was broken."

"Her consciousness, it seems, is part of this realm," Elred said. "Her Syntha flame permeates the very air and sky. The flame of growth. That is why this world is so green and has daylight though there is no sun."

Raelight nodded. "I know something of all five rays. For a moment, they were all inside me. Vitruvia always wanted to use the star's energy to nurture life. I believe this pocket, as you call it, is inside the green band, at least partially. As Romeon created the Nanj Cloud to straddle the Gnost, Vitruvia created a realm that straddles the Magna. It is not truly endless, but its frontiers are obscured by a vision of stars, projections from across the cosmos."

"If that's true," Kelmin said, "then if we go back in the ship and keep exploring, perhaps we will eventually come to the green band."

"I know something of visions," Falconhyn said. "If my ancestors hadn't remained on Edda, I might have been among Lord Raelight's followers, perhaps among those lured away by the Magna. I don't know why Vitruvia created this world; it seems to be a place of exile, cut off from the star. This green fire is pale, and I assume it lacks the Syntha's full power and vibrancy. The flame, the grass, even the stars, they all seem to pacify and lull, like the Gnost."

Auro rose to his feet. "Why did you join this expedition?" he asked Falconhyn pointedly. "The Stylights always treated the nebula like a tomb, to be viewed with sadness and awe but never disturbed, as if it held some terrible truth we weren't meant to understand."

"It is a frontier," the Stylight answered. "We believed we were not meant to enter it until we were ready, but we also perceived that Amphora's destiny lay within it. The nova affected the Eddans no less than the Empyreans. We are one people, united by one star. The Stylights have long known that some remnant of Soliere was shrouded within its clouds. The appearance of the bolides and the Noctarians gave us an opening to act."

"And now we know that we are not the first Amphorans to enter it," Auro noted. He turned to Jaimin. "Who was the third person in the prism with you and Haelia?" He knew the answer but wanted to hear it directly from him.

Jaimin had been dreading this moment but now felt glad that Auro had asked directly. "I met her in the Nanj Cloud," he said carefully. "She was from your city, the same being we encountered near the Pale. Her name was Armarna." He looked away from Auro to Bailyn and Falconhyn. "Do you know of her?"

"She is my mother," Auro admitted heavily. He stepped closer to the fire. He didn't feel as overwhelmed as he had under Raelight's dome, but the same emotions simmered. "My parents' ship was lost at the Pearl Stations. I believed that during the battle, they had been taken into the clouds. It was more than an intuition. I felt a presence from far away, heard a voice faintly calling. This was the real reason for my patrols along the Pale and for finally entering the nebula. At first, I thought it was your arrival, your energy, that set me going, convinced me that this was the right time, but really, it was her. I didn't recognize her when she attacked you outside the Pale, but I think even then, deep down, I knew. Did she recognize me?" he mused, reflecting that the flame that had struck him had come from the bolide, not her hand.

"The prism combined our powers to bring us here," Jaimin said. "Especially your mother's Magna. She has the yellow in her, too, but I think the red has captured her heart. I also suspect that she believes at some point in the future, you will join with her and be infused with the flames as she has been."

"What about us?" Shanna asked, referring to her, Jaimin, and Kelmin. "It seems time we looked to find a way back. Lord Raelight has his people to lead, the Amphorans have plenty to report back to the prefects, and we Gemmans . . ." She looked at her teammates, hoping one of them would pick up her thoughts.

"The dark paths are the only way back that we know of," Auro said, "but do they run through this pocket? Even if they do, could we find them? Perhaps Haelia can still perceive them, or Elred can pinpoint the one that brought him here. But what of Romeon? Is he still trying to break out of his band? He still has his prism, though he now lacks the Eternigy."

"For all we know, his bolides are attacking the Rae Citadels or Amphora as we speak," Kelmin said.

"No," Raelight countered. "At this point, there's nothing for him at either place. He only wants to go inward, to reach the star. He will exert all his power to reopen the rift."

"I cannot lead you back to the path," Elred said. "Vitruvia guided us here long ago, and here we will remain until she guides us away."

"I think we are meant to lead Romeon's way rather than him leading us," Auro suggested. "This world holds a glimmer of the Syntha flame. I say we harness it and follow Vitruvia's voice—if Raelight and Haelia can hear it. I would go all the way to the core star."

He waved his hands over the fire and then turned and strode away from the hearth, walking slowly down the hill. The rest of the company let him go off by himself while they finished their meal in silence. Then they, too, began to roam freely to mull over their predicament. Raelight took Haelia to watch a group of reindeer grazing on a nearby slope. Falconhyn stayed on the hilltop and strolled around the house and garden.

Jaimin, Kelmin, and Shanna slipped off to check on their ship. It was the first time they had been alone together since they'd arrived from Gemma. They shared a deep bond, which had given them a mission they had always struggled to define. Now they struggled with the meaning of what they had found. This nebula had great depth and rich energies; perhaps they were meant to explore it.

"I shouldn't have run off the way I did," Jaimin said finally. "I see that now. At the time, the urge was overpowering. The red fire drove me. It was searing, irresistible."

"Is it gone now?" Kelmin asked. "Did it all leave when you discharged your energy through the prism?"

"I'm not sure if any of it remains," he replied, "but I no longer feel any burning. Whatever its presence inside me, I don't believe it will continue to influence me as it did back there."

"If you still have some of it, we may have need of it yet," Shanna said. "It looks like we will keep going forward, toward powers far beyond ours."

✳   ✳   ✳

Hours passed, and the sky was beginning to darken again. Although Auro had wandered off alone, he knew that solitude would not solve any of his dilemmas. The notion of exploring the nebula, once exciting and mysterious, was now a looming descent into the depths of his own identity. Perhaps his mother had meant to entice him into the nebula. Was she still truly her former self? He didn't know what to think.

He paused in a sharp breeze and suddenly saw Bailyn coming toward him. Auro still felt guilty about leaving him alone to deal with the Gemmans and the intrigues of the Stylights and the prefects. In his unassuming way, Bailyn had risen to the occasion. Auro told him as much.

Bailyn shrugged at the praise. "I just tried to stay out of the way."

"If I had been there, I would have tried to steer things," Auro admitted. "There's no telling what problems that would have caused."

"What now?" Bailyn asked.

"I don't think I can leave the nebula while my mother is still somewhere in it. But if the Gemmans try to leave, I think you and Falconhyn should go back with them."

"I'm not sure they really want to go, either," Bailyn mused. "As for me, I just don't know."

As they mulled these questions, the tall figure of Raelight, with Haelia at his elbow, strolled down the hill ahead of them. They seemed carefree among the wild grass and roaming herds. Perhaps they were even glad to be free of the yellow star for a while and the price it exacted for the serenity it gave them.

"Did you see the deer in that westward valley?" Auro asked.

Raelight nodded and swung Haelia up on his shoulders. "I'm glad we were dropped in the middle of these vistas when her sight returned. Soon she will see our great domes again."

Auro stretched out his arms and looked around. "Is Elred really the same man you knew at the time of the nova? What do you make of the green flame . . . and all this?"

"Elred is taller than I remember. The Gnost could not create a place like this, nor the Magna. Yet Elred does not possess the Syntha's full potency. That exists in the green band." Raelight breathed deeply of the crisp air. "The Gnost quiets the mind and fosters self-reflection. The Magna heats the spirit and stirs courage to seek out the unknown. The Syntha spurs growth and nurtures life. Vitruvia kindled this world, creating the conditions for the life we see."

"Elred said we were in a *pocket*," Auro remembered, "like the dark path or the Nanj Cloud, a little realm of space carved between the bands. Vitruvia lured them here all those years ago? Maybe she thought you or Romeon would eventually find them, follow them here?"

"She has been closer to the star than either of us," Raelight noted. He added cryptically, "She has a darker flame."

"What was she like?" Bailyn asked.

"She was closest to Aris and the first of the Light Lords to join with him. She saw him reaching out to Soliere as our ancestors had to Sol, drawing in its energy, growing. She wanted to grow." His voice trailed off, as though afraid of drowning in long memories. Haelia seemed oblivious to them, gazing up at the sky and out across the slopes.

Auro suggested they go find the Gemmans. They still had to decide which of them would go back and which would press on. But just then, a commotion burst above them. Elred appeared at the hilltop, calling down to them and pointing up at the sky.

The green clouds were parting, broken by a red glow. Auro and Raelight felt an oncoming dread. Their quarrel with Romeon had followed them there, for the fiery sail of the *Dante* appeared in the sky. Behind it, two bolides also descended, one of Magna and one with the yellow aura of the Gnost. It must have been the *Meteor*, now part of Romeon's force.

Elred's voice sounded again from the hilltop. "She is with them!" he cried. "She has come!"

As the *Dante* descended, its sail searing the green clouds, they could see a figure of great size standing at the prow. It was not Romeon but a woman, bigger than human scale, nearly a quarter of the height of the mast itself, a giantess with long green hair.

Elred cried out again, but neither Auro, Bailyn, or Raelight could make out his words. The mistress of this little world had finally come to its surface, and Elred's visitors now had to reckon with a new fire, darker than any they had ever known.

# CHAPTER 10

# INTO THE PRISM AND BEYOND

The *Dante* burned through the clouds and glowered low in the sky, and the fire comets plummeted past it. Auro, Bailyn, and Raelight stood frozen on the slope. Elred, after shouting his alarm, disappeared into the house. The grazing deer darted away.

"That's my ship!" Auro cried, identifying the *Meteor* by its yellow flame. With its red counterpart, it descended to barely a thousand feet over the hilltop.

They realized Romeon must have reopened the rift despite the damage to his prism and the escape of his captives. But he was not the one at the prow of his ship. The giantess standing at the rail was another Light Lord of the Pentheon: Vitruvia of the Syntha Band.

What had become of Romeon, and why was Vitruvia on his vessel? And another dread filled Auro's mind: Was his mother among this host? Could she be on the deck of the galleon or in one of the fire comets, even his own? Auro shouted for the Gemmans, hoping they could unite and meet this threat together, but his cry fell silent.

The woman raised her long green hand, and the *Dante*'s sail flickered green so that, for a second, it blended with the sky.

With no conscious decision from him, the thrusters on Auro's space suit suddenly activated and lifted him up, ascending toward the fiery ship. Raelight and Bailyn remained on the ground. Auro was vaguely aware of them shouting as he took off. In a moment, he found himself hovering before the prow, directly before the green-glowing goddess-like figure. Auro guessed her height at some thirty feet. Lithe as a vine, eyes like emeralds, and hair like grass, she looked keenly at him and said, "You broke through the red band and entered my realm."

Auro's body was locked under her influence, like Kelmin and Falconhyn had been on the *Dante* by the wreaths of Magna fire, but this was a stronger grip that reached deep inside him. Unable to escape or even look away, he could at least answer her. "I am Aurorno Augustine of Amphora, a descendant of Eddans and Empyreans. My city came under threat from Lord Romeon and his fire comets, and we pursued him into the nebula. Romeon created a rift that opened a way here, but we don't even know what this place is."

"This is a part of my realm," she declared. "Just as tree roots burrow into soil, my roots reach deep into space. Long ago, they pierced one of the paths in the nebula where the starlight does not reach and grew it into this wider realm. I brought a colony here near the dawn."

"We know of the dark paths," Auro said, "though not that they could be expanded. But how did you come to be on Romeon's ship?"

"He has long sought to enter my realm. With your help, he finally broke through, only to be thwarted at the end. Once you were on your way, I took the step of inviting him in. Of course, I exacted my toll." She laughed with an unnerving satisfaction. "I reopened his rift and lured him in with his little fleet. Possessing the higher flame, I grasped him in its coils and entrapped him in his mischievous instrument, which he foolishly thought could cut a path to the star. None of us is ready to go back to Soliere. Only when the Syntha tells me that I have reached my full growth will I traverse the inner bands. Perhaps then I will find Aris, if he still exists."

"Romeon believed all the flames had to be united," Auro said.

"He needs the other flames to advance. The yellow and red are bright, but they can only heal and hope. The green and blue build and purify. Beyond them all, the purple holds the key."

"So what now?" Auro asked pointedly, still unable to move.

"Those of you from Amphora and the Gnost Band may return home. The Noctarians from afar will come with me. They provided Romeon with the additional power he needed to breach the bands. It will not do to have them wandering around the outer spaces, but I can help them develop their potential. As for Romeon and his people, I have had enough of fending off their attempts to enter my realm. They will remain here in exile, cut off from the red ray. Raelight may go back and preside over both the Gnost and the Magna. He is the least of us but the most introspective. He will be a wiser steward and may even unite those flames as Romeon desired. When he is ready, he may join us in the inner bands. Perhaps by then, Romeon will be ready, too."

At that moment, the lock on Auro's body released, and, sensing movement from below, he looked down to see Jaimin flying up from the surface, blazing in his red plasma, with the *Astraeus* following him. He came to a stop alongside Auro. "Bailyn and Raelight gathered us," he explained. "They are in the ship with Falconhyn. We left Haelia down in Elred's house." He addressed Vitruvia: "We know what you said to Auro. We heard you."

Auro was intrigued. Vitruvia had apparently communicated with them on the surface even as she had spoken to him. She was perhaps communing with Elred and his people as well.

"We may be visitors in the nebula, but we are no one's thralls!" Jaimin proclaimed. "Not to any of the Light Lords. We will go where we will."

Vitruvia's green countenance darkened. "Your only way forward is through me. I will show you what has become of your Magna foes."

With that, the *Dante*'s sail swelled, and the vessel lifted again, heading out of the planetoid's atmosphere, back to space. Auro and

Jaimin managed to grab hold of the railing and hung on to the vessel, with the tall woman standing over them. Once again, they were surrounded by darkness and stars. The little green world shrank below them. The *Astraeus* still followed them.

Romeon's prism came into view, gleaming in the distance, reflecting the *Dante*'s firelight on its glassy surface. Straining their eyes, Auro and Jaimin could make out the Magna lord hovering in its center, trapped in his own creation. Jaimin was silent, conflicted. But Auro, still driven by a motivation that went beyond discovery or growth, pointed up at the *Meteor* hovering just above the *Dante*'s sail. "That is my ship," he said. "Who is in it now?"

"Your mother," Vitruvia replied, with a flash in her jade eyes. "She had greater ambitions than Raelight, which is why she forsook him for the Magna. She has been helping Romeon, but with me, she can fulfill a greater purpose. I will bring your yellow bolide back to my band, along with the red galleon, and add their fires to my own."

As Auro and Jaimin pondered these words, two figures flew out of a port from the *Astraeus*. Jaimin recognized Kelmin's gleaming armor and Shanna, no less striking in her space suit reinforced by plates of her mystical marble. They both dove down to join them on the deck of the *Dante*.

Vitruvia fixed her mesmerizing gaze on the three Gemmans. Then, to Auro, she said, "They will not need their alien craft any longer. Take it back to your city."

Swayed by these words, acting without conscious thought, Auro found himself activating his thrusters and flying toward the *Astraeus*. Then, to his surprise, the Gemman vessel suddenly opened fire, its powerful guns shooting wide at the *Dante*, across the hull and directly on Vitruvia herself.

The galleon swerved and tilted as if nearly capsized by a tidal wave. Auro saw Vitruvia fall to the floor of the deck. Her massive body might have crushed her enthralled passengers if they hadn't suddenly gained enough of their senses to scramble out of the way.

Auro realized this unexpected attack had severed Vitruvia's control over him. He glanced back in midflight at the *Meteor*. It had been circling the mast, but instead of protecting the Syntha lord, it moved away and headed toward the prism.

Still determined to find out if his mother was truly in his old vessel, Auro veered sharply from the *Astraeus* and started streaking toward the yellow bolide. Yet he had not gone halfway when something held him fast. To his astonishment, the *Astraeus* had caught him in a towing beam.

Auro let out a silent scream, powerless to break the grip. As he was pulled back, the *Meteor* kept on until it was a yellow flicker in the distance.

✳   ✳   ✳

Down on the *Dante*, Kelmin recovered quickest from their own ship's onslaught. Jaimin had fallen beside him, and Kelmin helped him to his feet. Shanna had been thrown farthest, lacking heavy armor or shielding plasma, but got right back up and quickly rejoined them. They were also shaking off Vitruvia's influence, which had enthralled them to such a degree that Shanna and Kelmin had left the *Astraeus* to present themselves to her.

Now the three stood over the massive green body, sprawled prostrate across the deck. Kelmin raised his forearms and released a blanket of light that descended over her. He was trying to keep her down with a force field. "I think she could regain consciousness at any time," he said. "Hopefully, this will keep her immobilized."

There was a stir as the *Dante*'s crew, led by Thomoly, emerged from the lower deck.

"Did she commandeer the vessel?" Jaimin asked the captain. "What happened on your side of the rift after we went through?"

"The rift disappeared," Thomoly replied. "We assumed you had sealed it. Lord Romeon was enraged and entered the prism himself to try to reopen it, persisting in the attempt hour after hour. We still had the yellow bolide that the Amphoran brought into our band, and Armarna boarded it to contribute its fire. Then a new distortion appeared at nearly the same location. Something on the other side seemed to be trying to get to us. Threads of green light reached out, lashed around the *Dante*'s hull like tentacles, and pulled us in. Some of the bolides managed to come in after us. We fell unconscious as we passed through. When we revived, we were here, along with the prism with Lord Romeon still inside it. Then we saw Vitruvia and recognized her as the Syntha lord. She came onto the deck and exerted some hold on our minds, rendering us dumb and obedient. Taking her place at our prow, she bade us set course for the planet."

"She's not invulnerable," Shanna said. "It took a full blast from our ship, but we disabled her."

But Vitruvia was beginning to stir under the restraining field. Kelmin's arms tensed, redoubling the energy stream that covered the massive body. "I can't maintain it," he uttered through gritted teeth.

Suddenly, her eyes opened and looked up at them coldly. Now green-glowing appendages coiled out of her sides, like the tentacles Thomoly had described. Apparently, she could form her green flame into filaments of energy, and they wrapped around Kelmin's arms and waist. His force field gave way, and Vitruvia rose to her feet, even taller than before and more radiantly green.

"Fools!" her voice rang once more in their minds. "I brought you here to embark on a journey worthy of your power."

Jaimin fired a burst of his plasma at her, to no effect. A sword appeared in Shanna's hand with a wide blade and strong hilt, her favorite weapon to create from her mystical marble, and she swiped at one of the filaments that held Kelmin. It severed with a snap.

Vitruvia stepped back, shocked to see her appendages so easily defeated. Her body grew still more in her fury. Giant hands thrust down, grabbing Jaimin in one and Shanna in another. She held them aloft. Down the deck, the rest of the *Dante*'s crew members were coming under her surging influence again.

"Your energies are strong," she said. "It was bold of Romeon to merge your power with the Gnost and Magna. Let us revisit him before we depart."

Upon her command, the *Dante*'s sail swelled, and the galleon headed toward the prism radiating with the power of the Light Lord inside it.

✳   ✳   ✳

Auro had gunned his thrusters to full power, intent on reaching the *Meteor*'s yellow firelight. But for all his efforts, the *Astraeus* was pulling him in another direction. He only stopped struggling when the air lock enclosed around him and the heavy door sealed shut. He lowered gently to the ground as the chamber pressurized. The door to the interior opened to invite him in. Feeling thwarted rather than rescued, he stormed up to the flight cabin. Gathered at the main console were the remnants of their party: Bailyn, Raelight, and Falconhyn.

Bailyn came toward him, relieved. "I didn't think we'd get you back," he said. "Kelmin and Shanna got it into their minds to leave the ship. We could not stop them. That woman on Romeon's galleon put some hold on all of us. By the time we saw you try to fly away, the influence had abated enough that we were able to fire a salvo at her and activate the towing beam."

"I'd have broken it if I could," Auro replied sharply. Bailyn looked perplexed.

Then Auro softened. "You did the right thing. My mother is inside the *Meteor*, and I tried to follow it after it flew off, but that was not the way." His mind was racing as fast as the events that had just occurred.

"The *Meteor* and both bolides are near the prism now," Bailyn said. "Should we head toward it?"

"I, too, would like to contact Armarna," Falconhyn said.

Suddenly, Raelight broke in: "Something is happening to the prism." He pointed at the screen, where the bolides were converging on it. They were circling its apex, perhaps trying to figure out how to free Romeon.

"Yes, head toward it!" Auro cried. Carrying out his own order, he sprang upon the console and set a course. Although he regretted leaving the Gemmans in their struggle down on the *Dante*, the *Meteor* had become, for Auro, the lodestar for his whole expedition. He hailed the bolides but received no response. "They must see us," he said in frustration.

As they moved closer, the *Meteor* suddenly dove down along the side of the prism. It stopped before a physical distortion in the center of one of its sides. They realized that this was the hole that Kelmin had created when he had freed Romeon's captives. It was bigger now, and Kelmin's force field had been replaced by a green film of energy. Vitruvia must have put it there to keep Romeon in; incredibly, the *Meteor* passed right through it and entered the pyramid to float inside it beside the Magna lord. With the contribution of its light, the prism shone like a lantern.

"She brought the whole vessel in!" Auro exclaimed.

"She's not trying to free Romeon but join him," Raelight said. "They may be planning to focus their energies together through the prism."

Then the red bolide also swooped down and followed the *Meteor* into the hole. At first, it didn't look like there would be enough room, but as it poured through, it became apparent that the prism was growing. The sides were stretching, the base widening. Auro and Bailyn brought the *Astraeus* to a halt as the glassy structure expanded. Inside it, the *Meteor*'s yellow flame merged with the red of its counterpart.

"Is this Romeon's doing or Vitruvia's?" Auro wondered. "Someone seems to be gathering all the power they can into the prism."

"And now the *Dante* is heading our way," Bailyn said. "Maybe this is all part of her plan, or maybe our friends managed to subdue her?"

The fire galleon was indeed sailing into view. Their screen clearly showed Vitruvia standing on its deck, taller than ever, her hands raised high, and each had something in its grasp. The sail flickered with traces of green.

Vitruvia's thoughts now entered their minds as they had before: "I offered these travelers a chance to grow. That is the gift of my flame. But they rewarded me with assault."

*Maybe they would have gone with you if given a choice,* Auro thought and realized they had all heard it, as if his thoughts had been projected into a disembodied voice.

"I never thought I'd see you again!" Raelight called out to the green Light Lord. "I have dwelled in the yellow band since we were released from the star. Romeon sought me out. I suspect you could have reached us both, but you chose to remain hidden. Romeon could go no farther inward than the edge of the Magna. Now that he has broken through, you would trap him here? You would send me back, yet take these foreigners? Why?"

"You have not grown," she replied with a flash in her eyes and contempt in her mystical voice. "A golden fool is still a fool. Our fusion failed. These three from afar have brought us a new energy, the fertilizer my power needs."

Auro saw that Raelight was taken aback, perhaps reading an implication into her words that he did not understand. "My mother has taken the Gnost bolide into the prism," he said. "I don't know if she is under your control, but I intend to join her there."

With that, he brought the *Astraeus* closer to the prism, which was still expanding and glowing with an orange light. The energies emanating from it churned through the starship's fantastic engine, and in a move worthy of Kelmin's prowess, Auro channeled it through the laser emitters and fired into the hole, dissolving the green field, widening the opening so that even the Gemman vessel could enter.

✳   ✳   ✳

Still held fast by Vitruvia, Jaimin, Shanna, and Kelmin watched the *Astraeus* enter the prism. Jaimin and Shanna were clasped in her enormous hands, and Kelmin was immobilized on the deck by the coils of green energy. The *Dante* was also heading toward the prism. The light inside the glassy structure was flashing even more violently, and it appeared to be melting down. The Gemmans did not understand what was happening, but they were afraid that their friends on the *Astraeus* were now caught in a terrible cauldron. A new flash from the prism, brighter and more intense than before, brought a shock wave that hit the *Dante* like a gale, more powerful than the barrage from the *Astraeus* had been, nearly extinguishing the sail and sending it spinning.

Vitruvia had taken the brunt of the blast, and the concentrated beam of blended energies from the prism seemed too powerful a blow for even her to withstand. She stumbled, gravely weakened, and Jaimin managed to fly out of her hand.

He fired plasma at her, and to his surprise, his assault sent her flying off the deck and into the void. He doubled back to see that Shanna was also free and had fallen to the deck at the foot of the mast. The coils around Kelmin had lost their strength. Jaimin rejoined his teammates on the deck.

The prism was no longer a pyramid. The apex had melted down; the base was curving and bulging. It was morphing into something that resembled an hourglass, with two bulbs connecting at a narrow point. The yellow-and-red flames had separated, each filling one of the bulbs, and each bulb was discharging a beam of light into space that culminated in a colored distortion, like the rift the original prism had opened.

"Romeon's work?" Kelmin wondered.

"Evidently," Jaimin said. "Maybe Romeon and Raelight are working together in there, trying to use the prism to open portals back to their bands?"

"I guess the only way to know is to go in and ask them," Kelmin said. "Our ship is in there now, but on which side?"

"Can we really get in there?" Shanna asked.

They saw no way of taking in the *Dante*, and there was no time to discuss such a mission with its crew. Resolving to inspect the prism for themselves, the three Gemmans linked hands and, as a unit, propelled themselves off the deck and toward the burning phenomenon.

The fires raging within the bulbs were so bright, they could no longer see into the interior. The hole through which the ships had entered appeared to have been sealed as the prism changed shape, but the hot and morphing crystalline walls now had a weak molecular cohesion, like melted glass.

Scanning its properties, Kelmin grasped that if his force field could protect them, they might pass right through it like a membrane. He looked sidelong at his teammates. They understood his mind and trusted him to lead them in. Gripping their hands as tightly as they could, they plowed in unison inside the fantastic structure.

The brightness was overpowering. Even Kelmin shut his eyes despite his helmet's protection. His grip on his friends loosened. They were in the center of the hourglass, with the Magna on one side and the Gnost on the other. In the middle was a mix, not a smooth orange like the Nanj, but kaleidoscopic, as though the light had been broken into innumerable shards. After giving his senses a rest, Kelmin adjusted his visual system to filter the light. Meanwhile, Shanna had covered her whole head with a shell of her marble. Even Jaimin, his eyes blazing with plasma, struggled to see.

Kelmin tried to locate the *Astraeus* and found it on the red side, not the yellow. Taking Shanna and Jaimin again by their arms, he led them toward the opening to the Magna bulb. The light around them softened into the pure crimson tint of the Magna Band so that their normal vision was restored. The *Astraeus* was hovering in the center of the chamber. The red bolide was pacing around by the inner wall of the bulb, which was like a great window.

Cautiously, they approached the *Astraeus*. Kelmin opened the air lock. In an instant, they were inside, hurrying to the control deck. So far, their presence seemed to have gone unnoticed. To their astonishment, they found Romeon standing before the main view screen, with Auro seated at the console and Raelight and Falconhyn close at hand.

Auro turned toward them as they stepped into the room. "We dared hope you would find your way in," he said. "We saw some of what happened on the galleon. Are you all right?"

Jaimin was too stunned to respond. He pointed at Romeon. "What is he doing on our ship?" he demanded. "Are you helping him open new rifts? Where is the *Meteor*? On the other side?"

"Yes," Auro replied. "And Romeon has confirmed my mother is in it. When we entered the prism, he forced his way on board, but he didn't come to fight. He said he could get us home."

"Vitruvia sealed me inside the prism," Romeon explained, "but I was able to communicate with Armarna. She took your *Meteor* and my bolide into it. Then her son followed her in with this vessel. I was able to channel both flames through your engine, separating them again in opposite streams. They reshaped the prism."

"Have you seen your mother?" Jaimin asked Auro.

"Not yet," he answered. "Romeon boarded us almost as soon as we entered. We agreed that once we helped him transform the prism, I could go to her."

Jaimin didn't express his skepticism, but something didn't feel right. Bailyn looked worried, too, but Auro seemed giddy with anticipation.

"This pocket of space is between the Syntha and Magna Bands," Romeon went on. "It has interdimensional properties, and I believe from here, we can reach places we couldn't before. On this side of the prism, we are opening a new rift to the Syntha Band, and on the other side, Armarna is cutting a path back to the Magna. I will enter the green band and continue my journey into the interior of the nebula, toward the star. This time, Vitruvia will not be able to stop me. If you wish, you can take your vessel to the other side, back to the Magna. From there, you can go back through the Nanj Cloud and then home."

Jaimin looked at Auro and understood that his only goal right now was to reunite with his mother in the other bulb. That desire seemed to override any qualms the others felt about the implications of what Romeon was attempting, what conflict it might unleash with Vitruvia and whatever powers lay farther in the nebula. Just as the Gemmans were wrestling with these uncertainties, outside the prism, a new object passed before the red bulb, about halfway between it and the rift it was forming, a flickering green light. In an instant, they recognized the *Dante*. Its sail was no longer Magna red but Syntha green.

"It can't be!" Romeon exclaimed, staring at the new incarnation of his beloved vessel.

"Vitruvia must have returned to it," Shanna said. "She reignited the sail with her own flame. Look, she's steering it in the path of the beam."

Indeed, the beam issuing from the Magna bulb was streaming directly into the sail. It flashed on impact, its color darkened, and the rift behind it rippled. Curiously, its color changed as well, but instead of turning green, it became dark blue.

"We need to cut that beam off until we know what she's doing," Jaimin said.

"No," Romeon countered. There was an eagerness in his voice, and his body radiated like never before. "She will lead us to a new frontier. But she will not have my ship."

"Are you mad?" Auro cried, finally applying a critical eye to these precarious events. "Go through that rift if you will. It's time for us to go to the other side. Will you honor our agreement?"

"I will not stop you, but she might," Romeon said. "For now, farewell." There was a flash of red flame, and the Magna lord was gone. Those he left behind were dumbstruck.

"I guess he wasn't trapped in here after all," Jaimin marveled. "He seemed to be waiting for something. Did he expect this? Has he been in league with Vitruvia all this time?"

"No time now to figure it out," Auro said. "We need to get to the other side while we can."

They all heartily agreed. Kelmin veered the *Astraeus* back through the middle of the hourglass. But an obstruction suddenly appeared in their way. A cascade of green fire ignited at the entranceway. It seemed to be a wall of Syntha flame.

"Vitruvia again?" Kelmin wondered. "The scanners can't detect anything beyond it. What else can we do but plow through it and hope for the best?" But as he prepared to take them in, they noticed dark spots popping up within the rippling fire, as if some other power were drilling holes through it.

"Are those openings?" Shanna asked.

"I think so," Kelmin said, "but none of them is big enough for the ship to fit through."

"They are meant for people, not for ships," Falconhyn realized. "Vitruvia may have generated that flame to block us, but someone is creating little tunnels that individuals might get through. Perhaps Armarna?"

"She wants me to enter," Auro said.

"What about the rest of us?" Jaimin asked. "We can't all abandon the *Astraeus*."

"We may not be able to get there anyway," Kelmin observed. "Something is happening. We're being pulled back."

They all felt the jolt of the ship's thrusters reversing. They were being pulled back toward the Magna bulb. "Apparently, someone wants us to go through the other rift," Bailyn said.

"Or we all leave the ship and go through those holes," Shanna said.

"No," Jaimin declared. "I'm not leaving. If something is leading us farther into the nebula, then that is our course."

Kelmin and Shanna looked at him in surprise and saw the same resolution as when he had gone with Auro into the Pale. "Why go back now?" he added. "We came to find the farthest reaches of humanity. Perhaps we'll find it beyond that rift."

"We won't split up this time," Shanna insisted. "We belong together on our ship."

Auro pointed back at the gate of green fire. "My way is through there to find my mother."

Bailyn stood at Auro's side opposite the Gemmans. Raelight and Falconhyn were between the two groups.

"My daughter is still with Elred's people," Raelight said. "I believe she is safe there. I may not be able to go back to her yet. Right now, we have two roads from which to choose. I, too, will seek out Armarna. I have questions for her, as Auro does. Hopefully, after that, I will be able to go back for Haelia and take her home."

Falconhyn walked over to his fellow Amphorans. "I followed Auro into the nebula to discover the source and truth of the Stylights' visions. Like Jaimin and Romeon, I, too, want to keep on the journey inward."

Thus, two expeditions were set—and not a moment too soon, for the vessel started to shake. "Go quickly, then," Kelmin said to Auro, Bailyn, and Raelight. "We'll cover you. Good luck."

Jaimin saw them off to the air lock. Before he stepped out, Auro turned to Jaimin. "I'm glad your injury has healed. Now you can continue on as you should, with your shipmates. I would go with you, but I have a call to answer."

"I may travel farther, but I think your journey is deeper than mine," Jaimin said. "You'll find her, and when you do, you'll know for sure what all this has been for."

Jaimin watched them depart and stood at the door for moment, thinking of all that had happened to lead up to this fateful moment. Then a tremor rumbled through the ship. He dashed back to the flight cabin to find Kelmin working at the console and Shanna monitoring the phenomena outside.

"We're no longer in the prism," she said in surprise. "Whatever power has control of the engine just pulled us out where we came in."

The view screen showed the *Dante*, whose sail now looked to be a mixture of red and green, as if the two flames were contending for dominance, heading into the blue rift until it disappeared inside its maw. The *Astraeus* was heading toward it, too, at increasing speed. Kelmin had lost flight control but was still able to work the scanners. "I read no Syntha energy behind that rift," he said.

"What the devil is going on?" Jaimin asked.

"Our friends on the other side may be asking that same question," Kelmin said. "I'm reading a rift there, too, but it's not of Magna energy. That portal may have changed as well."

"Yes," Falconhyn said. "Vitruvia circled the prism and intercepted both beams with her flame, altering both rifts. It seems none of us will be going where we intended."

As they pondered their friends' fate, their own was coming upon them fast. The blue chasm widened, quickly edging out the black space and phantom stars. Then it enveloped them.

✳  ✳  ✳

Auro felt he was on the cusp of a new life as he and Bailyn followed Raelight toward the wall of emerald fire. They each sought one of the dark holes that cut through it and emerged instantly in the opposite bulb. It was filled with a pale-green light, and there was no sign of the *Meteor* or of any yellow Gnost.

Just like at the other end, the energy issuing forth from the prism culminated in a rift in space. It, too, was green. Suddenly, they all began to move again, as if caught in a current, passing through the gelatinous membrane of the prism bulb and out into space. The rift grew larger as they closed in on it. His body enveloped in yellow fire, Raelight called up all his power to fight whatever force had them in its grip, to no avail.

But there was new activity from the rift itself. Great arms reached out from its depths to seize them. Not arms but glowing coils of green energy, like those Vitruvia had wielded on the *Dante*. One for each of them. Cables, ropes, tentacles—whatever they were—wrapped around them, keeping them tight in their grip. Auro, Raelight, and Bailyn went limp, pulled in toward the rift as though caught by some cosmic beast: part animal, part plant, all energy.

Helpless, they were carried through to their altered destination by the roots of something that grew far beyond this pocket of space and flowered in the light of an alien star with a power beyond their comprehension.

# PART II

# CHAPTER 11

# THE GREAT WIDE BLUE

They had plunged into an ocean, or so it seemed. The three Gemmans and Falconhyn huddled in the flight cabin as the *Astraeus* pushed on into blue space that was like vast dark water. Kelmin adeptly piloted through the thick currents skimming over the hull. Gemma had seas that were mere lakes to Earth's oceans, but neither compared with the vast depths of the Thyrrenean Band.

For this was where they had come, the fourth ring of the nebula. The rift that Romeon's prism had opened and Vitruvia had altered with her fire had transported them farther than perhaps either had intended. Not only had they cleared the little pocket on the edge of the Syntha, but they had overstepped the green band altogether and gone on to the blue. The core star was larger than ever, glowing like a great sapphire. Its heavy light seared the region, and its great mass gave space a watery, even syrupy, feel.

There were no other vessels in range—no sign of the *Dante* or the *Meteor* or any bolides. Hopefully, Auro, Bailyn, and Raelight had reemerged in the Gnost Band. They had all made their choices back in the prism. Auro had resolved to follow his mother on whatever roads that journey would take him. The four of them who remained on the *Astraeus*, at the last moment and at Jaimin's instigation, had determined to keep going farther into the nebula.

Each new band was closer to the star, thicker and darker than the last, and their sudden immersion into the blue was jarring. What little they knew of it they had gleaned from fleeting visions on the pillars and vague descriptions from such sources as Leone and Raelight, who had either never been in it or had no memory of it. All they really knew was that it was the domain of Thyrr, the most powerful of the Pentheon, save Aris himself.

"What is out there?" Jaimin asked, overwhelmed by the abyss. "Can the sensors detect any planetoids, clouds, lights?" He was beginning to feel as helpless as a sailor adrift in a lifeboat. A glance at Shanna and even Falconhyn told him they were feeling the same. But unlike his first foray into the nebula, Jaimin was now in his own vessel with the friends who shared his formidable powers. He only missed Auro's intensity and resolve. In fact, he realized that Auro, more than anyone else, had helped shape his sense of purpose there.

"I only see the star," Kelmin said with a sigh. "Our course is fixed on it."

"But we know the blue star is a mere illusion," Falconhyn mused. "The Thyrrenean ray illuminates this band, but the real star is beyond. To reach it, we must find and cross the barrier between this band and the next."

"We can assume that somewhere there is a dark path to the next band," Jaimin said. "But will we ever be able to find it?"

"We'll have time to think it over," Kelmin said. "If the instruments are right, this band is wider than the yellow and red combined. But more than that, the cloud is getting thicker. Like diving into deeper water, the pressure will slow us down."

"Should we turn back?" Shanna asked. "Or just stay put and explore our options? In time, Kelmin may be able to find the dark path or adapt the engine to take us through the barriers. Maybe we could even re-create Romeon's prism?"

All were silent. No one disagreed with her reasoning, but for now, their vessel kept going, as if the band itself was luring them onward, a deep, beckoning voice from the blue.

The Thyrrenean cloud was neither water nor light but a strange fusion of the two, so thick they felt as though they could reach through the screen and scoop handfuls of it. Its color was darker than sky or sea, with an eerie brightness. As in the other bands, some stars from outside the nebula pricked through from vast distances and glowed faintly as if from an ocean floor. While the Gnost had shone with a reassuring benevolence and the Magna was an inspirational fire, the Thyrrenean simply made them feel small. Without taking away their hope, it imposed a sense of insignificance. Shanna supposed that this was how their ancestors felt when they had created the Bioplanes adrift in a vast, dark universe.

Soon, an unusual movement in the dense currents aroused their awareness of another moving object nearby. They could not yet see it, but it generated a vibration that Kelmin piped through the speakers. They heard an utterly alien sound, at once guttural and melodious, all the stranger in the way it was distorted in the clouds. Shanna and Kelmin suddenly remembered their vision on the pillar and seeing vague monstrous shapes in the blue space as they flew out from the star. Unnerved, they nevertheless followed the sound until the view screen showed them a peculiar light and shape. They were catching up to it now; it was not moving very fast. Gleaming a pale light, its long body swelled and contracted in a steady rhythm like a disembodied heart.

Cautiously, they approached this curious object and saw that it somewhat resembled a sort of organism that had once existed in Earth's seas. There was a gelatinous body from which several squid-like tentacles propelled it through the currents. The head was a bulb, and from it, a beam of light shone into the dark blue ahead of it. It was almost half as long as their vessel. Dumbfounded, they all stared at it in silence, wondering if they were looking at a truly alien life-form.

"Is it aware of us?" Kelmin wondered aloud. He looked back at his shipmates, uncertain whether or how they should try to contact it.

"I could go out there," Jaimin whispered, though by now, even he was wary of such a strategy.

"I sense something from it," Falconhyn said. "An intelligence."

Suddenly, the creature maneuvered with greater vigor, pushing on ahead, with the currents swirling and churning around it. Kelmin accelerated, straining the engine through the dense cloud. This bizarre creature became a sort of buoy for them, with Kelmin determined not to let it slip out of sight. While it appeared to be swimming through space on its own muscle power, it kept ahead of their starship.

Yet Kelmin had begun to adapt the engine to this strange band and was able to increase their speed, riding along the currents with greater ease. He also detected more objects ahead, including space rocks, some nearly the size of planetoids, suggesting this band was not as empty as it had originally seemed. The environment was changing so dramatically that Kelmin felt inclined to cease the pursuit and investigate their surroundings when, suddenly, the creature veered around and started coming at them.

For the first time, they saw it from the front, with its bulbous head, blue eyes, and toothless mouth gaping. The white light emanating from the head flashed at them in a beam that seared over their shields and rocked the vessel. Kelmin steadied them but did not fire back, recognizing the difference between this creature firing at their ship and unleashing an assault on its naked flesh. The others seemed to sense his mind.

"Let's change course and let it be," Jaimin said. "We're chasing it, after all." He looked at Falconhyn. The Stylight seemed to have some special perception of it and was studying it closely.

No further bursts came forth from the creature. Kelmin flashed the ship's forward lights in a basic pattern, trying to convey a nonhostile intelligence. As if in response, the creature's light dimmed; the eyes became visible again and blinked slowly. Then it turned and streaked away from them. This time, they did not pursue it.

Kelmin sat back and sighed. "Well, we know we're not quite alone here." He turned to Jaimin. "Did you see anything like that in the other two bands?"

Jaimin shook his head in disbelief.

They continued on at a steadier pace, scanning as they went. Their instruments led them to into a region where the clouds were brighter and exerted less pressure on the hull. This was an unexpected but welcome turn, a sign that the clouds were not bound to keep getting denser the deeper they went. It was as though they had come to a warm part of the ocean where the light penetrated farther and life teemed. The region extended out with a range of millions of miles, and within it, the sensors homed in on a large space rock.

They headed toward it. After several hours with the currents at their back, they came to a curious sight: more creatures swimming in warmer currents. Some were shaped like the jellyfish creature they had encountered, but others resembled tadpoles with flagella-like tails; some were upright like seahorses; others like octopi, round and with many limbs. All had gelatinous bodies that radiated an assortment of lights.

They kept their distance, and the creatures returned the courtesy. Kelmin steered the vessel steadily on until they came at last to the drifting island. It had a generally flat shape, though the surface was rough and even mountainous so that it resembled a small rocky Bioplane. A sliver of land jutted out of it that formed something like a peninsula or a headland. It was surrounded by a cloud that was a lighter shade of blue than the rest of the band and that, according to Kelmin's readings, seemed to form an atmosphere. Moreover, the scopes showed two human figures standing on the tip of the peninsula, and they seemed to be encouraging them to land.

Glancing back at his comrades and finding silent agreement, Kelmin hovered the ship over the pointing finger of the headland and slowly lowered them onto the surface. Their excitement grew at the opportunity to contact human beings in this band. They exited the air lock and stepped out into a chill wind that swept over them, and they stopped cold before the two mysterious people as the gusts whipped between them.

They were a man and a woman of similar age and youthful appearance, possibly husband and wife. Both were beautiful, with tall and lean bodies, flowing hair, and bright-blue eyes, dressed in furs and leathers. The male, though of muscular frame, leaned on a white staff that was even taller than he. The woman's face had the beauty of a sparkling pool. Their names were Adnan and Rishna. They declared that they knew of their coming to this band, that word of their arrival had spread across the currents.

Kelmin introduced their company, reciting their names and delivering a hasty background of where they were from and how they had come to be there. The man walked forward, anchoring his staff on the stony ground with each step, moving with an alien grace.

"And so, you could say, we are lost at sea," Kelmin concluded awkwardly, figuring that was as accurate a summation as he could manage. He had rambled a bit, but neither the couple nor his comrades had stopped him. They were all a bit disoriented, standing on this narrow stretch of land in an abyss of oceanic depth.

"You are at sea but not lost," Adnan said kindly.

"Our land is not bountiful," Rishna added, "but it does offer refreshment. Follow us."

Before any of the visitors could ask any questions, Rishna started back along the headland toward the mainland, and Adnan turned after her and beckoned them on.

Unlike Elred's lush planetoid, this was an entirely rocky landscape without a glint of green or growth. It really did resemble an island within this strange cosmic sea, a world of crags, caves, and pebbly paths.

"Who else lives here?" Shanna inquired as they walked.

"Just us," Adnan said. "Most of the others are out there." He gestured up to what, from there, was the sky, the great blue cosmos all around them.

"We saw creatures out there," Jaimin said. "Are they alien life-forms that came to dwell in this nebula?"

"We know of no aliens!" Rishna called back, turning around buoyantly, as though about to dance. "They are human beings, no less than we."

"We are all the people of Lord Thyrr," Adnan said. "We were caught in the blue wave of the nova, and now we live in this ocean that circles the star."

"It's not really an ocean," Jaimin said, "but this is certainly the thickest cloud we have encountered so far."

"Ah," Adnan replied. "The Thyrrenean is an energy unlike any other. Part fire, part water, both hot and cool. That is why so many of us have ventured out in it to swim the deeps. Over time, the waders took different forms. Rishna and I waded for a while, but we found that we were content to observe from shore. We wanted to retain our earthly bodies, though we, too, have changed in some ways. There are islands like these throughout the band. We settled here some time ago and took to exploring the caves and climbing the hills. At times, others lived here with us. Now we are alone. Some of the creatures, as you call them, swim up to our shore, and we talk with them."

They crossed through a ravine with two rises of rock on either side, and once or twice a mile, they passed a carved edifice that could have been an entranceway into a cavern. The blue clouds formed a deep horizon above and ahead that included the sapphire star. Here and there, they caught sight of one or more of the bizarre cetacean forms swimming in the sky.

But no distractions hindered Rishna as she bounded up the path. It gradually widened; the rock walls receded and then began to slope downward. Now they stood before a broader landscape that reminded the Gemmans of the plateaus of the Crystalline Mountains in which they had hidden after their immersion in the Eternigy. These mountains were solid rock and less steep, but they were, in their own way, just as awesome to behold.

Rishna led them down toward an opening in the side of a cliff. It appeared to be the mouth of cave, from which glowed a blue light. They followed her into it and walked through a dark tunnel that gradually widened and eventually culminated at a cavern with a pool of water resplendent with blue light. The walls rose some hundred feet above, and the pool was fed by a waterfall that flowed down from the dark recesses. Rishna went to the water's edge, where a set of cups lay along the stone rim, and started drawing water into them. A cup was offered to each member of the company as they gathered around.

"It seems radioactive," Shanna observed of the gleaming liquid. Despite this, she didn't feel alarmed, held the cup to her lips, and took a sip. It had the fragrance of tea yet tasted more like a broth.

"It has all the nourishment we need," Adnan noted.

They all sat quietly and drank slowly. The visitors could well believe that this was all the sustenance they needed, for it brought a restful peace of mind and an invigoration of the body, similar to the Gnost's effect but more direct and physical. The nourishment and the soothing sound of the trickling falls pushed their many questions to the backs of their minds. They sat restfully silent, but their hosts began to pose some inquiries of their own. Rishna finished her draught with a lingering swallow, tossed her head back, and said, "You came from the inner bands, but you are originally from even farther out, are you not?"

Jaimin found himself answering, even as he wondered if the drink was meant to put them in a mood to reveal more than they might be inclined to without it. "Shanna and Kelmin and I are from another world, not so far away in the cosmic scheme but enough to separate us for centuries until we could find a way to bridge the distance. We hoped to come in friendship and reunite the human family. To our surprise, we found people who were themselves separated by a nebula and its layered clouds, beings affected in different ways by the different energies of a star—"

Falconhyn set his cup down and broke in. "I am from Amphora, a city just outside the nebula, a remnant of Edda. Only now have we Amphorans been able to see what happened since the nova, beyond fleeting and cryptic visions. We know that the five lords of the Pentheon entered Soliere together; that their fusion was broken; and that as the nebula formed, they became lords of their respective bands. We have encountered Raelight, Romeon, and Vitruvia. This is the band of Lord Thyrr. Do you serve him?"

"How can we serve one we cannot know?" Adnan said. "We followed Thyrr in the time before the nova. When he joined with Aris and the other lords, we followed the Pentheon and were able to get closer to the star than any other of our people. As the star swelled outward, we were caught in the path of the blue ray, which became this Thyrrenean Sea. We have not seen Thyrr since, but we feel his spirit. At times, we hear his voice in the currents, even if his words are too faint to decipher."

"We remember the other lords," Rishna said. "Aris convinced them that fusing into the Pentheon, uniting their forms, would enable them to withstand the very core of Soliere. It seems they were wrong. I imagine they want to reunite."

"Romeon does," Jaimin said. "He has been in contact—and conflict—with Lord Raelight of the outer yellow band. The Gnost flame has cooled Raelight's desire for energy, but Romeon's belly is full of red fire, you could say, and he seems driven to reach the star. As for Vitruvia, what she desires, I couldn't say."

"You have felt these other lights and fires?" Rishna asked, her blue eyes glinting. "And you have a fire of your own?"

Jaimin looked at his comrades. They had not spoken of their own powers, of the Eternigy. "We have power, not from a star, but perhaps not unlike those of your Empyrean lords. Some believe our arrival here signifies something."

"It does!" Falconhyn exclaimed. "Our presence here proves it. Since they were split apart in the nova, the Light Lords have been divided. Raelight wishes to be left alone, Romeon to explore, Vitruvia to grow. It is said that Vitruvia and Thyrr were united in marriage before they united physically in the Pentheon. She undoubtedly knows this great sea lies beyond her realm, but I surmise she is waiting for some change to pass before she will be ready to unite with anyone again. What, then, does Thyrr want? What does he know of the band past his, where we can find Aris and his star? You say Thyrr's presence has been hidden, his voice faint, but you knew him once. Do you know any part of his mind? The ones who swim above us in their new forms—what insights have they gleaned?"

"The Thyrrenean is the flame of depth," Adnan explained. "Its band is broader, reaches farther than any of the others. The Gnost burrows into the self but dismisses the outer world; the Magna reaches into the unknown but forgets where it comes from; the green nourishes growth and thus pushes outward, yet it keeps its roots. But the Thyrrenean has true depth; its reach is ultimately limitless, and those who explore it can easily get lost."

The company sat in silence, trying to comprehend. But Kelmin applied his scientific mind to interpreting these mercurial worlds. "It bends space-time," he said. "Time and distance. Beings here can evolve quickly; that is why the ones out there changed so dramatically while traveling through it. And Lord Thyrr, he is both here and not."

"Fluidity," Rishna said. "Neither light nor water are easily contained. They flow where they will." She gestured at the falls. "Whether down walls of rock, across light-years, or through the passing of centuries. Where is Thyrr? Out in the blue. Some of us wait for him; some search him out. The barrier to him is not the distance but whether he is ready to be found, and we are ready to find him."

They talked no more. All their cups were empty. Adnan and Rishna led them out of the cave and along the rocky hills, the ocean-sky above them with its swirling currents and lights. The visitors realized that their hosts now meant to part from them.

"After taking nourishment, we walk the world," Adnan said, "just as the ones out there swim the sea. We are glad you stopped here. After so long a time immersed in the blue, it is a comfort to feel something of the warmer lights. Perhaps you would like to stay here as we have, but I think you have more roaming to do."

With that cryptic observation, the strange couple turned down a gravelly path, leaving the Gemmans and Falconhyn to ponder it.

Falconhyn sighed. "We came so far so quickly, carried by events."

"What is time or distance here?" Jaimin retorted with a smile. "They claim they haven't seen Thyrr since the band was formed, but I wonder if they are somehow steering us to him."

Jaimin had been in the nebula the longest of the company and compared Adnan and Rishna to the other characters he had met in the three bands he had seen—in particular, Leone of the Oriflamme, Romeon and his fiery galleon and crew, and Elred and his tall, aged people on their green hills. It seemed that all the Light Lords had their heralds who, wittingly or not, carried out the will of their flames.

"Do their motivations matter?" Shanna asked. "Back in the prism, we wanted to go on, but this band is so vast, we could end up like those creatures up there, swimming aimlessly forever. For all we know, this is just a big fish tank on Lord Thyrr's mantel."

The thought was amusing as well as disquieting. They started back toward the headland, where the *Astraeus* awaited them, and the thought of taking refuge in its walls and fine instruments was especially inviting. But instead, they found themselves walking past it, right up to the very tip of the peninsula, where they gazed out at an unfathomable sea.

It was not the sights that had lured them but a sound. As they had experienced before with the first creature they had encountered, the currents seemed to carry a peculiar vibration that washed over them like a tide. It, too, was guttural and musical, yet deeper and far more powerful and alluring. They felt an urge to follow it, a desire made all the more profound by the gentle rolling of the currents that reminded them of the water from the pool in the cave.

All thoughts of entering the ship dissipated from their minds, even Kelmin's, in the breath of this siren's call. The four of them linked arms and stepped off the edge.

The current caught them. Outside the protective atmosphere of the headland, they yet seemed to be breathing the same air, though it was colder. Jaimin energized his plasma, his body glowing red in the blue, and Kelmin activated his armor's jets, but neither propelled them forward. They were moving with currents that seemed to flow with the sound. Jaimin's plasma brought them some warmth, but even his power was unable to disrupt the currents that carried them, as it had done in weaker bands. He thought back to what Rishna had said about Lord Thyrr: He was out in the blue, where distance was no barrier. If the lord dwelled somewhere within this sea, could they ever reach him? The chill went to their bones, to their organs, and finally their minds. They lost consciousness in an icy slumber. But on they went.

Unknowable time elapsed across an unknowable distance. They awoke to find they had stopped moving and were now hovering in place, still surrounded by the blue. The sapphire star was bigger than ever in the distance. They seemed to have traveled far across the vast band and were near its edge. They saw what they believed was the barrier to the next band, a dark wall in space with a purple sheen glowing behind it. Yet there was another phenomenon closer than either. The currents that had carried them seemed to coalesce into a great spiraling mass. It was a storm and appeared as a spinning whirlpool, galaxy-like in shape if not in size. The spirals formed a large wheel, with layers moving ever inward until disappearing into a central point.

Shanna was the first to notice a small light flickering in the spirals. Kelmin lurched forward, activated his scanners, and let out a cry of disbelief that his comrades heard in the void. He recognized the fiery object caught in the storm and being carried into its eye like a firefly funneling down a drain. It was the *Dante*.

# CHAPTER 12

# TWIN TREES

Auro stirred groggily. His stiff body ached. When he opened his eyes, they were filled with a green light. He had just come from a pocket between the red and green bands, pulled through a rift created by Romeon's transformed prism, tugged by coiling ropes of green Syntha, the same sort of tendrils Vitruvia had wielded to great effect in her struggle with the Gemmans on the *Dante*. They had reached through the rift to seize Auro, Bailyn, and Raelight and carried them into what they presumed was Vitruvia's realm.

Now in the green haze, dizzy and disoriented, they saw the source of the arms that had seized and carried them. It was not a cloud or a planetoid but a massive object so strange that at first, Auro had no frame of reference to determine what it was. Gazing at it intently as his head cleared, his eyes followed its winding limbs up and out as far as he could see, with branches covered with what looked like shiny, draping leaves.

*A tree,* Auro thought in amazement. *Some sort of space tree growing in the green light.* He realized that the coils that ensnared them were appendages of the tree, like living vines, and they were pulling them toward it. In the distance, he saw a new incarnation of the core star. Of course, it was green there, like a gleaming emerald, and larger than it had appeared in the yellow and red bands. The Syntha was the flame of growth; this tree was perhaps a manifestation of it, as Vitruvia herself had looked like a nature goddess.

Auro set aside his wonder to focus on freeing himself from the vines. Bailyn and Raelight were on either side of him, also struggling. Raelight was thrashing about as the vines around him coiled even tighter. His body glowed yellow as he shifted from side to side, trying to loosen them. His flame then burst into a fury. Even there, far from its source, reservoirs of Gnost surged within him. The vines, too, were made of flame, which they had been led to believe was a higher power than the Gnost; nonetheless, they gave way before the Gnost lord's determined onslaught. Raelight broke free and veered over to Auro, attempting to arrest the progress of the coils that were slithering and tightening around his arms and legs.

It was at that moment that out of the green space, another blazing object suddenly shot past them. It was yellow, and from its shape and flight, Auro had no doubt that it was the *Meteor*. It had crossed into this band after all. Showing no interest in them, it sped on in the direction of the emerald star.

"Quick," he pleaded to Raelight. "Go after it! If it gets away, we may lose it forever!"

"What about you and Bailyn?" Raelight looked over at the great tree where the vines were taking them. "Even if I catch up with it, if you end up somewhere in there, how will I find you again?"

"My mother is in that ship," Auro said. "I know it."

He didn't have to say more. This was why they had come. They both believed Armarna was the key to the whole cascade of events that had led them into the nebula.

Raelight broke off and swelled his energy to its full power. Although he had imparted some of it to Falconhyn, he was still a Light Lord, and he soared through the green space as though he were a meteor himself. Soon, both the vessel and its pursuer were lost in the distance.

That left Auro and Bailyn still ensnared and heading fast for the tree. They were closer together now but too disoriented to communicate. Auro's line of sight was filled with a jumble of branches covered with glowing foliage. The vines that carried him were either incredibly long or could grow to suit whatever purpose they were put to.

They arrived just above one of the thicker branches jutting out from the trunk. They were now well inside the canopy. Shiny leaves draped over them, obstructing their view of the surrounding space, though the emerald star peeked through holes in the foliage. Auro managed to loosen his right arm enough to grab his laser emitter and aim it at the part of the vine that Raelight had seared with his flame. He fired; the coils shuddered, yet they set him down on the branch while keeping him in their grip. Bailyn's vine squeezed him tighter, as if aware of what had just afflicted its counterpart.

With his free arm, Auro grabbed one of the branches dangling above him, but the vine holding him pulled the other way, stretching his shoulder and leg. He managed to use the leverage to free his other hand enough to aim his laser at the tendril and sever it with a concentrated blast. The remaining piece around his leg withered off like a worm cut in half, leaving him hanging from the branch. He swung up and perched himself upon it. It was just wide enough to stand on if he braced himself against the branches above. Auro expected another vine to lash at him from any direction. None came. But when he thought to fly out to help Bailyn, he realized his jets were no longer functioning; the vine had crushed them.

Bailyn was still held fast and struggling. Auro couldn't get to him and was hesitant to shoot for fear of hitting his friend. He assumed Bailyn would be deposited on one of the branches as he had been, but if the vines destroyed his jets as well, how would they ever get out of the tree?

Despite having lost his power of flight, Auro leaped off the edge of the branch and grabbed at the vine not far below Bailyn's dangling feet. Gripping it hard in both hands, he felt the thing starting to wrap around his own leg. He reacted quickly, scampering up and grabbing at the coils that squeezed around Bailyn's upper body. "Can you activate your jets?" Auro called urgently.

Bailyn shook his head. "The thrusters are pulverized."

"So are mine."

Auro felt desperate. Too close to Bailyn to fire a laser, he instead released his cable and swung it up at the branch. It held fast to it, and once again, Auro felt his body stretch. But in the tumult, the vine's grip on Bailyn's arm loosened enough for Bailyn to wield his own weapon. Struggling to aim at the vine just below Auro, he discharged at the green tendril, and it snapped away like a burned finger. Then it disappeared into the brush and did not return.

Auro and Bailyn were both free, unable to fly but anchored by Auro's cable, and they managed to swing in unison back onto the branch. Bracing themselves, they stood for a moment in the glowing glade, collecting their wits and letting the tension drain away. They even laughed at their bizarre ordeal.

At length, they began to move around and examine their surroundings. Auro carefully trod the length of the bough, peering through the canopy, gazing out at the emerald star and the wider cosmos twinkling in the green depths. He looked out for yellow or red lights, signs of the *Meteor*, or anything from the other bands that might have found their way there. But there was only the green expanse of the Syntha. Compared with the Magna with its volcanic fury and even the Gnost so close to the stormy Pale, this band had a serene emptiness like a peaceful lawn.

They turned their attention back to the tree, or treelike phenomenon, that seemed to have grown its way through this band. Auro vaguely recalled myths of cosmic trees, representing life, dwellings of gods. The main trunk, to which the branch they stood upon was attached, was to them a massive wall they could not see around. The leaves glowed as if a little spark of the star ran through them. They were larger than earthly leaves, many several feet wide; some jagged like maples, others elliptical with rounded edges; others long and linear, willowlike, and hung in strips. All were interspersed with flowerlike bulbs lit in various soft colors.

Dazzled by all these sights, in a few moments, they became aware of a rustling coming from the branches above. Auro froze and listened. While Bailyn stepped farther out along the branch, probing the green horizon, Auro crept toward the trunk. As he passed under a cluster of draping branches, he was startled by the sight of two legs dangling overhead.

He jumped back. The legs belonged to a peculiar figure sitting on a shaggy perch with thick leaves drooping down. The feet kicked back and forth in a carefree manner. They belonged to an impish figure, long and lean but not large, with thin arms and legs, a green complexion, and grassy hair like Vitruvia's. It was apparently a young girl. She held one of the colored bulbs that grew among the branches and took a bite from it, letting out a little squeal of delight and looking down on Auro with gleaming green eyes.

"What's going on?" Bailyn called, hurrying back toward them. He halted, looking dumbfounded at the dangling creature. Auro didn't look back at him, nor could he quite bring himself to speak.

The girl finished off her fruit, wiping her mouth with her long fingers. Then she stood up on her springy perch, bracing against a higher branch that brushed at her back. "Did the Great Mother bring you here?" she asked with an innocent nature that took Auro aback.

"We came through a rift," he answered in dismay. "A rift formed by . . ." He stopped. "Then this tree . . ." He started again. "Vines grabbed hold of us and pulled us into it." Auro realized he wasn't making much sense, and the girl kept peering down at him with a detached curiosity.

"We're from far away," Bailyn said, keeping things simple. "Who is the Great Mother? Is this her tree?"

"Of course." The girl shrugged as if it was something any sensible person would know. She motioned for them to step back and jumped down to stand before them with her back to the bole, showing no sign of fear. She was only a little shorter than the two young men, though Auro guessed she was only a year or two older than Haelia, at least by human standards. She looked somewhat like an elf out of an old storybook. She wore tight, leaflike wrappings dyed with pastel colors. Her arms were bare, as were her legs below the knees, and she appeared very dexterous. Her long toes gripped the branch, holding her firmly upon it.

"We may have encountered your Great Mother," Auro said carefully. "In another part of this nebula, where the star is not green and there are no trees like this." His eyes probed her face to see if she understood. "What is your name? How did you come to be here?"

"I'm Sheraleth," she said. "I've always lived in the tree. My mother—my *real mother*, not the *Great Mother*—told me where the older ones came from before the tree grew. They followed the Great Mother before she went into the star. When she came out, she filled all the space with the green light and seeded the trees. She brought us here so that it could be our home and we could grow with it. We are Starboreals, the people of her trees. She told us outsiders would come someday. We've been watching for you."

Auro and Bailyn were certain Vitruvia was the Great Mother of whom she spoke. These were the true people of the Syntha, which Elred and his folk knew of only faintly. Clearly, they had spent the centuries since the nova in the full power of the green flame. Leone had hinted that people farther in the nebula might be changed, more than human, and here was an example of one who showed signs of having been transformed by star fire. This beguiling girl was evidently some sort of scout. No doubt, they had been observed as the vines had pulled them toward their tree. But why send a child?

Auro and Bailyn finally introduced themselves, telling her their names and a bit about where they came from, though Sheraleth seemed little interested in their backgrounds.

"You said trees. Are there others besides this one?" Bailyn asked.

"This tree is called Star Leaf," she answered. "There is another. We call it Star Needle. We can only see it from a distance. Its roots are where the green space ends. The trees are growing toward each other. Someday, they will touch. Then we will be able to cross all the green and go beyond."

"Does the tree move?" Auro asked. "The roots and branches? We were brought here by glowing vines."

"Everything grows," she replied. "Sometimes the branches and vines reach out to us."

They considered her words. At first glance, the girl seemed to be of a primitive people, possibly regressed from living in this vast organism, yet they may have accrued a wisdom that would make Raelight's ascetics and Romeon's explorers seem less developed in comparison.

"We, too, wish to grow," Auro said. "We are on a journey through this nebula. I believe your Great Mother led us here. We came with one other, a Light Lord like your Great Mother. His region is yellow as yours is green. He is somewhere out there. Could your people help us find him?"

"If he is out in the green, there is a branch where we might be able to see him," she said. "But it's a long climb."

She turned and scurried up the branches like a squirrel, then proceeded to jump from branch to branch until Auro and Bailyn could only see the wake of her streaking through the brush. They were startled at her sudden flight, and though skeptical that this waif of a child was really what she appeared to be, they hastened to follow her before all trace of her was lost. They were not as light and nimble, but the branches were strong; even the small ones gently gave under their weight but never broke. The Syntha seemed to run through them like sap, giving the leaves their glow and the branches their strength.

On they went like this for some time. Finally, Sheraleth stopped to wait for them. They caught up to find her snacking again on one of the glowing fruits and resting in the branches. That did appear to be a good place to stop, and the fruits there were larger and more enticing than the others they had seen. Bailyn grabbed one about the size of a grapefruit, easily ripping it apart and handing half to Auro. Its juice ran like sweet nectar down their throats. The flavor so engrossed them that they sat back dreamily and looked out at the green. Sheraleth continued lounging, but there was no telling when she would suddenly spring into a swift climb again.

The vista there was different from where they had first landed. The green was darker. Far ahead, just beyond the star, they thought they could see a faint gleam of blue. Auro wondered what would happen if he just stepped off the branch and fell into the veldt. Perhaps he would drift through the band until some barrier stopped him or a vine reached out to carry him back. The great trunk loomed over them. They weren't so much climbing the tree as running along it. The bole wound along in the general direction of the emerald star.

*How fast does it grow?* Auro wondered. *How big was it when Sheraleth's people first came to be here? Do all her people look like her, or do her elders, born before the nova, look more human?* The Gnost and Magna had certainly affected the populations of their bands, and this denser and darker flame would leave its particular mark. Each band had its light and fire, and each had its lord and inhabitants. Yet these disparate peoples were all Empyreans whose powers and exploits filled so much of Amphora's history.

Having now come into contact with Empyreans in three of the bands, Auro thought they seemed, in their own way, as lost as the Amphorans. Even the lords, who had once fused together in the belief that the star would promote them to a higher state of being, were not only scattered but scarred, perhaps irrevocably. The different bands they had formed, the different forms they had taken, were like shards of a shattered mirror or a prism. Romeon had made a feeble attempt to put them back together. Vitruvia was letting her growth take its course. Raelight had simply turned inward. They were all groping blindly, seeking something they could not know.

Sheraleth suddenly rose in alarm as if she sensed something disquieting. Auro stood up beside her. "What will we see when we reach this branch we are heading to?" he asked.

"The frontier," she answered. "The crown of Star Needle and the blue beyond the Great Mother's light. If the one who came with you is still here, we may see a sign of him."

"Do you know what lies beyond the green?" Bailyn asked.

"A place where we can drown," she said, as if repeating an old and frightening legend. It sounded strange coming from a child, just as it was odd that she was their scout. It seemed that Leone was right, that the peoples farther inside the nebula were no longer quite human;

therefore, perhaps it was fitting that children should be their guides, from Haelia, whose mystic blindness had set them on course, to this elfish dweller of a cosmic tree. They were all children of the star.

They started moving again. This time, Sheraleth kept just two to three branches ahead, and there were no diversions. Hours seemed to pass, but their eating of the glowing fruit had brought on a lingering lightheadedness that distorted their perceptions. Perhaps the girl deemed it necessary for their journey, for it seemed to have affected her as well, slowing her down and dampening some of her gaiety.

The foliage was thinning as they headed into younger parts of the tree that had not yet grown such great leaves. The branches were spread farther apart, making it more difficult to amble from one to another. Sheraleth led them over to the trunk itself and showed them how best to clutch it and climb. To their surprise, the ridges in the glowing bark bent slightly under the pressure of their fingers. At length, they came to a juncture where a very large branch split off from the trunk and extended out like a new road. Sheraleth hopped onto it, and Auro and Bailyn followed. Bare of foliage, it led away from the main tree, wide enough for all of them to stand abreast.

"This branch is no older than I," Sheraleth said. "My elders say it split off from the trunk around the time I was born." She seemed to enjoy the thought. "We can see Star Needle from the end of it—and other things."

Auro tried not to look down as they walked along the bough, thinking that he really could fall into the void. But gazing into the distance, across a gulf of green space, they saw a strange new light, different from the emerald star, with a silvery color. As Sheraleth had said, it was the crown of another great tree, with roots in a different band, infused with Syntha but also with another energy. They were seeing the very tip of it and could tell that it receded into a vast distance, like the tree on which they stood. They were evidently near the center of the band, where the trees were growing toward each other. It was an awe-inspiring sight. Nothing Auro had seen yet in the nebula quite compared to it. Vitruvia was truly a Great Mother, for she had nurtured life, harnessing the star's green flame to grow until she was mature enough to return to it.

Sheraleth turned back toward him. "Do you see it?" she asked.

"Of course," Auro said, still overwhelmed. Then he realized that she was not talking about the other tree, for he noticed a new light twinkling off to its side. It was not green, silver, or blue but yellow, and it was getting bigger, heading their way very fast.

Auro and Bailyn pointed and exchanged exclamations as Sheraleth looked silently on. There was no doubt it was Gnost fire. As it streaked closer, they saw that it had not the tail of a fire comet and seemed about the size of a person. Crossing the distance from tree to tree, it landed behind them on the bough not far from the trunk. By the time they turned around to look, they gasped to see the figure of Raelight, his eyes and beard aglow, with the grave look of a herald with a message.

"I have seen your mother," he said to Auro. "She is across the gulf in the other tree. Vitruvia is with her, and they bid you to go to them."

# CHAPTER 13

# MAELSTROM

At sea or in space, ships are lost in storms. That thought came to Kelmin as he pushed forward to get a closer look at the *Dante*. The vessel Romeon had dreamed of sailing across the nebula was caught in the currents of the storm before them. A strange call had lured Kelmin and his companions into the currents and carried them deeper into the band. They were hovering before a great whirlpool, and spiraling into it was the familiar fiery light of the *Dante*'s sail. It was red again, its true flame restored.

Jaimin flew over to Kelmin's side, and Shanna and Falconhyn joined them. They all felt sure they had been brought to the mouth of this storm for a reason, perhaps by an intelligence that lay somewhere within it. The *Dante* was being pulled inexorably into its dark center, assuming it was not crushed by the currents on the way. The galleon had indeed crossed into the blue band. Perhaps its crew had been exploring just as they had, only to be lured there and caught in these rapids. They felt powerless to attempt a rescue. If such a vessel could not escape this maelstrom, what chance would they have? Nevertheless, they felt they had to try something. Despite their past conflicts with the Magna, they were all foreigners and explorers there, and if Romeon or any of his crew were alive, they might come to a common understanding and purpose.

The *Dante* was shaking and floundering in the second spiral, on its way to the third. Jaimin suddenly noticed that the sail was flashing in a peculiar way. "I believe they are trying to send us a message!" he exclaimed. "They see us."

Without waiting for a reply and heedless of danger, he ventured in for a better look and was quickly caught in the pull of the outermost swirl. It was the largest and least forceful, but Jaimin was swept up instantly. Not since the bolide had pulled him into the Nanj Cloud had he felt such a force, so powerful that he could barely sustain his plasma.

Kelmin shot out a cable for Jaimin to grab, but he was already far out of range, and it lashed around aimlessly in the currents. But to Kelmin's surprise, Shanna grabbed the cable; using it as an anchor, she extended her other hand, and a pole of her marble grew from it and lengthened farther and farther into the storm.

At first, Jaimin was unaware of the lifeline, for he had shut his eyes, yet he did pick up her plaintive cries. Finally, he saw the pole and reached for it, holding it as tightly as he could. Not a moment too soon, for he had already been carried far, and the longer Shanna made it, the more difficult it was to keep steady. Now she began to retract it, using all her power to pull him from the currents. The strain on both was great, and Jaimin felt more buffeted than ever. Kelmin reached out to Shanna to help steady her, but she was oblivious to him.

Falconhyn looked on in awe. He had come to regard Jaimin as the most powerful of the Gemmans, for his crimson energy manifested most impressively, followed closely by Kelmin, who could do amazing things with technology. But now he saw this steely girl as no less than the others and realized that he could never have breached her wall back on Amphora had she not been distracted.

Jaimin at last felt the pressure lessening as he was steadily pulled from the currents. His plasma surged again, like a fire no longer smothered by wind. When he felt the time was right, he let go and lunged out on his own power, escaping the maelstrom and making straight for his friends.

But he also saw an ominous shape approaching behind them, of which they seemed unaware. Jaimin thought it must be another one of those strange cosmic creatures that Adnan and Rishna had insisted were humans. It was considerably bigger than any they had seen before, nor did it resemble the others; it was shaped more like a whale, with a grayish-blue hide that was thick and solid. The great head swayed from side to side, taking in the sight of them with enormous blue eyes that conveyed a deep intelligence.

By the time Shanna reached Jaimin, she saw that he was distracted by something in the distance. She turned and gasped to see the looming interloper. Kelmin and Falconhyn became aware of it as well. Kelmin started to scan the creature but could hardly analyze the data as he watched it with trepidation, expecting it to lash out at them at any moment. But it just continued to look at them curiously.

Suddenly, the great mouth opened. It had no teeth, just a massive gray tongue, and a guttural sound rumbled out of it that, to their surprise, began to form words. "The ship," it said. "I am afraid it is lost. Is it yours?"

The question was asked with the utmost earnestness, and Jaimin found himself answering as he and Shanna reunited with the others and they all huddled before it. "It is not ours," he said. "It is the vessel of Lord Romeon of the Magna Band."

"Ah, I see," the whalelike being replied, his head now nodding up and down. "That is Magna in the sail. I have not seen red fire since the star first shed its light. My name is Josep. My body was once like yours. I was a follower of Lord Thyrr, who brought the blue wave that formed this sea."

The explorers were still mystified that this was a human being—or once had been. Jaimin introduced them and explained how they had come to be there, as well as he understood it, and told of their stay with Adnan and Rishna.

"I know them well," Josep said. "They are among the few who have decided not to swim the currents. They still resemble you, mostly.

I took to the depths long ago and, over time, took this form. I roam the sea, but I cannot go beyond it. That sailing vessel came into this band not long before you followed. I believe it was heading toward the star, but I presume they know that the star we see is merely the light of the blue ray."

"They know," Jaimin said. "They are driven by the need to explore and probably felt compelled to cross the band until they were stopped here. What is this whirlpool that caught them?"

"This maelstrom is as old as the band itself," Josep replied, "created when the Thyrrenean first spun out from the star. Many of us think Lord Thyrr dwells within it, that it may be the source of his voice as it ripples through the currents. The storm calls to all who brave the sea."

"It called to us," Shanna said, reflecting on how the sound coming from the currents over the edge of the headland had sent them into a reverie. They could only conclude that the lord of this band knew of their presence. Had he also called to Romeon? Perhaps the maelstrom was some sort of test?

The *Dante* was now entering the third spiral. It was still intact, for it was no wooden sailing vessel but of solid ore tempered by the Magna. But it was shaking violently, its sail flickering, and there was no telling if anyone on board still lived.

"Can you help us reach it?" Kelmin asked Josep. "Your long immersion in the Thyrrenean has changed you, but you and the others just seem to go on swimming, never finding a destination. If we work together, maybe we can brave this storm and find your lord—end your wandering."

Josep's eyes glinted dreamily, and the cavernous mouth heaved in and out, perhaps in deep thought as well as breath. "I have always heard his voice but could never make out its words. Curiously, it is faintest by the maelstrom, yet I have always felt the storm is closest to where he truly is. I have wandered far, circled the entire band, visited all the islands, skirted the borders, but I have always returned here, hoping to find a way to pass through these wheeling currents to see if the lord is truly behind them."

He stared intensely at the whirlpool. The three Gemmans and Falconhyn saw that their fate there now hinged on a man who had been submerged so long in the blue light that he had become a leviathan, a creature of the depths.

At last, he decided: "Either we will free yonder ship from the currents, or all will pass through the storm together. I will be your vessel; you can be my sails."

He instructed them to mount his enormous head. They did so, grabbing hold of his blubbery flesh. The massive tail pumped up and down. Smoothly and swiftly, they lunged through the dense blue space toward the churning maelstrom.

Jaimin channeled much of his plasma into his right hand, which he held up to shoot a beam of crimson light ahead of them. He knew how powerful those currents were. They all felt Josep stiffen as they closed in. The pressure intensified. Yet they felt a strange confidence, anchored on a living vessel, on top of the massive head of a cosmic whale who had roamed through this band of nebula for many human lifetimes.

They passed the point of no return. The spirals crashed over them like a tidal wave. They braced themselves. Falconhyn was nearly thrown off, and Kelmin, redeeming his failure to rescue Jaimin, was able to shoot his cable in time for the Stylight to grab hold of it and steady himself. Kelmin then managed to wrap the cable around Josep's thick body, creating a harness for them all to latch on to.

Josep strained with all his might to defy the storm, his great tail pumping with a vigor he had not attempted in centuries of slow meandering. Bringing it down with a powerful thrust, he surged forward until they had plowed through the outer spirals and were heading straight toward the *Dante*. Gaining momentum from the current behind him, Josep came at the galleon at full speed and rammed it with his head.

It was well that Kelmin had created the harness, for all four passengers would have been thrown into the storm had they not clutched it as tightly as they could. The impact still knocked them around, and each struggled to get their bearings. Kelmin was the first to right himself and probed the sensors in his helmet to piece together what was happening.

They were no longer caught in the maelstrom, and neither was the *Dante*. Josep had not told them he intended a collision. He might not have thought of it until the moment came. Kelmin wondered if he had been injured. Thinking the same thing, Jaimin shouted Josep's name, trying to see if he was still lucid after such a blow. They heard the oceanic voice rumble again: "I did not have the strength to ride the storm, and neither does that ship. Its sail was giving out. Anyone on board would have perished before it fell into the center. All I could do was knock it away and use the impact to free us as well."

"Are you okay?" Jaimin marveled, equally concerned and impressed. "You must have a terrific headache!"

Josep only grunted.

There was little more to do than rendezvous with the *Dante*, now adrift some distance away, its sail faint but clearly visible. Josep moved slowly toward it. Kelmin planted his feet under the cable, scanning and readying his weapons. Jaimin surged his plasma. If any of the crew members were alive, would they thank them for saving them from the storm, or would they think they had been attacked?

Josep slowed, sensing something. The *Dante* had tilted up and turned. Kelmin detected life readings. He activated his force field and extended it around Josep. The *Dante* kept turning, showing its long side and the rows of circular openings along it like gun holes. And indeed, like canons on old seafaring warships, streams of fire issued from them, one rapidly after the other. The barrages burst over Kelmin's force field; the impact pushed Josep back. The *Dante* kept turning until its prow was directly before them, then charged them head-on.

Kelmin and Jaimin fired back. Their lasers and plasma crackled across the deck. Any normal human aboard would have been incinerated, but the *Dante*'s crew was infused with the Magna. Still, after a moment, there was no return volley. The vessel halted and lay still.

"Can you get to them?" Kelmin asked Jaimin. "I can maintain our shield here."

Jaimin leaped off Josep's back, and Kelmin released the force field for the moment he needed to exit. Burning crimson in the surrounding blue, Jaimin streaked toward the *Dante*, flying over the length of the deck and not seeing a single person. He figured the crew must be below, manning the gun ports. He circled once more and considered diving down along the side of the hull where he could peer into the holes, though that would expose him to a barrage. As he swung around the sail once again, a spark of red fire came at him, causing him to veer back in shock. It was Romeon.

The Magna lord hovered before the sail, ready to attack. "You came for my ship?" he asked accusingly. "Have you lost your own?"

Jaimin was perplexed. "We just rescued you from that maelstrom!" he exclaimed. "You brought us here, did you not? You and Vitruvia? She changed the rift, crossing her flame with yours."

"It was her doing," he answered. "She meant what she told you, that she wanted to keep me trapped in that little pocket between our bands. She thought me dangerous even before we fused. Since our separation, she has reverted to her old foolishness. *The flame growth!*" he scoffed. "She knew the Syntha would take her to the blue band in its own good time, but once she crossed over, she would need a vessel to take her through that vast sea. She could not grow a ship, so she tried to take mine. While you and your friends were deliberating where to go, I wrested the *Dante* back from her control, even cleansed the sail of her fire, drawing the Syntha into myself. She fled to the other side of the prism. I had already suspected that her injection of the Syntha into the rifts had altered them, making each a bridge to one band farther than I originally intended to take us. At first, my crew and I rejoiced to have entered the blue. In the Thyrrenean currents, we moved at great speeds and saw wondrous sights. In truth, I think these depths brought us into a peculiar delirium, but we kept on, drawn by an indistinct voice that I believed was Lord Thyrr himself."

"I think his voice lured us all to this storm," Jaimin said. "Is your entire crew alive and below deck?"

"All are well and at their posts. When we arrived here, the storm overwhelmed us and carried us in. Captain Thomoly took the crew below deck while I tried to keep the sail alight. We have failed in our first attempt to pass through, but we will reach Thyrr yet. He is waiting for me."

Jaimin looked at him skeptically. "Is that why you attacked us—because we interfered? We thought you were about to be crushed out there."

"They certainly were!"

The voice came from beyond the sail. Jaimin and Romeon turned to see Kelmin descending onto the deck, his silver armor reflecting the sail's light. Following him from farther back, approaching more slowly and cautiously, was the elephantine shape of Josep, with Shanna and Falconhyn still perched on his head.

Jaimin and Romeon had been so focused on their conversation, they had forgotten their respective vessels were embattled. The guns had been silent all the while, and Kelmin had finally ventured forth. There was also a stirring from below deck. Thomoly and some of the crew were poking up their heads, seeking instructions from their lord. Kelmin landed at Jaimin's side.

Romeon looked in disbelief at the leviathan on which his adversaries rode. "Does it speak?" he asked.

Jaimin signaled to Josep to swim up along the hull. He did so, wary of the fiery sail.

"You are one of Lord Thyrr's people?" Romeon asked Josep. He had known many of that cadre of Empyreans and had even drawn some of them into his following long ago when Soliere had been whole and they had all lived in the same light.

Josep's great eyes took in the sight of the Magna lord. "Thyrr saw further than anyone, save Aris," he said. "He knew the magnitude of the feat the Pentheon undertook. We saw the star break, as you did, and we were flooded with the blue light. This band became the greatest sea humanity has ever sailed. Those of us caught in its expanse have been swimming through its depths or huddling on its islands, but we have not seen Thyrr himself. The lord has made his home behind the storm, and none can reach him."

"If he is in there," Romeon said, "then we must rise to the challenge and pass through it to reach him. I did not come here to drift aimlessly for centuries. This blue is one shade of a larger spectrum that was shattered long ago. I intend to unbreak what was broken, reform the Pentheon, make Soliere whole again."

"It is the Aristar now," Josep declared. "If Aris created the bands, he included this sea as the final moat. Only Thyrr himself can help us cross it."

These words, uttered slowly by one long submerged in depths of contemplation, caused a silence to descend on them all. Jaimin thought he was beginning to see a larger truth and addressed Romeon again: "The Light Lords were thrown out of Soliere through the rays. If each band's flame is more potent than the last, then Vitruvia and Thyrr have higher powers than you. They understand the growth, the spiritual preparation, needed for the journey you would take. What if they are right? What if you are not ready for this? If Aris wanted to reunite with you, don't you think he would have sought you out?"

Romeon's immediate answer was the angry look of a thwarted missionary. But before he could reply, a stirring came from the *Dante*'s crew. Thomoly shouted to them, "Look, the storm is coming our way!"

Shocked, they all looked back at the maelstrom and saw that it had indeed changed position and now seemed to be coming right at them.

"The storm has never moved!" Josep exclaimed, injecting an urgency into his usual lumbering speech. "I now sense that the lord does mean for us to enter it."

"We've tried and failed," Kelmin said.

"Not all working together," Falconhyn noted. "We each possess some part of the other flames, save the Syntha. I have the Gnost; Romeon, the Magna; Josep, the Thyrrenean; and you Gemmans, of course, have your power, the Eternigy. If we can unite them, it may empower us to penetrate the storm."

"And we are not without Syntha," Romeon proclaimed. He raised his hand, and a fire erupted over it that had a green light mixed with red. "Have you forgotten that I absorbed the green that Vitruvia injected into my vessel's sail?"

With new possibilities in mind, they all looked back at the maelstrom. For the first time, they understood that it was, in a sense, another rift, somewhat like those made by Romeon's prism but wrought by the lord of that band from a power greater than any they had encountered so far. It could destroy them all, but sailors had always crossed dangerous seas in the hopes of reaching new lands and futures. All of them, including Romeon, now turned to Josep. He had to decide whether he would attempt to take them in again, the one route he had avoided since he had begun swimming the Thyrrenean Sea.

"I will take us in," he said. "After all my roaming, it is time I visited my lord."

Romeon instructed Thomoly to get the *Dante* to a safe distance and not to try to rescue them if they were overpowered by the currents. "If we fail," he instructed, "you will carry the Magna in this band, sailing this sea until another time comes."

Thomoly ushered the crew back below deck while his lord and the others mounted Josep. The *Dante* moved away from the approaching maelstrom, which now took up nearly their entire field of vision. They all felt its enormous power, its alluring central eye, as dark as space, with a peculiar depth, as though someone or something was behind it, just out of reach.

Bearing his five passengers, Josep made straight for the center, mustering all the determination and strength the Thyrrenean flame had infused into his powerful form. His great body glowed blue as he swam toward the culmination of his centuries of wandering. Romeon and Falconhyn joined hands, glowing red and yellow, forming an orange aura with a tint of green. Jaimin, still ablaze in his pure red plasma, joined his power with theirs, and their combined energies shielded them from the oncoming currents.

The maelstrom began to envelop them, the spirals hypnotic and overpowering. Kelmin adjusted his helmet's visual system and saw that they were approaching the center. Josep began to shake. His tail had stopped pumping. Kelmin inched toward Shanna, hoping she could hear him. "We need a path toward the center," he said. "Can you create something?"

Shanna forced her stinging eyes to look into the dark vortex. She had never created something for such a purpose. Drawing forth her power, the only one of them who could manifest solid matter, she outstretched her hands and concentrated for a long moment until she made real the incredible object she had formed in her mind.

A great tubelike tunnel of her marble materialized around them, leading straight into the center of the storm, keeping the currents at bay. The entire company looked awestruck. Their combined powers, spanning energy and matter, had helped clear the way.

Now it was for Josep to traverse the distance. Again, his tail pounded. The eye of the storm enveloped them in darkness. Quickly, they cleared it and entered a new frontier, the deepest part of that deepest of oceans.

# CHAPTER 14

# FIREBIRD

Auro stood still, wrestling with the news Raelight had brought him. He and the lord, with Bailyn and Sheraleth, were gathered on an outlying branch of Star Leaf, looking out at Star Needle. The light of the emerald star filled the gulf between the Syntha trees.

Sheraleth seemed unfazed by the yellow stranger's dramatic appearance and sat at the edge of the bough, looking out at Star Needle. Her people were waiting patiently for it to grow toward them. From somewhere in its glittering, silvery branches, Auro thought he could hear the strange call he had heard from the nebula.

"Who was in the *Meteor*?" Auro asked, walking slowly up to Raelight. "My mother or Vitruvia?"

"It was Armarna," he answered. "I could not overtake the vessel, but I got close enough to sense that it was her. I followed her up the length of this tree and out to the other. At times, I almost touched its fiery tail, my fire, which I could have absorbed. Armarna must have recognized me but seemed intent on keeping me at bay. I wondered how we all fit into Vitruvia's plans, which twist and turn like a vine. And I feared that Romeon might have made his way into this band and that Armarna may have been trying to reunite with him.

"We crossed the gulf and came to the other tree. As you can see from here, it has no draping leaves. Its branches are more coniferous, with needles and cones. The *Meteor* disappeared behind it. But Vitruvia was standing in its branches, as tall and powerful as when she stood on the prow of Romeon's galleon. I found I could no longer go forward. She held me fast, as you experienced. The Syntha has the power to make trees of us, to plant us down as if it were a universal soil. Here in her band, this power can affect even a Light Lord. We talked at some length. She told me how the green ray held the power of growth, both physical and spiritual. At the dawn of the nebula, as I was building my citadels and Romeon was kindling his bolides, she seeded her frontiers with sparks of her fire. On either side of her band, they sprouted roots and grew into these great trees."

At this, Sheraleth jumped up, catching Raelight's notice for the first time. "Did the Great Mother tell you about us?" she asked.

Raelight looked in wonder at the elf-like girl. "She did," he said in a whisper.

"You are a brother of our Great Mother?" She sounded quite like a child encountering a long-lost uncle.

"I was in the star with her long ago."

"Are you still friends?" she inquired brightly.

Raelight regarded her in his fatherly way. "There has been some changing and forgetting," he said gently. "None of the Light Lords of the Pentheon can be true enemies. We cherish different energies of the same star. I understand Vitruvia's love for her people. Since the nova, I have been as devoted to healing as she has been devoted to growth."

Auro and Bailyn were silent. They still regarded themselves as captives in this tree and assumed that Sheraleth's people were watching them from the recesses of its foliage. They thought of Raelight's long conflict with the Magna and hoped that they were not bringing strife to this serene band. It seemed that neither the Gnost nor the Syntha was aggressive, as the Magna could be. Both, in their way, fostered inner peace and outward growth, and Auro dared hope they might find both there.

Finally, Auro said, "Vitruvia is waiting for her trees to join. Star Leaf's roots lie in the border with the red band, and Star Needle's are in the border with the blue. She claimed she wanted to bring the Gemmans here and tap into the Eternigy as Romeon did, but they did not come here. Instead, she has us, and she seemed to have little use for the Gnost. But how does my mother fit into this?"

"I believe Vitruvia told the truth back on Elred's world," Raelight said, "though perhaps not the whole truth. It seems she wanted to bring your mother and the Noctarians here to her Syntha Band, along with Romeon's vessel and the *Meteor*, and leave the rest behind. But the Noctarians fought her, and while Romeon was trapped in the prism, Armarna entered it in the *Meteor* and brought the other bolide in as well. I think your mother was playing both sides, so to speak, fulfilling her last obligation to Romeon while also acting at Vitruvia's behest. She helped Romeon create portals to the Syntha and Magna Bands, but afterward, she was going to drive him out of the prism so that Vitruvia could exile him and his people on the planetoid while she moved on to the Syntha.

"Both plans took a different turn. Romeon indeed remade the prism and created the portals. But when Vitruvia reignited the *Dante*'s sail, she took the vessel into the path of the prism's beam. She didn't say so, but I presume she was trying to tap into the concentrated energy, perhaps thinking she would need the extra power to subdue Romeon and keep the Noctarians under her influence. But her green flame, combined with the interdimensional properties of that peculiar pocket in the nebula, unexpectedly altered the rift so that it opened not to the Syntha Band but to the Thyrrenean. When she realized what she had done and was unable to change the rift back to its intended destination, she hastily abandoned the *Dante* and made for the other side of the prism. There, she performed the same feat with the Magna rift, altering it to open to the Syntha. As a result, we all ended up one band farther than intended; we are here in the green, and the other group jumped ahead to the blue.

"While we were trying to escape from the prism, Romeon regained control of the *Dante* and entered the blue rift. Meanwhile,

Vitruvia and Armarna entered the green rift along with the *Meteor*, and we went in shortly after. Realizing the Noctarians were too powerful to handle, Vitruvia erected a barrier of her flame to prevent the *Astraeus* from getting through to her band, but she also created paths through it so that Armarna's son could follow her.

"While I was speaking to Vitruvia, trying to piece together all that had happened, the *Meteor* suddenly appeared from around the trunk. It hovered before us, and Armarna emerged from it in a blaze. She explained that once in the Magna Band, unbeknown to Romeon, she began to hear Vitruvia's voice faintly through the roots of her tree, which pierced the Magna. She did not know exactly what the voice was saying, but since she was aware of it and Romeon apparently was not, she took it as a sign that a higher power was inviting her to go into the Syntha Band, independent of Romeon's plans. By chance, Armarna had become the first of her people to enter the nebula and had, up until now, determined to keep traveling through it, absorbing its flames along the way, each deeper and richer than the last. She knows you are here, Auro, but Romeon kept you away from her until she had completed her part in assisting his escape from his band. She had fulfilled her purpose, and now, free of her obligations, she intended to turn back, across the gulf between the trees, and seek you out.

"But Vitruvia halted her, just as she had stayed me. She explained that her trees' growth had stalled of late, and she reached out to your mother for the same reason she had tried to rally the Noctarians: she needed new energy to spur new growth. 'All your time here,' Vitruvia said to Armarna, 'you have striven to grow. Would you now cut off your own journey to go back to your home and family?'

"Armarna admitted that she didn't think she could grow anymore. 'I have come too far,' she said. 'Nothing can be as it was. I don't want to grow beyond my son and my people but to create a path for them to reach me. Would you add your green flame to my yellow and red? If you did, what would it do to me? Will I become like a tree, planting roots, growing slowly for ages before I've grown enough to see the next light?'

"'Not a tree,' Vitruvia answered. 'You will do more than light a path for others to follow. My flame will give you wider wings, which you can pass on, the power to fly beyond any frontiers you have seen so far.'

"At that moment," Raelight went on, "I saw Vitruvia as her people evidently do: as a guide, a Great Mother. She surged with green light, and her long arms stretched out, showering her flame upon Armarna. The Syntha poured over her, mixing with her distinctive blend of fire. For a moment, even I had to look away. Then I saw two appendages growing out of her back. They were wings. Her legs shriveled; her body bulged; her head changed shape, assuming a hawkish visage, sharp-eyed and determined. She had become a bird!

"The wings reared back, and she flew, yet not across the gulf toward you but in the other direction, along Star Needle's trunk to the border with the blue band, and disappeared in the distance.

"*Where will her new wings take her?* I wondered. Then Vitruvia turned to me with a look of derision. 'She will soar, yellow fool. When she is ready, she will join her son, and he will find his way to the sea. Begone!' On this command, independent of my will, my own flame lit over me, and I was hurled across the void from that tree to this, as I was shot from the star long ago. And here I am."

Raelight's account had sent Auro's mind to another place. For a moment, he looked across the gulf and thought he saw a fiery bird flapping over the distant tree in the light of the emerald star. He shook his head and it was gone. He looked back at Raelight, whose yellow eyes were probing him.

But it was Sheraleth who broke the silence. "There is a story," she recounted, "first told by the Great Mother, that a bird will fly between the trees and help them grow until they touch."

"My mother?" Auro asked, half to himself. "She has journeyed through three bands and absorbed their flames. The trees are rooted in the adjacent bands; perhaps they need the other flames to connect—to cross-pollinate, so to speak?"

Raelight had no answer. Auro turned to Sheraleth and asked, "Do any of your people know more about this legend of the firebird?"

"The elders," she replied. "They were here when Star Leaf was just sprouting. Yggrid is eldest of all and closest to the Great Mother. She was the one who told us you were coming. Then we saw the tree pull you through the rift. Yggrid said that you were not a threat. She thought I might be the best emissary to send to you, that I could gain your trust, but others have been following us and listening. Since we came to this branch, they have gone back up to our home, but they're still watching from there."

This confirmed some of Auro's and Bailyn's suspicions about Sheraleth. The leader of her people seemed to know them in some way, perhaps from her connection to Vitruvia's mind. Auro found new strength in the knowledge that his mother was just across the gulf. He also felt unsettled about her apparent transformation. As determined as ever to seek her out, he was now more fearful of what he would find. Moreover, he wanted to learn more about Sheraleth's people, these strange Starboreals who lived in this tree.

From this bough, looking back on the trunk that wound outward and upward as far as the eye could see, the glittering leaves draping over the branches, it was almost like he was looking at the tree from space again. The foliage could be hiding anything and anyone. There was no rustle or any sign of life, yet he could feel eyes watching them all along its length.

"Will you guide us to your home up there?" he asked Sheraleth. "The Great Mother's prophecy may be coming to close to fruition. My mother may be the bird of your story, able to bring the trees together. I think I have a part to play as well."

"I was meant to bring you when you were ready," she replied. "But it's a long climb from here."

"Not necessarily," Raelight said. "Auro and Bailyn may have lost their power of flight, but I have not."

"Can you carry all of us?" Auro asked.

The Gnost lord blazed yellow. He beckoned the girl to climb onto his back. She hopped up on one thrust of her long legs and locked her arms around his neck. Raelight took Auro and Bailyn by the hands and then ascended from the branch with his passengers, slowly and steadily rising along the tree. At first, the foliage thinned as they reached the younger growths with their sapling branches, but as they entered the last stretch, the leaves became thicker than ever, folding in layers like the flaps of a tent. In a curious way, the canopy reminded Auro of Raelight's domes, though it glowed soft green with glints of brown.

Guided by Sheraleth, they came to a bulge where the branches wove together to form a circular floor extending out from the trunk, with another layer above it forming a ceiling, and more levels above. On this floor, a couple of dozen people were milling around. They shared many of Sheraleth's characteristics: green-toned skin and eyes, grasslike hair, long and slender bodies, large ears. The elders were more human-looking, whereas the younger ones, like Sheraleth, had more pronounced Starboreal traits. Some partitions divided the space. Hammocks draped from the ceiling, some filled with napping occupants. Steplike ridges were carved into the side of the trunk, providing a ladder to climb up and down the floors.

Raelight set his companions down, and Sheraleth led them into the camp. The occupants observed the procession, but no one said a word or made any movement toward them. Seeming pleased with being the center of attention, Sheraleth led the visitors to the trunk; they climbed up to the next level and the next, finally emerging at the topmost floor. The canopy they had seen outside sprawled above them. Unlike the floors below, this was wide and undivided, with no sign of living quarters, a space of ritual and business. Openings were cut into the leafy drapes, windows into the veldt, with clear views of the silver tree and the emerald star.

They stepped off the trunk and walked into the tentlike chamber. There, the people gathered around, mostly elders, quite human in their proportions, yet their eyes glowed as green as their elfish heirs. Sheraleth did not speak. The visitors came to see that she was somehow silently communicating with the throng, as she apparently had been even in the lower levels. Then she went off to the side. Auro sensed that her part in this was done.

A tall figure now stood forth: female, frail at first glance but more regal and imposing with each step. She glowed brightly with Syntha. Her hair was silver with an emerald sparkle.

"I am Yggrid," she said. "Matron to our Great Mother. I helped seed this tree long ago and have watched over her children here." She looked at Raelight. "I remember you from another lifetime, one of the five who entered Soliere with the Mother. We thought you were content to stay in the outer band with its yellow light."

"I was," Raelight replied. "And I have children of my own, you might say. I never thought of them that way, except for my own blood daughter. Romeon's machinations brought us here. He broke the starlight as it has not been broken since the nova, opening rifts to the inner bands. Some who were among us may have traveled even beyond the Syntha."

"We are growing into the blue realm," Yggrid said. "One day, Star Leaf and Star Needle will touch and open the way. But there has been little growth on either side for some time. I have tried to communicate with the Mother. Lately, she has not come to us as she did of old, but she has brought me peculiar dreams. I saw a vision of a great bird soaring between the trees. I believe the Mother herself will assume that form and deliver us as she has promised."

"There is such a bird!" Auro exclaimed. "It's not your Mother who has taken its form, but mine!"

Raelight nodded. "We encountered Vitruvia in a realm between the Syntha and Magna Bands. I followed her to the crown of Star Needle. There, I found her with Armarna, the mother of Aurorno here and a descendant of Empyreans and Eddans. She was the first of her people to enter the nebula and has since journeyed through the bands, absorbing their fires. I saw Vitruvia transform her into the bird of your visions and prophecies."

"Why hasn't she come here?" Bailyn asked. "You said she flew the opposite way, along the bole of the other tree."

"Maybe she needs something from Star Needle," Auro suggested. "Or maybe she's just not ready."

As they talked, Yggrid seemed to be communing with her people silently, as Sheraleth had when they had arrived. Then she said out loud: "The visions are vague. I have not known how the bird would be born or when it would come."

"I must cross to the other tree," Auro said. "My mother has been calling to me ever since she entered the clouds, maybe without even being aware of it. As she absorbed the yellow and red flames, part of that energy and part of her consciousness made its way to me. Whatever she intends to do, I believe I'm meant to help her."

Yggrid clasped her long hands together. "For the sake of both your mother and our Great Mother, I hope you can reach her and guide her flight. But can you cross the gulf? The Syntha does not grant us that gift. We are bound to this tree, wherever it grows."

Raelight turned to Auro. "I imparted some of my Gnost to Falconhyn, and though it would further deplete me, I could give some to you."

Auro felt the crushed circuits of the jets behind his back. They would not get him across the void. Then he looked at the yellow lord who had been his fatherly guide through the nebula ever since he had encountered him at the top of the golden dome. "Can you give some to Bailyn, too?" he asked.

Bailyn gave a start. "It will mean less power for you," he said.

"But I'll have you at my side. I'm more frightened of what lies over there than a thousand fire comets."

Bailyn was moved. Auro had always been steely and single-minded in pursuit of his personal missions and apt to leave others behind. Now, at the moment of most profound discovery, he was reaching out in need of help, loyalty, and trust.

"We will all go," Raelight said. "With my remaining flame diffused among us, we will have equal power. I believe it will carry us to the silver tree, though we may not last long against Vitruvia or Armarna if they should try to stop us . . ." He trailed off, not wishing to surmise they would have conflict. But certainly, there was no telling what seeking out Armarna would bring since she had been transformed into a fiery bird of dream and prophecy.

"There is another source of power," Yggrid said.

She gestured upward. In the canopy, hanging from branches like lanterns, were shining orbs of fruit, brighter than those they had consumed with Sheraleth, a source of nourishment and light. Some of the people around Yggrid reached up with their long arms and shook the branches until the ripened fruits loosened and fell to the floor. Auro, Raelight, and Bailyn each took one, tearing away the peels and biting into the glowing pulps. The juice seared down their throats, planting a seedling of energy in their stomachs, waiting to burst out in a spurt of growth.

Then the three travelers walked toward the largest opening cut into the drapery. Raelight summoned his golden flame. It covered him gloriously, much to the wonderment of the Starboreals. The Gnost, though perhaps not as potent, had a spirit that the Syntha lacked, as though it carried the power of the human heart and mind. Raelight stepped toward his young charges and pressed his flaming hand to their chests.

Auro felt the yellow fire burning into him and a greater connectivity throughout his body, from his head down his spine to the tips of his fingers and toes, a tingling vitality he had not felt since he was very young. He felt light, as though he could just soar away, yet retained a desire for more discovery, a healthy inner hunger. He presumed Bailyn was feeling the same. He looked back at Yggrid and the throng around her and spied Sheraleth gazing at him with a tilted head and curious eyes.

"Through the flame, you will come to know yourself," Yggrid said as she waved them on, "and through the tree, you will grow."

Raelight nodded and beckoned Auro and Bailyn toward the window. The three stepped through it and were soon soaring through the green, with yellow fire streaking behind them.

Star Needle shone in the distance. Like Star Leaf, it grew from its roots near the frontier with the next band and seemed poised to join with its twin. Perhaps there were inhabitants in that other tree, yet it seemed ghostly still as they drew in. Instead of wide leaves, these branches bore needles and cones that glowed in colors to dazzle the eye, flickering as though they were the nerve center of a vast intelligence. The travelers, tentative and thoughtful, hovered above the tree. Its trunk extended down and out as far as they could see. The emerald star was brighter than ever.

Auro lowered himself onto one of the sharp branches near the very tip. On contact with the needles, he felt like his body had plugged into some system and was compelled to close his eyes. When he opened them again, he turned to where he thought Raelight and Bailyn were, but they were gone.

Suddenly, he realized his surroundings had changed completely. He was no longer in the tree but standing alone on a gray, barren landscape that stretched out in all directions. The green star still shone in the dark sky above him. Then a new light appeared overhead, not a star or a vessel but something living. It passed over him in a golden-brown blaze with wide wings, in the shape of a great bird.

"Mother!" he shouted.

He surged the Gnost that simmered within his body, thinking only of flying up from this alien landscape into the sky. But now, after he had soared across the gulf from tree to tree, he found he could not ascend and was weighed down like an anchor on this bare, hard ground.

He looked into the distance. Not far away, the lands became greener, but farther out, they became the gray foothills of great mountains. The bird was flying toward the highest peak in the distance. There, it slowed and circled it, a prick of light on the horizon.

This was the moment of truth. Auro's eyes fixed on that light over the mountain, on the soaring entity that had baffled him and pulled him through frontier after frontier, unknown after unknown. The bird did not descend onto the peak but flew on, leaving him stranded and alone.

# CHAPTER 15

# FUSION AND SCHISM

The storm was behind them. What lay ahead was obscure. Josep, with the help of his powerful passengers, had taken them straight through the dark eye of the maelstrom. They emerged into what seemed to be a tunnel that resembled an underwater cavern. There was no sign of the storm or the sapphire star. The Thyrrenean blue was thicker and darker, but there were no currents to sweep them away. This new environment was placid yet baffling. A rocky wall circled them. Brightly colored in the manner of a coral reef, it provided a comforting light in the murk. Still, they could not see very far ahead or behind.

Josep lumbered cautiously on, exerting his formidable strength to propel them all through the thick blue. Finally, he broke the silence with his low, rumbling voice: "We are heading toward Lord Thyrr." He sounded very sure. "His voice has always traveled with me, and I hear him more clearly now. A hazy vision is forming in my mind. He awaits us at the end. The blue ray of the star is at his back."

"I suppose he's watching us," Kelmin said.

They went on. The tunnel was narrowing, and the coral wall was gradually closing in. To the Gemmans, the coral resembled the crystalline mountains of their world. Its warmer colors suggested other energies were mixing with the blue, or perhaps the Thyrrenean assumed other hues there. Moreover, peculiar objects floated out of the coral and into the center of the tunnel, gathering around them. Each was no bigger than a human hand and, like a hand, had five digits. Indeed, they resembled starfish, with white centers and points tipped with assorted colors.

"Friends of yours?" Jaimin asked Josep, half in jest, as they marveled at them. Surely these were not transformed humans like Josep. Were they alive? Their resemblance to the core star with its five rays was interesting.

"I have never seen their like," Josep said. "I hear no voices from them. I guess they are a manifestation of the energies in the coral. Perhaps they serve Lord Thyrr, looking out for anyone who might find their way in here."

Although they had no discernable eyes, the star creatures did seem to be observing them. They were not threatening, however, and the company became accustomed to them floating around. Their attention turned back to their dark passage. Even Kelmin's instruments could not penetrate very far into it, and his armor had gotten heavy to the point that even moving his limbs took effort; neither would his jets lift him up. The watery atmosphere also sapped the usual heat and vibrancy from Jaimin's plasma, and Romeon felt the same dampening of his Magna. Shanna tried forming a new shape of her marble and found that it would not conjure with its usual ease and substance. She felt like she was moving her fingers through mud, and the simple objects she tried to make dissipated unless she exerted all her power to keep their form. They all grew glum, feeling the atmosphere thickening and their powers weakening.

Josep's exhausted tail finally fell limp. Yet they kept on at nearly the same pace. The current had picked up and was carrying them along. The coral walls drew farther inward, their sides now just a few yards from them all around. The shiny starfish began to group in greater numbers, perhaps responding to some command. It was then that they all began to pick up a faint sound that Josep had been conscious of all along: low, guttural beckoning, like the sound of the sea.

Kelmin struggled to his feet and ambled to the front of Josep's head. With his scanners now of little use, he retracted his helmet and squinted ahead with his own eyes. They were coming to the end of the tunnel, illuminated by a brighter and warmer blue that overpowered even the coral walls.

"That must be the star's light!" Kelmin exclaimed. "The blue ray. Is this side of the maelstrom somehow aligned with the star? Or maybe it is simply a more intense manifestation of Thyrrenean energy?"

"This is where the lord has concealed himself all this time," Josep said. "He is bringing us to him."

Romeon stepped up and stood beside Kelmin. The Magna lord had never looked so human. Indeed, he was pale, with no sign of his flame or even a crimson tint in his eyes. Shanna, Jaimin, and Falconhyn stood behind them, brimming with anticipation.

The light they were heading into began to take a physical form: a massive statuesque figure situated at the end of the tunnel. Larger than human, like Vitruvia had been, it was seated on a ledge of coral, which served as a sort of throne. The entire body was covered in a blue shell-like material with ridged patterns, like a clamshell that had grown over a vast expanse of time.

They were sure it was no statue and was in fact a living being, presumably aware, possibly mobile. The face was hidden by the shell that covered it like a helmet, and across the forehead was an etching of the familiar five-pointed star. The left hand rested on an outcropping of the coral while the right held a scepter with a blue flame burning on its tip. Behind the figure was a blue light that pierced through an opening in the wall above the head, projecting into the tunnel.

Josep came to a stop. He and his passengers all gazed up at this new Light Lord, who truly looked more powerful than anyone they had encountered so far. Romeon seemed a lesser peer, dabbling with an inferior power. Yet after a moment of awe, the Magna lord was the first to speak.

"Thyrr!" he cried. "How little we resemble the lords of long ago, but I sense your old spirit! I have been trying to reach you ever since we left the star. I even built a ship to cross your sea. It ran aground in your storm, but with the help of this company, I found my way to you."

The Thyrrenean lord remained silent and still. Then a sound like a low horn vibrated along the coral walls until they could discern the words of a disembodied voice: "I know the heat of your flame, the wonders it can forge and the desires it can stoke. You were ever one to go where you were not ready to be, to push beyond frontiers you do not understand."

"But we have reached you now," Jaimin interjected. "You remember Romeon from another lifetime, but do you know us? We are from the Bioplanes. We, too, have absorbed great energies, crossed many light-years. We were told entering this nebula was impossible, as was crossing the bands, then passing through your maelstrom. We cleared them all."

"And I brought them here," Josep said. "I have roamed this band the longest of all your people, since the great wave came. I was the first to leave the islands and venture into the sea. Over time, I was changed into this form. I wanted to reach you, to seek answers I thought you must have."

"Your wanderings are done," the voice said. "If you tread any farther, let it be on your feet again."

The flame atop the scepter brightened, and the five figures on Josep's back, mesmerized by its piercing blue light, suddenly realized their mount was dissolving away. Josep was no longer there, and they were floating in the watery thickness in the middle of the tunnel. Then some force weighed them down, and they sank to the floor, not as fast as a free fall but enough to stun them when they hit the bottom.

Struggling to their feet, they saw that Josep stood among them. He appeared as he had long ago before the Thyrrenean depths had changed him. Even his clothing was restored. He cut a somewhat rotund figure, with a round face and large eyes, rather like a monk given to indulging in bread and ale when not off on some barefoot crusade. Josep stared at his hands, took small steps, walking for the first time in countless years, becoming reacquainted with his body like an old friend.

After a pause, as his visitors oriented themselves, Thyrr's voice sounded again. "Yes, you have reached me. My band is wide and deep. Beyond it lies the innermost circle before the core star where all the rays are joined."

"We have the chance to fuse again," Romeon said. "To go back to Soliere."

"The Pentheon was broken," Thyrr replied. "Soliere has become the Aristar. Beyond our reach. There is room enough here. Though my band has borders, its depths are unending."

"Romeon has devised engines to travel the bands," Jaimin said. "But you and Raelight and Vitruvia seem not to share his desire to reach Soliere again. You have each lost yourselves in your bands, submerged in energies that reflect your own spirits. We Gemmans know that feeling, living with the Eternigy inside us. It has changed us profoundly. I was also seared with Magna fire. I know what it is to be transformed by power and then to fear losing it or having it altered by another power. You know the Thyrrenean is only a part of the star, and I suspect its great depth is part illusion. The whole lies with Aris, who has been the jailer of you all inside this nebula. Yet you are closest to him, and I wonder if you have communed with him since the nova."

Romeon looked at Jaimin in wonder. This strange youth from far beyond his realm had just given a stronger voice to what had driven him than he ever had.

"At times, I can hear Aris," Thyrr said. "Faintly, just as my voice reaches my people through the currents of the sea. Just as they cannot understand me, I cannot understand him, nor can I see all the rays of Soliere, only the blue."

"We have gathered the other flames," Romeon said, "Gnost, Magna, Syntha, and we have the Eternigy, which will intrigue and tempt even Aris. You say you have heard Aris, if only faintly. Is he truly still inside the core star? Why was he not ejected like the rest of us?" He paused. "Was it truly he who forced us from it? Did he create the bands?" He pointed to the blue light shining into the tunnel. "Each band is lit by a different ray, but perhaps they are all watched by the same eye. This is our time. Finally, we can break the barriers that have contained us, even your Thyrrenean ocean. It is time to fulfill our old quest."

"And how will our fate be different than before?" Thyrr asked. "The folly of the Empyreans has ever led to disaster."

They were all silent. Jaimin wished Auro was with them, who knew all too well the folly of which Thyrr spoke. If humanity had stayed together in the exile, perhaps the Bioplanes would have been created near Earth and there would have been no divisions. But he had come to realize in his travels through this wondrous nebula that this branch of humanity had its own destiny.

At length, Falconhyn asked the question that had no doubt long burned in the minds of the Stylights: "What happened when you entered the star? What made you think you could survive such an act, and what so traumatized you in the core? Has the blue flame retained any memory of it, or have you forgotten as the other lords have?"

"For a brief moment, we were one," Thyrr said. "Body and consciousness. It brought a revelation: Our desire to tap its energy had come from the star itself. It had been calling to us, perhaps from the time of our growth on Earth. Luring us toward it, changing us slowly, preparing us to absorb its energy so that we could fulfill its purpose."

These words resonated deeply with Falconhyn and Romeon. Josep set his face impassively, whereas the Gemmans were bewildered. Romeon appeared to be in the midst of an epiphany, one so simple and yet strangely profound.

But it was Kelmin who spoke next, trying to understand. "Are we saying," he asked, "that Soliere, and even Sol before it, had a sentience? That the stars were, in some sense, life-forms and wanted to split apart, to procreate? That may be what you accomplished. You took some of the sun's energy, used it to travel across the galaxy, inseminated it with more energy on the way, then spawned a new star."

Shanna picked up on his thought. "Perhaps over billions of years, Sol absorbed something of Earth's biosphere, its life force," she said. "If so, could this relate to the Eternigy also?"

Another round of questions and another silence. The only sign of life around Thyrr was the flame on his scepter. Suddenly, the shell covering his head dissolved away, revealing a face. Thyrr was the only Light Lord who appeared aged. White hair flowed down his head like a waterfall. The face was lined and creased, though the eyes were blue and piercing, with a misty depth.

"Did Aris rob us of our rightful place?" he mused. It seemed to be a question he had long pondered. "We were not ready to be in the star. Only Aris could withstand it. The rest of us were dispatched into the clouds, sent to learn from the parts of the star that could best speak to us."

"I suppose you had the least to learn," Jaimin said. "You are closest to Soliere and to Aris if he is still within it. But as Romeon has said, we have brought a new power into the nebula." He looked back at his fellow Gemmans and then at Romeon and Falconhyn. "We are five, each with a power to rival the old Empyreans. Perhaps we can form a new Pentheon."

The others were stunned. The proposition seemed preposterous, yet somehow the logical culmination of their journey. Having crossed four bands and come nearly to the end of this cosmic ocean, in the eye of this great storm, the next step was the star itself. And what more fitting way to reach it? Of course, the last attempt had failed, but theirs would be a different fusion, formed from a different power. The star, too, was different now, the heart of a nebula. They all gazed at the blue ray shining through the opening behind the lord. It seemed they had only to reach out to it.

"I tried to merge our energies through a prism," Romeon said. "It led me to false hope and misdirection. The Thyrrenean transformed Josep over many years, but you are its lord, and I believe you have the power to shape us now."

Thyrr's scepter flared. "You presume to attempt what Aris himself failed?" At first, he seemed to speak in anger, as if offended by the audacity of a lesser peer. But there was a pointedness to the words; he actually seemed to be prompting the thought forward. "You presume to enter the star?"

"I presume nothing," Romeon returned. "I was of the Pentheon, as you were. I have a right to try to go back. If my original brethren won't join with me, I will join with others."

"You would merge with them? Your feeble body is nothing in my water. I can show you the enlightenment of mixing with such as these!"

Upon this proclamation, Romeon's body flickered and then seemed to lose its form. It looked as though his bones had suddenly disappeared, with the remaining flesh folding into jelly. The body squished, the limbs melted away, and the rest dissolved into the surrounding cloud like a red clot floating in water.

The rest of the company looked on, horrified. Jaimin, Kelmin, and Shanna huddled, as they had many times against powerful threats, but their own powers were still dampened, their movements weighed down in this oppressive water cloud. They could not conceive of how to counter the power wielded by the massive and forbidding lord. Josep, still feeling like an alien in his human body, now faced the dread of losing himself completely and finally drowning in these depths. But Falconhyn, no less appalled but more curious than the others, asked, "Is he still alive?"

"He lives," Thyrr answered. "In fact, he is ready to be fused with others, if any of you consent. Whoever joins with him, I will send the combined being beyond my sea."

The Gemmans looked incredulously at Falconhyn, who seemed to be considering the offer. "Is this how the Pentheon formed all those years ago?" the Stylight asked.

"Soliere was no ordinary star," Thyrr said. "Aris led us closer to the corona than anyone had ever gone. Our bodies melted away but did not die. We fused together to create a new being, one that could enter the star while retaining our combined consciousness. Although we are not so near the star, the Thyrrenean power, magnified in this little realm behind the storm, can dissolve you into each other if you so desire."

"Did Romeon consent to what you did to him?" Shanna asked.

"It would not have occurred against his will," Thyrr said. "He merely needed a push from a greater power to fulfill his desire."

"The Stylights become one when we meditate together," Falconhyn said. "We ascend on pillars in the hope of transcending our bodies."

He reached out to touch the amorphous mass that had been Romeon. He did not seem to realize, until the Gemmans shouted out at him, that he was undergoing the same transformation. Even more quickly than Romeon, Falconhyn's body dissolved away. His essence joined with the Magna lord, adding to it a tint of yellow.

The Gemmans looked aghast. Shanna and Kelmin remembered when they had first seen Falconhyn ascend off Simeon Tower. Now fused with Romeon, he had entered a whole other plane of consciousness.

"Are you going to send them across the border of your band?" Kelmin asked.

"They will need more power to make that journey," Thyrr declared.

"We will not join them," Shanna said.

"You already form a trinity," the lord replied. "You possess different facets of what you call the Eternigy, just as we Light Lords possess different facets of Soliere. You aspire to use your power to build bridges and cross frontiers. Why not truly merge and cross the greatest frontier of all?"

The Gemmans looked at each other, seeking consensus on taking this incredible step of merging their minds and forms, both with each other and with two more. "Once fused," Jaimin asked, "will we be able to separate again?"

"Enough!" the lord said, his quick temper beginning to rage again. "This is a transcendent path. I cannot tell for sure where it will take you. Some boldly embark on their voyages; others cower before the waves."

The scepter flashed again. The surrounding blue churned like it was beginning to boil, a primordial soup, and the Gemmans felt themselves melting away.

Kelmin's armor began to rust and disintegrate. No human body was visible as it wore away. He, too, became an amorphous form and joined that which had been Romeon and Falconhyn. Shanna shouted Kelmin's name, but that was the end of her reaction, for her body likewise dissipated into a shapeless mass the color of her marble, and her remains, too, merged with the larger cloud.

Jaimin expected to meet their fate at any moment and strained to keep his plasma glowing. He heard Josep's voice calling to him but could not discern the words. Channeling all his strength, he managed to rise against the heavy blue, levitating up to eye level with Thyrr on his massive throne. The great head alone was nearly twice his size, the blue eyes like tunnels to great depths.

"They're all gone!" Jaimin cried.

"They live. I told you they desired it, either consciously or not, each being fused into one. Look."

Jaimin glanced down and was stunned. The mass that had been four separate beings split into its constituent colors and then recombined, taking a new shape, analogous to a human figure. The legs seeped up to form part of a body, joined by arms that spread into shoulders.

Jaimin now heard Josep calling to him from the floor: "This is what we witnessed centuries ago, just before the nova. He is re-creating the Pentheon!"

But there was one piece missing, and Jaimin knew that he was meant to become the head. Still, he was of a mind to resist and summoned as much of his weakened plasma as he could to brace himself against the Thyrrenean power. This lord did not need a prism or a galleon to conquer his frontiers. He was a being of the depths.

So far, Jaimin had resisted the urge to join with his friends. He grasped that it was not his greater will but his wounding by the Magna and the scar that remained on his psyche that was sustaining his humanity, at least for the moment. He turned back to Thyrr for a last word. "We won't be the original. I see that you need our new powers to leave your ocean, to break out into the next band, as Romeon did. You may seem content to sit here on your throne until your depths swallow you completely, but I think you really do want to reach the star again."

The lord's mouth formed a smile that looked like it could bridge worlds. "I have learned something of fusion and schism. Only in combination could even the highest of the Empyreans enter Soliere, and only by fusion do you and your fellow travelers have a chance to ever find your way to such a star. Like the core from which it came, the Thyrrenean can distill living beings into the essence of their spirit. Is this not your purpose? But I will guide you, just as you can guide me."

These words confirmed Jaimin's suspicions that they had been maneuvered into this, that Thyrr really did want to harness their combined power without joining with them himself. In any case, fusing with his friends now seemed to be the only way to save them. He looked down at Josep. "Will you come with us?" he asked.

Josep nodded. He was a creature of this ocean. After lifetimes of wandering its depths, he would go with his lord and those strange visitors beyond its frontiers.

"Return him to his oceanic form," Jaimin said to Thyrr, "and I will become the head of your creation."

Again, the scepter flashed, and in an instant, Josep morphed back into the leviathan. Simultaneously, Jaimin felt his own body melting away. Without limbs to move or eyes to see, he was somehow still aware and floating downward, drawn toward a familial warmth, until he merged into the partially formed fusion.

Now he was seeing through reborn eyes, having taken his place as the head of a multicolored, multifaceted being. Shanna, Kelmin, Romeon, and Falconhyn were a part of him, and he of them. Their minds merged, but Jaimin's thoughts governed. The others slumbered willingly under his leadership, reflecting that he had spearheaded them through the nebula. He felt the weight of responsibility to get them all out of the depths of this band and to eventually split them into their individual forms again.

Thyrr stood up from his coral throne, perhaps for the first time in ages. Floating toward the new Pentheon, he touched its chest with the tip of the scepter, as Leone had once touched Jaimin with the Gnost. Now he and the others felt the blue fire-water gush through them like a hot liquid. Their fused form grew until it was equal in size to the lord. Josep looked too small for them to ride now but was still a welcome friend.

"Come," Thyrr said. "Let us go to shore."

The opening above the throne suddenly widened. Thyrr turned toward it, beckoning his visitors, now only two, to follow him back through the other side of the maelstrom and once again into the great sea. Soon, they were swimming again, following the light of the scepter toward the sapphire star.

Jaimin could see that they had exited through the eye and turned to see the great storm again, along with the star, the visage of the blue ray. There was also the purple sheen of the next band behind the frontier. Jaimin and the others, looking through his eyes, recognized the edge of the band where one light merged with another, forming an impassable wall.

Thyrr stopped and turned. Extending his arm, he handed over his scepter, which Jaimin grasped and held aloft. Energies of various colors channeled from his hand into the instrument, and the flame at its tip turned from blue to white. Josep observed this in awe, remembering when his five passengers had combined their powers to help him carry them through the storm.

Jaimin pointed the scepter toward the barrier, and it parted like a curtain on a stage, receding on either side and creating an opening that was initially dark, but then a new light emanated from it, a deep and beautiful violet. Through it, they could see a new view of the star. It was no longer only blue. Its center was pure white, with five rays extending from it: yellow, red, green, blue, and purple.

"Behold the Aristar," Thyrr said. "You have parted my sea and revealed the full core of Soliere and its five great rays. From there, the Light Lords came. There, the greatest of us remains."

# CHAPTER 16

# A LOST TRAVELER'S DREAM

**A**uro struggled to understand where he was and how he had come to be there. Dismayed by the sudden change in his surroundings and the disappearance of Bailyn and Raelight, he nonetheless felt that this was where he was meant to be. He had traveled the length of Star Leaf until he had come to the gulf between it and Star Needle. The roots of the silver tree reached into the border of the band beyond.

He and his companions had crossed the gulf in pursuit of his mother, who had assumed the form of a great firebird. But upon reaching Star Needle, he was apparently transported somewhere else. He stood upon a desolate landscape swept by a gentle wind, reminiscent of Elred's world. A mountain range loomed in the distance. The sky was dark and full of clouds, yet some light source above the peaks brought a pale incandescence down on the land.

The firebird had flown toward the mountains. So that was where Auro resolved to go, on foot since he could no longer fly. He started off, reaching into the flicker of Gnost that still burned within him to lift his spirits in the face of the many miles ahead. But then he felt a vibration in the ground. Something heavy was pounding upon it in the distance, heading his way.

He turned to see the startling figure of a horse galloping toward him, mounted by a rider with a billowing cloak. Auro stopped dead, waiting for the beast to overtake him. As it bounded near enough to make out the rider, he gasped to see that it was none other than Leone, bannerman of the Oriflamme. It was only days ago, by his reckoning, that he had visited that frontier station, yet he had passed such vast distances, through so many rifts and distortions, who could say how long it had really been? The glimmer of familiarity overpowered any trepidation at his baffling appearance, and Auro breathed in relief as Leone's steed halted and trotted up to him, the hoofs thumping the ground.

"I greeted you upon your passage through the Pale," Leone said, climbing down from the saddle. "You have called me to your side at the cusp of the final push."

"I called you?" Auro asked, perplexed. "If I did, I wasn't conscious of it. I don't even know where we are. If you have a horse that can gallop across the bands, you might have saved me a hard journey."

Leone patted the beast's neck. "Strange," he said. "My memory is fuzzy as well." His voice was casual, as if remarking on a change of weather. "You're right." He scratched his head. "What am I doing here? How did I get on this horse? All I have is a vague notion that you have come far since we parted. For some reason, I have a picture in my mind of a tree, a great tree growing in space."

"A tree!" Auro cried. "Yes, I flew to Star Needle. But it disappeared, and suddenly, I was here. Then you came galloping over the field. But are you really here?"

He reached out to Leone, and indeed, his hand passed through his body as if he was a hologram. Auro also saw that there was an ethereal brightness to Leone's form that he had not noticed before.

"Perhaps I'm not really here," Leone whispered, half to himself.

Auro stepped back. Alarmed as he was, he was still glad for the company of this apparition. He was actually afraid Leone would disappear at any moment and leave him alone again on this ghostly world. "Are you a figment of my mind, or am I somehow communicating with the real you?" He wondered if there was any way to really know.

"Remember, the Gnost is the flame of self, and you are in a Syntha tree with roots in the blue band, the Thyrrenean Sea. Here, the growth of life meets the depth of the mind. The branches and needles reach within you. I was the first person you met in the nebula. Trying to understand where you are, how far you have come, your consciousness is resurfacing what you encountered in the beginning."

"Then this is a sort of dream," Auro said. He realized there was no point in trying to assess the reality of what he was experiencing. What difference did it make? "Are Bailyn and Raelight experiencing their own visions?" he wondered. "Could I bring them into mine?"

"They may have landed on branches that sent them into their own reveries, or they may be in a dreamless sleep, waiting for you to come back. You are the one who has business here. This is why you entered the clouds. Isn't that what you told me back on the Oriflamme?"

"I came for my mother. You told me that the farther I journeyed toward the star, the less human the life would be and the more removed from my humanity I might become. I still feel human enough, yet my mother is always a step ahead. She has absorbed many energies, and now she has assumed the form of a bird. A bird of fire. Maybe she is not my mother anymore."

"She will always be your mother, but in some ways, she is not the woman she was. Of course, you are not the child you once were, nor even the person you were before you entered the nebula. This dream has long brewed in your mind, the vision you were denied on the pillars at the summit of Amphora. For this vision, you needed the star's energy. Armarna has had such dreams. Now she can take flight and reach the remote places you have yearned to go."

"If she can fly, why doesn't she come to me?" Auro asked.

"Because you will only be able to hear her if you reach her yourself."

As Auro pondered this, Leone whistled, and a new steed came riding up to them, conjured out of the horizon, the same kind of stallion that had carried Leone. It neighed musically at full gallop, came about, and pivoted around them, nestling right up to Auro. He felt its warm breath, even the pounding of its heart. Auro swung up on the horse, feeling a connection to it as if its legs were an extension of his own.

He and Leone began to ride side by side over the sprawling meadowland. The cliffs before them grew taller and grimmer, and the ground gradually hardened. As they approached the foothills, the horses finally halted.

"She is up there," Auro said, pointing at the mountains, remembering the image he had seen of the bird soaring over the peak he could no longer see.

"We have left the open spaces of your mind," Leone explained. "Plains, you can gallop over at speed; now we have come to where your fears and memories run high and the going is hard."

Auro swung down, but Leone stayed on his mount. The bannerman would not accompany him any farther. Auro's mind had conjured him from his first memory in the nebula to start him off once again. From there, he would proceed alone.

"I can't scale the mountains," Auro said, hoping the friendly apparition would at least have some parting guidance.

Leone grinned down at him. "How did you cross between the trees?"

"My Gnost is no longer strong enough to fly, and my jets no longer work."

"Sometimes we lose things along the way," he said. "We can find them again with a little help."

Auro looked at his hands and wondered what it would take to get them to glow again. He reflected on what the Gnost was and reached deep inside himself. The flame was still there, just deeply buried. He felt he had it within him to regenerate it, even grow it, to become like the Light Lord himself. For a moment, he felt lost, oblivious to all except the flicker inside him, encouraging it like a campfire on damp ground. After a struggle, as if against a cold wind, he caught his inner blaze. The yellow fire surged over him, stronger than it had ever been. He could fly again, perhaps not as high or as swiftly as his mother with her great wings, but at least able to follow her at speeds he had never attained before.

Leone seemed to sense his mind. "There are many peaks and canyons out there," he said, "containing lessons from your past and keys to your future."

Auro smiled. "Raelight was wise to plant a flag by the Pale to welcome visitors from beyond the clouds. He could not have chosen a finer steward to wield his banner."

The flame under Auro's feet boosted him like a rocket into the dark sky. He looked down and saw Leone and the two horses, tiny on the fringe before the mountains. They receded behind him, and he surged over the great range of towering rock.

These mountains were no more real than the plain, no more real than Leone had been. He was in some realm of the mind, as phantasmic as the images in the inner dome of Raelight's citadel or the stars around Elred's world. There were stars above him now, large and white. Below, one high peak caught his eye, with a peculiar twinkling on its summit. It was a temple-like structure with no roof, rectangular, with short columns lining the sides. Auro realized it was a near replica of Simeon Tower with its pillars. And indeed, there were people perched upon the columns, their cloaks twinkling in the starlight.

Arriving over it, Auro descended and landed in the center of the platform. The statuesque figures all around him looked much like the Stylights, but he did not recognize any of the faces. They could have been actual mystics of the past or anonymous representations in his mind. He called out to them, imploring them to wake up, to tell him what visions they were experiencing in this nameless place. He didn't know it, but he was having a vision much like Shanna and Kelmin had with the real Stylights.

Suddenly, they all stood at once upon their pillars and pointed into the sky. The firebird was flying high over them. Without another word, Auro flew up again, leaving the mystics still pointing. Desperately, he followed the bird, but it was still swifter, ever a distant point of fiery light.

Auro was now so high, he no longer saw any land below at all. Soon, he appeared to be fully in space, with bright stars all around. A new light pierced out ahead. It was the tapering shape of Amphora, with its gleaming city, and beyond it, the stormy clouds of the nebula. He had not set eyes on home since venturing into the Pale, yet it was strange to look on the clouds again from outside the nebula.

As he flew with all his might, he saw fiery bolides burst from the clouds. Then the Amphoran fleet came out to meet them, and the ensuing rage of lasers and red flames. Once again, he was reliving the Battle of the Pearls, as Leone had afforded him on the Oriflamme and Raelight under his dome, and he saw more of it now than he had in those brief glimpses. His subconscious seemed to keep returning to it, as if it held a lesson he had yet to learn. The crash and horror came over him anew, his beautiful city helpless before the dread fire. Yet those wielders of the Magna were no longer faceless demons; they were Romeon's people, and he understood the motivations behind their raid. His attention focused on one ship: the ship that had haunted his thoughts since that day, the ship his parents had been on.

Yet this was a mere memory. His father was gone; his mother was the firebird who, in this vision, was soaring through the battle, darting in and out among the ships and bolides. Not a laser bolt or a lick of flame came near her as she reached the Pale and disappeared into the clouds. Auro dove after her, navigating through the embattled vessels just as she had. As he approached the clouds, he saw the image of his parents' ship caught in the long tail of a comet, which pulled it into the Pale.

Surrounded by the stormy clouds, he could no longer see the ship or the bird. Though the currents were blinding, they did not buffet him as they had when he and Jaimin had braved them in the *Meteor*. He cleared them quickly, like running through a colorful fog.

But instead of finding the yellow glow of the Gnost Band, he saw black space and stars again. There was just a glint of yellow ahead, and he came to a golden dome, but with no citadel beneath it, just the dome afloat in space like an upturned bowl. A yellow flame still burned at its apex, and a small person sat by the plinth. It was Haelia with her glowing eyes. He called to her, and she seemed to reply in a voice too faint to hear. Before he could reach her, Auro felt intense heat beneath him. A red flame had ignited all around the rim of the dome and was spreading across it. Swiftly, it reached the girl, and she went up in the conflagration.

Auro feared this vision might be a manifestation of some terrible reality, that Raelight's daughter had indeed met some dark fate back where they had left her. But as he pondered the symbolism of what he was seeing, the red fire that had swallowed the dome took on a new shape, curving into the recognizable form of the *Dante*'s sail. Sure enough, the masts appeared; the hull materialized beneath them, manifesting the full galleon, bigger than it had been in life, with an even more ghostly spirit about it.

It began to sail away. Auro pursued and found he could match its speed. Soon, he was flying above the mast and then descended upon the prow. There were people along the deck who looked vaguely like Romeon's crew, but like the Stylights, Auro did not recognize them. They, too, were impersonal replicas, phantoms staring at him with ghostly red eyes. Suddenly, one of them raised his hand, pointing upward, and the others assumed the gesture until all were pointing as the Stylights had. Auro looked up and saw a flash above them, at first obscured by the sail. He feared it might be a bolide, but it was the bird again, twisting and turning around the sail and heading off into the stars.

Auro leaped off the prow, hoping that his mother would circle back to find him. Still, he could not catch up with her. He surged his fire to streak across the dark void faster than ever. He was no longer falling behind but still barely gaining. They were heading toward a new light that pierced from a great depth, and he sensed that this was their ultimate destination.

It was a star with five colored rays, the Aristar, just as its likeness depicted on Leone's mantel back on the Oriflamme. The rays were like spears shooting out all around it. Neither the rays nor the white light of the central core was blinding to his eyes, and he seemed impervious to the heat as he flew ever closer. The firebird kept up her flight, fixed on the core with an unbending will. Auro grasped her intention: She was taking him into the star, or at least its representation in this vision.

On he went, in his last hope of reaching what he had been pursuing, one way or another, ever since his parents had disappeared into the clouds. He felt at one with his Empyrean ancestors who had made much the same journey over many centuries, though only five had taken the great plunge. He was enveloped in white light. All sights, cares, and motivations passed away. He was free. He could no longer feel his body, as though he had been vaporized and was now just a consciousness and so could go anywhere. Then suddenly, physical sensation returned, and he had eyes to open.

He was lying on stone—apparently, the mountain peak that he had seen from afar and tried to reach at the beginning of this dream. His mother knelt beside him. The green figure of Vitruvia stood behind her. The Aristar shone in the sky.

Cradling his head in her arms, Armarna lifted him gently into a sitting position. "I knew you could do it," she said. "I knew we would meet here." She looked back at Vitruvia, tall and silent.

None of the star flames Auro had felt on his travels compared with the emotions that swelled within him now. Whether dream or reality, having come so far, he didn't know what to say. But no words were needed. He breathed deeply of the air he could hardly believe was real and looked up at the strange star, at the otherworldly women stooping over him.

"What has happened, Mother?" he asked softly. "You came into the nebula and stayed with Raelight, then defected to Romeon, helped him open the rift. But then you left Romeon for Vitruvia, and in the Syntha Band, you changed . . . became a bird?" He stopped. "Where are we?"

"In the branches of Star Needle," Vitruvia answered. "Through the power of the flames—yellow, red, green, blue—you have been exploring the depths of yourself and the journey of your growth."

"I'm still in the tree?" Auro was too overwhelmed by the strains of his journey and the emotion of reunion to begin to comprehend. Although Armarna was in her human form, she still seemed remote, as though part of her was still that bird flying far in the distance. "Do you see the star up there?" She pointed up at its piercing image.

"Soliere, or what has become of it since the nova. Its rays are the source of the flames."

"It exists in the Empyreal Band across the Thyrrenean Sea. It is still the star of our ancestors, Eddans and Empyreans alike."

"I brought you here," Vitruvia said. "Romeon's prism supplied the means. In my band, I could plant trees, give my people a home, but they had to grow at the Syntha's pace. I knew that someday, a power from beyond my band would speed the growth and make a bridge to the bands beyond. I thought the Noctarians might do it, but so could your mother, for she had set out on a journey to absorb all the flames."

Armarna helped Auro up. The three of them stood on the mountaintop in the light of the star.

"I was in the dark for so long," she said. "The daughter of a Stylight who saw fragments of his visions. Your grandfather foresaw the coming of a power from far away that could break down the barriers the nebula had erected, reunite Amphorans and Empyreans. Of this, I confided only to your father. We led the creation of new ships and stations along the Pale and urged the prefects to explore the clouds, not to wait passively for whatever threat lay within it. When the bolides came and your father lost his life, I was brought into the nebula, and in grief, I determined to keep pushing on toward the center.

"Lord Raelight healed me, but he had withdrawn into his yellow band and would not look beyond it. Romeon sought to break the barriers, but Vitruvia held him at bay. During my stay in the Magna Band, Vitruvia called to me through the roots of her Syntha tree. Her voice was faint, but after meditation, I came to discern the existence of one who could guide my growth. Meanwhile, Romeon sensed that the distant power was on its way, and I pledged to help him bring the Noctarians to his band and complete the prism he was constructing. I also directed my thoughts into the inner clouds so that the Stylights—and whoever else who heard me—might know that I was alive, that someone in the nebula was calling to them. When Romeon perceived that the Noctarians had come, he sent me to greet them. I went in a bolide through the Nanj Cloud, across the Gnost Band, into the Pale. When I found you with them, I guessed that my messages, however faint, had indeed reached Amphora."

"I heard your call," Auro said. "But I never knew if I was only hearing my own hope." He rubbed his head and eyes. The events that had brought him into the clouds were finally piecing together in his mind. "When you appeared outside the Pale, I didn't know it was you, or maybe I denied it to myself, but I had to follow you in. You were always one step ahead of me, even as the bird, always flying ahead; you would not turn back."

"Dear boy," she said, "we walk the paths of those who come before us. I had to strive to see my father's path. It fell to me to enter the nebula and bring new travelers in after me. In my time here, I have learned that our Empyreal lineage is the strongest of all the Amphorans and goes back to Aris himself."

"We are descendants of Aris?" Auro marveled. "Does he know of us?"

"He has been watching," Vitruvia said. "He can see through all five rays. He has been waiting for the Light Lords to overcome the trauma of the schism. Ever since the nova, the lords of the Pentheon have been trapped within their bands while Aris dwells with the star. But Raelight has been roused from his slumber, Romeon finally broke through to my band, and my trees are reaching their final growth. The Noctarians have ventured into my husband's sea. Aris is ready to move on. What is beyond the center of the nebula? Perhaps even he does not know. I am content to let you find the answer, for it will find me. If we are about to see a rebirth of the star, it may mean the end of the five rays and the nebula, and the powers that the flames have given the Light Lords may fade. But that is what our growth has been preparing us for."

"We are only in the third band," Auro said. "How are we to reach the star? You say there is a vast sea ahead of us."

"You will fly," Armarna replied. "Nearly all the power I have accrued since I entered the nebula, I will impart to you, and Vitruvia will channel more from her trees. You will become a greater bird, swifter than I ever was, and carry on the journey."

"What will happen to you?" Auro asked.

"We will tend to the trees," Vitruvia said. "We must prepare my Starboreals for the changes to come. The changes that you will help bring about."

"Then we can go home," Armarna said, "to guide our people in the new era."

Auro deeply inhaled the chill air that seemed to be on the mountain and looked up at the star. "That is where I will go," he concluded. "But this is still a dream."

Armarna rested her hands on his shoulders, and a blinding light channeled through her body into his. Great gusts of flame shot out of Auro's back, in the shape of great wings. Before he was even conscious of his transformation, he was soaring over the mountain.

He looked down to see his mother and Vitruvia waving up at him as he had looked down on Leone when this dream had begun. Then he looked back toward the star. He was about to fly into it again, just as he had when he was following his mother. As she had foretold, he was much larger of wing than she had been. Faster than the *Astraeus* or the *Dante* or any bolide, he streaked straight into the blazing core, into the center of the star and its blinding white light.

✳   ✳   ✳

He woke as if from sleep and found himself standing on a large branch, pricked with glowing needles, surrounded by the now familiar green of the Syntha Band. He was back on Star Needle. Bailyn and Raelight were perched on either side of him.

"Are you all right?" Bailyn asked. "You looked like you blacked out for a moment."

"A moment?" Auro said, disoriented. He looked around in wonder. This was indeed the majestic silver tree he had crossed a gulf to reach. The needles glowed and tingled his legs.

"We just landed," Raelight said. "Then the branches began to grow outward, which distracted us. When we called to you, you appeared to be in some sort of trance, but you just came out of it."

The tree had grown? Auro looked out and saw that the great branches of Star Leaf now stretched across the gulf and touched the farthest branches of Star Needle. The trees had connected and formed a great arch across the band.

"We saw the firebird flying back across the gulf," Raelight recounted. "The branches followed her, growing along the path of her flight until they touched the other tree. Then the bird took a new form."

Raelight was smiling. Auro looked out and saw that where the trees had joined, several figures were standing: Vitruvia, Yggrid with Sheraleth at her side, and with them, his mother, in human form, no longer covered in flame but still with piercing yellow eyes that conveyed hope, happiness, home. For the first time since he had entered the nebula, Auro felt at peace, in tune with his new power, certain of what to do.

"I am the bird now," he proclaimed.

They looked at him in wonder as a new fire swelled over his body, at first not so different from the Gnost, but more vibrant. Just like in his dream, the wings spread out from his sides, and he arose in the form of the bird. Spreading his great fiery wings, he said to his companions, "Come—we will fly from the roots of these trees into a great sea and then on to the central star!"

"Will you take us with you?" Bailyn asked.

As he spoke, a familiar light came streaking out of the green depths. It was the *Meteor*, covered in Gnost flame, its fiery yellow tail flashing over the tree.

Bailyn and Raelight understood and flew off the branches to board the bolide. Once inside, Bailyn fired the tow cable at Auro, which he caught in his blazing talons. Beating his wings, he flew along the winding bole of Star Needle, pulling the *Meteor* along at speeds Bailyn had never thought possible, the Syntha clouds parting before them.

At last, they came to the roots that punctured through the barrier of the band, creating a portal impassable to people and ships, even to a Light Lord, but not to a firebird. With his old vessel in tow, Auro made straight for that opening and found himself soaring through an endless sea of blue.

# CHAPTER 17

# THE EMPYREAL SEAL

"Step through!" Thyrr called.

They had come to the end of the ocean and the threshold of the innermost band. Jaimin, now the head of a fusion of five beings, peered through the rift he had helped create. It glowed with a purple light, and through it gleamed the full star with all its rays.

Jaimin looked back at the grim lord. His higher consciousness governed the conjoined form that contained himself, Shanna, Kelmin, Falconhyn, and Romeon. They were quite a different entity than the original Pentheon, fusing the Eternigy with the nebula flames, and the three Gemmans felt and understood each other's powers more intimately now. Jaimin believed that in this form, they were more powerful than Thyrr, perhaps more powerful than any being in this nebula or anywhere else in the wider universe. And now, near the very center of the nebula, they were within reach of the full power of the Aristar. Yet he hesitated.

Thyrr was waving him on. Josep, back in his whalelike space-faring form, was swimming back and forth behind him, with the maelstrom swirling in the distance. Jaimin still held Thyrr's scepter and gazed at the white flame burning at its tip. Calling on the guidance of Romeon and Kelmin, with their understanding of such instruments, he grasped what Thyrr's purpose truly was.

"You don't intend to enter with me," he said. "You want to send me through so that you can draw Aris out to harness his power."

"You wished to reach the star," Thyrr rejoined. "Why, if not to release its power? Since the nova, I have been submerged in this sea; together, we have pricked a hole in the dam. Aris may be able to hold back the waters, but he cannot stop me from siphoning the Empyreal flame."

Josep ceased his pacing and swam between them. "Before you act, think of your people here. We followed you when you fused with the other lords, almost to the star. When you were hurled back with the blue wave, you never emerged to guide us, and we slowly lost ourselves in the depths. You took no interest in our plight. Was supplanting Aris your ambition all along?"

"What could I teach you that ages of wandering could not?" Thyrr replied with a rumbling malevolence. "When did I ever say I would be your guide? You followed me because I was ahead of you."

The scepter suddenly ripped from Jaimin's hand and flew back to Thyrr, and he grew to an even greater size, as if the surrounding watery blue was seeping into and bloating his body.

Jaimin looked hard at the colossal lord. "I haven't sought the star for the purpose of giving its energy to you," he said.

And reaching into the powers of all the beings within him, Jaimin formed a great force field around his fused body, not unlike one that Kelmin's armor might have generated. Then, through both hands, he unleashed crimson energies, one of plasma, the other of Magna. Thyrr again held forth the scepter, drawing both streams into its tip. Yet sparks and streaks showered over him, and his massive body shuddered.

Jaimin lunged toward the scepter, intent on seizing it back. An enormous hand pushed out to block him while the other held the instrument out of reach. They grappled in a stunning clash. Jaimin's fused body shimmered yellow, red, green, and blue. Thyrr was a solid blue statue, as immovable as the sea. But Josep, circling above them, suddenly dove toward Thyrr's raised hand, clamped his teeth on the scepter, and ripped it from his grasp. Robbed of the chief instrument of his power, Thyrr reverted to his normal size. His grip on Jaimin slipped away, and Jaimin doubled back to unleash a new strike.

But something held him back. A distant force was disturbing the currents, something far away but of immense power and coming closer at great speed. Thyrr and Josep sensed it, too. Setting aside their quarrel, they all peered into the distance. A new light beyond the maelstrom shone in the blue and intensified as it approached, so fast it could not have been the *Astraeus* or the *Dante*. As it hurtled closer, they could see that it had two appendages, like a winged craft, and was covered with a flame of a different color and character than any they had seen. It was no ship or bolide. In shape and movement, it resembled a bird, like something out of myth. The wings spread wide, gliding along the currents. Curiously, it seemed to be pulling something behind it that looked like a ball of fire. Now it was almost upon them. They all froze, even Thyrr.

It swooped in closer, revealing its full majestic form. The talons held a cable that attached to the fireball, which it released, and Jaimin recognized it as Auro's ship, the *Meteor*. He also realized, perhaps from an intuition sprung from the multiple minds he now encompassed, that the bird was none other than Auro himself. The mouth opened wide like a dragon preparing to breathe fire, but before word or flame could issue from it, a white light suddenly streaked past Jaimin's head. He turned and saw that Josep, with Thyrr's scepter in his mouth, had discharged a blast of the fused energy at the strange invader. The bird let out a shriek.

Then the *Meteor*'s fire rippled in the manner that usually signaled that something was about to emerge. Sure enough, a yellow flare burst out to reveal the imposing form of Raelight. The Gnost lord looked hard at Jaimin and pointed at his whalelike ally. "Quickly!" he said in a commanding voice. "Destroy that scepter!"

Jaimin nodded back at Josep, and the leviathan champed down on the rod lodged in his teeth, snapping it in the middle. There was a flash as the broken halves dangled down his massive jowls.

Thyrr let out a cry of anguish, and his body shrunk even more, down to human size. Seizing on his diminishment, Jaimin and Auro, fusion and firebird, unleashed simultaneous streams of energy at him. Thyrr was thrown back. The blue currents, perhaps responding to his will, now seemed to carry him away. He receded into the depths until, caught in the spiraling currents of the maelstrom, he disappeared back into its dark eye.

The breaking of his scepter also had ramifications for those who had fallen under its power. Josep again reverted to human form, catching the broken halves in each hand. Jaimin suddenly became aware that the fusion he governed was becoming unglued. His great body shook, and its five constituent beings split apart. Auro, Josep, and Raelight watched in awe as the massive figure burst and seeded the clouds with its parts. Jaimin, Shanna, Kelmin, Falconhyn, and Romeon were themselves again, at once in grief at having lost their unity and exhilarated at the reemergence of their individuality. Jaimin, the most conscious of what had happened, was also the last to recover. He gave his head a moment to clear, then looked over to see his fellows converging on him. Their fusion into a single entity seemed like a spectacular dream.

There was no time to reflect upon it. Bailyn now emerged from the *Meteor* as well, his body also glinting yellow with the Gnost. But the firebird still commanded their attention. It folded its wings, leaned back, and was engulfed in a blinding flash. When the luminescence subsided, Auro stood in its place, a slight, raven-haired youth clad in a simple space suit. Yet in a way, he seemed grander than any of the lords they had met on their journey. They all perceived a deeper wisdom and resolve in him.

Kelmin's scientific mind reached into his armor, re-created as it had been before the fusion, scanning the maelstrom, trying to determine if Thyrr had indeed been banished back into it and was not lying in wait. He scanned Auro and Josep, too. But above all, he searched for something he knew he and his teammates needed now. Silently, he activated a beacon and hoped it would answer the call.

The nine figures hovered together in a circle. They were halfway between the still-spinning maelstrom and the rift to the next band, with the Aristar gleaming on the other side. Everyone was astir at this unexpected reunion. To explain his sudden appearance and transformation, Auro's voice rang out in the currents. "My mother came to this nebula before me and accumulated every bit of energy and wisdom that came her way until, ultimately, she took the form of a soaring bird. When I finally found her, she imparted her power to me."

"We have reached the last stage," Falconhyn said. "We have been able to study the Light Lords, each endowed with a fragment of starlight with its own spiritual drive. Thyrr sought to conquer the great depths of existence, and apparently, Aris created that maelstrom to contain him. With your help, he freed himself and opened this rift. He meant to use us not to find Aris but to siphon his power. Rather than trying to reach the star, I believe he was trying to draw the star's power back into him."

"He is imprisoned again," Jaimin said, pointing over at the silently spiraling maelstrom.

"We broke his scepter," Kelmin added. "I think he created it out of the blue itself, like freezing water, to channel and amplify its power. But he still needed our power to escape the maelstrom. Eventually, he may be able to escape again."

Josep held up the broken pieces. "Go through the rift," he said. "I will remain here and stand watch on the storm while you go out to the star." He looked at the travelers who had helped him to finally find what he had been searching for. Auro was a stranger, yet Josep felt a kinship with him, too, as they had both been transformed and traveled far, though one swam and the other soared. "I will not be alone," he continued. "I will tell the others of this band what has happened. For centuries, we searched for our lord across this sea. Now that we know where he is, we must determine what we are meant to do. If you succeed in reaching Aris, a new era may dawn for us. As you were fused together, you may reunify the five flames. But beware the lord of all the rays. Even Thyrr did not dare approach him."

"Raelight and I were joined with him long ago," Romeon said. "I have striven to reunite with him from the moment I was thrown from the star. Now we come to him with a new power. We will not be denied again."

Raelight was pensive. He wished, above all, to reunite with his daughter, but he believed the path back to her ran through the Aristar. Yet he, too, feared the danger of unleashing its power.

Shanna, for her part, was staring intensely into the rift. "How should we go?" she asked. "Fly in as we are, or in the *Meteor*, or could Auro carry us?"

"Our vessel was designed to brave the unknown," Kelmin noted. He pointed back toward the maelstrom, and they all saw a familiar object coming around it and toward them. The *Astraeus*, summoned by Kelmin's beacon, bore down upon them. Its silver hull gleaming and blue engine blending with the currents, it stopped just off to their side like a lifeboat.

Jaimin could barely contain his delight at the sight of their trusty vessel. "Your inventions always come when called, Quantus, and this ship has been the gift that has given over and over." His eyes passed over the whole group. "Shall we go together?"

There was agreement across the board, among such disparate and sometimes conflicting beings. The Amphorans and Raelight had once dreaded Romeon's red fire; Auro and Bailyn were once in awe of Falconhyn; they had all been bewildered by the Noctarian travelers who possessed a power to rival the greatest Empyreans. Now they were coming together on one vessel for a shared purpose.

Kelmin, Jaimin, and Shanna beckoned the others to join them in the air lock. They left the *Meteor* with Josep, still safeguarding the broken shafts of the scepter, and entered the *Astraeus*.

With its notable crew, the *Astraeus* made for the rift. Ahead lay the last band in the nebula, the Empyreal, where they would find the full star with its five rays, where all the lights and flames originated. Kelmin and Jaimin sat at the console with Shanna at the monitoring stations. Auro stood before the view screen, catching a last glimpse of his old vessel in which he had placed all his hopes for carrying him through the Pale and into the mysteries of the nebula. He was not sad, for he had reunited with his mother and become a vessel himself, imbued with power such as no human being had ever wielded, save perhaps Aris and the Gemmans.

The change was acute as they passed through the rift and blue gave way to purple. They had not thought it possible for space to be thicker than the Thyrrenean, but now the ship seemed to be gliding along the surface of a velvet carpet or within the folds of a purple robe, space itself bending and twisting around them. But this was no dyed cloth. Lit with a rich light, radiating like stained glass, something between matter and energy sparkled and crackled as their vessel pushed through it like static electricity in rolling fabric. Kelmin had to continually channel power into the shields to maintain their integrity.

"Matter and energy are converging," Shanna said. It was not lost on her that the Empyreal clouds were nearly the same color as her marble. What was its character? If Gnost connected to the self, Magna to discovery, Syntha to growth, and Thyrrenean to depth, what was this final energy so close to the star?

"Life!" Auro exclaimed, leaping to an answer. Becoming the firebird and soaring through the last two bands had given him an intuition even the Light Lords could not articulate. "The Empyreal is the Flame of Spirit!"

All the minds in the company took in this thought as though it filled a vacuum.

"Stars have lives," Romeon noted. "They are born and grow. Some create new life. The same could be said for fire."

"And the Eternigy as well," Jaimin mused. "The energy of life. Yet everyone we've met in the nebula has said that our power is different from that of the star. How? For all the mysteries of the five flames, at least we know their source. Some mystics on our world made the

Eternigy appear with a few chants and relics; they thought finding it was the culmination of ages of meditation and transcendence. Could there be any connection between our power and what we are engulfed in now?"

They were all absorbed in these questions as they sped on toward the great star, which shone brilliantly through the screen. Some of them had seen glimpses of it in visions; its true visage looked much like the depiction Jaimin and Auro had seen on Leone's mantel. The purple ray pointed straight up, the green and blue to the sides, the yellow and red downward. Each ray gradually darkened from the white center to the tip. The center was like a white eye that cut through the purple and roamed the narrow band like a spotlight.

Kelmin tried to anticipate the roving eye but could not discern a pattern to its movement. He wondered what might be controlling it and was so absorbed in its mystery that he did not notice another disturbing phenomenon about the star. Shanna called out from her monitoring station, but Auro's voice overpowered hers as he pointed to the main screen. "The star," he said urgently. "It's getting smaller."

Indeed, their destination was receding even as they accelerated toward it. The rays were shrinking; the white light was becoming fainter, easier to evade. There was also a new distortion ahead in the velvety space. This was no storm like the Thyrrenean maelstrom. Lines were creasing and folding in the purple cloud and seemed to be forming an object. The sensors read the phenomenon as not fully solid, but it had the appearance of matter, and though Kelmin tried to steer around it, the ship did not respond to his commands.

The streaking lines curved and formed a circular shape that covered their view of the star. It resembled a great coin, minted with the star's combined energies, and they came to believe they were looking at some sort of sigil, the seal of a ruler. Within its circumference formed many shapes of different colors and changing patterns, twinkling and scrambling like a kaleidoscope. It was as though all the lights of the preceding bands were gathering within it, mixing, overlapping—all the flames of the other bands as well as blends like the Nanj and the colors of the Syntha trees. The patterns were dazzling and seemed to be communicating something as though this was a visual manifestation of the thoughts of a powerful mind.

Strange though it was, it was eerily familiar. Shanna, Kelmin, and Falconhyn remembered glimpsing something similar in their vision back on the pillars. Raelight and Romeon also felt a flicker of recognition. It was Raelight, the most in touch with his own memories, who said: "It is Aris."

"Is that really him?" Auro asked. "Is this the form he takes now?"

"It is his seal," Romeon said, comprehending. "He is still in the star. His sight and thoughts reach out through the purple ray, the Empyreal light, the very fabric of space in this band, the ultimate fusion of matter and energy. This is a representation of his presence, the final barrier between us and the star, a manifestation beyond any one state or form."

As he spoke, the patterns on the seal took on a new dimension. Many of them leaped off its surface and swirled around them in streams of vibrant, multicolored fire.

Each occupant of the *Astraeus* felt an urge to leave the ship, to go out toward the seal, drawn to particular colors and vibrations. Knowing they were being led on by a higher power, as they had been before at various points along their journey, they filed out the air lock and ventured into the purple space. The great seal loomed over them, its surface a stage of dancing lights. The streams it had sent forth were all around them, circling, darting near and far, drawing in close, evincing an intensity of heat that none of them had felt before. Their energies seemed to have a consciousness all their own.

Romeon was the boldest, reaching out to grasp a dart of pure red Magna. First, to his shock, it burned his hand. Then, to his horror, it assumed the shape of a serpent, snapping at him with a fiery mouth and lashing tongue. The others watched as all the little streamers, from the brightest yellow to the deepest purple, assumed such totem-like forms, from snakes to various grotesques with multiple limbs, all with angry eyes and fiery teeth.

A Gnost entity in the form of a spider bore down upon Raelight. Kelmin fired at several others, but the lasers passed right through them. A purple one that looked like a bat with a long snout collided with Kelmin's force field. Its fire crackled, and some of it seared into Kelmin's body. Shanna formed a sword in her hand and slashed at the bat. To her surprise, it exploded upon impact in a shower of sparks.

Jaimin, too, was busy, for a green fire in the form of an octopus grabbed hold of him with all its tentacles, stronger than Star Leaf's vines. Jaimin had to maintain all his plasma to keep the arms from squeezing the life out of him.

Meanwhile, Auro assumed his bird form, and his glowing wings seemed to overawe their swarming foes. But then several lizard-like forms pounced on him and tore into his wings with their claws and teeth, shaking from side to side like a crocodile with prey, as Bailyn and Falconhyn tried to help him.

So far, Shanna's sword was the only effective weapon they had against these entities intent on burning and devouring them. Surrounded now by several insectoids, she slashed at them desperately, but they evaded her blade. Recovering from his assault, Kelmin flew to her side. His lasers were useless, but encouraged by the promise of her sword, he called out to her: "Shanna, make a blade for me!"

Reflexively trusting her stolid teammate, she hurled her own blade over to him, and a replacement immediately materialized in her hands. In that moment, the entities encroached on her, but before their fiery mouths could bite, Kelmin channeled his sonic power through the sword, turning it into an antenna and amplifier. Waves coiled off the blade, widening into circular emanations that disintegrated the entities on contact.

Simultaneously, Bailyn and Falconhyn managed to dislodge the demons that were tearing at Auro before themselves being thrown aside. Auro folded his tormented wings, tossed back his head, and exhaled a great stream of flame from his mouth. Now Falconhyn and Bailyn ran for cover as the firebird unleashed his full fury. The lizards in the path of his barrage were destroyed as Kelmin's foes had been.

Now all the entities withdrew. The octopus released Jaimin and scampered off, as did the rest. They reverted to simple streamers again. No longer in their nightmarish forms, they darted back toward the great seal like a school of fish, becoming once again part of its kaleidoscopic surface.

The seal itself stood firm, still blocking their view of the star. The company regrouped and looked hard into it. They sensed they could not go around it or through it, that it was as formidable and confounding as any of the barriers between the bands. They would have to find a way to shatter this last manifestation of the starlight. Auro began the task by unleashing a new blast of his fire directly at the center of the seal. It had no effect. Powerful though it was, Auro's flame was of nebula origin and could not extinguish the fires of the seal.

But even Aris had never reckoned with the Eternigy. Kelmin stepped in first by releasing new waves of his armor's sonic power through Shanna's sword. Jaimin joined in by shooting a full blast of his plasma, and their alien energies combined with Auro's. The seal began to shake. Its lights dimmed and flashed, sparks crackled, and the pressure intensified. Now Auro drew forth his greatest power. Once more, he spread his blazing wings; welling up with a brilliant burst of light, he sprang forward like a missile toward the very center of the seal, where Kelmin and Jaimin were still joining their fire. The bird seemed to explode on impact. In a great flash of light, the seal broke apart into millions of glittering shards.

Shanna managed to create a gigantic wall between them and the explosion. After a wary moment, she dissolved it so that they could see if Auro was still out there. They indeed saw him, hurling back toward them in human form. Bailyn and Falconhyn lunged forth to catch him as the others surveyed the area. The seal was gone, with no trace. The purple blanket of the Empyreal clouds stretched out before them, and the five-pointed star shone directly ahead.

Whereas before the star had receded before them, now it was getting bigger; the five rays were lengthening. Their eyes were drawn to its white core, their bodies paralyzed in its glare. It seemed to be looking back at them. In the great blaze, they could discern two dark spots that looked like eyes and, below them, a gaping orifice like the mouths of the entities that had attacked them from the seal. But this mouth had a voice, and it began to speak.

# CHAPTER 18

# THE VOICE OF THE STAR

At long last, they had arrived at the Aristar in the very center of the nebula, having traversed many clouds filled with gleaming citadels and flaming volcanoes, winding trees, and oceanic depths. The great seal had dissolved. There was the core star, whole and unobstructed, immersed in a purple nucleus that straddled the states of energy and matter.

The Gemmans had felt nothing like it since their immersion in the Eternigy. The seal had bedazzled the eye; the star itself bedazzled the soul. Its rays, still spread in a vaguely human shape, now appeared as mere ornaments, like jewels on a crown. From the white center, they sensed something resembling a consciousness. It took a visible form in dark creases across the blaze, a roughly drawn etching of a face—the eyes defined enough to project wisdom and a searching intelligence, the mouth an abyss that conveyed no clear expression yet seemed ever on the verge of speaking. The sun that had glared upon all their ancestors had been reborn in Soliere, and the one remaining human being who had been on that journey, who may have created this nebula, gazed forth from within it. They were looking into the eyes of Aris.

In his glare, each of their energies was revealed as if by ultraviolet light. Romeon's body glowed with Magna; Raelight, Bailyn, and Falconhyn with Gnost; Auro once again took the form of the firebird, as robust as ever despite his exertion in shattering the seal. No less impressive were the Gemmans. Jaimin's plasma burned bright red. The marble that augmented Shanna's space suit gleamed, and Kelmin's armor surged with power, every circuit tingling.

The star's eyes scrutinized them, the mouth heaved, and a deep voice blared forth. It was directed toward his two former followers who had once been fused with him.

*"My lesser disciples, farthest from the core and least worthy—on the wings of an alien power, you crossed the bands to return to me."*

They were all stunned by the cosmic voice, pondered the references to wings and an alien power. The company looked to Raelight and Romeon. It was the Light Lords that the voice had addressed and belittled, and it was Romeon, the striving explorer, who dared reply.

"Who could be more worthy than I?" he declared defiantly. "It was I who gathered us here, the first to break the confines of my band to try to reassemble the Pentheon. The other lords shrank from bringing our powers together again and seeking you out."

All the hopes and frustrations that had festered within the Magna lord poured out with a desperate sincerity. Of all the lords, he had felt the most outcast and fought hardest to break free of his band. But the star's features assumed the countenance of one listening to a lie.

*"Have you not considered why those who were once joined with you would refuse you now? As a follower, you gave us strength; as an appendage, you were a lame limb, a disease in the body, seeking power over harmony. Nonetheless, I always saw your usefulness. I knew your ambition would spur others to action."*

Romeon looked deflated in the wake of this cruel dismissal. Now Raelight, gleaming like a golden statue and reflecting on his long conflict with the Magna, spoke plaintively. He sought peace and understanding, as befit the Gnost fire he had carried since leaving the star.

"We doomed our people when we brought on the nova," he said. "Most of them were swept into the outermost band and dwell there under my care. The yellow flame has sustained and healed us. We are content in our citadels far from the star. When Romeon breached the barrier between our bands, I shunned the Magna's temptation and resisted his ambitions. Yet I also knew that we could not remain sheltered forever. Therefore, I am glad to come before you again. But after all this time in the core of Soliere, what have you to offer the peoples who have known only broken facets of its light?"

*"Your instincts were always true,"* the voice from the star replied. *"You saw that the coolest flame could warm the heart. It must have saddened you to see so many lured away by another, but you always knew that one day you would be pulled back to me."*

Raelight and Romeon looked at each other, struggling to come to terms with their place in this cosmic scheme, whether all this time they had merely been playing a part written in the clouds by Aris, now a strange fusion of star and man.

"We all did what we could with the powers we had," Romeon said. "So again, I ask: Were Vitruvia and Thyrr really more worthy? She was waiting passively for her power to grow. He was lost in his own depths and seemed to be lurking for the chance to steal away your power. You had to imprison him within his prison! I alone remained a true part of the star, and I will not be denied my place!"

With this final uncompromising declaration, Romeon's Magna swelled even beyond what it had been when he had stood at the apex of his prism. Suddenly, in a red streak, he charged toward the great star like a spark returning to its spawning fire.

*"Stop,"* the great voice commanded. *"You cannot enter the star against my will!"*

There was no turning back for the Magna lord. Those left behind in his mad dash lost sight of him in the blaze. Straining to see into the core, they could not tell if he had truly rejoined his old master or had burned up in the attempt. The star was silent.

Raelight leaned back in the void and sighed. He seemed certain that his fellow lord, with whom he had long quarreled but stood alongside in the end, was truly gone. The Amphorans and Gemmans looked on gravely. Auro spread his wings and broke the silence, calling out across the void into the inscrutable light.

"Hear me, Aris! I am from Amphora but descend from your line. The Eddans never wanted to forsake Soliere, only to cease striving for energy they were not meant to possess. They barely survived the nova and used their ingenuity to save their greatest city. Today, they dwell on at the edge of the nebula, intrigued by its mystery. When powers inside it breached the Pale, it looked like a renewal of the old struggle between the Eddans and the Empyreans. We found a way to penetrate the clouds, but we could not have made it all the way to you without a new power that appeared from afar." He indicated the three Gemmans huddled near his side.

The voice spoke again: *"I have watched your city in its quiet repose outside the clouds. My only contact has been with those who retain a spark of Soliere and congregate in its highest towers, striving to extend their sight. Their thoughts ripple through the clouds, make their way to me, and I have answered them, though they could not have been aware except in their deepest dreams."*

The company looked to Falconhyn, but he remained silent and stoic before the star.

"My grandfather was a Stylight," Auro said. "My mother became the first Amphoran to enter the nebula. With help from these Noctarians, I followed her, traveling through the bands all the way to you. Like her, I absorbed the great flames along the way. I appear before you now as a firebird whose wings soar with all the energies of the star. I shattered your great seal." He said this with pride, yet he turned toward the Gemmans. "They made it possible."

The Gemmans had listened while the Light Lords and Auro had addressed the Aristar and sensed their turn had come. Their arrival was the random element that had led to this momentous meeting. Jaimin, particularly, had pondered a question ever since he had first seen the fireplace and tapestries in the Oriflamme. He floated forward, his crimson plasma reflecting the white of the core. "Do you know the nature of the energy we carry?" he asked. "Has your eye reached all the way to the Bioplanes, to see the power that lately surged forth from them?"

For the first time, the face in the star looked uncertain, as if they had come to a matter long anticipated but not entirely understood. *"There was a schism after the exile. Those who stayed close to the sun lamented that most of their brethren had ventured out into the cold. Finally, after the Great Journey and the creation of Soliere, it fell to me to fulfill the Empyreans' quest. It was only when I was alone inside the star that my senses turned outward. From here, I can see through the five bands all the way to the outer clouds, and from there, the light of the core shines into the cosmos, and my sight goes with it. I have seen the marvelous continents your ancestors built. Yet I knew how they ached for the sun. That desire pushed them, through science and mysticism, to search for what they had lost. For long, their search seemed fruitless. Then suddenly, a star appeared by your world."*

"We made that star!" Kelmin cried. "It was formed from the Eternigy, just as the Empyreans formed Soliere. You know that our power rivals yours. Do you fear that we could take your place in this star?"

*"Does one star fear another? You fancy your energy is life itself, but you know not its true source. I am in the very wellspring of mine. None can remove or supplant me. Yet our energies are indeed akin. Life on Earth sprang from Sol and grew in its light. Like my Light Lords, you each possess fragments of a broken light. I know that since you acquired it, you have been searching for its purpose, for the meaning of its manifestations within you. That is what has brought you here. Your people looked to Sol in the night skies of the Bioplanes with regret and remembrance, and here you stand before its heir. Do you not realize the purpose you have served by reaching for what your people have long desired?"*

At these startling words, the Gemmans remembered their recent fusion and saw that the white center of the Aristar, but for its peculiar face, seemed much like the vortex that had enveloped them back in that crystalline cavern. Aris was right: They had been searching for their true path and purpose, but above all, they desired that immersion again. Now, with that pure unifying starlight beaming into their eyes, they perhaps had a chance to do just that.

Auro, Bailyn, and Raelight also realized what the Noctarians were considering: to follow Romeon into the star. But this would be no presumptuous charge. The Empyreal lord now seemed to be inviting them in. Where would that leave the rest of them? If they joined together in this greatest plunge, who among them could withstand the power of the star?

Before anyone could speak, Falconhyn drew himself into the thick purple cloud with his legs crossed as though perched on his pillar. "You have not been alone, mighty Aris, in watching the cosmos from your fastness in the star. The Stylights of Amphora have seen much, even across the nebula. Now, with you before my eyes, I can complete the vision I began with these travelers when they arrived."

The star's eye fixed on the Stylight; indeed, it seemed to be feeding him energy. Kelmin and Shanna remembered the vision they had shared with him on the pillars and could well guess what was coming. The others looked on in trepidation, and Auro reared up and spread his wings. The light around Falconhyn began to sparkle in the colors of the five flames, which coalesced to form an image that filled all their minds. It was indeed the vision that some of them had begun on Simeon Tower, and it now took them all into the star itself.

They were about to see the nova through the eyes of the one who may well have caused it, the eyes that were watching them now. Surrounded by the star's blaze, they saw the outline of a great human-shaped figure, the Pentheon. Having entered the star, it had come at last to the stellar core. Here was the astonishing feat of a living being who had come to stand in the very center of a star, submerged within energies unimaginable.

Moreover, they saw what that great fusion of the Light Lords had found there. In its farthest depths, all the star's energies seemed to converge into a great circle of pulsating colors that resembled the Empyreal seal. The vision took them in closer, and as they approached the circle, it morphed into a new shape—polygonal, with five sides and five corners, each corner glowing a different color, the beginning of the five rays. Then, one by one, each corner began to flash into the surrounding white. Caught in this sudden eruption of energy, the figure of the Pentheon seemed to shatter, and the five smaller beings that had comprised it burst out and showered down upon the core. The four lesser lords were each drawn to one of the corners and followed the path of its light out of the star, each hurled into exile in the stream of a colored flame. But Aris himself remained before the core, which, emptied of its spectrum of colors, became black as space, a dark pit in the center of the vast white light.

Thus did the single consciousness of Aris remain in what was left of Soliere. Having tried and failed to absorb and draw inward the densest of energies in the very core of the star, the Pentheon's fusion had broken, the star's light had broken, and the shattered parts of both were sent outward in the nova. As the bands swelled, the star compressed; the only part of it that got bigger was that mysterious dark pentagon that remained at the heart of a multicolored pentagram: the core of the core.

Everyone in the company struggled to find the meaning of what they had seen. There was no doubt the Pentheon had reached the culmination of a journey begun millennia ago when the first exiles had started moving toward the sun, getting closer with each generation. But the star had apparently used the fused form as a sort of living antenna, drawing its deepest energies through it and then outward to form the nebula, leaving Aris in the center of the star with the dark core he had helped it create. But to what end?

Aris no longer had a true body, but his essence dwelled by that core even now, and his form could manifest there, just as his face seemed to appear on the star's surface. The company, in this vision, moved toward him, and Aris seemed to beckon them to approach the core. They followed him and were enveloped by its darkness. But the vision could not lift that veil; there, it finally ended, and they all opened their eyes to see the purple cloud again and the Aristar before them with all its rays.

Falconhyn was still lost in the reverie, sitting cross-legged above them in the cloud. Kelmin boosted himself up to where he sat in his strange vigil. The Stylight's body was glowing; the surrounding colors intensified into a flame that swelled up around him. When the flame subsided, he was gone, consumed by a fire that dissipated as quickly as it had come, leaving nothing in its wake. Falconhyn had completed the vision that his mystical order had long been trying to decipher: the cause of the nova and the nature of the power that dwelled deep within the nebula. But it came at a great cost. Perhaps he had extended his sight too far, looked too long into the sun.

"He burned up," Kelmin said. "Just like Romeon."

They all felt a chill run through them. Was he truly dead? Was Romeon? The face in the star had looked on while they had been immersed in the vision. Whether or not Aris had shared in it or knew what they had seen, he had not impeded it.

Auro believed he was finally beginning to see what lay behind the Empyreans' obsession with entering the star that went back to the first exiles and their unbreakable bond with the sun. "Something opened in the core," he said. "It was the heart of the star, the power that drew the lords here. Soliere was just a means to an end. Well, not so much an end, but a new beginning."

"We created a new kind of life when we fused into the Pentheon," Raelight said, reaching deeper into his memory than he had ever dared. Then, in entering the star, it was like we entered a kind of womb. Perhaps in some part of our combined mind, we sought to be reborn."

"In a sense, you were," Jaimin said. "The star split you up again and then pushed you out. Much like we were reborn in the Eternigy. But Aris somehow defied that great force and remained inside."

"But if you had succeeded in drawing the energy inward," Kelmin asked, thinking more scientifically, "would that have collapsed the star? Did you not think that would create a black hole?" Even as he formed the question, he suddenly felt he had come to a revelation. "Is that what Aris meant to do, invert the star and then go through it, to be reborn into a different world, perhaps even a different universe?"

"Yes!" Raelight cried, as if the truth had all along been hidden in a little corner of his mind. "It took a scientist to see it!"

They had become so engrossed in unraveling the mysteries of the vision, they had forgotten that Aris was still watching and listening. The voice of the star reverberated again in their minds.

*"The door through which I meant to pass was deep within the star. I thought our fusion would make it through. I was as surprised to end up alone in the core as the other lords were to be thrown out of it. But that was meant to be. They became emissaries to the others outside."*

"The Light Lords were insane to fall under your spell," Raelight said. "All of us except Romeon came to see our folly! We, too, were enticed by the great energies and foolishly fused with you, subsuming our minds and bodies under your will. Only after our expulsion did we realize that we had destroyed all that our people had built. Since then, I have found peace and atonement."

"Did you intend to collapse the star, even though it would mean certain death to the Eddans?" Auro asked.

*"What is death but a new beginning? That is what I sought for all. I opened a door that I meant to bring everyone through. I thought that doing so would reverse the nova and sweep all humanity inside with me."*

"Except the door did not open," Kelmin said. "The star was broken. The nebula was formed. Edda was destroyed. And you were left in there to burn."

*"The work was incomplete. I have remained in the core ever since, watching and waiting for someone to cross the bands, to come to me with a new power. But the other lords withdrew into their little realms: Raelight into himself and his flock; Vitruvia into the path of growth and the whims of time; Thyrr into his deep waters, plotting to supplant me. Romeon retained the spirit of discovery but lacked wisdom. As I despaired over the centuries, I came to sense a new power from afar that rivaled what the Empyreans had unleashed."*

"We created a star near our Bioplane," Jaimin explained. "A dwarf star of white light made from the Eternigy. If the Stylights like Falconhyn could sense it, surely so could you. Unless you are actually the source of the power that our mystics found?"

*"Neither your power nor the star it created came from me. To create a star where there was none before is a feat beyond even the Empyreans. Your people have lived long in the cold, and through sheer force of will, they tapped into energies coursing through the very fabric of the universe. I sought to draw you here, for you are the new spark we need."*

"We only meant to reach the farthest human colony," Kelmin said. "Here you are, in the center of this nebula, but I don't believe you are truly human anymore. You went too close to the sun, too close to a power beyond your ability to absorb, and it imprisoned you. The mysteries of the nebula kept driving us on to reach you, or perhaps it was merely your siren song. But we have seen enough."

"I, too, was drawn in," Auro added. "By the desire to know the fate of my parents, to understand the madness that drove the Empyreans. Now I see you at the center of it all. You claim to want to open a door for us, but your ambitions have only brought tragedy. Even you are not ready to go where the star would take us. Vitruvia was right, at least about the importance of not forgetting our roots. The Empyreans will continue to live in our exocities and citadels, our trees and islands, or else we will roam until we grow beyond them."

The star flashed. The features evinced a surging wrath, and those before it knew they were looking into the emblazoned face of a lord gone mad.

*"If you were not meant to enter the star, you would not have heard my call. This is the heir of the sun that gave us life, that governed Earth, that, when absent, opened our eyes to other stars. Some of our kind always favored the night. The sun was too bright for them, too judging, and when the time came to leave Earth, they were drawn into the cold depths of space. But our destiny always lay with Sol. This even the Eddans and Noctarians knew. The Empyreans slowly earned the right to approach the sun. By fusing with my followers, I brought us closest of all. But our fusion was broken, and I was left as a singularity, stranded in this burning purgatory, unable to complete the journey. Here, our chance has come again. You have heard the call, you have the power, and none of us will be denied."*

The velvet clouds swirled around them as though they were an angry breath. It recalled the Thyrrenean currents that had carried the Gemmans toward the maelstrom, yet these were even thicker and felt like gripping hands taking them toward the star. The discourse with Aris had ended; now they would serve his purpose. For he was right—they had striven all along to come there, drawn by the mystery of the nebula, with all its lights and flames, the different facets of a shattered power. The core of Soliere, a relic of Earth's sun, was now inhabited by a former human being who, after much evolving and striving, had dared to enter it and had become a part of it. None of them, alone or in combination, could overcome the powerful force that had taken hold of them or slow the speed at which they were moving. As they were pulled closer and closer in, the same thought occurred to each, spontaneously and independently: they might do what the Pentheon had done before them, enter it as a fusion.

The currents swept them along in two groups. The Gemmans were huddled together while Auro, in his bird form, formed another trio with Raelight and Bailyn. Jaimin had briefly been the head of a fusion created with Thyrr's ancient power. Did they still need that power to come together?

The Gemmans linked hands. Jaimin's plasma glowed in the heavy clouds, and he opened himself to the star's energy. Kelmin and Shanna, in turn, opened their minds and powers to him, too, and to each other, as they had at times when meditating together. A great light obscured all of them. When it dimmed, they were a single form: a massive being clad in Kelmin's armor, glowing with Jaimin's plasma, and crusted with jewels of Shanna's marble.

Separated by a gulf of rolling Empyreal clouds, Auro, Raelight, and Bailyn drew inspiration from their feat. Auro spread his wings to encompass his two fellows, both blazing in yellow light, and absorbed them into his form. The bird grew yet greater and grander, shining like gold. Now the clouds were shepherding two fusions along toward the star, one of Eternigy, the other the embodiment of all the nebula flames.

The Aristar grew larger, its incredible heat thinning the currents. Without even being aware of crossing a boundary, the two fused beings found themselves inside the corona, with its oppressive heat, crushing density, and overpowering light. Yet they lived as though this were another vision. In their fused forms and minds, they could see into the blaze, the white light that was as limitless as the darkness of space.

There was no sign of the face that had scowled at them from the outside, but they felt the same presence, the strong will of Aris.

Deep as they went, for a long time, they saw nothing but white. Then, at last, something appeared: a dark mass in the distance, etched in the surrounding light, a marker that gave them something to travel toward. They had seen it in their vision. It had straight edges and five sides, and though the shape was black, at each corner was a colored dot of light, the same as the five rays. The fused beings hovered before it, sensing that this was the very center of the star and should have been its hottest part, yet the dark shape dampened the light and heat like water on hot coals.

Then they sensed something nearby. An immense human-looking figure revealed itself. They could see it clearly in the white, as they could also see one another. The body shimmered with the kaleidoscopic colors of the Empyreal seal, surrounded by the aura of the purple flame. The head was crowned with five tall points tipped with the colors of the rays.

"Aris at last," the firebird fusion said in Auro's voice. The fused Gemmans heard him, even here in the star, just as they had been able to speak to one another in the clouds. Aris heard him as well, for he answered in the now familiar voice: *"Here we have our consecration. You are now part of the star as I have been. Great fusions are here again, where it all started, the great womb."*

"Is this truly a womb?" The question reverberated in Jaimin's voice. "Has there been any growth here? If there had, would you have needed us, or are you a mere prisoner?"

*"We have all been imprisoned by the fire."* Aris came toward them, shining before the dark core and pointing back toward it. *"But this is the way out. The nova was necessary for the star to seed its energy. Now we can draw it back inward to fulfill its life cycle. The cycle of existence plays out throughout the scale of the universe, from the atom, the cell, and the organism to that which we call mind and soul. Humanity was born on Earth by the energy of the sun. For our sins, we were compelled to leave, but we have returned to the core of the star, and we can open its door for the final transcendence."*

"Then it is another rift, a portal?" the Gemmans' fusion asked. "Like a black hole might open a path to some other realm?"

*"This star is the culmination of the human story, the end of the path that your Eternigy opened you to. With me, you were meant to take the final step."* Aris held out his great hand. *"Together, we can draw the rays inward and ignite the dark core."*

The six beings in their two respective fusions considered the weight of the moment. Even in their godlike forms, immersed in the center of a star, they felt very human now, like children, and like a child, they felt impelled to take the extended hand. Whatever motivations stirred in the strange heart of the Empyreal lord, he had dared to go where no other human could have even conceived. At this culmination, they accepted him as a guide and father. The right hand of the combined Gemmans rested on top of the hand of Aris, and the firebird curved its wings inward and touched theirs with both wingtips. Aris then placed his other hand to create a junction of five glowing limbs.

There, the five rays began to stream back into the core and converge, as long ago they had streamed outward, tearing the Pentheon apart. These new fusions were drawing them back toward the center like sheathing blades, reunifying the light. The five streams streaked into the dark core as if into the depths of a well. The dark shape curved, and its five sides rounded until it took on the oval form of a black eye, perhaps the eye that had been watching them all along.

Then the streaming ceased, and the voice of Aris spoke once again: *"The prison becomes the door."* He withdrew his hands from theirs. Facing the great dark eye, he looked intent on stepping through it with the determination, if not the foolhardiness, of Romeon. The fused beings also moved toward it, whether by their own will or that of a higher power, plunging on to their final fate.

But Auro, in a sudden moment of cold clarity, cried out, "Aris, stop! It truly is a black hole! It will destroy us and the star!"

The words were lost. They felt themselves on the edge of a precipice and tried to lunge back but could no longer resist. They were all falling into the gaping hole, with Aris ahead of them. The light of the star gave way to a dark abyss in which their own glowing bodies were the only light.

# CHAPTER 19

# RISE AND FALL

They seemed to be falling down a great pit, as though all the gravitational force of the core was descending upon them, the same force that had once sent the five rays out of the star and was now drawing them back in. Aris had jumped first and was below them, falling just as fast. Even he, it seemed, did not know where they were going. But all that the supreme Light Lord had experienced since he entered the star, and perhaps since his birth at the time of the Great Journey, had compelled him to take this plunge.

The five rays were streaking down around them like colored ribbons and resembled the staves of a cask of light forming around them in the darkness. They no longer appeared to be flames but had a glassy look like tinted windows, and they showed images and scenes of human history. Perhaps these were the star's memories, for while the sun had been too bright for human eyes, it had watched them. For the Gemmans, they especially recalled the pageant of the human story they had seen when first immersed in the Eternigy.

Each ray, each color, depicted a facet of the human spirit and development. The introspective yellow showed spiritualists in caves with their totems and incantations, with earthly fire only recently harnessed. There were stone temples and houses of worship, monasteries, and libraries. They saw knowledge accumulating, eventually burning to ash but destined to be rediscovered in time. In the red were ships like the *Dante*, but with cloth sails crashing on dark seas. They saw workshops and laboratories, wondrous mechanics, from clocks to spaceships, at once ingeniously intricate and childishly simple, and behind it all, the urgency to create and the boldness to explore. In the green, they saw the passage of life from young to old. Billions of mothers birthing billions of souls, sacrificial nurture, and guiding hands. Growth that moved at its own pace, but move it did, and the organism might look back but could not go back. The blue showed the creation in which growth takes place, the limitlessness that is yet somehow contained. It showed no people but took them through wide lands and deep seas, over tall mountains, through broad skies, up into the stars, and into the depths of cosmic space. Only the purple was bereft of anything to see, a solid color, as much a shroud as the Pale had been to those outside it.

Falling into the dark abyss, the eyes of the two fused beings passed from one color to another, trying to piece together a unified picture. Now they felt their descent slowing, as if some new current was obstructing it, until they hung suspended in the great tunnel with a seemingly infinite expanse above and below, surrounded by the five colored windows. Aris, too, had come to a stop below them, his body surging with all the lights. Perhaps he had been able to defy the force pulling them downward, at least for a moment, for he drifted over to the purple, as if straining to see something in it that he could claim as his own.

Auro pointed his right wing toward it and said, "It was the light of spirit, of life, but there is nothing to see in it, no picture to comprehend."

"The answer is not here but down there!" Aris called up. His voice was clear, and his hands pointed downward.

"How do you know what is down there?" Jaimin asked. "What if there's nothing? What if we fall forever?"

"A long fall it is," Aris agreed. "What is there is not to be seen; it is beyond light. Do you not feel it, in the core of your being, where your own flames burn?"

Auro and Jaimin, the heads of their fused forms, looked up and down along the colors, from the highest reaches to the lowest depths that they could see. Where was it all going? Then, as if in answer, a vague sound seemed to echo up to them. It was a voice, far and hidden, like Armarna's faint call through the clouds or Thyrr's whispers across his sea. *"Come,"* it seemed to say, though they could not be sure. Then, finally, the purple ray contorted as if something was warping its color and shape, like a vibration echoing from far below.

"Who is calling to us?" Auro asked. "That is not any human being, not even a Light Lord. Is it the star itself?"

Aris looked exhilarated. "It is here?" he asked. "The essence of the star, beneath our feet."

"Or a being beyond," Jaimin said. He could sense Kelmin's mind behind his words. "We are in the aperture of a black hole or something like it. Who knows what lies on the other side?"

"A new life!" Aris declared. "This is the call I have heard, the journey I was meant to take, yet even I could not make it alone."

"What kind of life?" Jaimin asked, now speaking with Shanna's sensibility. "Every intuition in my combined being tells me the pressure of this pit will eventually crush us."

"Were you crushed when your bodies fused?" Aris rejoined. "Or were you given a new body and an expanded consciousness?"

"The star is moving on," Auro insisted. "Maybe it intends to release its energy somewhere else, but do we belong with it?"

"The star needs us to reunify its light," Aris said. "We are the prism here! We will fuse, and all the rays will flow through us. At that moment, we will pass through the horizon."

"We have already lost ourselves in these fusions," Auro said. "Even if this is a threshold to a new existence, what does it matter if we lose our humanity?"

Aris was unmoved. "All of humanity will join us," he replied. "At least the Empyreans scattered throughout the five bands, the people of Amphora, perhaps even those even farther out. They will be drawn in with the rays and join with us here at this juncture, join into one great fusion. As one life-form, we will cross through the final door to the other side."

These words sounded like madness. Jaimin and Auro now felt more human than ever, even in these godlike forms in the core of a collapsing star. Jaimin remembered what Thyrr had said, that none were merged against their will. That was a lesser lord in a lesser realm. Still, it was Jaimin's will to resist despite the odds, and he knew it was Shanna and Kelmin's as well. He looked over at the firebird to see that Auro was spreading his wings in defiance.

Jaimin's massive arms swung back, his hands almost touching the rays that were now closing in as though they meant to bind them and take them down to their fate. But his fused form combined the powers of the Eternigy, and as he exerted multifaceted energies through his hands, the rays rippled and were pushed back. Auro spread his wings so that they also touched the rays, helping Jaimin stay their advance. His mouth unleashed a breath of white fire down upon Aris himself. The supreme Light Lord cried out and fell limp. They could not tell if he was truly hurt or in the process of absorbing the energy that, however concentrated, still came from the star from which he derived his strength.

Then the cryptic voice from the darkness again sounded in their minds: *"The ring circles round the few, all begins anew!"*

Strange, whimsical words. Jaimin and Auro both felt an acute strain and despaired that they could no longer keep up their strength. Below them, Aris appeared to recover from the firebird's onslaught. The eerie verse uttered from the depths seemed to have invigorated him. "Yes!" he shouted up. "We will all come to the other side as one, the greatest fusion of all, the seed of new life, perhaps in a new universe."

Jaimin and Auro stared down at him, dumbfounded, intrigued, and overwhelmed. Aris meant for them, for all humanity, to be pulled into the collapsing star, to merge with it into a single life, to pass through to wherever it would take them. To where? As what?

As they felt themselves drained of the strength to resist the star's pull, the downward pressure came back upon them and they began to fall again. Yet something within them, in a voice less distinct but no less real than the one from the darkness, insisted that this was not the time or the way. They still had this life and, eventually, death.

They were in the grip of a mad lord, in a fevered star, being forcibly taken to a destiny that was not theirs.

Surrounded by energies they could not control, the six beings in the two fused forms felt they had a final chance. Just as fusion had enabled them to enter the star, schism could help them leave. As the colored cask closed in on them again, the two great forms began to glow but also separate. Each split into three bright orbs that flashed and were revealed as human beings again. The powers they released counteracted the crushing might pulling them down. The core shook, and the rays began to widen around them again.

Amid his descent, Auro called down to Aris: "You thought you created Soliere. In truth, the sun was on its own journey. It lured the Empyreans toward it, prepared them to take a part of its energy where it could grow again. It is using us now for a similar purpose, but we are not ready to go with it. We may be its children, but our life is outside of it."

Aris looked up at them in fury. "No! I was born in the star's energy, bound to its fate. So are we all."

He had barely spoken when the cryptic voice reemerged from the abyss.

*"A journey delayed, a choice is made; light the beacon, sound the horn; through the womb to be reborn!"*

These words reverberated in all their minds as they hurtled to a fate beyond the dreams of the exiles when they had first drawn forth from Earth. More than ever, the three Gemmans understood that their power was rooted in human life, not godly stars. Their journey had been to find life, and life as they knew it did not lie at the end of this abyss. The others, too, had lives outside the star too strong to forsake. Raelight had Haelia, whom he had left in haste after she had been healed of the red fire, and the quiet community he had worked so hard to tend and protect. Bailyn, an ordinary Amphoran, had gone far beyond where the greatest Empyreans could envision, had seen what lay within the nebula, and now wanted nothing more than to see his shining city again.

Auro was perhaps the most conflicted. He was the culmination of the Stylights' journey, which Falconhyn had sacrificed to help him complete. In his dream on Star Needle, his mother had helped him become the firebird and led him to new frontiers, just as his ancestor, in this great plunge, was about to take him through another threshold. But why? How far was too far? Like Bailyn, he now longed to return home, to see his city again, to see his mother outside the confines of a dream, to use whatever powers he retained to help the Amphorans and Empyreans to reunite and grow together—not to drag them, as Aris would, to a destiny they could not know or reach themselves.

Although no longer fused with Raelight and Bailyn, Auro still had the power of the firebird. Even as he fell, his wings again blazed forth, and he plunged into a dive, falling faster amid the transformation, and managed to steady himself just above Aris. Flipping over onto his back, Auro flapped his wings against the force pulling them downward, and in doing so, opened a moment for the others to try to escape. Raelight and Bailyn surged their flames, and Jaimin surged his plasma. Kelmin reactivated his armor's circuitry, and Shanna materialized a platform beneath her feet to steady her. They all started to rise again, all but Auro, who was still flapping in place, generating the counterforce but unable to rise himself.

Then something shot up past him like a torpedo: Aris, his body straight as an arrow, with his arms practically grafted to his sides. He had flung himself up, heading not toward the source of the obstruction but to the others now trying to rise with it.

"You cannot go back!" he cried. "You carry the energy of the star." He shot straight at Shanna's platform, shattering it. She lost her footing and began to fall again until Kelmin caught her.

"We've had enough of this star," Jaimin declared. "Our ancestors left Earth's sun, and we didn't come here to become its pawn or spawn." He unleashed a full blast of his plasma at the Light Lord.

"You're mad, Aris!" Raelight cried. "I always knew, as did the others, even Romeon, though he could not resist the drives you aroused in him. Our fusion failed because Soliere's power was too much, even for you." With this, he fired streams of his yellow flame and was joined by Bailyn and Jaimin. Their three-way assault staggered Aris, holding him fast at the juncture of their light.

Kelmin was about to join them, but his sensors alerted him to another purpose he could put his power to. The force that Auro's wings were generating below them could be amplified by his technology. He felt he had found a key, as he had when he had opened the diamond door and blasted through the side of the prism. Through his scanners, he could see the waves as they funneled up from the wingtips, over and around them, into the reaches above. He amplified them into a force to rival that which came from the pit of the star. More quickly than he would have thought, the colored stripes of the rays that had been moving down with them reversed and began to streak upward.

The star seemed to shudder. Aris, seeing the rays streaking away, blazed forth, blindingly white. No longer held in place by his adversaries, he prepared to launch himself up at Kelmin. But Shanna intervened, plummeting down on a platform, this time colliding with him. Again, her platform broke, but the blow from the mystical matter stunned even the Light Lord, and he fell back into the pit. Jaimin swooped and caught Shanna. Joined arm in arm, they looked up at Kelmin, Bailyn, and Raelight and realized they were all rising along with the rays around them.

Auro was still below. As Aris fell back down, he grabbed the bird's wingtips, arresting their movements, intent on pulling at least the two of them down into the aperture. The others watched the lord and the firebird struggling below and found that now they were neither rising nor falling, for the rays and the star were exerting opposite forces that held them in place.

"Go!" Auro shouted up to them. "Fly out while you can!"

They were hesitant, torn between ascent and descent. Shanna was the first to break the impasse and created a new platform beneath her and Jaimin; then she widened it so that it nearly touched all the surrounding streaks of light, conducting their energies across its surface. On it, they arose as if on one of Falconhyn's pillars, catching their three friends under their feet. Now all five were on its solid, blazing floor and ascending at increasing speed.

Auro watched them go as Aris continued to weigh them down, gripping both his wings. The streaking lights continued to shoot up around them, pulled along now by the upward momentum. They were all Light Lords now, in fact, even greater, for they had been inside the star longer than any except Aris. The old lord of the Pentheon remained unique, in touch with this strange star entity. He had helped bring about its birth and boldly entered it, and it was now difficult to tell where his essence ended and the star began.

Aris had his own special destiny, and it lay down where this dark pit of a core would take him, but he did not want to go alone. He had always sought to bring others whom he could enlighten and guide, but that was perhaps a mask, a resistance against the otherness to which the star had consigned him. Auro's friends had risen beyond his grasp, but he still had Auro, the greatest of them, and now they, at least, could fuse before undertaking their greatest journey.

"There is nothing down there!" Auro shouted as he felt his form melting away, knowing he would soon be fused with Aris and under his control. "The rays are going out again. Neither you nor the star can bring them back. They are returning to space, to the nebula, leaving nothing but void in the center."

"There will be no nebula!" Aris said. "The star is moving on. We will go with it as the wise who braved the light and flame. I wanted to bring all our people in. Those fools have robbed the rest of that destiny, but we may still fulfill ours."

As he said this, Auro thought he could detect another voice, faint from the deeps. *"To the other side we go; what awaits us, we shall know."*

Yet those words only spurred Auro to muster the last of his strength. He looked up again at the five rays streaking upward. Now, by each one, he saw a human figure. All the Light Lords—Raelight, Romeon, Vitruvia, Thyrr—seemed to be hovering before their respective rays. Then Jaimin, Shanna, Kelmin, and Bailyn appeared as well, in the center of the ring—all the beings who had been in the star, living and dead, much like the ghostly figures he had seen in his Syntha dream, and like them, they all pointed up. That was the way.

Auro was still fusing with Aris, and the lord shared his vision—not a vision of the star but of the power of life that still resided outside of it. Pointing up with their right hands, with their left hands, the apparitions all released energies down at Auro and Aris. As the energies hit them, Auro could feel himself disengaging from the grip and fusion, becoming a full individual again, still in the form of the firebird. He broke away, and his great wings spread wide over Aris. The lord looked small, even lost.

"Go where you will with your beloved star," Auro said. "It was meant to be. You helped the rest of us reach for the great fire, but we can go no farther."

Aris looked up at him in resignation and fought no more. He had been driven to pursue the core, perhaps by the star itself, and believed it was his mission to bring humanity where it would take them. But they were now at the end, the end of all reflection, exploration, and growth. Auro hovered in the dark with his wings wide and watched as Aris continued to fall until he was lost to the depths. The strange words of the star still echoed in his mind.

The force that had brought the lord down was still strong, and Auro could feel it begin to grip him again. But the five rays, streaking up all around him, were passing beyond his sight. He strained again to beat his wings, to ascend along with the rays. The higher he went, the faster he rose, until he outpaced even the lights.

Blindly, he flew on and came out of the darkness into the white. Even that quickly dimmed, for the white heart of the star seemed to be sputtering out, swallowed up by the dark core. This was not the sort of nova that had created the nebula; the star was truly collapsing. Perhaps, as Kelmin had suggested, it had been on the way to becoming a black hole, but at the last moment, they had reversed its implosion and the flow of the rays. What that meant for the star and for Aris, he could only guess.

Had his friends made it out? He flew into darkness again, but this time, it was the starry gloss of open space. Gone was the purple fabric of the Empyreal Band. There was only space and bright stars. Auro felt a sense of deliverance, a lifting of a burden that he and all his people had carried from times none of them remembered, to which the last living link had just fallen beyond reach.

As he soared ahead, he looked back to where the star had been. The white center had not held, but the colored rays shone all around him. No longer anchored to a star, they formed no clouds but shot straight out, like great pillars of light, far into space.

# CHAPTER 20

# NEW WORLDS FROM OLD

Five refugees from a collapsed star, who had survived fusions, schisms, deep descents, and much else besides, huddled on a little drifting platform, looking out from what was once the center of a nebula. All the clouds were gone, all the colored layers that had fanned out from the core. The purple fabric-like Empyreal Band and its great seal, the vast Thyrrenean Sea with its swirling maelstrom, the inner bands, the Pale: All seemed like a distant dream, as did the star that had shone at the center of it all.

Shanna widened the platform and stepped up to its edge. There was no fear of falling off into the void, for her power anchored them to it, and Kelmin generated a force field with life support around them. They puzzled over what they surveyed. They had ascended from the star just as nearly all its energy had been sucked back into its dark core.

The five rays were all that remained. No longer rooted to a celestial body, they looked like colored laser beams stabbing out in different directions as far as they could see, like the hands of a giant clock.

Raelight gazed longingly at the yellow ray, whose energy had once filled his band. Now, like the others, it remained a single concentrated line, on a new journey. Who could tell how far it would go?

They all felt that a world had ended and time itself had stopped as they drifted through space in the aftermath of a cataclysm, ghostly yet peaceful, with a sense of rebirth. Indeed, in the absence of the clouds, space looked more beautiful than ever, black depths and bright stars with all their remote mystery.

Where the star's core had been, where all the rays had touched, was now empty space. From that void appeared a new speck of light, blinking and moving toward them. They tensed and strained their eyes, and Kelmin trained his sensors on it. "It's a bird," he gasped with a guarded hope.

Before long, they could see that the light was not blinking but flapping, and they could make out the wings beating up and down, getting bigger with each exertion. Was this truly Auro, or a fusion of him and Aris, or another being entirely? They sensed a familiar spirit as the bird came closer and hovered above them. Its breast flashed with a new burst of light. When the blaze subsided, a simple human being emerged in its place. Auro Augustine fell into the arms of his friends.

They set him on his feet and bombarded him with questions—what had happened to the star, to Aris, to the nebula and the five rays? Auro had only been in the star a little longer, but he had seen the lord's final fall, and his time submerged in its energy, as well as his past visions and dreams, had perhaps given him a brighter glimmer of intuition about what had transpired.

"There was a reason the core became so dark," he said. "It was truly devoid of light, inscrutable. Even Aris did not know where it led. I believe the star did have a consciousness of a sort and lured the Empyreans toward it. Aris was its ultimate instrument—or victim."

He paused thoughtfully, looking both troubled and relieved. Sol had been one star among countless trillions but had done what, for all humanity knew, no other star had—spawned a sentient race. That race had used up its home and departed. But some, perhaps an elect few, were drawn in by its light. Eventually, they drew out some of its energy and brought it to a spawning ground. Then its seed prepared to move on to its next stage of growth and once again turned to its children.

But even the Empyreans, except for Aris, were not ready for such a journey. And so the Pentheon was split apart; the star released the greater part of its energy to form a nebula in which the Empyreans could develop until they found their way back to the core. All this, Auro explained, working it out in his own mind as he spoke. "Aris seemed terrified of going alone," he mused. "And I think the star itself wanted to bring us along. Perhaps it had plans for us on the other side, wherever it is now."

They knew they would be reflecting a great deal about Aris's fate, and there was the lingering question of whether he was truly gone. Might he reappear someday, more powerful than ever, with even bigger plans?

But for now, they were adrift in a broad sector of space and wondered what had become of the nebula's people. The first thing they thought to do was recover the *Astraeus*. Kelmin summoned the vessel, and it was not long before it arrived. As grateful as they were for Shanna's platform, they heartily abandoned it to board the greatest instrument of exploration humans had ever devised. Once in the control room with its awesome technology, they could scan the region properly, no longer blocked by layers of clouds with their storms and barriers and interdimensional pockets. All was open, but the nebula had been broad; it would take the *Astraeus* some weeks to cross, even at its formidable cruising speed.

They set out, manning the stations in shifts, ceaselessly scanning and analyzing. As they departed the old Empyreal Band and entered the region where the Thyrrenean had been, their anxiety grew over whether anyone they had met throughout the clouds was still out there. Raelight was the most anxious; Elred's world, where he had left Haelia, had been sustained by the Syntha, and then there were the people of his citadels. There was also the question of Josep's fate; of Adnan and Rishna; the Starboreals and Armarna, if she was still among them; of Captain Thomoly and the *Dante*'s crew; and what had become of Thyrr and Vitruvia, who had presumably lost their flames and realms.

After studying the properties of the space around them, Kelmin declared, to their relief, that people who had been touched by the great flames would still be able to live, for a while, in the void without conventional life support. For although it could not be seen with the naked eye, an afterglow still permeated the region that, as long as it lasted, would sustain the atmospheric properties of the old clouds. This raised their hopes that the inhabitants had survived, and the sensors indeed began to pick up multiple and varied life signs.

The *Dante* was the first familiar thing their sensors were able to identify, and at length, they came upon it adrift in the dark. The fire sail no longer blazed over the masts. Its crew had followed Romeon's directive and kept on exploring the sea, little expecting that its blue depths would condense into what had looked like a great river flowing back into the star, leaving the inhabitants in cold space as if beached after a tide. All the crew still lived, as Jaimin, Kelmin, and Raelight discovered when they visited the deck. And they were surprised and delighted to find Josep there among them.

He had observed the maelstrom dissipate as the band drained out, and even the yellow flame around the *Meteor* was swept away. In his human form, he had ventured out into the tide, and as the last of the Thyrrenean Sea had drenched him on its way to the star, he willed himself to become the leviathan one last time.

"I swam out and gathered my fellow waders," he explained. "Without the cloud in which to swim, many were already starting to change back into human form. It was only a matter of time before I did as well, though the sea had given me this chance to help them get to land while their bodies could still get them there. I managed to lead them to Adnan and Rishna's island. Then I thought I sensed some other being out here we had not accounted for, so I ventured back out, only to find the *Dante*. Its sail had been extinguished. It was then that I finally changed, permanently, I believe, right here on the deck, and the crew welcomed me to stay."

"Any idea what became of Thyrr?" Jaimin asked. "Can you still hear him?"

"No," Josep replied. "There are no longer any currents to carry his voice. He may have been washed into the star or died in the flood. He was always mysterious, perhaps conniving, but never a tyrant, and he gave us a great realm to explore."

They were all relieved to find each other well, though the *Dante*'s crew was aggrieved to hear about Romeon's apparent demise. Thomoly took some comfort that his lord had met his end as he would have wished: leading the way into the unknown, however recklessly, spurring on his fellow explorers to take the next forbidden step.

"We should take you in tow," Kelmin said, a little ruefully since it would slow them down. "Without the sail, this vessel might as well be a log floating on a pond. I suppose the *Meteor* is adrift somewhere, too. Over time, this whole region will become more like regular space, and at some point, it will not be habitable without life support. Ultimately, we'll have to get the others to safety, perhaps to the Rae Citadels or Amphora."

"I think you should go on ahead," Thomoly replied. "Everyone on this deck, and throughout the old bands, for that matter, has been immersed in the clouds for so long that what is left of them will sustain us for a while. I sense that it will be some years before space here becomes too cold for us. But we are aware of your abilities and resources and will not refuse a helping hand."

The *Astraeus* stayed two days by the *Dante* as Kelmin labored to attach to the aft hull a makeshift engine with which they could travel where they would. He also left them a navigation device that could lead them to Raelight's citadels, and he surrounded the vessel with a force field that could regulate their oxygen, temperature, and gravity if they should perceive any slipping out of normal range. "We will watch for you from the domes," Kelmin said in parting, and the *Astraeus* left the galleon to its own course and ventured on.

After another long stretch, they came to the end of what had once been the great sea and arrived where the Syntha Band had begun, where Auro had last seen his mother and Raelight had last seen his daughter. The Gemmans had not seen the great trees outside of fleeting visions, and under the guidance of the others, they set their sensors on the lookout for the roots of Star Needle. But they found no sign of them. Perhaps the trees had dissipated like the maelstrom. But if so, what had happened to the elf-like Starboreals who had lived and grown along the boughs of Star Leaf?

Cautiously, they reduced their speed and continued until they approached what had once been the center of the band where the trees had joined. There, they saw a new light. Not only was it clearly not a star, but it even registered as solid while giving off a strange and beautiful glitter. As its intricate form took greater definition on the main screen, it was Bailyn who recognized it as a fusion of the crowns of Star Leaf and Star Needle. Shorn of their trunks, which had apparently melted away into the cloud and returned to the star, the crowns had merged, the leaves of one intermingling with the needles of the other, forming a luminous chrysalis. And to their relief, it was still inhabited. A new space colony, quite unlike any other, home to a people unlike any other, had come into existence. Although the Syntha Band was no more, it had left this curious structure behind that still had some of the old power flowing through it.

The Starboreals did not recognize the *Astraeus* but welcomed its crew. Yggrid received them in her new hall. Auro introduced the Gemmans. The elder seemed even more powerful and splendid than she had appeared in her more rustic camp in Star Needle. The travelers had more questions for her than they had had for Josep. The trees had indeed formed the great arch, as Auro, Raelight, and Bailyn had seen when they had departed the band.

"They joined at last," Yggrid explained. "Then the Great Mother joined us in the flesh, but only to guide us through the final stage of our growth as the fertile light was called back to its source."

Yggrid described how the trees connected. Vitruvia, with the help of Armarna and Yggrid, wove their topmost branches together as their trunks bent and curved below them. Space darkened as the green light was drawn into the star. An era had ended. The Syntha Band, the nebula itself, had passed away. That much the visitors knew, but they wondered what had become of Vitruvia and, even more, Armarna.

"At the end of our labor, I gathered all of our people here," Yggrid said. "The last of the Syntha departed, and the boles of both trees slipped off into the void to join the rest of the light on its journey to the star. Throughout our history, the Starboreals have grown with Star Leaf as it wound out into the veldt, ever looking toward the day when it would reach its twin. The trees will grow no more, but our growth will continue. The Great Mother declared so as she stood before us, on the very spot I stand now. She had guided our growth, but we had reached the limits of what the Syntha could develop in us. From here, we would find our own fields and frontiers.

"This new dwelling took shape around us. We call it Star Tree. It is a fusion of the old twins. The Mother opened her arms, her fingers grew longer, and green lighting flashed out from them into the branches as they intertwined. 'The trees have joined,' she said, 'and I will join with them, fulfilling my own growth. For now, you will dwell here with me, but someday, you will grow in a different field.' With that, she seemed to disappear, but she is all around us."

Auro turned around and ran his hands across a branch that formed part of the wall around them, studded with glowing needles and wrapped with leaves. He felt a peculiar charge of energy coursing through them that was like the old Syntha yet was something more. "She's in here," he said. "Most of the Syntha was pulled back into the star, but she ensured that some of it remained in the joined crowns, so concentrated that she was able to absorb her body into it."

"And she will continue to guide us while we are here," Yggrid affirmed. "But she said we will go to other places." She indicated the stars they could now see clearly. But that was a matter for another time.

"What of my mother?" Auro asked. "Did she also disappear like Vitruvia?"

Yggrid shook her head. "She helped the Great Mother fulfill her final growth. But she, like Sheraleth, is a scout, the emissary that the Eddans were bound, eventually, to send into the nebula. When she finished here, she departed to the little world of refugees whom the

Great Mother had adopted and tucked away just beyond the roots of her trees."

At this, Raelight stiffened, and his eyes welled with a deep-yellow light. "Elred's world?" he asked. "I left my child there after we restored her sight. What happened to it after the nebula dissipated? It lay in its own little realm."

Yggrid led them over to an open part of the chambers where a portion of the wall of interwoven branches opened like a window. In the distance, far and faint to the naked eye, was the pale-green light of the strange exoworld where their journey had taken such an unexpected turn.

"The other remnant of the green flame," Yggrid said. "The Great Mother made sure it was preserved there. That will be the first step of your growth from this day forward."

✳   ✳   ✳

Sometime later, Jaimin, Shanna, and Kelmin gathered together in an isolated section of the sprawling dwelling that looked to them like a vast treehouse. Auro, Raelight, and Bailyn had taken the *Astraeus* to Elred's world. The Gemmans had deferred to stay behind and retire in private, where they could take stock of all they had experienced and discuss what they would do now that the nebula was gone. The last time they had conferred together, three bands had lay before them and the core star beyond. Their choice then had been whether to keep on the unexpected journey they had started. Now their questions concerned the significance of the astonishing events they had witnessed and helped bring about and where their path lay now.

"We came to explore space and unite people," Jaimin said. "It seems we ended up fulfilling some sort of prophecy as though we were pawns."

"Not pawns," Kelmin replied. "Our choices and our power got these people out of a limbo they had existed in ever since they took, once again, to meddling with powers they could not handle."

"I wonder what the Organon will make of our adventure here," Shanna said. "Should we try contacting him, like we did on Silva?"

"Would even he understand all of this?" Jaimin asked. "I don't think we can rely on mentors far away. From the moment we ventured out from Gemma, we were on our own. He told us we would have to find our way."

Jaimin turned away in thought. Until now, all the turmoil they had left behind on their home world had been far from his mind. Taking stock of all they had seen and done since they had arrived in the nebula, he began to fill the silence again, speaking his thoughts. "Maybe we were too presumptuous when we set out. Back on Gemma, we were transformed by a great source of power, which we didn't find but seemed meant to have, power to defy Borno and his government, to travel to other worlds. Even the threats we faced, like Umbra and Trance, sprang in some way from the Eternigy itself. We thought we were meant to bring humanity together. I suppose we did fulfill a purpose here, but now that it's done, what do we have to offer these Empyreans, who absorbed the energy of the sun and helped it to spawn? We could bring some Amphorans back to Gemma, but that will not help them adjust to the new life they face now." He hoped his friends would pick up his thoughts and find a way back to their purpose, but he realized he had only led them further down the path of uncertainty.

Shanna turned to Kelmin. "Was this the only place you were able to detect human life outside the Bioplanes?"

Kelmin nodded. "Or any life, for that matter. But even my instruments aren't perfect. There may be others out there whom we can't detect or who have hidden themselves."

"So where does that leave us?" Jaimin asked. He paused. "Remember what the Organon once said: 'Some lights you will seek, and some will guide.'"

"Lights," Shanna repeated. "Stars. We created one near Gemma. Here, we roamed a nebula to find its core. They called us Noctarians, wanderers of the night. Maybe that is what we are meant to do: simply travel through space. Maybe something is waiting for us out in the dark."

"We could wander the night for a while," Kelmin agreed, "but it need not be an aimless voyage. There is a course we could set that could bring us truly full circle." He stopped there and let his teammates come to his meaning.

"Go to Earth?" Jaimin asked in amazement. He could almost see the nearly mythical blue world spinning in Kelmin's dark eyes.

"It's a cold hearth," Shanna said. "There's nothing there."

"Do we know that?" Kelmin asked. "No people, perhaps, according to our observations and histories, but nothing? Look what we have seen here: new worlds from old. Not knowing where to go, we might profit by going back where it all began, where humanity began. The Empyreans took a great deal of the sun's energy. It may not shine as bright and Earth may indeed be cold, but in its ruins, we may rediscover ourselves."

Jaimin and Shanna both smiled at the thought: a journey of rediscovery, on paths taken long ago rather than frontiers never crossed. A journey of rest and reflection. The Gnost path.

"Our friends are due back with the *Astraeus* shortly," Jaimin said. "It's time for us to move on. For them as well. I think their paths will be brighter lit."

# CHAPTER 21

# COLORED ROADS

Elred's world looked the same as before, only now the stars that surrounded it were real. This time, the *Astraeus*, minus its actual owners, landed on the very hilltop where Elred's house was perched, not far from the green hearth that had been their camp. This world was still a refuge. Its refreshing air and rejuvenating fire had given them the strength to continue on.

Raelight was quickest to rush out to the soft grass. Auro and Bailyn had never seen the self-possessed and dignified lord in such a state of anticipation. Even Auro, who had as much reason to be on pins and needles, was less hasty and more contemplative as he followed. They made right for the house, but Elred's voice cried out from the wayside. They turned to see the old man emerge from the slope, his long hand high in greeting.

They had a heartfelt reconnection, struggling after all they had seen to know where to begin. Elred understood the immediate concern. Before Raelight could utter Haelia's name, he warmly directed their eyes back toward the house. There she was, sitting on the front steps.

Raelight had never looked so radiant as when reuniting with his child. The two went off together, walking among the hills and flocks as they had before.

Elred led Auro and Bailyn back toward the hearth and rested with them in the grass. They filled him in on their experiences since their departure and asked him what had transpired there and how much he knew of the great changes that had occurred around them.

"We know the stars we see at night are real now," he answered. "And we see a peculiar light made from great trees where our cousins dwell. More distant are the colored lines left from the star. Our mistress spoke to us before she took you away. She said that if things went as she believed they would, all the barriers that have separated our peoples since the nova would break down, including the little pocket that had sheltered our world. The greater part of the green light and flame would move beyond us, but the part we have here would continue to sustain us for years to come. She told us of the trees she had been nurturing, which had grown toward each other and conjoined. She would fuse her own form with them, and her children would continue to live there with her for a time."

"We just came from there," Auro said. "We could take you back to meet Yggrid and the Starboreals. Having lived so long with the Syntha, in very different worlds, I'm sure you would have much to learn from one another. And you could be close to Vitruvia there, if only in spirit."

Elred shook his head. "She meant for us to be apart until we could find our way to her. Her children have never ventured out of their tree. It grew through the cosmos, and they grew with it. We are not so very far from one another. In time, we will develop other means of growth; then, like the trees, we shall come together."

Elred stayed with them as the sky darkened and the stars emerged. Raelight came back with Haelia in hand, and they, too, sat in front of the hearth with its dancing green flame. They could see Star Tree in the night sky, which was quite close, as Elred said, yet appeared as a little light. Farther out but much clearer, the five rays stretched across the firmament, each growing fainter until fading into the black depths.

It was time, Auro felt, to finally ask Elred his question. "Have you had any other visitors since the changes?"

"Yes," he answered, his ruddy smile barely visible in the firelight. "She flew down in a blaze of flame, faint but with gleams of yellow, red, green, and blue. She went off into the hills saying little, but I believe she will return. That is her affair . . . and perhaps yours."

He went back toward the house, bringing Raelight and Haelia inside. Auro and Bailyn remained by the hearth. Soon, Bailyn was asleep in the grass, and Auro felt the flames lulling him into a slumber.

He didn't know how much time had passed, but he opened his eyes to find it still dark. The hearth was green, but an amber glow was softly shining a few paces away. Auro gave a start and turned to see his mother standing on the hill, radiating with a residue of Gnost. He wondered if this was another sort of dream, then decided that it hardly mattered. He could see her clearly in the glare of the stars, the flickering green flame, and the yellow aura of her own body. She seemed to remember their last encounter.

"I used the wings you gave me," he said. "They took me far. In the end, I did not go where Aris meant to take us." He pointed at the five rays in the sky. "Is this what you wanted?"

"It was time for the nebula to end," she replied. "For the divisions to end. Growing up, I saw glimpses of the Stylights' visions. When I came into the nebula and began moving from one band to the next, I felt that the star itself was watching, reaching into our minds, trying to draw the energies in the bands and the people in them back into the core. Aris was acting on behalf of the star itself. It wanted to move on."

"When the Pentheon entered it, the star went nova and expanded outward," Auro noted. "When we entered, the opposite happened. It turned in on itself. We defied its pull, and we seem to have freed the five flames as well."

"Aris was desperately alone," Armarna said. "He was trying to reunify the starlight, perhaps a task that was set for him. But in the end, only he passed through the portal that, for centuries, the core had been cutting through space. The broken facets of the starlight will remain in our universe. They are not infinite, but they will travel a long way, lighting paths through the cosmos."

"Where is Aris now?"

"Maybe someday we will know. He was too far ahead of us, in the end. An instrument of a power we cannot truly fathom. He was all too human, yet not human enough."

Auro fell silent, thinking of the fate of such a grim, strange, otherworldly man. "What do we do now, Mother?" he finally asked. "What of Amphora?"

She rested her hands on his shoulders, her eyes full of memories. "You've come a long way, little Auro."

"So have you."

"Waiting for you here, I thought a lot about my father and your father. Our ancestors paved the way for us, all the way back to Aris and his forebears. If only Torro could have seen the wings you sprouted. But he didn't have to."

Auro didn't know what to say. His voice stopped with a rise of grief, his eyes full of sparkling tears. Armarna shared his feeling but tempered it with the purpose she had set for herself since she had given her husband to the yellow fire. "I've done my share of mourning. It never ends; it becomes a part of you. Sadness will come, but the strength of all we have lost will be with us. We can impart it to our people who need it now."

"You are going back to Amphora?"

"My next stop! I have always wanted to learn from the Stylights. Now I can guide them, and the prefects and scientists as well, though they may be a different challenge."

She smiled. It was in that moment that Auro realized what she had known all along: He would not be going with her.

"I know now why you made me the firebird," he said. "It wasn't just to fulfill our mission in the star."

She kissed his cheek and patted his chest. "We'll see each other again, in real dreams. Until then, fly."

She turned and walked into the dark hills. And the tears came again.

✳   ✳   ✳

The *Astraeus* returned to Star Tree and picked up the Gemmans. They were delighted to see Haelia reunited with her father and to hear that all was well on Elred's world. After paying their last respects to Yggrid, including a sweet farewell to Sheraleth, they took off and pushed on toward what had been the outer bands of the nebula. The Magna seemed desolate now, bereft of the vibrant red. The Nanj Cloud, too, was gone, and all the great rocks that had seared with scarlet flame were cold and dark, like a hearth whose last embers had died during the night.

Most of Romeon's people had been aboard the *Dante*, but they found a few stragglers still inhabiting some of the crags, no longer the great furnaces and foundries they had been in the time of Romeon's power. They gathered as many as they could and told them what had become of Romeon and the star. As they had found with the *Dante*'s crew, the distress at the loss of their lord was soothed by the knowledge that he had met his end attempting to cross the ultimate frontier. For all any of them knew, he still lived and was with Aris now.

All of them declined to be taken to the Rae Citadels or Amphora. Ultimately, they were deposited together on the great asteroid on which Auro had once been imprisoned. There, they could ponder their future and wait for Thomoly, however long it took the *Dante* to reach them. The crew of the *Astraeus* respected their wishes, left them supplies and provisions, and said that someone would be back to check in on them before long.

And so, finally, they came into view of the golden domes of Raelight's five citadels. Hovering just above the central one, they saw that the streets and hills below were full of cheering crowds, in contrast to the emptiness Auro and Jaimin had encountered when they had docked the *Meteor* in the same spot. Somehow, Raelight's people knew they were coming, and the lord revealed that he had been communing with them as they drew closer. The welcome was heartwarming, but they were surprised to see that they were not the only arrivals. Two Amphoran ships were also hovering above the dome opposite them. The people of the exocity had not waited long to send an expedition now that the storms of the Pale no longer blocked the way.

Soon, they were climbing the silver steps that led into the great atrium under the central dome. Raelight took his place again at the head of his community and welcomed his guests. The Amphoran delegation included the Stylights Etemeena and Sumero, as well as the prefects Ormonde and Sultaan. Leone was there as well. Auro and Jaimin nearly ran to greet him, and they marveled to see him standing by Raelight under the dome, for he had always seemed to them a person apart.

Many councils were held over the ensuing days. Raelight had always been wise, but after all he had experienced in the inner bands, he was a gracious host and took up the mantle of transitionary leader and fatherly guide, as he had after the nova centuries ago. Space was no longer tinted with yellow light, but each of the five domes still had its plinth and flame, the last vestige of the Gnost that was now within Raelight himself and those he had touched.

The Oriflamme was no longer covered by fire; its great hearth was bare, and so its bannerman was recalled home. Auro had a long talk with Leone that first night, telling him of his adventures in the nebula, including the strange vision in which he had appeared. Leone revealed that he, too, had experienced that peculiar dream one night, which began with him riding a horse across a rugged land. Auro marveled at the shared vision, and they agreed that their encounter had indeed been real.

The Amphoran delegation and Raelight and his elders worked out what amounted to a treaty, a framework for building a new life in which each community could benefit from the resources and knowledge of the other. In the years after the nova, the Amphorans had relied on their practical know-how to survive, turning to their scientists, engineers, and administrators to sustain them, relegating the old solar spiritualism to high towers. In contrast, those in the nebula were sustained by mystical fires, and their lives revolved around learning their mysteries and allowing them to transform their bodies and spirits.

They recognized that they had much to offer one another. As the ambient energy of the old nebula cooled, the Empyreans would need the technologies that the Amphorans could bring to the Rae Citadels, to Elred's world and to Star Tree, to the various asteroids that contained people throughout the old bands. And the Amphorans could touch what was left of the old flames and regain some of their Empyrean heritage. But for now, probably for a good while, all would have to live in cold space without a sun or a nebula.

It was agreed that Amphora would be moved toward the Rae Citadels, activating its engine for the first time since it had escaped the expanding clouds of the nova and fixed its position outside the Pale. And they would send their ships out across the expanse to account for all the souls who lived in the far-flung spaces of the old bands and either bring them back to the citadels or see to their needs.

Individuals such as Bailyn, Armarna, and Raelight, who had achieved high status, would be key figures in the nascent government that was already starting to form in those long councils under Raelight's dome. There was hope that the three Gemmans, who had helped bring about this new era, would stay and employ their formidable abilities to nurture their development, yet the Noctarians politely evaded making any promises and hinted more than once that their task there was done.

The biggest puzzle was Auro, who, in some ways, was the most esteemed of anyone. Yet everyone sensed, as his mother knew and Raelight first perceived, that he would not be staying, either. They came to see that he retained the power of the firebird, made even more potent by his extended immersion in the core. He stayed quiet throughout much of the deliberations, sometimes offering his insights when asked, but he was often seen walking by himself to look up at the dome or gaze out at the five rays.

On the last eve of the council, Raelight held a feast under the dome, and the throng of elders, prefects, Stylights, scientists, and other dignitaries filled rows of tables and toasted their future. Auro slipped out onto the steps under the stars and then ascended the great dome to stand at the plinth with its Gnost fire. There, he looked out at the void where the star had once shone, where the five rays now started their journeys.

He prepared to spread his wings. But as he did, he sensed movement behind him and turned to see Jaimin, along with Shanna,

Kelmin, and Bailyn. They all seemed to understand this was goodbye. None of them spoke until Auro himself broke the silence.

"I have my flight path," he said. "Not just one but five. Each ray was part of the star; each leads somewhere." He paused. "I may be back, or maybe not." He smiled with a steely determination.

"I head back to Amphora tomorrow," Bailyn said. "Your mother is already there. I thought you would be joining us. I thought leading our world would be next for you."

"I'll leave that to you, Bailyn. You'll be a prefect in time, as my mother will lead the Stylights. But she set me on a journey through the nebula and its five lights. They are still out there and still have places to take me."

"Maybe one of them will lead you to Earth," Jaimin suggested. "That is where we are heading. We may see you there."

Auro shook his head. "I don't think so. The rays do not seek to reunite with the old sun. Maybe Aris knew where they were going. I will find out, perhaps even find him along the way."

Auro's body blazed, and the wings spread out from his back. His body took the majestic form of the great phoenix, with all the rich color and strength he had derived from the star. For a moment, he stood there at the apex of the dome, dwarfing the plinth and fire. Then he reared back and launched off, flying into the starry horizon toward the five colored streaks until his wings were only a twinkle and he was lost among the stars.

One by one, Bailyn shook hands with the Gemmans and bid them farewell. Although not in the way they had expected, they had indeed accomplished their mission of reuniting disparate branches of humanity. They, too, launched off the dome toward the *Astraeus* and gathered on the flight deck, together again, alone again, to embark on a new journey.

They set course from both the Rae Citadels and Amphora, putting some distance between them before activating the engine to make the journey to Earth. It was very far from there, much farther than it would have been from Gemma. Kelmin trained their sensors out toward the rays, trying to get a last glimpse of Auro.

"I wonder where he'll end up," Shanna said. "What he'll find."

Jaimin sighed. "He may have escaped the fate of Aris, but he is still his heir. He might simply be continuing his journey."

"Well," Kelmin said, "we can only continue ours."

✳  ✳  ✳

Auro arrived at his starting point, where the five rays streaked out into the galaxy and perhaps beyond. Each presented a path, a road that he was determined to travel. He would tread the length of each, return to this point, then tread another.

He would start with the Gnost, still yellow, still the ray of self. Where in the universe would such energy go? He spread his wings and flew into the dark center where the core had been, then straight into the yellow ray, as he had once flown the *Meteor* into the dark path. The ray was not dark but expectedly yellow, soothing as the flame had been but more powerful, charging through his wings and body like the old flame multiplied manyfold.

Now he found he didn't need his wings. Like a vacuum tube, the yellow took hold of him, and he shot through it like a pulse of light; indeed, faster than light itself. Hovering on the edge of consciousness, he yet felt safe, heading into the unknown, very far away, on the kind of road that would not fail him, created by the star his ancestors had made, the part of it most in touch with the human heart. When and where would he arrive? Perhaps in mere moments, he would know. But in a sense, there would be no end. Such roads went ever on.

www.ingramcontent.com/pod-product-compliance
Lightning Source LLC
Chambersburg PA
CBHW020608110726
47899CB00002B/425